More Than Legend

More Than Legend

More Than Life
Book 2

Bethanie Finger

WISE WOLF
BOOKS

WISE WOLF BOOKS
An Imprint of Wolfpack Publishing
wisewolfbooks.com
701 S. Howard Ave. 106-324, Tampa, FL 33609

Cover design by Wise Wolf Books

Paperback ISBN 978-1-957548-29-6
eBook ISBN 978-1-957548-53-1
LCCN 2024931467

More Than Legend

For Lindsey and Samantha and twenty-eight years of SBT. Here's to many more.

Talian Sea

SCAPA

Talian Sea

ALA

Mikirian Forest

MIKIRIA

Mikirian Capital

VALES

Talian Sea

KERU   Deserin

Talian Sea   Ostan

chorage Inn

Woodvale

Cay

Talian Sea

Prologue

Prologue

JASPAR TOOK CONFIDENT STEPS ON THE SHIP THAT WAS as familiar as his own, letting it rock back and forth on the waves but never letting it knock him off his balance. A cool breeze chilled his bare neck, and he missed the six inches of hair he'd trimmed away the night before.

"Kimbal?" Jaspar called his mentor's name in a singsong voice, eager to tell the old captain of his new findings. "Wait till you see what I've brought you!" But as Jaspar made his way down the dock to the captain's cabins, the ship remained silent.

"Did you fall back to sleep, old man?" No answer.

"Oi!" Jaspar leaped down from the hot deck to the shade of the cabin. The door was already half ajar, and Jaspar rapped it lightly before entering.

"Kimbal?"

The room was eerily silent, and instinctively, he summoned a ball of flames in his hand. Something was off. The room seemed perfectly ordinary, but it wasn't early morning, it was midday. And yet...

The bed wasn't made. The windows were still locked closed. An abandoned pot of coffee hung over the dying fireplace. The

1

captain's blouse was laid out on the bed, comb resting on top, boots sat on the floor below.

"Kimbal?" Jaspar stumbled, his fire extinguishing as his knees collided with the floor. He cursed, narrowly avoiding the bed frame as he fell to the floor. His hands shifted and met the mass he'd tripped over.

"Kimbal?" But the name died on his lips. The great captain was motionless, a leather-bound book in his hand. He was half-dressed, donning only his pants and undershirt. It was as if he was preparing for the day, readying for another adventure out to sea, but the adventure would never come.

Jaspar clutched the chest of his mentor, but there was no heart-beat, no breath of air, no hitch from his lungs. His body had grown cold, hard. He could have been there for hours, laying alone and forgotten. Clutched in his hand was a journal. Jaspar noted the backing had been ripped and something had been clumsily hidden in the lining. The captain had dozens of journals, hundreds even perhaps. Why was this one clutched so tightly?

A thunderous blast from outside the cabin sliced through his grief. The windows burst open, glass flying in all directions. Jaspar's lifetime of covert instincts took over his body and he ducked under the bed. He saw the boots of an enormous human, thundering and loud on the ship's wooden boards. A billowing, vermilion-colored fog blew across the floor, and Jaspar fought the cough lodged in his throat. A growl escaped the person above and Jaspar bit his cheek to keep from screaming out.

The mysterious person kicked the fire, threw the coffeepot, and tossed the chair and desk and every content in the room until the bed that had been hiding Jaspar lifted. Jaspar forced himself to stand on shaking legs, refusing to appear fearful in the eyes of the monster.

The demon stood nearly nine feet tall. It had shaggy, dark hair, somehow greasy and coarse. His skin had a sickly, red and gray hue, as if it were made of day-old meat. A strange and deadly crimson haze silhouetted his grotesque frame. His eyes were deep maroon, red, like that of the color blood, and in their depth, he only saw darkness and evil and all that was wicked in the world.

Jaspar recalled the journal, clutched tightly in the captain's hands, and made to pretend he'd fallen over. The demon was prideful, thinking he'd startled the young man into losing his footing, and Jaspar used the moment to tuck the journal into the waterproof satchel on his waist. He turned the satchel around and under his cloak just as the demon approached.

The demon yanked Jaspar to his feet by the hem of his cloak, and Jaspar swallowed back the terrified bile in his throat.

"What isss it you've brought to the *dead* captain?" His accent was eerie in its foreignness. He tried not to focus on the way the demon had described his friend, tried to ignore the pain at hearing the word.

"Nothing." Jaspar was proud of the strength in his voice, and with a stab of guilt, he hoped the captain would be too. Or would have been.

"Liesss!" The demon slapped Jaspar across the face, the motion sending him flying into the ship cabin's walls. Without thought, a fire lit in Jaspar's palm, a glowing orb ready to defend its maker.

"Hagan." The demon's mouth twitched. "Who are you?"

Jaspar ignored him, building the ball of fire bigger in his hands.

The demon laughed, its great head lolling back and shaking. He made eye contact with Jaspar and smirked before lighting his whole body aflame. Jaspar's mouth parted at the sight of the monstrous man now glowing with embers. Flames licked his skin and trickled from his nostrils and ears. When he opened his mouth, smoke and fire emerged as if freed from the demon's chest.

Jaspar swallowed but held his ground. He snuffed his fire, bitter that he couldn't use it. He felt a stab of anger at his Hagan power; it had never failed him before, and yet, when he needed protection the most, it was useless to him.

The demon took two steps forward and snapped his fingers. From out of the shadows, two men appeared, both with slimy, green-tinted skin and webbed hands and feet. Sidons, fish hunters who usually targeted water creatures and those with waterpower, like Danthems. What did they want from an old sea captain? Or a forgettable Hagan?

The Sidons approached, and each grabbed one of Jaspar's arms and despite his best efforts, the Sidons held Jaspar still as the demon riffled his pockets.

The demon smiled, exposing muddy black teeth, and Jaspar gagged at the stench. He pulled from Jaspar's inside pocket a folded parchment, yellowed with age. Jaspar fumed in fury as the demon unfolded the parchment to reveal a crudely drawn symbol, one Jaspar had yet to identify and now tried to commit to memory.

"What have you found indeed?" The demon grinned, holding up the parchment, revealing a rose compass. But where there should have been a circle was the outline of a shield, and each of the compass's four prongs were shaped like swords. "Where did you find thisss?"

But before Jaspar could refuse to answer him, loud shouting echoed, and the ship shook with the boarding of several people. One of the Sidons holding Jaspar abandoned him and ran to the window. "It'sss the Talian Sssea Guard, my lord." The slimy, green man spoke with the same strange accent as his master.

Jaspar was certain the demon would not care for a few extra men to toy with, but the demon rolled its eyes. Sounds of the sea guard searching the ship reached his ears, calling out to anyone aboard, seeking to find the reason for its abandonment at sea.

The demon's body shook and trembled, emitting smoke and ash. Fire boiled from its skin, building higher and higher until it was an enormous ball of flames, as tall and as wide as the demon himself. The flames went from red to blue, and the man walked forward, leaving the blue flames behind him. A sphere of the blue flames churned, and Jaspar was hypnotized by its swirling pattern.

One by one, the Sidons went into the strange fiery portal and disappeared, until only the Sidons holding Jaspar were left.

"What the blazes—"

The demon cracked its neck and dropped its heavy hand onto Jaspar's head. Jaspar screamed as a throbbing pain began to pulse from the man's palm and fingers. His skin burned, and he felt the beats of his heart in his head as his skull began to splinter.

"You will forget you ever sssaw thisss sssymbol. You will forget you found the dead captain. You will forget you ever sssaw my face." The demon's voice had taken on an intense quality, like a burning, crackling fire, each word turning to ash on the wind.

"Throw him out." The demon said, removing his hand and snapping his fingers once more. The last thing Jaspar remembered was the Sidons' slimy hands on his arms before he was tossed from the ship's windows, splashing into the cold, unforgiving depths of the ocean.

1

JASPAR'S LIPS WERE TURNING BLUE AND PURPLE, AND Cordelia wondered if they'd grown as numb as hers. Her chin wobbled as she tried to rise to her toes, to stand as tall as possible, to keep her head above the water that was rising higher and higher and higher.

How had this happened to her? Why? Four months ago, she was a lady of society with a promising future and a home and a family. And then she'd lost her father. She'd lost her title. She'd lost her home. She had been forced to adopt a new name, a new life, a new job.

But through it all, she had found Jaspar, her soulfate. And he had shown her the world anew. A world filled with magic and fire and water and possibilities. And she had been happy, truly and really happy, and now she was sinking to the bottom of the Tilerian Sea. And Jaspar was with her. And her happiness would soon be drowned in the endless depths of the ocean.

Cordelia felt the water rise above her lips and she breathed in as much air as she could hold, and then breathed in even more, until her lungs felt like they would burst. Jaspar stood several inches taller than her, telling her to hold on, telling her it would be alright.

Jaspar heaved in a deep breath before disappearing under the water, swimming down. He was trying again to free her from the cage, to open the latch that held her hostage. The latch that'd been dented in on itself. The latch that was currently embedded in the bulwark of the ship. The ship of their friends, three brothers who traveled the waters of the world with kindness. And Jaspar and Cordelia had put them in danger.

Kevin cried out, the bodies of his two younger brothers floating beside him, their weight nearly pulling him under. Kevin. Poor, innocent Kevin, who only wanted to help two stranded strangers. Who only wanted to offer safe passage along the Tilerian Sea. Who had never thought his ship would be attacked and destroyed by a group of angry Sidons.

The Sidons weren't hunting Kevin. They had no interest in him at all. They were hunting Cordelia and the water magic she held deep within herself. Cordelia tried again in vain to summon her magic, to seek within herself that powerful orb of energy. But she was simply too exhausted, too injured. Her skull still throbbed and ached, and her hair was congealed in blood. The entire left side of her body felt as if it'd been crushed beneath a rock. Her fractured rib made it hard to breathe, and she could barely hold up her dislocated shoulder. She swayed on her feet, her head dizzy, pulsating like a hammer in her mind.

Jaspar's head broke the surface for the briefest moment, gulping in more air before swimming back below. The water was rising too high, and she could barely keep her head above it. She tried to touch him, to fit her fingers through the cage, to tell him once again to leave and save himself while he still could.

I love you. I love you. I love you. It was the only thought in her throbbing skull until a high shriek invaded her eardrums, the pain like a needle in her brain.

Caws, loud, screeching caws, drew her attention as a large black bird soared into the room, flying in a circle overhead. Frân, a theurgist messenger bird she knew belonged to Hygonia the demigoddess, landed precariously on Cordelia's head.

She winced as the birds' talons dug into her scalp, into the cut and welt from smashing her head into the deck. Her pain felt impossibly worse. A whirring sound filled her ears and darkness encroached her vision. But the bird didn't stop, it stood on her head and cawed and cawed and cawed.

Frân pushed his talons deeper, using the momentum to push off. The bird's usually dark eyes had turned a strange, milky-white color, and they stood out stark among the dark feathers. The bird flew in a circle above her head, soaring and cawing.

Cordelia slipped under the water, her eyes open to see Jaspar's lungs had given out in his futile attempts to open the cage. His eyes were closed, unconscious, and her heart constricted when she saw his chest wasn't moving.

No. No, no, no, no. It was like losing her father all over again. Like losing the only thing in the world that gave her joy and hope. Cordelia's hands clenched into fists, and then she felt it, she finally felt it.

She reached deep inside herself, feeling the tiny orb of power in her chest, only it wasn't the small orb she'd used before. Now the orb was strong, expanding until it expelled into the water around her. The water churned, swirling faster and faster and faster until it was nothing more than a vortex, a tornado of waves expanding over and over. She had created a bubble of water so large it encased her entire cage.

The ship bent and cracked under the pull of the vortex until it split apart completely. The cage burst open, and Cordelia was thrown from under the water, rising high above to the surface before coming back down in an impact so heavy that waves rippled around her in great torrents.

Cordelia turned, the cold air chilling the water on her skin. She swam below, searching through salt-stung eyes. Minutes passed, and she thought about seeking the surface, about gasping in more air, but she found she didn't need it. Her lungs felt full. She swam in circles, up and down, left and right, but Jaspar was nowhere to be seen.

She broke through the surface, scanning the waters around her, panic threatening to pull her down to the depths of the ocean, and then Kevin was there. Trevyn, Iverson, and Jaspar were all floating on a huge plank, Kevin gliding them through the water. Her lungs relaxed. They were safe. They were alive.

She had found her magic at last; she had freed them all. Cordelia coughed and fell forward. She clutched her chest and felt a sharp snap in her heart. The pain in her head and body came back in an attack so aggressive it stole her oxygen, her energy, her soul. Her magic was fading, and her body was returning to its broken state.

The water was growing high again, rising at an alarming rate, overtaking her clavicle, her neck, her chin. But, no, the water wasn't rising. Cordelia was sinking, her legs no longer kicking, her body no longer able to tread the waters.

She heard the caw of Frân and saw the sparkling haze of a blue moon high above them in the sky. And then the world went black.

2

KEVIN'S BODY ACHED IN WAYS HE NEVER COULD HAVE imagined. If he'd known helping two stranded strangers on their honeymoon would destroy his ship and nearly kill him and his brothers, he would have gladly left them astray. Now, the five of them were marooned, and he was the only one still conscious.

Trevyn and Iverson had been knocked out when the broken beam of the ship had struck them. The man's lungs had given out as he'd tried desperately to save his beloved. The woman's lungs had given out when she wasn't able to free herself from the fishing cage she was trapped in. And all that was left was Kevin.

The woman had been freed from the cage during the tornado vortex phenomenon. Kevin had no explanation for what strange weather had caused it; he'd never seen a hurricane rise and fall so quickly. The vortex came from nowhere, pulled the ship apart, freed the woman, and then disappeared.

It could have been a magic user, but there was no one around except the five of them. He'd heard the cawing of a bird but hadn't caught sight of the creature until it was soaring away, disappearing into the night sky.

Kevin pushed with as much strength as he could manage, shoving the wooden plank against the current of the waves. It was all that remained of their once great vessel, and it was barely large enough to support the four unconscious bodies he now felt responsible for.

They'd been drifting along to Keru at a fast but manageable pace. Years on the water had given him enough knowledge to navigate his surroundings, he took a moment to orient himself. Lucky for him, it was well past the twilight hour, and a starry sky of constellations told him they were traveling northwest.

Based on the constellations that were visible, they were close to the central west shoreline of Keru. And based on the height of the moon, it was nearly nine in the evening. He worked every muscle he had to force himself and his companions to continue to float. Every kick of his leg in the water was like a stone, pulling him down, but he carried on.

Hours passed, and the moon told him it was nearly dawn when land finally came into view. By the time they had reached the shore, the sun was peaking up, and his brothers were just starting to stir. The man and the woman remained unconscious.

Kevin pulled the plank as high on the shore as he could before collapsing on his back. He lay in the sand with his arms and legs sprawled out, heaving in huge lungfuls of air and letting his weary eyes rest. He heard a groan and, unable to fully sit up, rolled his head to face his brothers.

Iverson's dark-brown hair and beard were shimmering in the early sunlight. His movements were slow and lagging, but eventually, he shakily sat up, his arms above his head to shield his eyes. "Kev?" His voice was a croak and he looked around him slowly.

"Over here, Ive," Kevin panted.

"Trev!" Iverson's voice panicked as he shoved their younger brother, tugging on his ginger beard and slapping him in the face. Trevyn shifted, his eyelids sagged, his pupils red and bloodshot.

"It's alright, mates." Kevin crawled across the sand and the three brothers huddled in a somewhat unbalanced hug. "We're alive."

"Valia!" Iverson suddenly shouted, looking around and seeing nothing but the large plank Kevin had used to drift them to shore.

"She's with the sea, mate." Kevin cursed, a hand over his chest in tribute to their sunken ship. The boat had been in his family for three generations; she had survived decades of war and storms and swashbucklers. What would they do now? How would three traveling fishermen earn wages without a ship?

His brothers hung their heads and fisted their chests. Kevin was the first to collect himself. "What about these two then?"

"Who are they?" Trevyn asked.

"We picked them up in Woodvale, don't you remember? Offered to help them get to Keru?"

Iverson scratched his beard. "It's all a little fuzzy. But they do look familiar."

"Well we can't help them now." Trevyn scoffed. "Not like we're in a position to rescue anyone."

"I think I've done enough rescuing for the moment. Why don't one of you take over?" Kevin bent forward and stretched his aching back.

"Not their fault we were attacked by pirates. But we can't do much stranded on the beach." Iverson looked around. "Where the bollocks are we?"

"Central Keru if my constellation mapping is correct." Kevin tipped over a boot full of water.

"Well, we need coin if we're to find a way back to Vales, though Alaro may be safer if the storms continue." Iverson shook his head to rid the water. "But we shouldn't leave them; it wouldn't be right."

"Doesn't matter." Trevyn was inspecting his arms and legs, noticing the many scratches on his freckled skin and tears in the fabric of his clothes. "Without a ship, we ain't going nowhere."

"Well, at least we can make port here until we figure things out. Anyone managed to keep their coins?" Iverson asked after pulling out his empty pockets. Trevyn shook his head, but Kevin pulled out a small pouch, discovering enough coin for a room for a night or two but not nearly enough to travel.

"Well, better hope they got some gold on them." Kevin tossed a thumb at the man and woman. "We don't have a lot to share."

Iverson shrugged. "Wouldn't be the first time. Remember that summer we—" Trevyn slapped Iverson's shoulder, shushing him and pointing to the woman now stirring in the sand. She clutched her injured arm at the elbow and winced in pain. Her ocean-blue eyes locked on his seaweed green, and she tilted her head.

"Kevin?"

3

CORDELIA'S EYELIDS WERE HEAVY, HER HEAD STILL throbbed. Breathing caused sharp pain in her lungs, like tiny needles. Her eardrums pulsated a painful rhythm that nearly drowned out the noise around her. She heard the wind whistling, the ocean waves crashing.

She sat up, a little too quickly, her limp arm pulling her down. She cradled her elbow close to her chest to take the weight of her arm off her dislocated shoulder. She shifted and something heavy clunked under her dress. She tapped a hand over her heart and found her talisman, cold and wet on her skin, keeping her protected.

Around her was an unfamiliar sand, a dark-brown color so unlike the beige sands of Alaro. The brothers eyed her with suspicion, remaining several feet away from her.

"Kevin?" Her voice wheezed, so raspy she could barely understand herself. She tried to clear her throat, but it burned, causing her to gag.

"Miss." The brothers didn't move. She hoped they suspected the attack from the same pirates that had plagued the Tilerian Sea for years and hadn't been able to recognize the ship belonged to Sidons. But where were the Sidons now? Her thoughts continued to throb in her skull, slowly sorting themselves into cohesion.

"Jaspar!" He was several feet away from her and she moved

15

awkwardly, shuffling on her knees while attempting to keep hold of her arm, the soaked skirt of her dress dragging across the sand. "Jaspar!" She shook him, but he didn't wake. "What's happened to him?" She cried desperately, beseeching the brothers.

Kevin took slow steps toward them, inspecting Jaspar's unconscious form and shaking him several times.

"Is he..." She couldn't bring herself to say it; it was too cruel a thought.

"He's alive. Just concussed." Trevyn gestured to a large gash and welt on the back of Jaspar's head. It had been covered by his dark hair and had little bits of sand stuck in it. The arrow that had lodged in his stomach during the attack was gone with barely a trace of its embedment. Had it merely been a flesh wound?

"Will he wake?"

"Dunno, do I?" Trevyn mumbled.

Iverson picked sand from his nails. "Just give him some time."

"I'll get a fire going." Trevyn stalked toward some driftwood not far off. Cordelia was about to ask where they'd shipwrecked when Iverson and Kevin sat beside her. They'd arranged themselves in a small circle, Jaspar lying next to Cordelia and her hand absentmindedly stroking his chest.

"Where are we?"

"Keru." Iverson said as Trevyn returned and made quick work of starting a fire. It was obviously something he'd done several times, and Cordelia and the brothers all scooted a little closer, drying and warming their clothes.

Cordelia was surprised to see her clothes were as wet as the brothers. Perhaps it was because she'd stopped using magic while still in the water. Did she only stay dry if she controlled the water source?

She felt her head, remembering Frân and wondering where he had flown off to. She had aligned her thoughts enough to understand that the bird's attack on her head had been to help her find her magic, but she had no explanation for how he could do that, how he had found them, or how he had known they needed help.

"Is your ship..." She couldn't bring herself to ask, ashamed that it was her fault they were stranded here.

"Sunk. Bloody swashbucklers." Iverson grumbled.

"You got any coin, miss?" Trevyn asked, and for the first time, Cordelia remembered her valise. Cordelia examined the sand around them...her bag was nowhere to be seen. Her bag which had the last letter from her father, his journals, and her clothes and belongings. She rubbed her eyes, opting to deal with the loss later when she was alone. She picked through Jaspar's pockets, pulling out a small leather pouch with several coins and coppers.

She hoped it was enough to get them two rooms for the night and enough food to tide them over. And hopefully, by tomorrow, she and Jaspar would have a new plan.

"Yes. I can get us two rooms for the night and some food. I'm not sure if I'll have enough for longer than that though," she said. "Do you...will you be alright?" Cordelia wondered if she should share their coin. After all, it was her fault the brothers were without a ship, and she realized with a twinge that they were also out of jobs.

"We'll manage, miss, but thank you." Kevin nodded. Cordelia returned the leather pouch to Jaspar's pocket, and he stirred, rolling on his side and expelling an alarming amount of the sea.

Cordelia held his bicep as he shook and slowly lifted his head. Jaspar stared at her, head cocked to one side. His shoulders pulled him back, and he jerked out of her grip so hard she fell forward in the sand, landing painfully on her injured shoulder. His eyes, usually so brown and warm, turned dark and almost deadly. He reached down to his boot, pulling out his sharp dagger, aiming it at Cordelia.

"Who the blazes are you?"

4

CORDELIA FELT HER STOMACH DROP. JASPAR WAS holding a knife, wielding it at her, ready to slash or stab or worse. His eyes were wild, grim in a way she'd never seen before. Words rushed to her mind, but none of them seemed to make any sense. She got to her feet slowly, not wanting to startle him further.

"Jaspar?" Her murmur earned her nothing but a low grunt from him.

"Who are you? How do you know my name?" He slashed the knife back and forth, as if preparing to use it, or perhaps just showing that he could.

Cordelia opened and closed her mouth twice, unable to form words. What name had she given the brothers? And what was she to tell Jaspar? Why did he not recognize her?

Jaspar's eyes darted around. "What's happened?"

"Pirates. Sunk our ship." Iverson said, and Cordelia was grateful the brothers were there because she had yet to find her voice.

Jaspar spun, sand flying in all directions, his knife now pointed at Iverson. "Where am I?"

"Keru," Iverson said, voice slow with forced calm. Kevin and Trevyn remained still as statues.

"Keru...why am I here? Did you...did you trick me? Abduct me?" He brandished the knife at each of them, turning in a circle.

Kevin gave a nervous laugh. "Abduct you?"

"Why the blazes am I in Keru?" Each time he spoke, his voice got lower, sharper, unrestrained and deadly.

"Jaspar?" Maybe it was the brothers he didn't recognize or trust, but a dark voice in her mind wondered why he didn't recognize her. Had her talisman been damaged? Was she a blurred shape to him that he couldn't identify? "Do you...please, tell me you know who I am?"

Her body took a step toward him and instantly regretted it when he slashed her arm, the knife slicing through her dress sleeve and drawing blood. Kevin pulled her back before Jaspar could cause further harm, and Trevyn and Iverson crowded around him.

"Stay back, all of you!"

Air bobbed in her throat, unable to break free and replenish her lungs. Jaspar showed no remorse for cutting her, in fact, he looked ready to take on all four of them.

"Easy, Mate." Iverson held up his arms. "We're all friends here."

"I don't have any friends," Jaspar's voice was menacing, and he cocked his head once. "Wait...the captain. Where is he? What have you done with him?"

When no one answered, he slashed the knife again and took a dangerous step toward them.

"Where is the captain?" He snarled. "Did you capture him too?"

"Er, which captain, mate? Maybe we can find him for you?" Trevyn said.

Jaspar blinked several times as if the name was on the tip of his tongue but could not be found. "Kim-Kimbal," he stuttered out.

Cordelia saw the brothers all sag, and Trevyn placed a hand over his heart.

"Sorry, mate. Really, I am. He died last July."

"No," Jaspar shook his head, and Cordelia relived the moment she'd found out about her father. The screaming and crying and denial she knew all too well.

Iverson's voice was low, haunted. "It was a heart attack."

Jaspar snapped. "Wait. What did you just say? July?"

"Yeah. Heart attack in July." Trevyn repeated himself a little slower this time. It felt wrong for Cordelia to stay silent, but she'd never been able to utter the words, never actually said that her father was...

"He's not dead. I just talked to him last week, and he certainly hasn't been dead for a year."

"A year..." Trevyn's expression went neutral. "What day do you think it is, mate?"

"June twenty-fifth," Jaspar said without hesitation.

"No, mate," Kevin scratched the back of his head. "It's November fifteenth."

Jaspar convulsed on his feet, the knife trembling in his hands. The knife dropped to the sand, and Jaspar keeled over, catching himself with his hands on his knees. His face turned green, his eyes full. His neck lurched, throwing his head forward in a violent motion as he emptied himself before falling face-first into the sand.

5

KEVIN EXAMINED JASPAR'S HEAD, TURNING IT SIDE TO side. "Amnesia?"

"Dunno, do I?" Trevyn shrugged.

Cordelia fell to her knees, unable to hold her body up any longer. "But then why did he retch? Can you get sick from amnesia?"

"No. I suspect that's halensickness." Kevin said.

"Halensickness?"

"It's what we call saltwater poisoning in Vales."

"He probably took too much in when he drowned," Iverson said.

"Is it...can it kill him?"

The brothers shared a look but didn't answer her.

"Did you say your name was Cordy?" Kevin squatted next to her in the sand.

Cordy? Right, the cover story. Jaspar and Cordy were recently wed and were taking a tour of the continents to celebrate. "Yes."

"Sorry about your husband."

"It's nearly morning now; we should try to find a town," Trevyn said.

"Come on, then." Iverson tucked one arm under Jaspar, and Trevyn reluctantly helped. The three walked in a strange huddle but didn't make it far before the brothers dropped Jaspar.

21

"He," Iverson panted, pointing at Jaspar, "is too heavy."

"Well, we're not leaving him here." Cordelia frowned, her hands fisted at her side.

"Alright, calm yourselves." Kevin scratched his beard. "There's a house up the way. Let's just get him there, and we can ask for help."

This time, all three brothers dragged Jaspar down the shoreline, leaving a trail in the sand. They took a break when the sand turned to grass and another when the grass turned to pebbled road. They walked nearly an hour before they arrived at the house Kevin had seen from the shore.

The smell of fresh flowers grew strong as they made their way to the large farmhouse with blue shutters. Near a wraparound porch sat an old man with long braided hair tending a garden.

"Morning!" Kevin let Trevyn take the weight of Jaspar and approached the old man, who looked at the group with unease.

He removed a worn pair of gloves, letting his tan hands rest on his hips. "Help you?"

"Please. We were hoping for an inn nearby."

The man pointed north. "Up the road, three miles." The man stood, his graying braid swinging behind him as he walked. He nodded to Jaspar's comatose form. "What's happened to him?"

"Halensickness," Iverson grunted. "Where in Keru are we?"

"Ostan."

Trevyn quirked a brow.

"You need help? I got a wheelbarrow out back."

Trevyn nearly dropped Jaspar in relief. "That'd be great, thank you."

"Wait here." He walked to a small shed next to the house. The shed was the farmhouse in miniature, with the same blue shutters and small porch.

"Where is Ostan?" Cordelia asked as they waited for the man to return.

Kevin rolled up the sleeves of his blouse. "Central west border. It's a large city; there should be plenty of people and inns."

"Central west border, eh?" Trevyn's face brightened. "Only a day's sail from Alaro then."

"Suppose it is," Iverson said. "If we had a ship."

"Perhaps we can buy passage on a fishing ship headed that way."

"I suspect Gladys'll let us work for a meal or two," Kevin said before turning to Cordelia. "Will you two be alright?"

Cordelia wasn't sure how to answer him, but the old man had returned, saving her from having to make a decision. He pushed an orange and rusted wheel barrel, the wheel squeaking sharply.

"What's happened to him?" He gestured to Jaspar, and Cordelia's throat ran dry. Cordelia swore under her breath. For one moment too long, she'd forgotten that Jaspar's curse would take his remembrance from the old man.

"Halensickness," Iverson said slowly. The old man grunted, shook his head, then shoved the wheel barrel to Iverson and Trevyn, who still held Jaspar aloft.

"Six coppers."

Kevin blinked. "What?"

"That's six coppers."

"Oh." It was clear Kevin thought the man would simply let them borrow the wheel barrel, but Cordelia fished through Jaspar's pouch and handed him the coins.

"Greedy scoundrel," Iverson muttered once they'd deposited Jaspar into the barrel.

"And senile." Trevyn pushed the wheel barrel down the pebbled road, the wheel squeaking with every turn. "How do you forget the unconscious man you got the wheel barrel for but not the wheel barrel?"

Kevin shrugged. "Not my job to know or understand the minds of others. I can barely use my own somedays."

6

"It'll be a few days for the halensickness. I don't know much about amnesia, though." Kevin said.

"What can I do for him?" She wished she could see Hygonia; her demigoddess soulmother could heal Jaspar in seconds.

"Lots of water and rest for halensickness."

"And the amnesia?"

The brothers shared a look, but it was Iverson who answered with sorrowful eyes. "Don't know much about it, but I can say to give him time. Amnesia's a trauma thing, probably from that blow to his head." Iverson pointed to the bump on the back of Jaspar's skull.

"Just have to wait it out, I'm afraid," Kevin said. "But...I'd be careful."

"He won't hurt me."

Kevin looked at Cordelia's arm where she was sporting a gash courtesy of Jaspar and his knife.

"I mean, once I tell him who I am, he won't hurt me."

"I don't know, miss. If he don't remember you..." Trevyn didn't need to finish the thought; she knew what he was going to say, and she didn't have the energy or heart to consider it.

"Do you need anything from us?" Kevin asked as Iverson and Trevyn laid down the still-unconscious Jaspar. The room they'd found was cheap, but they had enough coin to stay there for at least a week. She wasn't sure how long they'd be stranded or how long it would take Jaspar to heal, and she figured it was better to err on the side of frugality.

"You've done so much already. I can never thank you enough." Cordelia offered them several coins from her purse, but Kevin refused. "Please. I feel dreadful about your ship and the circumstances."

"That ain't your fault. Pirates sank our ship. We're all just lucky to be alive."

"That's deep, Trev." Iverson smirked. "You sure you're not sick?" Trevyn rolled his eyes, stalking out of the room, and Iverson followed him. Kevin lingered by the door for only a moment before offering her a small wave.

And that was it. How long after leaving the room until they forgot her and Jaspar? She didn't know. But she knew they would only remember the shipwreck, the pirates. They had been friends once, the five of them, and it felt like a betrayal to leave the brothers stranded here with nothing and not even the memory of how they'd really gotten here.

And they were going home, they were going to Alaro. There was a part of her that longed to go with them. They could drag Jaspar back to Anchorage Inn, they could find him another talisman. She could see Taylor, Diarmuid, and Gladys and sleep in her own bed, and they could reset the clock. Go back in time. To a time when they were happy and their lives were easy, safe.

For the moment, they were mostly out of harm's way. There was no sign of the Sidons, and they had enough coin to stay at the inn for a week, maybe longer. She'd had to check into the room for an entire week, just to be certain no one would notice. She considered removing her talisman, it would make things so much easier. But what if the brothers recognized her? What if the Sidons returned?

She stretched out her sore muscles and decided as long as Jaspar was asleep, she could have a moment for herself. She bathed and changed into fresh clothes, a blue and white maid's uniform courtesy of the hotel staff. They'd also provided an old cook's outfit for Jaspar. She brushed her hair with her fingers. She gathered the rations they'd received upon arrival: bread, cheese, dried meat, and fruit. It would be enough for the day, especially if Jaspar continued to sleep.

What did he need to recover? Kevin had said the only cure was rest and lots of fresh water, so that's what Cordelia planned for. She snuck out to the well and filled two buckets before realizing her dislocated shoulder could not carry them back. She had to carry one bucket at a time and make two trips.

The bed was small, and she took time to ensure Jaspar had plenty of space, blankets, and pillows. She wasn't sure what to do with herself while she waited. She didn't know how long he would sleep, how long it would take him to recover. But she knew when he woke, he would want her by his side. And that's where she wanted to be.

7

Cordelia startled awake, her eyes slowly adjusting to the dimly lit room. She wasn't sure the time, but Jaspar was still sleeping, hand tucked under his head. There was a small tapping noise on the window behind her. Cordelia rubbed her eyes. She peeked at who was outside the glass and grabbed a handful of fruit from the basket by the fire. She threw open the window, and a large black crow flew inside. It soared in one circle before landing on her arm.

"Hello, Frân." Cordelia stroked the bird's head, tilting her thoughts when she saw his eyes were still milky white. The bird nipped her affectionally on the finger. "Are you alright?" She gave the bird an apple slice, which he ate with relish. He seemed to be the same as he was before, only the eyes had changed. Perhaps this was a side effect of him helping her to channel her magic.

"Thank you for saving us." The bird didn't answer, of course, but she knew he understood. She assumed Hygonia had sent him to assist with her magic and that it was on Hygonia's orders the magnificent bird was here now.

"Can you get a message to her, please?" The bird scratched an invisible ear, which she took to mean *yes*. "I'm alright. And we're in Keru." The bird gave a loud caw and Cordelia held out a small cube of cheese. The bird ate, nipped her finger, and blinked its still

27

white and creamy eyes. "Thank you." She nuzzled her head to the birds, and then it was off, and the room felt alone again.

She yawned and stretched, noticing the height of the moon. She leaned onto the sill. The air was cold, but she could stand it for a short amount of time. Long enough to take in the brilliantly blue moon, hazy and lighting up the night sky. Jaspar's voice coaxed her mind. *"I like reading by moonlight. In the bright sun, I have to squint, but the moon is...peaceful."*

8

JANUS GRIPPED THE TALISMAN IN HIS FIST, TWISTING IT tighter and tighter until it crumbled under his strength. He dropped down to the ship deck, landing with impossible grace and brute force, the magnitude of his power weighing down his unworthy human body. The ship trembled beneath his steps, and he took pleasure in the instant gratification of his power.

The ship looked like a broken toy. As if thrown against a rock by a child, it lay in shattered pieces with jagged edges, some sinking beneath the waves, some floating, trying desperately not to drown in the depths of the ocean. His lip curled at the smell of ash and salt and the acid of rotting, dying flesh. Vultures circled around and around the ship, swooping down for feedings and returning to the skies to wait for the next meal to succumb.

Janus kicked boards and buckets, tins of emptied foods, and bottles of unfinished whiskey. The bodies of his fallen men lay scattered around, blocking his path, and he shoved them away with a careless flick of his boot. Vapors of smoke, crimson red, and obsidian black encased his body, a waft of sulfur trailing behind him.

The ship had been wrecked by cannons, left hallowed out and barely floating, smoke and cinders flying from it like a mist of disappointment. He kicked carcass after carcass, his eyes finally finding the one body he sought.

The Sidon, green in skin, blond in hair, dark in ambition, red in blood. His face was marred by boils, a sign of yet another failed attempt at his promise to Janus. Janus kicked him away, the boot of his toe colliding with the dying man's chest. He sat up, coughing blood.

"Where isss it?" Janus's voice was a low, dangerous whisper. The man looked down, moving his cloak to reveal a coral-carved quiver with eleven arrows, all tipped with quart stone Janus had worked tirelessly to malign. One arrow was missing, one flame left of disgusting hope.

Janus grabbed the dying man by the neck, pulling him up with ease, watching as his body hung limply, blood spurting from his nose and mouth. "Your arrow." The man's head drooped, and Janus shook him. "Did it find itsss mark?" The man coughed, blood spurting out, and Janus felt the dampness of it hit the collar of his shirt. "Did it hit itsss mark?" he hissed.

"Yesssss." The man slurred out, and Janus felt his lip curl.

"You have ssserved me well. I shall not let you die a long, sssufferable death." The man's eyes widened. Clouds of black flowed from within Janus, slowly flowing out into the man, reaching into his eye sockets and nostrils and swirling inside him before pouring out of his mouth like liquid smoke.

Janus threw the dead Sidon into the pile with the others, uncaring, unfeeling. His eyes scanned the ship of lost men. They had all served their purpose, some more than others, but no matter. He had plenty more at his disposal.

"My lord." A croak, a wheeze from behind an upturned barrel of gunpowder. Janus kicked through the dead and then the barrel. A young Sidon, barely more than a child, missing a left eye, an empty socket staring unseeingly at the world. It was haunting and wicked in a way Janus only slightly envied. The boy was clutching his stomach, keeping his insides as close to his body as possible.

"I do not wish to die. I can still ssserve." He bowed his head and Janus admired his bravery, his devotion.

He knew the boy's loyalty was intertwined with self-preservation, but that could easily be crushed. Janus inspected the young Sidon, pointing to him and raising a finger. He stood on shaky legs, arms still clutching his guts inside. Janus conjured a fire in his palm, wielding it hotter and hotter until it burned blue. He took two steps forward, yanked the young Sidon's arm back, and thrust the fire into his gut.

The Sidon screamed so loud and shrill Janus felt his ears twinge. Janus gripped his shoulder, keeping him as still as possible. When nearly a minute had passed, Janus let the flames slowly recede, and the Sidon swayed on his feet. His one eye lingered on the enchanter before spinning down to his now cauterized abdomen.

"Who do you ssserve?" Janus growled as the boy stood straighter on his feet and bowed his head.

"Lord Janusss."

Janus released the man, scanning the oceans, the quiver of arrows still clutched in his hand. He reached for the bow, arching a single arrow to the skies above. His mark hit a vulture, who tumbled to the deck of the ship with speed. Janus pictured the arrow arching above the seas, between the ships, and into a man's gut, and he laughed, mirthless, wicked, and victorious.

9

KEVIN HAD BEEN RIGHT ABOUT THE LONGEVITY OF halensickness. Jaspar had been recovering for nearly a week. By the second day, Cordelia had sought the help of an apothecary, as there were no healers nearby. She'd considered contacting Hygonia, but she didn't know how long it would take for a letter to travel; by the time it arrived, the sickness could have passed. Or worsened...

The apothecary provided them with a rehydrating drink, though Cordelia wasn't sure it was more than aloe and water. The potions master could do very little for the amnesia, except offer advice for Cordelia to be patient and withhold necessary information so as not to overwhelm the traumatized mind.

Cordelia's injuries were all physical, scratches and bruises here and there. Her bruised rib was a painful nuisance, and her dislocated shoulder ached after being shoved back into its socket. She was a little worse for wear, but at least she had her mind. The apothecary gave her a tonic for the pain, and she acquired a bandage wrap to secure her ribs and a sling for her shoulder.

For seven days and seven nights, Cordelia watched by as Jaspar slept, drank, asked who the hell she was and why she was there, and then fell unconscious again. He didn't seem to be fully lucid, like his cognitive functions had been delayed, and all he could currently think of was sleep, water, bathroom, and then back to sleep. Cordelia had grown restless, but she'd managed to secure their room.

It hadn't been as hard as she'd feared. She requested their room, paid the coin, signed the logbook for the entire week, and then requested a *do not disturb* sign. She snuck out for food and fresh clothes every day or so, and she visited the hotel library for her own entertainment, and though she always searched for books on memory loss, she never found any. Mostly, she sat with impatience by his bed. The waiting was the longest, and no matter how many stories she read from the library, the time stretched on and on and on.

Jaspar would get better, he just needed time. But her greatest fear was that when he woke, when he finally was himself again, he wouldn't remember her. She wasn't sure what that would mean for her, for them. On the one hand, she was terrified of the man who'd woken on that beach and immediately reached for a blade. But could she blame him?

On the other hand, she wasn't sure that man would want to keep her around. She was a stranger, and he owed her nothing, and what would he want with her? But could she really leave? Could she say goodbye to the man who held her heart even if he didn't know it? What would it be like to return to Alaro, spend each night at Anchorage Inn? Go back to the days of working and the nights of loneliness that she'd had before Jaz had come to town.

She could live a life like Gladys, running the tavern, never having let go of her past love, remaining alone all her life, still clinging to a time when she'd felt loved. She knew she wouldn't really be alone, but Cordelia felt that even surrounded by others, she would still feel the absence of Jaspar. And, like Gladys, she would bury her feelings and hide behind her work.

She would spend her days with her family and her friends and learn more from Gladys. And she would spend her nights missing Jaspar. Because that's what a future back in Alaro meant: years and years and years of missing Jaspar, of seeing him every time a new fisherman came to town, of hoping he'd walk through the door at the end of every day or the start of every morning.

It was like the night of the storm all over again, except this time, Cordelia hadn't the slightest hope. Because that night, when he'd finally came home, he'd remembered her. And now, when he finally woke, he would see a stranger.

10

JASPAR DREAMED OF SOFT HUMMING, FINGERS RUNNING through his hair, a gentle lap beneath his head. He could smell the salt of the sea and lavender. He heard the crackling of a fire, the soft cadence behind the humming.

His eyes opened slowly, seeing but not comprehending. An unfamiliar room, a hotel maybe? The ceiling was a beige clay mix, like the mud of the earth. A woven rug lay across the floor, a chair in front of the fire, a pile of clothes, and two water buckets on a table by the door. The humming continued, soft fingers brushing along his scalp.

His body went stiff, and he shot up, leaping out of the bed, the wood floor cold and hard beneath his bare feet. He blinked several times; his head spun, his stomach churned.

"Jaspar?" The woman's voice was sweet, like her humming.

"Who are..." Wait, did she just call him Jaspar? How could she know his true name? He carefully took in her features, looking for something he might recognize. Her lips were pouty, and her eyes were the deepest blue he'd ever seen.

Long, dark curls cascaded down her back. She had a heart-shaped face and nose that seemed a little too small for her cheeks. She could be pretty, he supposed, but he'd never given much thought to physical features. What was the point when no one

35

would ever remember him long enough to stick around? Except she had just called him Jaspar.

"How do you know my name?"

There was a pause, a long one, before she took a deep breath. "My father was Captain Kimbal."

"Was?" Scenes of the shipwreck came back. He couldn't recall details, only small components, like the booms of the cannon, a large metal cage, and thrashing waves. And he felt...something akin to loss? What had he lost? Had he left something aboard the ship? Something precious? But what did he have that was precious?

"Yes." Her face smoothed out, but her eyes were like a mirror to her soul. He saw sorrow and panic and maybe just a little fear. "Four months ago."

"Right." He didn't want to appear weak, didn't want to let his guard down. But this news was hard to digest, and his usual defensive nature came out. He reached for his knife, but he wasn't wearing his boots. Where were his boots?

The woman saw his eyes roam the room and she walked to the front door, returning with his boots and his knife. She dropped the boots in front of his feet but held onto the knife. "If I give you this, can you promise not to hurt me?"

"Why the hell would I do that?" he snarled, and she recoiled.

"Because I would never hurt you." Her voice grew firmer, but it sounded forced, like she was uncertain of her words. "And you've already hurt me once; if it didn't scare me off then, it won't scare me off now." She threw the knife at his feet, and he saw a three-inch-long gash on her right forearm. Had he done that?

He picked up the knife, the motion making him lightheaded. He fought back the bile in his throat and clutched the knife tight in his grip.

"Where am I? Why did you capture me? Why did I nearly drown in the Tilerian Sea?" He could feel his head growing sick, his body starting to sway. He leaned into the wall, feigning nonchalance while trying to hold himself up.

"Jaspar." His name fell from her lips like velvet, like silk, soft in a way he'd never heard it spoken before. It was...unsettling.

She took the slightest step forward. She didn't approach him, but he could tell she wanted to. "You've suffered from sea water poisoning and a concussion. You've been resting for nearly a week, but you should still sit down." She stepped away from the bed, keeping to the edges of the room, putting as much distance between them as possible.

"Sea water poisoning...and...a concussion...a week...a week?!" He shook his head. "Why don't...why don't I remember the last four months?"

"You suffered a concussion during the wreck. I believe the injury has disturbed your memory."

"Amnesia?" What a cruel gift from the world that he, of all people, should get amnesia. Wasn't it bad enough no one could remember him, now he had to live without memory as well?

She nodded. "Please, sit down." It wasn't a command but a plea.

"No. I'm out of here." He turned to leave, but the floor shifted beneath him, and her arm was suddenly there, catching him on her shoulder. It was the shoulder of the working class, firm and solid, muscled from labor. Not the shoulder that would belong to a captain's daughter.

He shoved her off so hard she actually fell to the floor. She winced and clutched her left side. "Who are you?"

She hid her pain well, schooling her features and using the frame of the bed to pull herself up. "I told you. I'm Captain Kimbal's daughter. My name is Cordelia." She enunciated every word as if afraid he wouldn't understand her.

His nostrils flared. "You're not Kimbal's daughter. His daughter was a lady; she'd never have the muscle or strength to support a grown man."

She wrapped her arms around her torso, as if holding herself together. "It's been several months since...my life has changed a great deal. But I assure you I am his daughter."

"Prove it," he snarled, and she flinched back. Her body moved with restraint, her feet a little stiff as she took tiny, hesitant steps forward.

He stepped away, leaning his body against the wall. She held up a hand. "I would never hurt you."

He cocked his head a little, the word seeming almost familiar, but not quite. An image returned to him of the fireplace from the cay...he shook his thoughts clear, fighting back the nausea that came with them.

"I have proof. Just let me show you."

His eyes narrowed. "Fine. But keep your hands to yourself." He tipped his head to the hand she held up to him and saw they were covered in tiny scars, and for some reason, he thought of oysters.

She moved to stand in front of him, and he recognized the smell of lavender and seawater. She was inches away, and the closeness tugged at something in his chest, something he'd never known before. She pulled her hair to the side, revealing her neck. She pinched her left ear to her head and turned her side to him.

"What? Is this supposed to be proof?"

"Look behind my ear," she said carefully.

At first, all he found was the tiny strands of her curling brown hair. But just beneath the roots was a symbol. Not quite like his own, but there was only one difference. Where his mark was a compass overlaying the shape of Qualaris, hers was a compass overlaying a heart with an unusual, three-pronged dagger piercing it.

Running footsteps echoed outside in the hall. He took two long strides to the door, the woman close behind him. The sound of footsteps was getting louder and louder, approaching their room.

He waved a hand, extinguishing the fireplace instantly. The girl had no reaction to his use of magic. Had she been around Hagans before? Was she one of the few who didn't believe the tales of horror associated with his kind? Or was she telling the truth, and she wasn't surprised by his magic because she'd seen him use it before?

He scanned the room, made a dash for the long-draped windows, and tucked himself between the curtain and the wall. The woman's shadow was visible from his hiding place, and he watched as she squared her shoulders. The doorknob was rattling, people were pounding, and she didn't have the time or forethought to hide. Should he have helped her?

Her posture became one of the noble class, and she fumbled with a necklace, a starfish with a blue stone. She opened the door, casual, expectant.

"Yes?"

"Er, excuse me, miss." Jaspar could see only the shoes of the man at the door. "We heard reports of shouting from this room. And I noticed this room was reserved for a single. A Cordy Marlow." Marlow? She had used his name? Were they married? Had he gone off and gotten married in the last four months?

"Yes, I'm Cordy Marlow." Her voice rang true, and if he didn't know better, he'd believe her. Maybe he didn't know better...was the woman he'd slashed with a knife and believed to be his captor actually his...wife?

"Apologies. I must have forgotten when you checked in." Jaspar's blood ran cold. That was a comment he'd heard before, but why was she hearing it? Why didn't the man remember her? Was she as cursed as he was? Had he gone off, gotten married, and cursed his betrothed?

"That's quite alright. But I'm in perfect health and would like to rest for the evening. Good day, sir." There were mumblings from the man, confusion that Jaspar couldn't hear, and then he heard the lock click shut. He saw her lean against the door, her hand still on the handle. She closed her eyes, sighing. Her face fell, full lips pouting, and she laid a hand over her chest.

Jaspar appeared from behind the curtain, and her fallen face cleared instantly. How did she do that?

"You gave him my name." He pulled his knife back out, more for something to do than because he'd planned on using it. She nodded. Her face paled, and she remained standstill, her back pressed against the door, her eyes on his blade.

"Are we...did I *marry* you?" He couldn't hide the antipathy in his voice. It wouldn't be so terrible to be married, but it wasn't something he'd ever expected to do, wasn't something he'd planned for. And the idea of being married to someone he didn't know, someone he had no recollection of marrying, was unnerving.

Her eyes sort of wrinkled, regretful, showing her every

emotion in that one brief slip before her expression cleared again. "No, Jaspar. It was simply a cover. You did not marry me."

"But I let you use my name? I *told* you my full name?"

"You didn't *let* me." She rolled her eyes. "It was your idea."

His jaw went slack. "To pretend I was *married*?" He swayed on his feet again, but this time, she didn't try to help him.

"Please sit down."

Reluctantly, he dragged his feet to the bed and sank into the soft, cushioned mattress. "What's wrong with me?"

"I told you." She grabbed one of the buckets from the table, and he saw it was filled to the brim with water. "You have seawater poisoning. You need to drink this." She shoved the bucket in his arms. Suddenly, he was so thirsty he felt he could drink the entire ocean. He ladled spoonful after spoonful of water, and the bucket was nearly half gone when she returned.

"Eat this." She handed him a bowl of tomato soup and a plate of fruit. "I know you don't like soup without bread, but right now, you need to rehydrate, and that means only eating foods that contain large amounts of water."

Despite the amount of water he'd just ingested, his mouth went dry. "How do you know that I don't like soup without bread?"

"Because I know you." She pulled a chair near the bed and sat down. "Now eat."

"Have...have I really been asleep for a week?"

"More or less, yes."

Jaspar forced down the food, taking breaks in between each bite so as not to irritate his raw throat. "And you've been here all that time?"

"Yes."

"Why?"

She shrugged. "Someone had to look after you."

She pulled out a cloak and needle and began mending the cloth, sewing back together tiny rips and holes. He recognized the material as belonging to his concealment cloak. Where had she gotten that? He ate and she sewed, and he tried to understand the mess that was his life. The food made him sleepy, and by the time he'd finished eating and drank the rest of the water, his eyes were drooping.

"You said you were the captain's daughter."

"Yes." She continued to sew.

"I've never met her, yet you know my eating habits?"

"I'm not just the captain's daughter. We're..." She bit her lip. "Acquainted."

Acquainted? "And you remember me?" He whispered this more to himself than to her. Her words bounced around his aching skull, but he couldn't make sense of any of it. She put down her sewing and took his food bowls and his now empty bucket.

She shivered. "Do you have enough energy to bring back the fire?" With very little effort, he pointed his hand across the room, and the fireplace crackled once more. "Thank you." She was carrying a heavy quilt now and sat back in her chair.

He wanted to sleep, but he wanted to ask so many questions, and he wasn't sure he could let his guard down around her long enough to rest. And yet, hadn't he slept already? His body laid itself down, the pillow catching his head. He heard soft humming, the blanket moved and was suddenly pulled up to just below his shoulders, and he could smell the ocean and lavender.

11

Taylor had spent most of his life after the war working during the day and reading during the evening. But as of late, he found himself spending more and more of his off hours at Anchorage Inn. Sometimes, he told himself he was hoping for word from Delia. Sometimes, he told himself he merely wanted to socialize for a bit. But deep down, he knew it was her.

Tonight was no different, though the tavern was a little less busy than usual. Gladys was wiping tables and tucking chairs back in. A group of sorts were putting together a puzzle in the corner booth. A young couple danced by the fire. A few straggling fishermen sat at the bar.

The night was quiet, and though he had brought a book, Taylor mostly pretended to read, sipping his tea while stealing glances at Gladys. Watching her strong arms arrange and rearrange the furniture. Watching the curve of her hip as she used it to push crates behind the bar. Watching the way her auburn hair swayed behind her whenever she reached for something. He cataloged every detail of her, every feature of both the girl he knew and the woman she had become.

Gladys poured Taylor a fresh mug of tea. "Dare I ask if you've any news of Delia?"

"No." She frowned. "I take it you haven't heard anything either?"

"No. I can't imagine why she hasn't returned. Or why no one's heard from her." Taylor kept his eyes on his book.

"I didn't think it would take more than a day or two."

"We shouldn't have let her go alone."

He could practically hear the annoyance in her voice. "Taylor, not this again, you and Mary both. She *wanted* to go."

He snapped the book shut. "She was upset, she wasn't thinking clearly. She kept going on about that boy no one ever found."

"She's a grown woman." Gladys's green eyes flared. "I know you and Mary still see her as a Lady, as incapable, but she's a young woman now, and if she wants to do something, nothing in this world will stop her."

"*You* should've stopped her."

"And done what, Taylor? Dragged her back here kicking and screaming?"

"Just because you've hardened yourself to the world, doesn't mean she has to." Taylor's mouth soured, and he wished so bad he could take the words back. Gladys's eyes were wide, hurt clouding the expression of her stunning features.

"Gladys, I'm—"

"Why are you here, Taylor? Did you come all the way down here to yell at me and make me feel bad about myself and tell me I'm a terrible person?"

"Of course not."

"So, why are you here?" She enunciated each word individually.

To see you, because I have to see you, because I miss seeing you every day and this is the only time I can spare to spend with you, even if it is from afar. "I don't know."

"Then maybe you should go home." There was the smallest break in her voice, and Taylor rose from his stool.

Before he could reach for her, the energy in the bar shifted. Diarmuid, the cook with a permanent scowl, hobbled into the bar, face red with fury.

"Pirates! At the innhouse. Trashing the damn place!"

Taylor moved without thought, his footsteps urgent, his long strides catching up to Diarmuid. Horses were running about in all

43

directions, released from their tethers in the stable. The innhouse door was flung open, half off its hinges. He ran up the stairs, taking them several at a time.

The halls were filled with the clutter of guests and residents: clothes, food, personal belongings. Dresser drawers had been removed and dumped, tables upturned, mattresses flipped over. Windows had been smashed in, broken shards of glass littering the floor.

Walls were scratched and the floor was streaked with slime and sand. Mirrors and pictures had been ripped from the walls. Taylor checked every room, but no guests were there, and he couldn't find a single thief. He couldn't find any responsible party.

And then his entire universe collapsed. A scream made his blood boil, and he pulled a blade he never used from his belt. He was down the stairs in two jumps, outside in one step, at the entrance in twenty paces, and kicking the door open before a minute had passed.

Slimy, green-skinned men in matching green robes held the bar hostage, each holding a different group of people by the threat of a bow and arrow. Hooded faces lined the room, and each man had a jörmungandr pendant on their chest. *Sidons*. A black-haired one missing his left eye stood in the middle of the room, a knife in his slimy hand pushed into Gladys's throat.

12

A DARK AND LOW REVERBERATION ESCAPED TAYLOR, like an animal hunting prey. Blood pooled on the floor by Gladys's knees from a cut far too deep along her collarbone. Her mouth was in a firm, hard line, her eyes pinned to the wall.

"I warn you, I'm not a patient man." The one-eyed Sidon pulled Gladys back by the hair; her face never wavered. The Sidon seemed to be addressing both her and the bar as a whole. "I'm only going to ask one more time, and then I'll spill every drop of her blood on this floor."

Gladys's expression did not change, she didn't move, didn't even blink, but her eyes swiveled slowly to Taylor.

"Drop the knife." Taylor's voice was deep, resounding around the bar. The Sidon met his gaze, blade still in hand, Gladys's blood dripping from its sharp tip.

"I wasn't talking to you." The one-eyed Sidon returned his attention to Gladys, but before he could stab the blade to skin, Taylor spun his knife, aiming it at the Sidon, the bladed dagger finding its mark in his throat. Blood spurted, and the man gurgled more of it from his mouth. He stumbled forward, falling to his knees, his lonely eye wide and bloodshot. His body oscillated once left, then right, before collapsing to the floor in a lifeless heap.

A deadly hush fell over the bar, like a wind sweeping away all sound. Gladys's eyes stayed locked on his, and he forced himself to remain the man he must be in this moment: deliberate, in command, an unmovable force. Reluctantly, he released Gladys's gaze with a single blink. He met the face of every Sidon in the room.

"Leave." When they didn't move, Taylor reached for the closest thing he could grab, an empty whiskey glass, and hurled it at the head of the Sidon holding the dancing couple hostage. Glass shattered as the Sidon tried to deflect the spinning cup. Before the Sidon could bend back, Taylor threw a heavy tankard at his head. The Sidon was forced down by the weight and momentum of the tankard, his eyes rolling into the back of his head, blood pooling from his scalp.

One by one the Sidons panicked, lowering their bows, eyeing the door.

"You heard the man!" Diarmuid shouted from behind Taylor. "Leave!"

The Sidons shared wide-eyed looks but didn't move. Taylor's control slipped. His eyes twisted fast, then he heard a light rustle, and Diarmuid's cane came into focus. He shot out an arm, catching it with ease. His body bent left at the middle, and the cane was airborne, slamming into the chest of the Sidon by the fireplace. The man toppled over, landing in the flames and screaming in pain.

The remaining Sidons stumbled, rushing to the door, leaving their fallen cohorts behind. Taylor was stiff, fists at his side. His insides churned with desperation, but he couldn't show even a hint of weakness until the Sidons had gone.

It was the most prolonged two minutes of his entire existence, but the Sidons finally exited and Diarmuid signaled when they'd ran out of eyesight. Taylor took three fast strides to Gladys, who was already trying to wrap her wound with a ripped sleeve from her dress.

He lifted her with the ease and strength of a much younger man, an arm behind her shoulders, another tucked under her legs. "Do what you can, Diarmuid." The old man stumbled around the bar, and a few patrons who'd found their wits helped him remove the bodies and clean up the space.

Taylor set Gladys on the large kitchen island counter, searching around the room for medical supplies before finding a small basket in a cupboard. He locked the doors to the bar and the courtyard. He stood next to her in one quick stride.

Her eyes were white as snow, her blouse crimson with a four-inch gash along her clavicle. Blood slowly seeped out of the wound that Gladys tried to hold a drenched sleeve to. Taylor caught her gaze, and she nodded, rolling out of the sleeves of her dress, revealing her slip beneath. He swallowed the desire that bloomed from her nearly exposed body.

Gladys had grabbed a bottle of whiskey and tossed back a shot before handing it to him. He took an alcohol-soaked cloth and gave Gladys a curt nod before wiping it gently across her wound. Her chest convulsed, but Gladys kept her composure as Taylor cleaned the wound, sewing stitches tightly.

He used a healing salve from the basket to gently coat the top of the wound, watching as Gladys's face eased a little under the numbing agent. He wrapped her chest tight, ensuring the bandage would stay in place, feeling the contours of her body as he did the only thing he ever wanted to do: take care of her.

A quarter of an hour later, she was fully bandaged. He washed his hands, throwing the bloodied clothes and rags in the fire beneath the stove. The barest groan reached his ears, and he was beside her in two strides. Her hair was wet, sweat-soaked to her neck, tendrils loose by her temples.

His hand moved her hair, lingered on her neck, his palm on her throat, his thumb stroking her jaw. "How are you...Gladi?" Her face reddened under the freckles, and he convinced himself it was from the ordeals of the night.

"I'm alright, Taylor." His name from her lips nearly did him in.

"What did they want?"

He felt her swallow under his palm, and he tucked his hand back in his pocket. "I don't know. They were talking about magic and power and something called a Celarestar. It was fairly easy not to tell them what I knew because I didn't know anything."

"You weren't just being stubborn?" He allowed his eyes to crease.

"Thank you."

"For?"

"You saved my life." Her eyes were tight, watchful, perplexed.

He fought the urge to embrace her. "You think so little of me?"

"Taylor, I..."

"What?"

Some of her fire returned. "What would you expect me to think?"

He opened his mouth to speak, but she clambered down from the counter, and in two heartbeats, she was nearer than she'd been in almost thirty years.

"You walked out and never came back to me. Even after the war, even after you moved back to Alaro. I've been waiting here for half my life." Her voice was sultry, as young as the kisses they'd once shared.

Waiting for half her life... "Why would I have come back? You didn't want me anymore."

He found resolve in the remaining adrenaline from the night. If he didn't ask her now, he may never have the courage to do so again. "Why did you let me leave, Gladi? Why didn't you come with me?"

He felt the absence of her warmth as she strode back. Her voice waned. "My parents died while you were training in Scaparo, and I was needed here."

"Why didn't you tell me?"

"I told you I couldn't go and that I'd wait for you. But before I could tell you why, you walked away. I called after you, I followed you outside, nearly chased you down the street, but you kept walking."

A deep sense of disgrace coiled in his abdomen as he flashed back thirty years to the night he'd proposed. Gladys had been in near tears, the first and only time he'd seen her show such open despondency. She'd told him to wait. Told him to listen. He'd pushed her away, shrugged out of her grasp, slammed the bar door in her face. Then he had left, and he'd never looked back. He'd spent half his life blaming her for breaking his heart when, all the while, he was the guilty party.

"I stayed behind because I had no choice." Her voice was back to normal, assertive, tantalizing. "But I would have followed you anywhere."

She was still so breathtaking. Auburn hair that formed tight ringlets. Green eyes that had haunted his dreams. Full, perfect lips that he'd longed for.

"I owe you thirty years of apologies, Taylor."

She was everything he had ever wanted, strong and bold when she needed to be, sweet and compassionate when she wanted to be, fiercely loyal and genuine to her very core. And he'd wasted thirty years resenting her when he should have been holding onto her, showing her how exquisite and timeless and rare she was.

He moved to her, anchoring himself to her body on the precipice of an embrace he should have held every day of his life. Unsaid words passed between them, and Gladys raised her chin ever so slightly, but Taylor's hardened heart broke through the haze. He took two heavy strides back. Hurt and rejection flashed her features, but Gladys hid them quickly.

"Gladi, I—"

"Thank you, Taylor, for your assistance, but I think I can manage from here." She corrected her posture, leaving him with her head held high. Taylor watched her go, and maybe he should have gone after her, maybe he should have kissed her. But too many years had passed them by, too many days of misunderstood pain, too many nights of restless sleep. Maybe in another life, maybe if he'd known back then, but now it was too late, it was simply too late.

13

Jaspar dreamed he was sailing under a dark sky. He pulled tight on the sails, his ship nearly keeling over in the storm. Wave upon wave crashed, flooding his deck. He spat out a mix of rain and ocean water, though more was streaming down his face.

Something shifted, and Jaspar was below deck on a foreign ship. It was sinking, with water nearly so high it covered his head. The woman was there...the captain's daughter. She was trapped tight in a fishing cage wedged into the corner of the ship. Jaspar watched curiously as another version of himself tried to free her. It was as if he was on the outside, looking in, seeing himself with Cordelia.

Dream Jaspar yanked at the cage until his fingers bled, trickling into the water in tiny red bubbles. And then her finger was poking through the cage, and she stroked it along his lips, and a pained look filled his expression.

Dream Jaspar spoke, the sound of a desperate man, affirmations of love and devotion. *He'd never leave her. Never.* He slipped beneath the ocean, and Cordelia soon followed. Bubbles escaped her as she tried to shout his name under the water.

Only now, it wasn't dream Jaspar with her, it was him, the real Jaspar, and he was swimming away from her.

"I don't know you," he gurgled. She stopped, holding her

hands in front of her chest, and the water around him started to move, and then he was pushed through the surface, as if an invisible wave shoved him up.

He was on a board now, a large plank from the ship, and Cordelia, still trapped in her cage, still palms up, was staring at him, forcing the water right up to the shore.

There was a whisper, a voice he knew, a voice he...adored.

He was lying on a beach, sand and dirt and grass beneath him. Cordelia was there, beautiful and shining like the sun. She hummed to him and stroked his hair. He blinked, now in a lumpy bed, he blinked again, and words he didn't hear, but he knew she said them. He touched her cheek. "I know you."

14

CORDELIA SHOOK AWAKE, RECALLING HER surroundings almost immediately. Jaspar was still asleep, his bed feeling miles from her chair though it was only two feet. It may as well have been an ocean, an ocean of lost memories that separated her from the man who was meant for her.

She stretched, bathed, dressed, checked once more on Jaspar, and was out the door in five minutes. She was still wearing the maid's uniform as she snuck through the halls. She didn't know what they would do next, where they would go. But she knew they'd need food and supplies. Jaspar would know what to do, would know what they needed, but he wasn't the Jaspar she knew. This man was wild, untrusting, and angry.

She kept as quiet as she could, down the hall and toward the kitchens.

"About time!" A stern woman with golden hair approached her, practically running down the hallway. "I can't believe how behind we are. What was your name again? Never mind, doesn't matter. Take this." She shoved a basket of linens and hops into Cordelia's arms. "To room seven. Their child had an accident, and they'll need fresh linens in the morning as well. You can leave it by the door."

"Yes, ma'am." Cordelia immediately followed orders, and by the time she'd dropped off the basket, the woman was gone. She

52

blended in with the staff? That could work to her advantage. She didn't waste any time, sneaking down the halls until she saw two maids heading to a large portraited wall.

They opened it to reveal a servant's stairwell. Cordelia rushed after them, pretending to be another maid who was late and needed a spare apron. They pointed her to the hall closet, and she made quick work of finding uniforms for her and Jaspar. Fresh clothes would do them good and it wouldn't hurt to don the look of the working class.

Walking through the kitchens was easy now. She simply grabbed a satchel from a pile of them hooked by the door. There were rows of bread rolls, fruit, cheese, a little coffee, and bacon. She took another satchel for good measure, shoving the clothes inside, and then made her way back to their rooms.

"Do you need help with that?" A short man with wispy white hair offered her an arm for one of her satchels.

"Thank you, but I can manage." She waited for him to turn down the hall, knowing that if her talisman still worked, he would forget her as soon as they parted.

SHE RETURNED TO A STILL SLEEPING JASPAR, HIS ARM behind his head, his blanket pulled up to just below his shoulders. The scene was so familiar, yet it felt like it no longer belonged to her.

While he slept, she started clearing the room, not wanting to leave any evidence that they had been there. She picked up the floor, fixed the rug, put the chair back exactly the way she'd found it. She left the washroom in case Jaspar needed to clean up. She was wiping the earth and fireplace when she heard him.

"I almost forgot you were here," he grumbled.

"Did I wake you?"

He looked past her, out the window to the moon, indicating that sunrise was a mere hour away.

"We're leaving?"

"Yes, I only had coin for a week."

He rubbed his eyes and stretched.

"There's peppermint leaves in the bathroom, and some soap shavings. I didn't want to use the bar in case—"

"It looked like someone was here."

She nodded, finishing the fireplace as he went to clean up. She made the bed while he readied himself, dressed, and looked refreshed when he emerged ten minutes later. Jaspar drank nearly half the bucket of water and ate most of the fruit while she continued to clear any trace of them. By the time he had finished eating, the room was back in its pre-guest state and Cordelia was packed and ready to leave.

"Are you feeling better?"

Jaspar nodded but didn't speak. Instead, he put on his boots and his newly mended traveling cloak.

"Do you have somewhere for us to go?"

He raised a brow to her. "I have somewhere *I* can go. I don't know where you're going."

"I'm going wherever you go."

"Look." He rolled his eyes, "I appreciate...whatever it is you did for me, but I don't do partners. You go home, and I'll pick up where I left off."

"But...but you said you believe me, that I'm—"

"Kimbal's daughter, yeah, but that doesn't make me responsible for you." His words were curt, so unlike the happy and carefree Jaspar she knew.

"Not responsible for," Her face fell. "the letter," she mumbled to herself. He never got the letters because he didn't remember going home and reading them. He didn't remember her father dying. He didn't remember what her father asked of him. All he knew was that Kimbal *had* a daughter.

"What letter?"

"Nothing." What could she say? Would he believe her? Hard as it may be for her, keeping him in the dark might be what was best for him.

He shrugged his shoulders. "I wish you luck and all that. And thanks for," he waved his hand toward the bed, "when I was sick. But I gotta get going."

"But." She hated the whine in her voice. "I have to go with you. You need—"

There was a knock at the door, the doorknob rattled. "Is someone in there?"

"They won't remember us," she assured herself, a comfort she still hadn't come to terms with. She grabbed her satchels, tossing them over her good shoulder.

"They won't remember *me*." Jaspar's eyes narrowed. "Why won't they remember you?" The door rattled again, and now someone was clicking with the locked knob.

"I don't have time to explain; we have to leave!" Cordelia rushed to the window, pulling it open with great effort. She looked down, the second-story bedroom suddenly felt alarmingly high.

Gracefully, Jaspar ran to the window and tossed himself out, landing on the ground in a crouch. Cordelia seethed but straightened her back and tried to mimic his jump. She landed hard on all fours, the air rushing out of her lungs, her injuries screaming from the impact.

She wobbled a little before getting to her feet and spinning in a circle. Jaspar was yards ahead, running east. She huffed, chasing after him, her small strides keeping her far behind.

She lost sight of him after nearly half an hour of running when her feet slowed to a jog. Another half an hour and her jog slowed to a walk. Two hours of walking, and her feet were practically dragging behind her, until after five hours of chasing Jaspar, of following the path she hoped he was on, she finally stopped. Her shoulders sagged and she bent over, her hands resting on her knees.

Her breaths came in quick, her throat dry and her eyes seeing small flecks of light. Her body might have grown strength as a bar maiden, but she certainly hadn't built up an endurance, not to mention her injured body was hardly in any condition to run for so long. Jaspar was nowhere to be seen. And she was too far from the inn to remember where it was.

Where in Mikiria am I supposed to go now?

15

JASPAR HADN'T EXPELLED MUCH ENERGY OUTRUNNING Cordelia. He hadn't seen or heard her for nearly two hours and had to assume she either couldn't keep up or had gone back to town as he'd suggested. Cordelia had said he'd spent an entire week recovering, but his body still felt weak. His head felt heavy on his neck, and his face burned hot despite the cold winter air.

His lips were chapped, his throat parched. How long would it take to rehydrate his body? How much of the sea had he swallowed? How long did it take to recover? *The captain would know,* he thought. A new pain seized him.

Could the captain really be dead? How? He had just received a letter from him not two days past. Had just spoken to him last week. The last thing he remembered was Scaparo and preparing to meet with the captain. He had a new mission for them, some new lead to follow. How had everything gone so wrong?

It felt like no time had passed, and yet snow covered the ground, and the air was chilled with winter winds and temperatures. How had he lost four months of his life and his friend in no more than a week? Only one person had ever remembered him, he'd only had one friend in his whole life. Was he really to believe that man was gone?

Jaspar coughed and stumbled, his face hitting something solid. The small pond he'd been traveling next to had dried and all the water was floating in front of him, a solid, immovable wall. His blood ran cold, and he dared to search the lands for the Danthem that created it. Hagans had very little power over water mages, particularly one powerful enough to dry an entire pond.

"Jaspar." A winded and red-faced Cordelia appeared, her body looking as if it may give out at any moment, her chest heaving up and down.

"Why the blazes are you still following me?"

"Look, I'm sorry you've lost your memories, and I realize this must all be a bit hard to bear. But I'm going wherever you go, so you may as well stop running," she panted out.

His eyes shifted from the wall to the woman and back. "Did you make this?"

"What? Oh, that." She shook her head and waved her hand, the water splashed as it returned to the bedrock. "Sorry, but I had to get your attention."

"Who are you?" He stumbled back, his feet plunging into the wet-again pond.

"How many times do I have to tell you? I'm—"

"Kimbal never mentioned anything about his daughter being a Danthem!" Jaspar's shout reverberated in the empty fields around them. He heard splashes as a group of pond turtles ducked back into the water to hide from the noise.

"Yes, well, he never bothered to tell me either, and I wager I had more right to know than you."

"I don't believe you."

"Well, that's just too bad because I'm not going anywhere." Her mouth set into a hard line.

He clutched a stitch in his side. "How do you even *remember* me?" He'd been confused by so many things but by nothing more than that. He could tell himself she was a late bloomer with her magic, that maybe Kimbal had kept it a secret for her safety.

He could explain away forgetting a few months from some concussion. Maybe he was even capable of letting himself believe the captain was gone. But how the hell did she know him? Captain Kimbal had been able to remember him. Had that been a gift his daughter had inherited?

"My mark," she wheezed.

Right. Behind her ear. "Why?"

Her shoulders sagged and she wrapped her arms around her torso. "Why what?"

"Why do you expect me to take you with me?"

She sucked in a ragged breath and winced, clutching her left rib. "Did you trust my father?"

He'd never been one for lying in conversation unless necessary. Afterall, why bother when everyone would forget they ever talked to him? So it didn't surprise him when he answered her truthfully. "Yes."

"Then trust me. Please." Her voice was small, feeble.

"Why should I—"

"For one thing, I've spent the last week nursing you back to health. Isn't that reason enough for you?"

He stared at her for a long moment, trying to find the truth in her words. But he felt nothing.

"No, it's not." He took off eastward, knowing she wouldn't be able to keep up with him, hoping she'd take the hint.

Guilt pricked through him like thorns. He wasn't one for a partner, particularly one he didn't trust. It would probably hurt her feelings, but it would be for the best if she just returned to her life and he to his. He had no intention of taking responsibility for this woman, he owed the *captain* his life, but he owed nothing to his daughter.

Jaspar didn't even make it half a mile when he stalled in his steps, nearly toppling over as a blood-chilling shriek pierced through the air and an unfamiliar feeling of concern twisted in his chest.

16

CORDELIA'S BLOOD RAN COLD. HER BREATHING CAME TO a near stop. *No. Please no.* She reached inside herself, testing her orb of magic, furious when she found it dimmed. The pond was too far away, she couldn't tap into her magic.

She did all she could to stand tall, proud, and brave as the Sidons came into view. It wasn't the same group as before, the blond-haired leader was nowhere to be seen. She counted slowly, forcing herself to breathe. One. Two. Five. Ten.

"What do you want?" she asked as the slimy green men started to encircle her. The clearing was almost completely open, with sparse trees and foliage. No houses or people in sight. The fields of wheat still barren with winter weather.

"Nothing from you." A Sidon so tall she had to crane her neck to look up at him smirked, slinking toward her. His long strides had him standing a foot in front of her in three steps. His skin, slimy and green, shimmered in the sunlight, and she flinched when his webbed hand touched her face, skating along her cheekbone. "We were looking for your friend, your magical friend."

"Who..." Cordelia cleared her throat, hiding the tremor in her voice. "Who is this friend?"

"Goes by the name...Jazzz."

All the blood drained from her face, her eyes widened so much she could feel air from the wind. "I've never heard of him," her voice shook, and she could practically feel their disbelief in her words.

"Oh, come now. Sssure you have." The Sidon ripped Cordelia's satchels from her person, breaking the straps and throwing them to his comrades. He twirled a dagger in his hand, reminding Cordelia of her first encounter, when the other Sidon had slashed her cheek. She hadn't answered his questions then, and she wouldn't answer them now.

They shouldn't even know the name Jaz. What could they want with him? Hadn't Jaspar and Hygonia said they were looking for a Danthem? They were hunting Cordelia. Sidons hunted water users. What would they want with a Hagan?

"You have me at a disadvantage, sir. I don't know a *Jaz* any more than I know any of you." Her voice was stronger this time as she toed the line of truth and lies.

"I think you do." The Sidon's slimy fingers squeezed her mouth tight, and she shook her head.

The cold blade of the dagger slid from her cheekbone to her brow, to her hair. It left little trickles of blood along its path, and Cordelia squeezed her hands into fists at her side.

"All you have to do isss tell usss where he isss, and then we'll leave."

Water, I need water. But despite her best efforts, she could summon no orb of magic. She resigned herself to her circumstances. If she was going to die today, let it be so that Jaspar could live another.

Cordelia clenched her mouth tight, the Sidon's hands still pinching her face. But he could squeeze her face all day, he could cut her as much as he liked, she would never, *could* never, tell them anything about Jaz or Jaspar.

The Sidon smiled, ominous, and tightened his grip so hard her skin pulled across her face. He slid the knife across her forehead, and now the blood was slowly dripping into her eyebrows. He tilted his head, quirking a brow, but she just stared back. He moved so fast she didn't have time to intake breath. He released her face, and his arm came down, the knife piercing her skin, just below her left collarbone.

Unprepared, unable to fight back, she screamed against her own will, her lungs deciding before she could stop them.

"Now, now." The Sidon started shushing her. "I don't want to hurt you. But I need to find your friend. Where...isss...Jazzz?" He said each word with a dig of the knife.

Cordelia's teeth clenched, and though she tried, she couldn't stifle her sobs as the blade burrowed deeper into her chest, causing more pain than she'd ever felt in her life. Her head grew light, her vision suddenly clouded by darkness. Somehow, she refused to speak. Blood warmed her skin, soaking into her blouse. The Sidon held her recently dislocated shoulder in his hand, gripping her in place as the knife stayed lodged.

"Bossss, I think I can perssssuade her to looosssen her tongue." A round Sidon walked forward, his bald, green head shining in the sun.

The tall Sidon yanked the knife out, and a new pain spiked down her arms and her chest. White spots clouded her vision, and a buzzing sound danced in and out of her eardrums. She was thrown forward, and the bald man caught her with his wide stomach. He yanked her up by her hair, digging a hand into the cut on her shoulder with a filthy, slimy fist.

"The way I sssee it." His fingers slithered from her shoulder wound, across her collarbone, to her the shoulder she'd only just taken out of the sling. "You've got two arms." He squeezed her arm tightly, leaving tiny bruises under his fingers. "And two legsss." He kicked her left kneecap, and she fell forward. "Ten toesss." He stomped on her foot, and another yelp escaped. "Ten fingersss. And ssseveral other appendagesss you can live without."

Abruptly, he yanked her back, her hand held firmly in his. He kicked her injured shoulder, forcing her to her knees. She heard her voice again, so loud and piercing and so unlike her nightmares when screams wouldn't come to her. She wished she could hide her terror, wished she hadn't given them the satisfaction of knowing how much they'd hurt her.

The man held her hand in front of her face and pulled one of her fingers, bending it the slightest amount. Her lips trembled and she bit them down, hard, so hard she tasted iron on her tongue.

"We'll ssstart with the fingersss then. And I'll go nice and ssslow." He pulled her finger farther back, then twisted it to the side, and she felt hot tears warm her face. "One." Another pull. "By." Another pull. "One." A snap, a breaking of bones, her head pulling her to the ground.

The man shook her, slapping her face, keeping her conscious.

"Lassst chance, pretty girl. Where. Isss. Jazzz?"

Cordelia's mouth had filled with blood, she was seconds away from expelling her pain or passing out or both. She reared her head back before spitting in the man's face, her bloody saliva coating his left eye and dripping down his nose. He snapped another finger, hard, the bone breaking instantly.

She inhaled as much air as she could and channeled all the strength that her father, Taylor, Mary, Gladys, Diarmuid, and her lost Jaspar had ever given her. She made sure her voice was strong, loud, and could be heard clear as day.

"Break them all."

17

JASPAR COULD BARELY UNDERSTAND THE SCENE AS IT unfolded before him. Why were Sidons hunting his alias? When was the last time he'd used that name? Why did they think this woman knew where he was? Why the blazes was she willing to let her body be ripped apart piece by piece to save him?

He pulled two knives from each of his boots and let his fire build inside him, ready to be used when necessary. But he didn't want to play all of his cards just yet. He flipped the dagger in his hand and let it fly. It found its mark in the neck of the fat man currently breaking Cordelia's pinkie.

Howls erupted as the Sidon clutched his oozing neck, dropping Cordelia to the ground. The other Sidons didn't move to help but instead searched the clearing with suspicious eyes, seeking the enemy they couldn't see.

Jaspar sought the man who had slapped and stabbed Cordelia and let another dagger loose, this one landing in the man's thigh. Cordelia followed the path of the flying daggers, and when her eyes met his, the pain was replaced with panic. "What the blazes are you doing? Leave, leave now!"

Jaspar was mere steps from her and came to a stop. Leave? She had been tortured to tears and trauma, and she still wanted to protect him?

"And who might you be?" A woman stepped out from behind

the group of Sidons. Jaspar was slightly taken aback by her appearance. At first, he'd thought she was a woman traveling with the Sidons, but upon closer inspection, he realized she *was* a Sidon.

Her skin was dark, and he couldn't see the Sidon green tint, nor did it appear oily or sticky. She wore her dark purple hair in tight dreadlocks that fell just above her shoulders. And where there should have been the large gills of a Sidon on her neck, she merely had two narrow rows under her ears, so small he wondered if she could still breathe underwater with them.

Unlike the Sidons, whose feet and hands were shaped like fins, this female wore black boots. Her hands, only a small web at the centerfold of each finger, gripped a tight spear with a large gold tip. And behind her sauntered a great Tigraige, orange and black and deadly.

The Tigraige stood at least twelve feet tall and two feet wide, with a head as big as Jaspar's whole body. The beast's shoulders moved up and down as it stalked them like prey. The great creature threw its head back, letting out a thunderous growl. The sea tiger's scaled and striped skin gleamed in the sun, its neck of gills flapping faintly in the wind. Mouth unhinging, it shook its head, letting out another great roar.

Jaspar gripped his last dagger. "I'm no one."

The female Sidon snapped her fingers, and the great beast attacked. Guilt wound its way around his chest as Jaspar took the knife to the creature, stabbing it in the shoulder. The howl the beast let out was deafening, and a paw collided with Jaspar's face, slashing claws into his bare skin.

The attack knocked him off his balance and he turned his fall into a roll. He stumbled to his feet, putting distance between himself and the beast. There was blood dripping from his face, and he wiped it with the back of his arm, soaking his sleeve in red. The Tigraige shuffled forward, its injury making its movements jagged and clumsy.

The beast swung another clawed paw, and Jaspar hated himself as he took the knife and plunged it deep into the creature's paw. Spit flew from the Tigraige's jaw as it yowled in pain. He couldn't bring himself to kill the great beast, though it attacked him with a fervor.

Tigraige's were sacred sea creatures and the Sidons had broken this one. They had turned it into a killing beast. But Jaspar refused to be like them, refused to take away the urgency and life of this majestic animal. Even injuring it twisted his gut with shame.

He took a step to the Tigraige, making a point of eye contact and lifting the knife once more.

"Stop!" The female Sidon's shout alerted both the creature and Jaspar to her presence. The creature, trained to obey its master, stopped mid-attack, landing all four paws on the ground with a tremble.

The female Sidon had Cordelia by the throat, the blade of her spear digging into Cordelia's neck, tiny drops of blood trickling from its sharp point.

"Let. Her. Go." It was a hushed command, a dangerous one, because the remorse Jaspar felt about killing an innocent creature did not extend to a Sidon.

"Step back." The Sidon hissed to the Tigraige, who followed her orders and retreated to the forest it had come from. The creature whimpered slightly with each step, no doubt from walking on its injured paw and shoulders.

One of the Sidons began rubbing the beast's shoulder and paw, a thick, cream-colored salve slowly healing its wounds. It was a strange comfort to know these evil fish hunters at least cared for the creature.

"Where's Jaz?" The female hissed and Jaspar noted to himself that she didn't have the typical accent of a Sidon.

"Who wants to know?" It occurred to him that the Sidons only knew his name but did not recognize him.

"A...friend is looking for him."

"Well, I don't have any friends by that name," he spat.

The woman eyed Cordelia with greed and bloodlust.

"What about her?" The female Sidon smiled at Cordelia's mangled body.

"She's not a friend of mine."

"I see." She twirled her spear like a baton and slammed

Cordelia to the ground. "If she means nothing to you, then I suppose you won't mind if I kill her." The female dug the spear into Cordelia's already bleeding shoulder wound.

A low growl escaped Jaspar, and he involuntarily took a step forward.

"Ah." The woman smiled. She pouted her lips at him. Two Sidons stepped to her side, aiming their bows at Jaspar.

"Who the hell are you?"

"I'm of no importance, and neither are you." She snapped her fingers, and the Sidons wrapped Cordelia's hands behind her back, tightly binding her wrists together. "Bring the girl."

"What do you need her for?"

"Is that any of your concern? I thought she was no friend of yours." She pouted her lips again. Cordelia remained astute, her heavy eyes and pale face the only indication of her pain and suffering.

Jaspar searched his mind. Stranger or not, he couldn't let her be taken by these monsters. But what could he say in her defense? He didn't know anything about her. Why did the Sidons want her anyway if they were searching for Jaz? And if they remembered Jaz, why didn't they recognize him? Who were they really searching for?

"The girl comes with us." The female repeated, licking her lips. She approached Cordelia and raked a hand through her hair. "Pretty girl," she tsked. "Feign your ignorance all you like, but Jaz will come for you soon enough. And when he does, Janus will be ready."

"He's gone!" Cordelia's voice was firm. "The man who...the man you're looking for is gone."

"Ah, so you *do* know Jaz." The female Sidon dragged her sticky fingers across Cordelia's shoulder wound, glaring down, her face marred with disgust. "Where is he?"

"There was a shipwreck. Our boat was attacked." Cordelia spoke in sharp rasps, panting from her injuries. "He didn't survive."

The female recoiled in disgust before slapping Cordelia hard across the face. Cordelia's limp body was thrown back by the blow and blood trickled from her lips.

"Lies," the female whispered. Cordelia didn't speak again and the Sidons yanked up her nearly unconscious body.

"On second thought." The female Sidon smiled and snapped her fingers, and the Sidons dragging Cordelia stilled. "If Jaz is gone, then I have no need for you." She kicked Cordelia over, thrusting her booted foot onto Cordelia's throat. Cordelia gripped the Sidon's leg, trying to pull her throat free. She gagged and choked, suffocating slowly.

Jaspar tried to resolve the scene, hoping to distract her long enough to come up with some kind of plan. He may not know Cordelia, but he couldn't let her die.

"Who is Janus?"

The female Sidon looked Jaspar up and down, her eyes narrow. She took one more look at Cordelia before kicking her foot off.

Jaspar took a step forward and the female Sidon snapped her fingers again, and a Sidon Jaspar hadn't heard or seen suddenly lifted him by the throat, squeezing and tightening. "I'm warning you," he growled in Jaspar's ear. "One lie, one wrong move, and I'll snap your neck like a twig."

Jaspar's nostrils flared, and swirls of smoke erupted from him. "I don't give warnings."

Fire sparked in his hands, a glowing orb of energy, chaos, and flames. The Sidon's hair was smoking, the smell of it toxic. He dropped Jaspar, who landed on perfectly solid feet. The Sidon screamed, slapping the flames on his head and jumping up and down.

Shouts erupted in the clearing. "Hagan!" one of the Sidons cried, and another hid behind the already damaged Tigraige.

"Leave. Now." Jaspar could make them stay, could torture them all. His own heart had hardened to such violence long ago. But the captain's daughter looked on the verge of death. The Sidons all stumbled, scattering from the clearing, shoving into one another and looking over their shoulders as they ran.

The female Sidon stood her ground, her spear over her shoulder. She snarled at Jaspar before reaching for Cordelia, grabbing her by the hair and attempting to drag her away. Jaspar lit a flame, hurling it at her. The female shrieked when the flame lit her slimy skin. She stared at her burning flesh in disbelief before she dropped Cordelia. She frantically started rubbing her arms, attempting to squash the fire.

Two lingering Sidons approached the woman, pulling her back and dragging her from the scene as she shrieked. "We can't! We need her!" But the Sidons weren't listening to their leader, they were fleeing, seeking to save themselves.

"I'll see you soon, pretty girl." She spat at Cordelia's feet before turning on her heels and following the other frightened Sidons.

Jaspar snuffed his fire, squatting down and helping Cordelia to her feet. Her face and shoulder were bloody, her dress ripped, and three of the fingers on her left hand were bent at odd angles, clearly broken. Guilt he couldn't explain weighed in his gut and he clenched his fists to his side.

"Thank you." Her voice was fragile. "How do they know about Jaz?" she asked, looking over her shoulder at the spot where the Sidons had run off.

His jaw clenched. "That's what I was going to ask you." She balked. "They shouldn't know I exist at all."

"Hey, I just—" But as she tried to stand, her legs wobbled, and she nearly fell over again. It took what looked like great effort, but she finally rose to her feet.

"Are you alright?" It seemed a restrained question given the state of her.

She coughed, and a small trickle of blood leaked from the side of her mouth. She rolled her eyes, wiping it on the sleeve of her dress. "Depends."

"On?"

She shook her hair back, the movement twisting her eyes. "On your definition of alright. I'm alive, at least." She pulled off the top layer of her dress, revealing some of the formfitting bodice underneath. Jaspar gulped and averted his gaze.

Uncaring about her state of dress, Cordelia attempted to wrap the cloth around her stab wound.

"Here, let me help." He tried to reach for the cloth.

"No, thank you, I can manage." She steered herself away from his touch, wrapping the gouge in her chest awkwardly, rotating the cloth between her uninjured arm and her wounded shoulder.

"What is your definition of alright?"

"I have what I can only guess is a fractured rib, a severed tendon, three broken fingers, and several cuts on my face. Not to mention my previous injuries from our recent shipwreck. Angry Sidons are hunting a man who shouldn't exist. And you show up, ready to give them exactly what they're asking for!"

He glared at her. "I just saved your life!"

"It wasn't yours to save," she spat.

"What was I supposed to do?"

"Have a sense of self-preservation?"

She tied off her wound wrap, using the left-over material to wrap her broken fingers together. She cowered and whined at the pain of it but still did not ask for help.

Jaspar removed his cloak. "Here."

She looked at the cloak and her shoulder and back at the cloak. "No, thank you. We should get going. I don't think they'll come back, but even still, I'd like to be as far away from the pool of my own blood as possible." She pursed her lips, and he thought she might retch, but then she exhaled.

"You're not coming with me," he sighed.

"After what I just went through you're going to leave me here?"

Cordelia's hand fell from her side, her body wobbled, her eyes lost, almost white.

He took one step forward, arms outstretched to what? Catch her? "Are you alright?"

Cordelia ignored him, breathing in her nose and out of her mouth. When she spoke again, her voice was hard, forceful, as if it took all of her energy just to speak. "I know you have hideouts in every country. Where's the closest one to where we are?"

Anger and frustration and something akin to concern warred in him. Beautiful, ocean-blue eyes suddenly turned grim, and she stumbled forward in an attempt to stand straight.

"You listen to me, Jaspar Marlow." The use of his full name hit him like a slap in the face. "I've had it. I've officially reached my limit of shit I cannot deal with right now. I went through hell and back for you, more than once, and Mikiria be damned before I let you walk out on me again."

The guilt he'd tried to keep at bay invaded his thoughts, and her screams from the clearing came back, the Sidon attack, her self-sacrifice.

He nodded. "There's a bunker not far from here. It's been over a year now, but I've stayed there in the past when I've needed a place to lie low."

"Lead the way, then."

Jaspar hesitated, wavering foot to foot with his hands in his pocket. Cordelia stood as tall as her injuries would allow and squared her shoulders. When she spoke, her voice was hard and clear.

"Lead. The. Way."

18

THE WALK TO JASPAR'S HIDEOUT HAD TAKEN SO LONG the sun had nearly set, and Cordelia wasn't sure what was more painful: her ribs and bruised body, or the aching silence that haunted the hours of walking with Jaspar. They'd only stopped once, nearly three hours ago, to eat. But Cordelia's injuries and raw throat kept her appetite light.

"This is less secluded than the cay," Cordelia's feet crunched on leaves and twigs as she followed Jaspar to an old wishing well.

"You've been to the cay?" Jaspar pulled at a stone beside the well, revealing a long rope. He tossed the rope over the wall of the well, and Cordelia watched as it slowly fell into darkness.

"Of course." How long until he remembered? "How far down is it?"

"Scared of the dark?"

"If you're trying to frighten me into leaving, you'll need something much scarier than a dark well."

The tiny mirth in his eyes was so like before, so like *her* Jaspar. "It's only about twenty feet down."

He lowered himself with the rope, leaving Cordelia at the top. With a sprained shoulder, a knife wound in her collarbone, and three broken fingers, how the hell was she meant to climb down the rope? She shook hair from her face, forcing out a breath and commanding her body to ignore the pain.

She propelled down as quickly as she could, ignoring the agony in her shoulder and hands as she practically slid down the rope, the frayed edges burning her palm. When she finally felt the ground beneath her, it had only been seconds, but her body felt ready to drop. She leaned on the wall of the well and turned to see Jaspar with a second rope over his shoulder.

"I was coming back. I was going to carry you down." He seemed...annoyed? Confused maybe?

"Oh," she tried not to be surprised. The Jaspar she knew would've helped, even if she was a stranger. Though this man was much angrier than the man she had met last summer.

"I've never had anyone in here before." His cheeks pinkened slightly, and she realized he wasn't just uncomfortable, he was anxious. Did she make him nervous?

Days ago, she would have reached for him, stroked his arm or his back. But now... "How can I put you at ease?"

"How can you *put me at ease*?" He scoffed, tossing a fireball in the air. The light opened to the space, and he started to lead her down a longer stone and clay tunnel. An odor of earth and mildew reached her nostrils, the cold air felt oddly comforting on her wounded face.

"What can I do to make you feel more comfortable around me?"

"I suppose you could start with telling me why I should be in the first place."

"Perhaps because I almost died for you?"

"Right." He smirked. "And are you going to explain why you were such a willing sacrifice?"

She bit her lip. How much should she tell a man who didn't remember her?

"Because I'm not going anywhere, and we may as well try to make the best of it."

"Why do you care so much? About me?"

"I—" She stopped herself, her true feelings too much to share with someone so indifferent to her. "We're friends." She finally settled on the word, but it felt like a lie.

"Huh."

"What?"

"Never had a lot of those. Actually, never had any of those, except Kimbal." He ran a hand through his hair. "He's really gone, then?"

It was hard for her to put him through this again. The grief was such a painful but necessary experience, and he'd already had to endure it once. Now, his memory failing, he would have to suffer all over again. This time, he wouldn't be alone, he would have her, but he didn't want her, so what could she do?

"Yes."

He cleared his throat. "And you've been to my home? I took you there?"

"Yes."

"Huh." He scratched his chin. "How long?"

"How long what?" The air in the tunnel turned warmer.

"How long were you there?"

"I don't know. A few days?" She shrugged, the movement causing a sharp pain in her shoulder.

"And how long did we know each other?"

"About four months."

"I suppose that makes—" he stopped abruptly and spun to face her. "Did you say four *months*? Not days. Months?"

"Yes, Jaspar. Days. Weeks. Months."

"Weeks with another person," he mumbled to himself. "Months...?" His pronunciation felt forced, like he'd never heard the word before.

"Yes. Months."

His eyes were wide, bewildered, before he returned to walking. Silence engulfed them, and the cold tunnel slowly grew brighter as they approached a solid clay door. There was no key for this one, just Jaspar finagling the handle in a very specific way before it hatched open.

She followed him inside, taking in the small space, Jaspar's orb of fire flying across the room and lighting the fireplace. This bunker was nothing like the one on the cay. It was tiny, only one room with a small closet she assumed was the washroom. There was no beautiful blue ocean-haze filtering the space, just the orange glow of the fire. Jaspar walked around the room, lighting a few sconces on the wall.

The room couldn't have been bigger than hers back at the inn. There was enough space for a tiny table covered in old newspapers, the fire, and one bed. A large sheep's rug lay in front of the fireplace, beside it was a small sink, a counter, and a cupboard. Jaspar kicked off his boots and hung his cloak on a hook by the door.

She took two steps to the washroom then stopped.

"Do you, er, need help?" He gestured to the washroom.

"No." She bit her lip. "I need clean clothes."

His neck flushed, but Jaspar rummaged in an old chest for several minutes before returning with a large white blouse.

"Sorry, this is all I have. We can get you more clothes tomorrow."

"Thank you." She made her way to the washroom, heaving out a huge sigh when she finally closed the door behind her. She leaned her head back and shut her eyes.

There was a knock on the wood behind her head. Grateful she hadn't undressed yet, she slowly opened the door. Jaspar handed her a small pot filled with red, hot stones. "For your bath."

The gesture was so subtle, so thoughtful, so the kind of thing *her* Jaspar would do. She swallowed. "Thank you."

She cleaned her wounds first and pulled from her pocket the small sewing bag she had used to mend Jaspar's cloak, painfully stitching her wounded chest back together as best she could.

Her bath should've been a nice reprieve after all the walking, but it wasn't easy to manage. Her legs were shaky and lifted like lead as she slipped into the hot water. Her ribs had been an annoyance at the inn, but the exertion of the day had reignited the injury. Not to mention how difficult it had been to bathe at all with only one hand. By the time she felt clean, her entire body ached. All she wanted was sleep.

All of her clothes had been in the satchels that were destroyed during the Sidon attack, and all she had was her dress and slip. They were covered in mud and dried blood, with rips and tears in various places. She wanted to burn the dress and the memories that haunted it. But it was the only clothing she had at the moment.

She used her remaining energy to clean them as best she could in the bath water and tugged Jaspar's large blouse over her head. She brushed her fingers through her hair before heading back to the main room. She was surprised to see Jaspar sitting by the fire, staring at the dancing flames in clean clothes with wet hair. *He must have bathed in the sink.*

He lifted his eyes when she joined him on the rug, and though she worked hard to sit far away from him, she saw his mouth part slightly. She watched as his eyes widened and his throat bobbed, the action making her scoot away even further.

His eyes followed her body up and down, and she realized he must be uncomfortable with her state of dress. His borrowed shirt sleeves hung past her hands, but the neck was loose, and her injured clavicle was exposed. The blouse material was loose and only reached her knees when she sat down.

He cleared his throat and rubbed his eyes. "Are you feeling better?"

She nodded, though it wasn't entirely true. He handed her a small mug, and she smelled alcohol.

"It'll help with the pain." He pointed to her knife wound.

"Thanks." She forced herself to drink the alcohol, even though she hated the burn. Haunted memories returned at the smell. She thought of the night Jaz drank her unfinished whiskey in one gulp. He'd left town the very next day, but when he'd returned, he'd declared his affection to her so freely. And now he saw a stranger in her eyes.

"Is there another bed? Or a cot?"

He shook his head.

"A sleepsack?"

"I have an extra quilt, I think."

She looked down at the fluffy rug by the warm fire. "I'll just rest here."

"I'm not letting you sleep on the floor," he sighed. "You're terribly injured."

"You're injured, too. And I don't mind, really. I'd just like to sleep." She felt empty. It wasn't just her body that had lost all energy, it was her heart, her mind, and the very predicament they'd found themselves in.

"Look..." He stared at her.

"Cordelia."

"Right." He scratched his neck. "Cordelia. Take the bed. I don't mind the floor, and we can find other arrangements later."

She didn't want to impose, but she also didn't want to argue with a man she knew had made up his mind already. Her Jaspar was the same way: kind, considerate, thoughtful.

It was the comfort she didn't know she needed. A soft reminder that although this man was angry at the world and mistrusting of a woman he didn't remember, the Jaspar she knew was still there. Maybe she couldn't bring his memories back, but maybe someday, they could make new ones.

But the fear that he may never get his memories back troubled her as she tried to prepare her mind for sleep. When she made her way under the blanket, she felt at home. Not because it was particularly comfortable, it wasn't.

The real reason she felt at home, the real reason she drifted to sleep within minutes, was the smell: driftwood and sea salt and something just a little bit sweet.

19

JASPAR WAS ABOVE, OR OUTSIDE, OR PERHAPS WATCHING through a fog. He could see himself, but it was a version he didn't remember. He had a small, still-growing beard and hair that was shaggy and unkempt. The bed he lay in was as simple as the room, and though he'd never been there before something about the space felt familiar.

A knock rustled, and a bar maiden in a maroon dress padded into the room carrying a tray and a large blanket. The woman turned her head to close the door, and he saw her face for the first time. Cordelia covered him in the blanket, tucking in the edges. Dream Jaspar lay by a stove heater, sweated brow and pale cheeks, and Cordelia sat beside him.

Her hand ran through his hair, humming beautifully, like the sweet song of a morning bird. His eyes opened, and dream Jaspar's world shifted until he saw Cordelia. The dream was so real he could practically feel his parched throat, his chilled body, his too-warm face.

She lifted tea to his mouth, helping him drink. The tea was both soothing and unpleasant against his raw throat. He summoned magic to the stove and pulled her closer, his grasp loose around her wrist. He coughed, and Cordelia helped him lay down, pulling the covers up and stopping at his shoulders.

Her features were soft, expression concerned. When was the

last time someone had cared for him like that? Had they ever? And yet, she clearly did. Somehow, Jaspar could feel what his dream counterpart felt as Cordelia patted his forehead with the back of her hand before letting it fall to his cheek, her face frowning. Dream Jaspar leaned into the touch, letting his lips rest on her palm, a chaste kiss he could hardly believe was stolen.

Dream Jaspar spoke, something heavy between him and Cordelia, something neither one of them were ready to admit. Jaspar couldn't hear her words, but it made dream Jaspar smile, and then laugh. He was playful and at ease in a way Jaspar couldn't ever remember being. And then he was lying down and holding her hand to his chest. And then he was asleep, and she was humming softly again.

The dream shifted, and Jaspar watched himself wake, jerking out of sleep unexpectedly. The dream Jaspar smiled when he saw Cordelia's closed eyes, her head resting on the bed by his stomach, and Jaspar watched from above as his own hand threaded through her hair. Dream Jaspar bent down awkwardly, leaving the barest of kisses in her hair, and he felt happy, content, and it was because of her, because of Cordelia, that he also felt at home.

20

Jaspar jerked awake. His heart ached from the longing of his dream. It lingered in chest, like the ghost of a feeling he knew but didn't recall. His eyes searched the room. Cordelia was still asleep. It was strange to see someone in his bed. His head fell back on his propped arm, and he wondered if it was real. The dream had been inconceivable, but then again, weren't all dreams?

He didn't understand the where, when, or how of the dream, all he understood was the impossibility of it. He didn't know this woman, she was merely the daughter of his mentor. She claimed they were friends, but where was the proof of that? It could be in the proof that, despite the strange dream, he'd slept through the night. He was comfortable enough with her that he was able to sleep, fully sleep without trepidation, his guard down for the first time since he could remember. Did that mean his subconscious remembered her? Trusted her?

And what of the captain? He should have been meeting with the captain now, should have been telling him there may be answers in Scaparo. He was going to tell him about the map and the lost library. Three days ago, the captain was fine and alive, and yet somehow he'd been dead for four months?

He'd never see his mentor again. Never confide in him, ask his advice, laugh at some mutual joke, or revel in some shared secret. He'd been alone for twelve years, ever since his parents died, and the captain was the only person who remembered him. He was the closest thing to a friend that Jaspar had ever had. Which should mean that Jaspar was alone now, but then what of Cordelia? If she could remember him, then Jaspar wasn't alone. But did he want her in his life? Did he want her as a friend? Would she be someone to replace the hole that was left by the captain's loss?

He believed so much of her story, and yet none of it felt true. Something about her was trustworthy in a way he couldn't explain, which only made him that much more suspicious of her. Why should he trust her? It wouldn't be the first time he'd been tricked. What if Cordelia wasn't the *same* Cordelia that was the captain's daughter? Come to think of it, he wasn't sure that was even his daughter's name.

Or she could be an impostor. And yet his dream lingered...her hand in his hair, his lips on her palm, her humming voice...

He stretched, trying to think of what he would normally do if she weren't here. He washed up, chewing peppermint leaves, the stinging in his eyes and tingling in his mouth helping restore him from his sleeping state. He found stale coffee but didn't want to wake her by boiling water over the fire. He made quick work of heating the water with a small fire in his palm.

He rummaged through a mostly empty kitchen and resigned to a quick trip to the square market. He was moments away from taking off when he realized: should he tell her he was leaving? What would she do if she woke up and he was gone?

"Cordelia." Her name felt oddly soft on his lips. He squatted by her sleeping form. She didn't stir. Should he poke her? Shove her? But she had suffered so many injuries. Should he let her keep sleeping?

"Cordelia." He spoke louder this time, and she slowly stirred. Her eyes sleepy, her voice drowsy.

"Hmm."

"I need to leave."

She yawned, "Not this again.""No"—he fought back a smirk —"it's not that. I need to get some food. And you need proper clothing and medical supplies." He stood up.

"Okay." She closed her eyes again.

"There's coffee in the kitchen."

She nodded.

"I'll be back soon."

"Be safe," she mumbled, eyes still closed.

He shifted on his feet. "You'll, er, be safe, too. Here. No one knows about this place."

"Hmmm." And then he was certain she was asleep again. When he closed the door, he breathed in deep. It felt like he'd inhaled his first lungful of air since he'd awoken on that beach.

21

Hazy blue lights lit her path, and Cordelia hopped from stone to stone. Glowing embers and tiny fires danced around her like drops of orange. She heard her name, a prayer, a whisper. She knew that voice...

Jaz!

She ran to him, but she fell through his body when they tried to embrace. She landed on a lush field of daisies, and then the world shifted, and she was standing on the ground again.

Hey beautiful.

Jaspar was there, his long hair and beard flickered in and out of focus. His body was translucent and cold, and her fingers slipped through the mirage when she tried to touch him.

You're not real. But I miss you so much. Her voice was garbled and distorted, but his was clear and strong.

I'm still here. He looked down, and she saw the Jaspar from the shipwreck floating and asleep.

She shook her head.

He's so different.

Jaspar reached to touch her cheek, but his fingers only lingered above her skin.

He just doesn't know you. He doesn't know our story. But he's still me.

82

Empty tears evaporated from her skin, almost like they were never there. She looked back and forth between the two Jaspars.

It doesn't feel like you're still here. It feels like I've lost you. Like I'll never get you back.

The mirage Jaspar spoke with a voice stronger than his slowly fading image.

You'll never lose me, Cordelia. I'm here, and I'm trying to find my way back to you. Don't lose hope. Don't give up on us.

Jaspar started to fade, and she reached for him, desperately trying to cling to the mirage of her soulfate. But he was already gone, and Cordelia was falling to the ground, the lush field of daisies ready to catch her.

22

CORDELIA GROANED AS SHE TRIED TO LIFT HERSELF from the hard floor, her visions of Jaspar slowly fading until all she remembered of her dream was a feeling of longing. She did what she could for her injuries, though without any medicine, she mostly cleaned her wounds and used her slip to make a new sling.

She felt desperate and restless waiting for Jaspar to return and tried to keep herself busy. She cleaned the washroom, swept the floor, and cleaned the small, makeshift kitchen. It all took less than an hour, and her usually busy workload adrenaline was still pumping through her, though her many injuries helped slow her down.

On a day like this at Anchorage Inn, she'd already be halfway through her morning chores. Breakfast would have been prepared, served, and cleaned up. Rooms would have been stripped of all linens, cleaned, and ready for new guests. If she were home right now, she'd be handwashing laundry, Diarmuid would be preparing for that night's dinner, and Gladys would be helping both of them while simultaneously running the inn and bar.

Her shoulders sagged. It was easy not to think too much about the life she'd left behind when she and Jaspar were at the cay, together. She had Jaspar to spend her time with, and they had adventures ahead of them. But she didn't know what awaited her now. When Jaspar returned, what would he want to do? Where would he want to go? Would he take her with him?

If Jaspar chose to leave, chose to separate from Cordelia, what would she do? Would she try to continue on alone? Would she seek and fight Janus by herself? Would she return to Anchorage Inn, to her home and life before she knew about Qualaris and Danthems and Soulfates and Hagans? Would she seek out Hygonia's guidance? Try to shape an entirely new path for herself?

It was so overwhelming it was unmanageable. She had too many choices for her future. Every single option she had would lead to a life of something worth having, whether that be a simple life with her family back at Anchorage Inn, or a life spent traveling and seeking the wonders of the world. And yet she really didn't have any choices because the future she wanted, the future she had planned for, her future with Jaspar, was no longer an option.

She sat on the rug by the fire, enjoying the feel of the soft material on her bare legs. She had decided to stay in his shirt. It was comfortable, and despite her attempt at cleaning it, her maid's uniform had not survived the attack from the Sidons.

She twirled her fingers around on the rug, feeling the texture on her skin and thinking what it would have been like to come here with a reminiscing Jaspar. He would have been excited to show her another bunker, he would have made a joke about how inadequate this was, and he wouldn't have slept on the floor, they would have slept side by side.

Her eyes wandered the room, silently cataloging all the ways this bunker was different from the cay, right down to the tiny kitchen sink and cupboard. She tilted her head; then she took a second glance at the cupboard. She hadn't seen it before, but there was a tiny door beyond it.

The door blended in with the wall so well that she had to dig her nails into the frame and pry it open before she fully believed it was real. It was a pocket door, lightweight, and it slid into the frame of the wall with ease. The room beyond was dark. She retrieved a candle from the kitchen, letting her eyes adjust to the dimly lit space.

It was the same size and shape as the washroom, but instead of a basin, there was a large writing desk. Like the tables at the cay, it was covered in papers, maps, journals, and illustrations of strange creatures. There was a large book made of old leather and papyrus and something that smelled sweet. Cherries? Years of tutorship came back, and she recalled an old Latin text, so old it was made of goat skin bindings, papyrus paper, and iron gall ink.

Cordelia examined the book, sensitive to the delicate pages and bindings. The language was one she didn't recognize. Ancient rune symbols, like tiny pictures. Each page had a map of some region, most of which she was familiar with, even if she'd never been there.

Her home country of Mikiria, which was mostly farming communities and local fishermen. There was Scaparo, a north-western country known for goods and materials. There was also Keru, where she was now, a neighboring country that mostly exported plants and alchemist medicines. And there was Vales, where Kevin, Iverson and Trevyn had been raised, which mostly exported lumber and paper but was also known for fine wools.

The map she currently inspected, however, showed a small island, this one in between southwest Vales and northwest Keru. The island shape was outlined in red, so dark it could be dried blood, and there was a tiny X next to it. The island was not named, but a tiny piece of parchment pinned to the page read *J26P13*.

It took Cordelia some reasoning, but she deduced what the message meant: journal twenty-six, page thirteen. She flipped through the journals, turning them over in her hands and searching for a number system. It was on the fifth journal that she noticed a tiny line on the binding. Other journals had similar lines, she had originally thought them a design or material flaw. Now she realized the number of lines was the journal number.

She sifted through eleven journals, some with as many as a hundred lines, before she finally found the journal numbered twenty-six. She reassured herself that Jaspar was gone and that if he were *her* Jaspar, he wouldn't care she was in here, and that if he didn't want her to find anything, he shouldn't have left her alone. Really, what was she supposed to do while he was gone? Stare at the walls and count the number of times her life had fallen apart in the last four months?

The journal pages were covered in neat, tidy writing, the kind one would expect from someone who documented their whole life and was raised by people who'd done the same. The pages weren't numbered, and she counted each page turn until she reached thirteen. It was dated almost a year ago, to January.

> *I don't think it's the island at all. I mean, what are the odds that my family spent thousands of years looking for an island that sank to the bottom of the ocean before the years of the man? Not to mention, an island that close to home would have been noticed at some point, right? And there was no evidence that Qualaris had sank, that it wasn't still surfaced and inhabited.*
>
> *The book Is an amazing piece of history, but I'm not sure it was worth the price, considering I only needed it for this one map, which has turned out to be useless. If I make a trip to northern Keru, perhaps I can gamble for a few nights, earn some more coin, and make my way to Vales. Just because I don't think the island on the map is there, doesn't mean I'm not going to check it.*
>
> *I've mapped out a route to take and prepared the ship for traveling. If I can get out to sea by sunrise, I should arrive in Vales in twenty-four hours. It's a long trip, and I may need to drop anchor and rest along the way. With any luck, I'll have a few more answers by the end of the week.*

The entry trailed off there, logistics about travel and the likely longitude and latitude of the unknown island. She grabbed a journal at random, seeing an entry from four days before her father died. She nearly dropped the book when her eyes flashed on the name *Kimbal* in big letters on the page.

Kimbal seems on edge, not his usual cheerful self, in fact, he's almost as taciturn as I am. He's been asking me a lot of questions I wasn't expecting. Am I happy? Do I wish people would remember me? Do I ever want to break my curse? Had it occurred to me to spend my time and resources on breaking the curse and not finding the island? But it all felt disjointed, as if he read each question from a list somewhere in his head.

I answered as honestly as I could, that's how it has always been between us: honesty and adventure first, friendship and mentor second. I was happy, relatively speaking, as happy as anyone with my curse could expect to be. And of course I wished someone would remember me, but I've never known any difference, so it's not something I spend a lot of time dwelling on.

But the curse was what really captured my thoughts: I had never thought of my curse as something that could be broken without the island. My family and I had always thought that by finding the island, we could prove the word of our greatest grandfather, and that would break the curse. But why had no one ever thought to seek another way?

Surely a talented theurgist somewhere could overpower this curse? Or could they? It's lasted nearly three millennia already. Don't curses get stronger with every passing day? And the curse has never weakened and has left its mark on every descendant without fail. And even finding the captain, the one person in the universe who could remember me, had been an unexplainable coincidence. Even if I did want to break this curse, how could I do it? Where would I start?

Her fingers let the book fall, her emotions running dry, as if she'd used them all up. Of course Jaspar would be used to his life and wouldn't want anything to change. Of course he would have accepted his fate years ago, made his peace with the hand he was dealt. And that was the Jaspar she was living with. Not the one who'd lost a friend and found a partner and gained a whole new perspective.

Cordelia rearranged the room, returning each item to the spot she'd moved it from and letting the door close softly behind her, blending perfectly with the wall. She could have kept reading, could have kept sifting through the room and learning more about Jaspar and Qualaris and possibly even her father. But she also couldn't fathom another emotional attack, and she was exhausted, so sleepy.

She had rested to the best of her abilities, the alcoholic drink before bed helping with the pain. But she longed for the peace and serenity of something soft under her aching body.

With no idea of when Jaspar would return and the bed's inviting cushiony warmth, Cordelia rested her head and let sleep find her once more.

23

"WHAT SIZE DOES THE LADY WEAR?" A SKINNY, FAIR-skinned female asked Jaspar, her sharp chin jutting out as she sifted through piles of clothes.

"Er, not sure." He looked the woman's body up and down and she glared at him. "She's, um, bigger than you, but shorter."

The woman went back to sorting through clothes before returning with several dresses, all casual. If their designs were different Jaspar couldn't tell, and the colors were typical—black, purple, red, white, gray, blue—but various shades of each.

He tried to recall what she'd been wearing the day before, but all he could picture was her maid's uniform and his shirt from the night before, the one that hugged every curve of her body.

"Er, just any two dresses will do."

"Color?" the woman asked.

His eyes flickered, a blue dress coming in and out of focus. And his voice, strangely calm and carefree in his mind. *I think my new favorite color is blue.*

"Blue."

"Which ones?" she asked a little impatiently. When he didn't answer, the woman sighed. "What does she look like?"

"Huh?"

"Would she look best in dark blue or light blue?"

"She'd look best in anything." The voice that muttered the

90

words was not his own, and yet it had come from his lips. The woman smiled before selecting one dark-blue dress and one light blue. He paid her two coppers for the dresses and a pair of women's boots that looked more decorative than practical.

She started to bag his purchases. "Anything else?"

"Yes. A bed roll and a blanket." He paid the woman another copper for a reindeer-lined bed roll. The woman snatched the coin quickly. She ducked beneath her counter, returning with a fluffy quilt. His breath hitched, memories from his childhood filling his mind. The taste of hot cinnamon, the feel of soft fur. But the nightmare of his childhood returned, the screaming, the loneliness, the smell of burning wood and ash and skin.

"How much for the quilt?"

~

SIX HOURS AFTER HE LEFT THE BUNKER, HE RETURNED with clothes for each of them, the new bed roll and the quilt, a few food supplies, basic medical supplies, and a bar of fresh soap. He tossed the many totes of supplies into the well, arching and stretching his back and shoulders before lowering himself.

He reluctantly heaved the totes over his shoulders again and began the long walk down the hall. The bags were laden down and heavy, and he could have put a few down and made multiple trips back and forth, but it was nearing afternoon, and he was weary and hungry.

He opened the door awkwardly with his hand, still gripping one of the totes. Once inside, he dropped everything, allowing his back, shoulders, and arms to finally rest. Cordelia was in his bed, fast asleep, his blanket tangled around her torso, her bare ankles and feet exposed.

He looked around the bunker, at the freshly cleaned counter and sink and the recently swept floor. It was strange to have someone care for him and his home in such a way. Had she woken, cleaned his home, and then returned to sleep?

It made sense she would be fatigued, her injuries had been

quite severe, and Jaspar thought she was hiding the bulk of her pain. The cut in her collarbone had been quite deep, and she'd suffered abrasions on her face and arms. Is it possible her cuts were infected? Could she have a fever?

He removed his boots, pulling his feet out instead of kicking them off like he normally would. Not wanting to wake her, he took his time, small steps on the hard floor. She seemed perfectly at ease, and he kneeled by the bed, leaning over to see if she was sweating or breathing heavily. He very reluctantly touched a hand to her head, and a strange spark pricked his finger where skin had met skin.

Cordelia rolled over in her sleep, and his hand was in her hair, soft and curly as it wrapped around his fingers. He tried to pull back gently, not wanting to wake her, but his shirt button got stuck in her hair. He disentangled it and was about to pull his hand away when she whispered his name. It was rare to hear it said aloud, especially in a voice as smooth as velvet.

"Sorry, I woke you."

Her eyes lingered from his to the hand he still had in her hair, now partially cradling her head.

"I"—his hand fell to the bed, and he cleared his throat—"you were asleep, I thought you might have a fever."

"Oh." She tried to rise from the bed, still wearing his shirt, her thigh brushing his other hand. Her touch should have bothered him, but he was more put off by how it didn't. There were small bruises on her legs, and one of her knees was slightly swollen. He felt the strange urge to touch her, to soothe her injured skin.

He swallowed back his urges and returned to their totes in the kitchen. Cordelia straightened his blouse over her body before following him.

"I was able to get you two dresses and a pair of boots. I had to guess on the size." He handed her the tote from the seamstress, and she peeked inside the bag.

"They're blue." She shuffled the bag, as if checking for more contents. "All blue. Did you remember?" She leaned forward, almost next to him, but not quite.

"Er, no. Why?"

Her face fell and she backed away. "Never mind. What else did you get?"

Shrugging it off, Jaspar pulled out the food, medical kit, blanket, and bed roll. She took the fluffy green plaid quilt from him, her lips a soft, sweet smile. "It's almost as soft as your mums."

His arm stilled in midair. "What did you just say?"

"Oh, nothing." She quickly tried to shuffle past, but he stepped in her path.

"Not nothing. The fluffed quilt. My mother's quilt. How do you know about that?"

Her cheeks burned crimson. "I've slept..." She cleared her throat. "I mean, I've seen it."

His mind twisted. "Right." Of course she had. She had said she'd been to the cay for days, it made sense she would have noticed a blanket.

"And you know where it came from?" His voice was guarded.

She walked away, laying down the blanket and bed roll, arranging them beside his bed. "It was your mum's. You've been keeping it sewn and mended as best as you can. And you've been wondering if you should find a tailor theurgist, someone who could mend it properly and help you preserve it and make it last—"

"Until the end of my days." Time stopped, suspended in the air between them like a wall, a slowly breaking wall. "I've never told anyone that. Never had anyone to tell." They were quiet for a long moment.

"Thank you," she finally said, gesturing to her new bedding. She didn't bring up the blanket again, and neither did he, but it lingered in his mind, adding another mystery to the already mounting pile of unanswered questions.

24

"Marcel?" A pale young boy skipped into his workshop, his clothes only slightly filthy, and Marcel recognized him as the gazette boy. Marcel didn't say anything by way of greeting, he just took off his mask and let his hammer rest. He was wondering how the morning gazette got here so early in the day, when Liam handed him a small roll of parchment wrapped in wheatgrass. "Urgent post arrived for you this morning."

Urgent post? Who'd be sending him a letter?

"From who?"

"How should I know?" The boy shrugged, peering into Marcel's cauldron and watching the fires and vapors curve around the iron he'd been wielding. "Have I told you before that you need an apprentice?" he asked, hopeful.

"When you're older, Liam." Marcel tossed a coin to the boy before taking off his gloves and unrolling the letter. He didn't recognize the handwriting, and his eyes peeked at the bottom of the parchment. His mind stilled at the signature.

It had only been a month since he'd started spending more time with the fisherman, though he'd thought of him much longer than that. Much. Longer. But Marcel knew he wasn't an easy man to care for. He was of few words and often kept to himself. He'd join friends for a round of pints, but he'd never stepped outside of his usual social circle. Until Trevyn.

Trevyn who was boisterous and loud, eager to be in the middle of a fight or a game of cards. Trevyn, who spoke as little as Marcel and yet managed to say far more in just as few words. Trevyn, who'd gone from just another fisherman traveling to Alaro to someone else...someone to look forward to.

> *M,*
>
> *Don't know if you'll be surprised that I'm writing to you. Suppose you probably will but couldn't help it, could I? I almost died. And that can really change a man.*
>
> *First, you should know that I ain't got no interest in blacksmithing.*

An exhale of mirth escaped Marcel's nostrils.

> *I came round your shop for one reason and one reason only: I wanted to see you. Maybe I should have just sought you out on my own, maybe I should have asked for your time. But you've always been hard to read, and I'm not a confident man.*
>
> *Second, today, my brothers and I shipwrecked someone outside of Keru.*

His neck stiffened.

> *She's resting at the bottom of the Tilerian Sea, and my brothers and I are stranded in Keru. I don't know how long we'll be stuck here with no ship and no money, but I'm sure we'll make do, we always have.*
>
> *I lost my ship, my livelyhood, and nearly lost my own life and the lives of my brothers. But I only thought of you.*
>
> *Do with that what you will. Just thought you should*

*know I'm making it my top priority to come back to
Alaro. And when I get there, all I want is to see you.
Byth
-Trevyn*

Marcel didn't know the last word and it took up space in his mind, along with everything else in the letter. Marcel had never imagined Trevyn's feigned interest in blacksmithing was simply an excuse to see him. Or that Trevyn had thought of him as much as he'd thought of Trevyn.

As for the rest of the letter, well, he supposed that could wait until Trevyn got back. Marcel reread the parchment and was close to putting it in his pocket when he thought someone else may have an interest in reading it. Or at least parts of it.

He stopped his work, dropping his apron, shield, and gloves, and made his way to Anchorage Inn.

25

TAYLOR HAD COME TO SIT IN THE BAR EVERY MORNING for the past two weeks, waiting for Liam to deliver the daily post. So far, he and Gladys had both been disappointed when each morning came, and nothing had been delivered. As if worrying for Delia hadn't been enough strain, the leftover feelings from their last conversation hung around them like vapors.

The night of the Sidon attack haunted her for more than just the violent reasons. Taylor had tended to her injuries, and she'd admitted her feelings had never wavered. She'd bared her soul and practically her body to him, and he'd rejected her, again. She'd never been more vulnerable in that one moment than she had been in her whole life.

He'd been here every day since. Long ago, she would have dreamed of nothing better than spending her mornings with Taylor, and if she were honest with herself, that dream had never gone away. But mornings spent with awkward detachment from the man she loved were hardly something she looked forward to.

"Morning, Miss Gladys!" Liam called, wandering into the inn and up to the bar. Taylor stood, walking over to where Gladys was scooping a bowl of mush for the young lad.

"Anything today?" Gladys and Taylor asked at the same time.

Liam's usually boisterous attitude dimmed a little. "No, ma'am."

Gladys huffed. "That girl better be damned near stranded not to write. Could be lying in a ditch somewhere for all we know. Why isn't she home yet?"

Diarmuid hobbled in. "Anything?" When Gladys shook her head, the cranky man cursed under his breath before heading back to the kitchens.

She sighed heavily and Taylor took a step toward her. It startled her, the way he leaned his head toward her, a slight tilt. Days spent in his arms and nights spent by his side clouded her vision and she busied herself, wiping the counter and refilling the coffee, and all the while, Taylor barely moved. Was he hoping for more news or avoiding going back to a job he no longer enjoyed? A small voice she couldn't ignore wanted him to stay there to be near her.

A throat clear pulled her from her wishful thinking.

"Morning." Marcel, the young blacksmith in town, closed the door behind him. A tall, portly man with blond hair and few words, Marcel hardly made an appearance in the bar, at least not unless a certain fisherman was around.

Taylor returned to his seat, and Gladys started to pour Marcel a coffee but then thought better of it, something telling her the usually quiet man might prefer tea. "Morning, Marcel. What brings you around?"

"The brothers have been traveling." Marcel didn't bother to explain who the brothers were, and Gladys didn't bother to ask.

"They were supposed to send word of Delia." Taylor scoffed.

"Well, I er got a post this morning."

"Good for you." What did Gladys care about the blacksmith's correspondence?

"It's from Trevyn." He scratched the back of his neck.

"Pardon?" Taylor turned to Marcel.

Gladys's gaze swiveled to Marcel's hands and she ripped the parchment from him before he could stop her. Marcel reached for the letter, but she slapped his hand. She quickly scanned the words, feeling embarrassed when she realized the intimacy of their nature. But her eyes picked up on the few things that mattered.

"He didn't mention Delia." She shoved the paper back to Marcel a little too forcefully.

"He mentioned they were shipwrecked."

"Hmph."

Marcel clenched his jaw. "He mentioned they almost died."

She brushed it off, hiding her concern for the brothers behind forced confidence. "He also said they were alive and fine." Her eyes dropped to the bottom of the page before widening and looking back to Marcel. "I..." it wasn't often that Gladys owed someone an apology, and she had to remind herself of the words. "I didn't read the whole thing."

Marcel didn't speak, just narrowed his eyes at her. After a moment, he offered her one nod before dropping a copper for his tea, though he'd never touched a drop. He made it across the bar and all the way to the door when he stopped.

"Do either of you speak Velsh?" His tone gave nothing away.

The language was one spoken in the northern country of Vales, and while she knew a few words from the varied bar patrons, Gladys was hardly fluent in the language. Taylor, on the other hand, had been stationed there for nearly a season.

"Why?" Taylor asked.

Marcel's shoulders stiffened and he peeked at the letter. "What does *Byth* mean?"

Taylor's eyes softened, but he spoke in his usual, deep timbre, "forever."

26

"WHAT EXACTLY ARE WE LOOKING FOR?" CORDELIA scanned the dark trees as Jaspar pulled vines from the building window. They'd walked nearly two miles to an abandoned schoolhouse where Jaspar was certain they would find valuable information. He was most interested in a library he'd been searching for last summer. It had taken almost an entire week in the bunker for Jaspar to let his guard down, and even now, it was still a formidable wall between them.

"I'll know when I see it," Jaspar said, hopping through a broken window and landing easily inside the decrepit, mud-made building. He took a few steps forward, then stopped and returned for Cordelia, lifting her with ease. Her heart raced at the closeness, the smell of him, the feel of him, but it ended quickly. He set her down and moved into the room without a backward glance.

The space was covered in growing vines and wild plants, the once mud and clay ground had sprouted grass and dandelions in various cracks through the stone-tiled floor. The walls were fractured and spindled, and the roof seemed ready to cave in at any moment. The only source of light came from a ball of flames Jaspar was idly tossing in the air as he walked.

Tables and shelves were overturned, books and scrolls of various conditions scattered around, parchments and ripped quills with upturned and dried inkwells littered the floor. Jaspar rummaged around the room, nudging shelves and drawers and random debris as he went.

Cordelia thumbed through the books on the floor, looking for she didn't know what. Mostly, they were scholarly, medicinal logs with various potions and healing explanations. She flipped through pages, wondering if any of the instructions would come in handy during their travels as they seemed to be prone to injuries.

"Grab whatever you like," Jaspar said, pointing to the pile of books she was sifting through. Jaspar already had an armful of scrolls and two books, but he was still searching the room.

Cordelia sighed, setting aside a book on herbal cures for restless sleep when her eyes lingered on a word. Inspecting it closely, she saw an entire entry dedicated to the study of memory and memory loss. Could she be so lucky? She scanned the pages, searching for keywords, her heart racing, daring to hope.

Cordelia let out a shriek when a mouse fell from one of the upturned drawers, landing at her feet, tangling in the hem of her dress. Jaspar rushed to her side, flame in hand, eyes narrowed in suspicion.

"It's alright," she panted. "It was only a mouse." She pointed at the large rodent, now scurrying quickly and hiding behind what was once a fireplace.

"Potato..." Jaspar mumbled, eyes crossed.

"Pardon?"

But a yell and the neigh of a horse caught her attention, and she whipped her head back to the broken window. Jaspar was there in an instant, snuffing his flame and jumping to the windowsill above.

"Guards," he cursed. "Time to go."

"What? Why?"

Jaspar was tossing his books and scrolls into his bag, he held two parchments side by side, eyeing them and then deciding to pack both. "We're not exactly supposed to be here."

"It's just an old schoolhouse." Cordelia struggled to fit her books in her bag and was shoving it as tightly closed as she could.

"Er, technically, it's an old parochial."

Cordelia stumbled as she followed Jaspar back to the window. "Holy ground? We've snuck onto holy ground and stolen property from the clergy?" she whisper-shrieked as he climbed to the windowsill with ease, tossing his bag on the other side.

"Yes, so you can understand why we're in a bit of a hurry." Jaspar lowered an arm, helping her up and out of the window.

"Halt!" A shadow in a blue and white uniform shouted as it rode up on a large, brown horse. "By order of the crown!"

"Damn." Jaspar tossed his bag over one shoulder and Cordelia's over another, eyeing the trees and shrubbery around them. "If I set a fire, I could burn down the whole forest." His voice shook, and Cordelia recalled how ashamed he was that other Hagans had used their magic to destroy and that a forest fire had been what killed his parents.

"Come on." Cordelia tore off, marching north of the path they'd used to get to the abandoned parochial and back to the lake they had passed.

"Where are you going?" Jaspar followed after her, catching up quickly with his much less injured body.

"Shh!" They ran nearly half a mile, the horse and guard stumbling through the thick forest after them. The lake was finally in view, and Cordelia sighed in relief at the same time that Jaspar scoffed.

"Great, now we're trapped." He looked over his shoulder, searching for the guard and his steed, their pace slowed by the winding and overgrown path. Cordelia ignored him, holding her hands in front of her chest and channeling her magic and every ounce of the support *her* Jaspar would have given her in this moment.

The edge of the forest was close, rocks and trees and bushes providing a border around the lake. Cordelia inspected the largest tree and used her magic to pull the water high above, arching it over the branches like a waterfall.

"Halt!" the guard yelled again, hoofprints getting louder and louder as he and his steed thundered haphazardly through the trees. Cordelia kept her hands in front of her chest, noting that her magic felt controlled, steady, as if it were a part of her. Wouldn't her Jaspar be so proud? She looked at the Jaspar who accompanied her and saw he was slack-jawed and unmoving.

She rolled her eyes, shoving herself behind the waterfall, pressing her body against the trunk of the tree. "Jaspar, get over here!" she hissed, and though it took a moment for him to pull himself together, he shuffled behind the water.

The guard strode up not a moment too soon, searching the lake and the trees with his eyes. His steeds's heavy breaths could be seen in the cold air and the guard's furrowed brow was just barely evident in the moonlight.

Cordelia caught her breath, but she channeled even more of her strength, determined to control the water, worried the slightest slip would give them away. After far longer than she had expected her magic to last, the guard turned his horse south, heading back through the trees. Cordelia forced herself to wait several minutes before letting go of the water and allowing it to flow back into the lake.

Cordelia panted, her body drained from the magic use. She swayed on her feet, an arm jerking to the tree behind them to steady herself.

"Cordelia?" Jaspar's voice seemed to come from far away, her vision was turning, was it getting darker outside? Had the moon hidden behind a cloud? She heard her name again, or maybe she felt it, because it was *her* Jaspar that was calling her, telling her she was brilliant, so powerful and controlled, telling her to hold on just a little bit longer.

"Cordelia." Jaspar's voice was concerned, strained, and she wished she could go to him, but her body found the dirt instead, landing on the muddy earth with a soft cry as her eyes slipped closed.

27

Jaspar grunted, setting Cordelia down as gently as he could before collapsing on the floor. He lay sprawled out, chest heaving, arms and legs aching beyond exertion. He'd been forced to carry Cordelia and their pilfered items all the way back to the bunker, and though he'd had to take several breaks along the way, he'd managed to get them there in just over an hour.

Cordelia had been incredible, frighteningly powerful. In fact, if it weren't for the nosebleed and loss of consciousness, he'd be asking how she was even human. He'd met plenty of theurgists in his travels, but never had he seen a Danthem who could convert an entire flow of water, much less bend it to her will.

The Danthems he'd heard of before had been one with the water, able to breathe longer under its depths and swim with the grace and ease of a water creature. Some stronger ones might have been able to shift the water, separate small amounts, but none could have created the formidable waterfall that Cordelia had.

It was no wonder her body gave out as soon as the magic and adrenaline had left her veins. It was more a wonder how she'd managed to control it long enough they could escape. He wasn't sure how long she'd need to rest. If her overuse of magic was anything like his, it could be an entire day before she fully recovered.

He counted his breaths, a palm on his chest, letting his heart rate slow. When he finally felt his body ease, he rose, sorting through their many findings from the parochial. He'd found several small maps, some unfinished, some that might be too damaged to decipher. He'd also found a few historical texts with ruins and descriptives that would hopefully help him to translate the tome in her study. And two letters that chronicled a local records hall. It wasn't much, but there was always something in the nothingness that others couldn't see. Except the captain.

Would his daughter share his understanding and curious mind? Would she too see answers in chaos? Would she seek them? That had to be her reason for staying with Jaspar, right? She was determined to fulfill the captain's mission herself. But what had the great captain left behind?

He hadn't included Jaspar on his last mission, and Jaspar was due to meet him any day. Or he had been. It was hard to grasp the concept of time when he'd lost so much of it. He could barely understand the loss of the captain at all, for it seemed he'd spoken with him only a few days past.

He took a peek at the books Cordelia had thought to grab, curious which texts would have captured her attention. He was surprised to see nothing but practical choices, he would've thought she was more the leisurely reader than the informative type. He piled their resources into the study but couldn't find the energy to dig through their findings just yet.

He wanted nothing more than to sleep, but he wondered if he should check on Cordelia first. Was he responsible for her now that she was unconscious? Should he ensure her safety and well-being? It was a new concept for him as he'd spent so much of his life only thinking of himself, only having himself to think of. He'd never needed to look after the captain, a man more capable than Jaspar.

He sat beside her gingerly, not wanting to wake her. Her face was still pale, her already fair skin looking sickly. It was nearly two in the morning; she could just be drained from the magic use, but what if it were something worse? Jaspar clenched his jaw and resigned himself before moving her hair from her eyes. Her forehead didn't warm under his touch but stayed cold and clammy.

In a life where no one could remember you, it wasn't often that he felt the touch of another person. And eventually, it had become something he didn't really think about. So when it happened, whether a bump in a crowd or a shake of the hand, it was a foreign feeling, one that, in the past, he had found unnerving. So why was he drawn to her, like something inside him craved her touch?

He was about to get up when Cordelia turned, her head rolling onto his leg, her eyes still shut tight. What was he supposed to do now? Would she wake if he shoved her off? Was he supposed to just sit there like that?

She shifted in her sleep, and Jaspar used the opportunity to roll out from under her head, letting it drop gently back on the pillow. He pulled the covers up to her neck, wondering why the sensation of her touch was unyieldingly familiar.

28

JANUS LET HIS FINGERS DRUM ON THE CHAIR AS ALARIA kneeled before him, her voice nasal and whiny, echoing off the cave walls. He half listened as she gave one pitiful explanation after another. Three of his Sidons were dead after failing to kill Cordelia's guardian in Alaro. And Alaria and her unit of Sidons had not only allowed his Tigraige to be attacked, but they'd also let Cordelia escape.

He had been too lazy, too trusting in the abilities of his followers. He had never confided in Alaria the value the girl had; he was relying too much on her fear of disappointing him.

"We were surprised by an attack from—"

"Enough, Alaria." She halted her speech immediately, her lips trembled as she waited for him to speak. He reveled in the fear he caused, knowing that every second he kept her waiting, she would grow more and more frightened. When her eyes started to water, he lost interest. "I do not have time for any more of your excusesss."

Alaria opened her mouth slightly, as if to interrupt, as if to defend herself. He watched her shut her lips tight, her practically gill-less throat clenched. It would have been so easy if she'd talked back, to punish her further, to silence her words with the flames of his powers. Perhaps he still would.

"You were in charge, Alaria. You let three of my men be

besssted by a mere homemaker and then let an already bound girl essscape."

Janus had often wondered about employing a Sidon who was half-human, but Alaria had proven herself very useful because she could blend in. He was disappointed, but he didn't want to replace a valuable asset.

Alaria kept her head down. She didn't answer right away, instead, she stayed silent and still for several moments until Janus grew impatient and lit a tiny flame on the hem of her dress.

"My lord," she stamped the flame with her hands and met his gaze. "I made a poor decision."

He rolled his eyes. "You may explain."

She took a deep breath, her shoulders rising high as she did so. "I wanted to find Jaz, sir."

"You what?" Flames came unbidden, lighting his chair and the cave floor. Janus ground his teeth and let the fire dim. "I gave you very clear instructionsss, you were to leave the Hagan to me."

"I wanted to find him, for you, my lord, to deliver him—"

"For me? You do not think I could capture him if I wanted to? I sssent you to retrieve the girl, nothing more."

"I could have if it weren't for the bloody Hagan."

"I am sssurprised, Alaria, that you could let a simple Hagan defeat you. Isss your skin not impenetrable to magic? Have I not gifted you a ssspear of the greatest caliber?"

"But his magic broke through, my lord! He lit us all aflame." Alaria leaned forward, her hands digging into the ground, pleading in her voice.

"What?" Janus growled. His mind ran fast, pieces falling into place, facts that shouldn't be true.

"He wasss there..." He fought back bile at the realization that the attacker who protected Cordelia was no mere Hagan, he was the offspring Janus had been searching for. All this time, he'd thought he'd been hunting just another Hagan, hoping to steal the man's power for himself. Could it be *Jaz* and Janus's greatest grandson were the one and the same? His mind spun as new thoughts and plans swirled like smoke.

"My lord?"

"When did the Hagan attack?"

"After we captured the girl, my lord."

"But why..." He wasn't asking Alaria, but himself. A curiosity that was slowly forming. "I removed hisss memoriesss of her, why would he care for her sssurvival one way or the other?" He mumbled.

He had thought separating the two would make the Hagan easier to attack, that the Hagan would no longer be burdened by the care for another person. Cordelia should have been easy prey, and the Hagan shouldn't have been there at all. He had thwarted Janus's trap, even with no memory of the girl?

"We tried to take the girl, but he was too strong." Alaria pleaded, ignoring the curious mumblings of her master. "His powers were—"

Janus clenched a tight jaw and lunged forward in his chair. Flames burst from the ground, climbing the walls of the cave and engulfing the air with smoke. Alaria choked back the fumes, awkwardly dancing to keep from the flames. Janus snapped his fingers again, and the flames were no more.

"Hisss powers are nothing, nothing compared to mine. And you'd do well to remember that, Alaria. You will not be given a another chance."

"Yes, my lord." Alaria bowed her head, cheeks streaked with tears, eyes red from the smoke.

"Clean yoursssself up; we have work to do." He waved a hand, dismissing her.

"*W-we*, my lord?"

Janus stood from his chair, his height nearly level with the ceiling of the cave. "You have proven yoursssself incapable, Alaria." He pulled a heavy cloak tight around his neck, red waves of smoke and fume following his silhouette as he left the cave and Alaria followed.

"If I want to capture that Danthem, I'll need to find her myself." His flaming silhouette lit the night air around them as they left the cave, emerging in a clearing of trees and clayed walls.

"And what of the Hagan, sir?" Alaria's voice trembled. Any

other Sidon would know better, but he knew she was too curious to not ask questions, a trait he both admired and loathed.

"The Hagan isss far too important to leave in your handsss." He let a new plan form in his mind, the mirth of a smile growing. "It'sss time to bring my grandssson home."

29

"WHAT ARE YOU READING SO INTENTLY?"

"Hmmm." Cordelia reluctantly pulled her gaze from the book. Jaspar was sitting across from her in the tiny study of his bunker, his feet resting on the table between them, his arms crossed behind his head, his brows knit together.

"I asked"—his voice laced with impatience—"what are you reading so intently?"

It had been three days since their trip to the parochial. She'd rested most of the first day, as her overuse of magic had completely drained her still untrained body. And she'd dedicated nearly every other second to this book. It was a few decades old, old enough to contain obsolete information, but young enough that parts were still accurate and relevant.

"Oh..." Cordelia pondered over the sections she'd read so far. "Just something of interest to me."

Jaspar tapped a booted foot to the cover. "You have an interest in brain psychology?" He seemed disbelieving.

"Er...yes?"

Jaspar leaned forward slightly and used his boot to kick the book out of Cordelia's hands and catch it in his outstretched fingers.

"Hey! Give that back!" She jumped from her seat, but Jaspar

was already flipping through the pages, his eyes growing steadily wider, his lips slowly parting.

"Cordelia," Jaspar rose to his feet and stood in front of her, eyes never leaving the book. "What have you found?"

Cordelia swallowed her panic. "It's a tome on memory loss."

"I see that." He flipped through more pages. "What have you learned?"

"It's hard to tell you that."

His eyes finally left the pages. "What? Why?"

"Because it could make things worse." She'd been absorbing everything she could from the book for days, and each page had brought more fear and less comfort. "The amnesia is your brain's response to trauma."

Jaspar rolled his eyes. "You don't say?"

"Jaz, please, I'm trying to be sensitive." His eyes crossed a little, the way they often did when she let the nickname slip.

"Fine." He dropped the book, and she followed him to sit by the fire while he prepared a mug of tea for her and poured a whiskey for himself. "What *can* you tell me?"

She sipped her tea, prolonging the inevitable. "I can reveal anything from the past that you have forgotten, but the more I tell you, the more emotional toll it will take."

"Emotions aren't exactly a concern for me," he shrugged, and it stabbed her chest to know that before she'd met him, Jaspar had completely closed himself to the very idea of having someone to care for. Someone to care about. Someone to care about him.

"What?"

She tried to school her features, but he'd already noticed the sadness there. "They grew to be a concern before."

"Huh." He tipped his head as if genuinely curious about what a sensitivity to emotions would feel like.

She understood why he had a hard time grasping this. Since she'd met this version of Jaspar, the one who'd awoken on the beach, he'd been taciturn and curt. How had he become Jaz all those months ago? Was it just the loss of her father that had made him so vulnerable? Coupled with his remembrance talisman and the comfort of familiarity?

"Can you stick to the facts, then?"

She nodded, eager to avoid revealing the emotional depth they'd shared. "My father left letters for you, he wanted you to look after me. You came to Alaro to find me, and it took longer than you thought."

"How long did it take?"

"You spent four months in Alaro."

"Four months?" he whispered as if he still couldn't fathom such a long amount of time.

"Yes." She bit her lip.

"Go on." He leaned toward her in urgency.

"I..." She had to tread carefully. If emotions could further the trauma, surely the passions of their relationship would cause more harm than good, right?

"I came with you to the cay, and we were on our way to Keru when we were attacked by Sidons and shipwrecked." It was a vast understatement of what they'd been through, but perhaps that meant he'd be sheltered from any pain.

"Why were Sidons after us?"

She chewed the inside of her cheek. "The Sidons work for an enchanter who is seeking us for our magic." Did she dare tell him the true identity of the enchanter?

"Why would an enchanter want *our* magic enough to hunt us down? There's theurgists all over the world."

She cursed under her breath. How do you tell someone that their greatest grandfather, whom they've idolized their whole life, was actually an evil sorcerer? "I think...I don't know if I should tell you that, Jaspar."

"You're worried I can't handle it?" He sneered.

"This isn't a matter of pride," she hissed, disregarding his wounded ego. "Trauma isn't something you can control."

He sighed. "Just tell me."

She nodded reluctantly. "The enchanter is your greatest grandfather, the lost captain from the legend, and he seeks our magic because he thinks it will lead him back to the island."

Jaspar's forehead smoothed, his face suddenly stock white, eyes unblinking.

"Jaspar...?" Damn. Why had she told him? She'd known it could be too much, and yet she'd let him talk her into it.

"I don't understand."

Cordelia inwardly chastised herself, gripping her skirt to ease her anxiety. She told him the story Hygonia had shared about how Jaspar's grandfather was wicked, and the curse was a deserved punishment, a punishment inflicted by her mother.

She tried to keep it light, sharing only the facts, leaving out any emotional connections to the story or people. Jaspar grew paler and paler with every newly revealed secret until his face was practically translucent.

"Cordelia..." his voice was strained. "That's just...it's not possible."

"Everything is impossible until someone proves otherwise."

Jaspar choked on his coffee. "What did you just say?"

She bit her lip. The words were out of her mouth before she'd been sensical enough to stop herself.

"My father used to say that."

"I know," she said gently.

"Right. And you know because *I* told you before?"

She nodded her head.

"I can't believe I shared so much with you."

It was on the tip of her tongue to tell him just how much they'd shared.

"And I believed this...this nonsense before?"

She nodded.

His eyes lingered on the book sitting between them. "Will I ever get my memories back?"

Cordelia's hands ached for him. Not that many days ago, she would have wrapped her arms around him, comforted him with her affection, but now she was trapped sitting beside him, forced to let him deal with the pain on his own.

"It's...rare. The more time that passes, the less likely it is they'll come back. But anything can trigger small memories; they'll come back in disjointed flashes, maybe a word or a smell."

"I think I'm going to be sick." Jaspar covered his mouth with a fist.

"Yes, the book mentioned physical side effects."

"Such as?"

"It's why I was so hesitant to tell you anything. The trauma is painful and unpleasant for your mind, and it spreads that discomfort throughout your body. It can cause nausea, headaches, mood swings, identity crisis..." She let her voice trail off, the shattered look in his eyes telling her she had already said too much.

She got to her feet, helping him to stand and walk to his bed. It was a true mark of how distracted he was that he let her walk with him, shoulder to shoulder.

"Should I not have told you?" she whispered as he tucked an arm behind his head.

"No, I'm glad you did. At least, I think I am." His eyes blinked, slowly closing and opening, as if fighting back the emotional exhaustion. She kept her movements slow, not wanting to disturb him any further.

She turned her head halfway back to her sleep roll.

"Thank you for telling me." His eyes met hers from across the room. "I'm starting to understand why you're not supposed to reveal too much when people lose their memories."

"Are you alright?"

"I need all the facts, Cordelia, whether my body can handle them or not." He licked his lips. "But, maybe from here on out, we just stick to *need-to-know* information?"

"Of course." She bit her lip, choking back her sob. "Whatever you need."

"Cordelia..." He swallowed. "You being here, the reason you were willing to die for me...is that *need-to-know*?"

She blinked, slow and painful. It would be easier for her to tell him the truth, but worse for him and harder, so much harder for both of them in the long run.

"No, Jaspar, it is not."

30

Jaspar dreamed he was in an unfamiliar courtyard, and Cordelia's eyes were red and puffy. Her dress was inside out, and Jaspar was fighting back a laugh. She showed him her collar, and it was tangled in her curly hair. He took out his knife, cutting her dress free, letting his touch linger on her neck.

He watched as if from far away as a dark, damp cellar came into view. He saw himself and Cordelia, her hair a mess and hands bandaged. She hesitated on the staircase, and he approached her, steering her down the stairs. And then her hair was in an immaculate braid, and her hands were clean, and she was lifting a barrel. She struggled on her feet, and his hand was on her back, and his face was by her neck, her cheeks flushing.

There was a table of men, all with beards, and a card game with money on the table. Jaspar looked natural, like he knew these men, like they knew him. They joked and placed bets, jesting when they lost, celebrating when they won. Cordelia dropped off a round of drinks, and Jaspar let his hand brush hers, intentionally, but played off as accidental. The men laughed and dream Jaspar threw his cards on the table, his eyes following Cordelia as she walked around the bar.

Cordelia was sitting on a dock, wincing with unshed tears. His hands stroked hers through the pain. Tiny nicks and cuts covered her hands and fingers. Then they were in a courtyard and he was sitting in the mud. She reached out to touch him, and he flinched. A moment later, he could feel the dream Jaspar soothe and calm and reach for Cordelia himself.

The dream shifted, flashing from one scene to the next. He was on his ship, journals scattered around him. He jumped to his feet, following a crudely drawn map in the journal. He was in Scaparo, and the town square was filled with loud, busy villagers. He was at a door, yelling at a man who kept shaking his head. Jaspar summoned fire, and the man slammed the door in his face. He was angry and frustrated, but then he was smiling at the sight of Cordelia, all frustrations of the day forgotten at just a look from her.

Cordelia and Jaspar walked from one building to another, slowly, talking. He smirked, and she sort of laughed with just her eyes. She said something, clever maybe, because the dream Jaspar raised an eyebrow and shook his head. She shivered in the cold, and he looked around, as if to see if anyone was watching. He reached an arm around her, and she leaned into him, their steps matching pace.

Cordelia was pouting, throwing a tray of rolls into a bin, while a man and a woman howled with amusement. And Jaspar was smiling, stifling a laugh behind a thick beard. He held up a jar filled with white powder, and she smelled it, and he laughed, and she frowned. He blew the flour in her face. And then he was wiping the flour from her forehead and cheeks and chin and nose, everywhere except her lips.

Then they were in a kitchen, his arms wrapped around her while she stood by a sink. He laughed when she deboned the fish. His heart stilled when Cordelia leaned into him. So close that dream Jaspar could have turned his neck and stolen a kiss.

A lute played and fireworks burned bright. He shielded his eyes and saw dream Jaspar dancing with Cordelia, and she looked almost like she was smiling but not. But he was smiling, big and untroubled and genuine. And they were eating something that soured her mouth, and he laughed again, always laughing with her. They were walking now, sampling food, and there was a strange puzzle that made him uneasy.

Cordelia was on the dock now, her eyes taking in the moonlight, sadness crinkling at the edges. He wiped her tears, cupped her cheeks, and then she left a chaste kiss on his palm. He helped her stand, letting his hands linger along her dress, and the tension was clear even in his dreamy state. She said something and he stared at her, and then he was running his fingers through the fabric of her dress again. He watched as the dream Jaspar trailed after Cordelia, his expression one of pained but hopeful longing.

31

CORDELIA LET HER ORB OF MAGIC SWELL WITHIN HER, expanding and contracting with each breath. The oceans she'd practiced with before were too far away now, but she'd been itching to test her magic, to learn more about her powers as a Danthem. Jaspar wasn't with her this time, and she felt lonely without his experience and encouragement. Sometimes, she heard his voice in her head, a whisper urging her on or reminding her not to push herself too far.

Close your eyes and think only of the water. Standing in the lake was nearly the opposite of the ocean. The sea's waves had crashed into her calves, but the lake was calm. The sea's temperature had chilled her skin, but the lake was warm. Even the smell had shifted from the salt of the ocean to the scent of fresh water.

Since the shipwreck, since Frân had stood on her head and clawed into her hair, her magic had felt closer than ever. When she was exhausted or injured, fatigue would slow her movements and control. But the feel of it was tangible. Almost like it had a texture of its own.

Focus on the water. How does the water feel on your skin? She waved an arm left, and water rose high above her, arching in a perfect oval shape, before returning to the lake. When she'd first started practicing, the water would splash and crash back to the surface. Now, she had learned to control the rise and fall of the water so that the movements were graceful and effortless.

She'd been practicing water movements for days, and her injuries were finally starting to heal in a way where she almost felt like herself again. And if she were being honest it was nice to take breaks from Jaspar, from the one without memories who treated her with apathy. She knew it wasn't his fault, but it hurt so much that the man who had once held her gaze with adoration now only showed indifference.

She closed her eyes, let the water seep into her skin, and smoothly slipped below the surface, the water barely rippling in her wake. She'd found she could open her eyes easily under the water. Her vision was as clear as on land, and no sting or irritation came. It was as if she had invisible lenses shielding her eyes from full exposure.

She had better control of her breathing underwater. She couldn't take in more oxygen, she didn't have the same gilled lungs as creatures who walked the land and swam the seas. But she could hold her breath for extended periods of time.

She'd been training her body to stay under as long as possible. To date, the longest she'd held her breath was just shy of fifteen minutes. Today, her goal was to stay below for a quarter of an hour.

She twisted, diving deeper into the lake. It was not so much swimming as it was gliding through the waters with ease.

Fish did not flee as she approached, plants felt soft on her fingertips, and the lake's pebbled bed rock felt sturdy beneath her feet. She counted her breaths; only five minutes had passed and she'd already reached the depths of the lake.

She walked along the benthic as effortlessly as if she were walking along the ground above her. She let her eyes wander, enjoying the view. The life beneath the water was like a different world, and yet parallel to the one above.

The land's ground was mud and grass; the lake's floor was made up of clay and rock. Above were bushes and trees; below the surface of the water, cattails and puffs of algae littered the benthic, and reeds swayed in the water's current. She wanted to share this with Jaspar, wanted to tell him of every beautiful thing she saw, but would it mean anything to *this* Jaspar?

Vibrant colors faded to unique shades without the sunlight to illuminate them. A red-eared turtle swam in front of her, its strong legs thrusting it through the water, leaving tiny bubbles behind. She'd often seen the brightly speckled turtles swimming, sometimes even sleeping on the bedrock under her feet.

She walked further along, finally reaching the patch of algae that was home to a coral-pink axolotl. The tiny creature had fascinated Cordelia and its cheeks puffed to a happy smile when she approached. She bent down, collecting the salamander and letting it nuzzle while she petted its head.

When her chest tightened, she was proud that her lungs had held for over a quarter-hour, but she was reluctant to leave behind the beauty of the lake and its creatures. Forlornly, she returned the axolotl, whom she had named Gus-Gus, back to his home in the patch of java moss. Cordelia allowed herself one last look at the new world around her before swimming to the surface, returning to the oxygen of the land above.

32

VALENTINA LOCKED THE DOOR, THE BOLT SNAPPING against the wooden frame. The candles were still lit, but the late night hour and lack of moonlight gave her shop an eerie dimness. She returned to her chair by the fire, sipping her tea and reading through the letter from Cordelia's guardian in Alaro. Valentina didn't know much about the woman, just that she ran a tavern and had handled ensuring Cordelia drank her tonics to keep her health up.

She read thoroughly, learning that Cordelia was traveling somewhere in Keru and would no longer have her tonic available. That was hardly a concern as the tonic mostly kept infections and common sicknesses away. What was strange was the mention that no one had heard from Cordelia in a month and that she was last seen making her way to Woodvale.

The door flew open, the candles snuffing out in a gust of wind, the fire flickering as the wind tried to stall it but failed.

Two men stood in the entrance, both wearing dark-green cloaks clenched together by a gold Jörmungandr pendant. Their hoods hid their faces and they both held bows, arrows knocked, aimed directly at her. She rose to her feet, shaky, the letter still clutched in her hand. She worked hard to control her eyes, terrified they would wander above her head and reveal the sleeping child upstairs.

"Evening, missssss." The word trailed off like the hiss of a snake. Sidons?

"I'm so-sorry, but we're clo-closed for the night." She hated the tremor in her voice, but her eyes kept darting to the arrow-knocked bows.

"We're not here to make any salesssss." One of the men took a step forward. "We want a Celarestar."

Valentina's mind whirred, but the word had no recognition. "The wh-what?"

"Tsssssk-Tsssssk." The other man took a step forward, and now they were crowded in the doorway so that she could neither flee nor could anyone come inside. "Feigning ignorance won't help you any. Where is it?"

She shook her head, eyes dry from the gusting wind billowing around her shop. She prayed they wouldn't be loud enough to wake Zasha.

"Why don't I have a talk with her?" A growling voice spoke from behind the men, and Valentina's fears grew impossibly darker. The Sidons stepped inside, walking around and encircling Valentina with their bows.

A man, more demonic than human, entered her shop. He was at least eight feet tall, with sunken eyes and skin that was gray, like burned cinders. Smoke of crimson and ash billowed around him, as if suffocating the air in the space.

"You've never heard of a Celarestar, have you?" His voice was a mirage, as if he were trying to sound pleasant but the wickedness inside him masked his ability.

"N-n-no, sir."

He nodded his head, taking a step inside. The smell of sulfur and coal and something sour invaded the room and she fought back a gag. "I believe you." She didn't have time to feel relief. "But there isss sssomething you *do* know," he sneered, revealing yellow teeth. "Where isss the girl?"

She clamped her mouth tight.

"Hmmm..." Janus placed a hand on her head, heavy and firm, and squeezed. Her mind flashed with visions and memories, and he threw her back.

"I'm not the first to ssseek the girl, am I?" When she didn't answer, his voice thundered louder. "Am I?"

She froze, blood running cold, heart stilling in her chest. Before she could answer, before her trembling nerves and stuttered voice could give her away, she threw herself at the fire, shoving the letter into the flames.

Arms, slimy but strong, gripped her biceps, yanking her back and throwing her body to the floor. Blood oozed out of the cuts left by the clawed Sidon's webbed hands. They aimed their bows again, arrows knocked, her chest a clear target.

"Ssstop." The demon held a hand, and the Sidons took a step back. He inspected the flames and Valentina followed his gaze, relieved and proud when she saw that the letter had burned. "Who isss Klingbeil?"

Valentina's relief vanished, her heart thudding so loud in her chest he would surely hear it. The letter was charred but had not burned fast enough to hide the identity of the last of Cordelia's guardians. She bit the inside of her cheek, refusing to speak, refusing to give away one of her own people, refusing to break the vow she had sworn her life to.

"Mama!"

"No!" Valentina screamed, jerking her arms and trying to reach out. "Go back upstairs, Zasha!" But the demon was already approaching her son, already squatting down to eye level. His evil and wicked face transformed, and though she could tell he was adopting an air of innocence, the malice lingered in his features.

"Zasha? What a ssstrong name." His voice, so deadly only a moment ago, took on a singsong nature, like a teacher speaking to a child.

Zasha eagerly shook his head, his cropped brown hair waving around him. "I'll be a defender of the people someday."

Valentina's spine stiffened; if only she had never told Zasha the meaning of his name, perhaps this man wouldn't know how valuable he was, how valuable their whole family was. But now he would know everything.

"Yesss, you will." The man patted her son's head, and Zasha, oblivious to the danger, smiled broadly.

"Ssso..." The demon turned back to face Valentina, rising to his feet like a pillar, leering over her with great power, casting a shadow so dark, it made her squint. "You're not an *alchemist*, are you Valentina?"

Her name...no, no, no. He couldn't know her name. Her eyes darted to an unassuming Zasha, who watched the scene with confused but curious eyes. She tried to imagine how this might look from the perspective of a four-year-old; did he think they were playing?

"Yes," she breathed.

The man's smile was curled and twisted, like a muscle he didn't use often was strained. "And what generation of guardian are you, Msss. Valentina?"

Her tears streamed down, and she shook her head, willing him to understand the boundaries of her vow. She bit her tongue, suddenly so swollen that she could not speak.

"Open your mouth." The demon growled, grabbing her by the jaw. Zasha let out a scream and ran toward her. "Ressstrain him." A Sidon grabbed Zasha by the biceps, and he started to cry.

The demon yanked Valentina's jaw so hard she heard a small crack and her too swollen tongue fell out. "You have made a binding vow," he assumed, and she nodded her head eagerly. He growled and shoved her aside before turning back and lifting a finger to his lips. "But...he'sss too young." The demon pointed to Zasha. "You haven't made any vowsss yet, have you?"

Zasha's eyes were wide as he shook his head. "N-n-no, sir."

The demon clasped his hands behind his back and began to pace in front of the fire. He adopted a low voice and spoke in song. "I am in need of a guardian, I ssseek the bravest of mankind."

"I am the strongest there is, and I will protect you for all time." Zasha recited the words with conviction, unaware of the noose he was tightening around his mother's neck.

"Yesss, you are, aren't you, my boy?" The man lowered himself to the height of the child again and extended his hand. "My name is Janusss, and I am a very powerful...man." He spat the last word as if it were poison on his tongue. "I'll be taking you on a little trip."

Zasha's eyes spanned between Janus and his mother, war and indecision evident in his young and innocent expression.

Janus patted Zasha's head again and strode toward Valentina. His steps were light yet thundered in the room as if his power were so strong his body couldn't contain it. Smoke escaped him from where she could not see, and soon, it was invading her every orifice. Her eyes, her nostrils, her mouth, even her ears were asphyxiating, suffocated by the invading smoke.

She choked and gagged, and then it stopped, and the man's eyes were on hers. They were red, currant as blood, and the pupils were a strange, undulated oval shape.

"Please..." she croaked, but the demon snapped his fingers.

"Grab the boy."

Valentina screamed and jerked, desperate to escape her bindings. The demon glared and turned to leave, but the Sidons didn't move or lower their bows. Janus stopped at the door, snapped his fingers, and the fireplace snuffed out.

"And bring the witch. I want to know more about her encounter with my greatessst grandsssson."

33

A MONTH HAD PASSED SINCE THE SHIPWRECK. A MONTH since Jaspar had lost his memory. A month of awkward silence and halfhearted conversations. A month of Cordelia trying desperately to heal the constant ache in her chest, the one that had nothing to do with her nearly healed ribs.

Each day, they'd eat breakfast by the fire. Cordelia had taken to visiting the nearby pond, practicing her magic, honing her skills. The more her body healed, the more she practiced, the more she felt connected to the water.

Sometimes, Jaspar would accompany her, but mostly, she went alone, eager to have a moment to herself so she could miss the Jaspar who remembered her. Then she would return to the bunker, happy to see a man who was indifferent to see her.

Cordelia had sort of pictured Jaspar's life as adventurous; running from one destination to another, sailing the open waters, meeting new people, learning exciting secrets of the world, but it was mostly...dull. A lot of sitting around and looking at the same books and journals over and over. She kept herself busy and entertained by reading but mostly by observing Jaspar.

Studious and so focused, his face revealing every emotion. She would watch it change from searching to evaluating to frustrating and then back to searching. Sometimes, his expression would clear just a little, and she could see the toll it was taking, and she wanted to go to him. She wanted to wrap him in her arms and allow him a moment of peace and ease his always-busy mind, and it broke her that she couldn't be that for him.

She took care of him in the ways that she could, bringing him coffee and reminding him to eat, and she hoped that if any part of him remembered her, no matter how subconscious, he would feel his burden eased just a little and for now that would have to be enough.

Cordelia let her eyes wander between reading an old gazette and watching Jaspar. The papers only held so much information, and life in the bunker was as mundane as it was lonely. But watching Jaspar work had been fascinating.

The way he chewed on his quill when he concentrated. The way his chin tensed when he stifled a yawn. The way he would have small bursts of excitement when he saw something interesting, scribbling furiously in his journal.

She'd realized the pattern of the journals now. Each year had its own mark, and the number from that year was scratched to the spine. His current journal was relatively new, though more faded than he had remembered, marked on the lower left corner by an X. This was the tenth year he'd had journals of his own, and this journal was the twenty-eighth one written.

It was the journal he'd left off with, the last one he'd written before traveling to Alaro for her father's services. Every journal after that was at the cay, or the bottom of the Tilerian Sea. Jaspar was searching for his last lead: the one he'd been working on when her father died. Something to do with an old book that had disappeared or burned or been stolen. A book that could have a map he desperately needed.

He was sifting through his notes, trying to find another way. She saw the bottom of his coffee tin through the liquid and took it to the fire to refill it. When she returned, he hadn't moved.

She set the coffee down and continued to read her gazette, this one from ten years earlier and featuring a particularly interesting story on new whiskey preservation practices. She made mental notes to take back to Gladys, if she ever found her way home. Of course, this being such an old paper, Gladys may already have learned of these tricks.

Cordelia had never done much with the whiskey, except over-pour it and complain about the heaviness of the barrels. She ignored the memory prickling her mind, of being in the cellar with Jaspar, his breath warm on her neck, the feel of him supporting her back, the sweet, tender moment she should have appreciated more at the time.

"My coffee?"

"Hmm?" Cordelia lifted her head to see Jaspar standing in front of her, coffee in one hand, journal in the other, an expression of dumbfounded curiosity.

"You filled my coffee." Did his voice ever *not* sound irritated?

"Yes."

"Why?"

What a silly question. "Because it was nearly empty."

"But I didn't ask you to fill it."

"So?"

He returned to his work, and she returned to her reading, and the usual awkwardness settled around the room again.

"Do you..."

His voice trailed off and she set down her paper, giving him her undivided attention.

"Aren't you curious about what I'm working on?"

"Of course."

"But you haven't asked."

She shrugged. "If you wanted me to know, you would have told me."

He exhaled through his nose, almost a laugh but not quite. "Come here."

She joined him at the table, she had planned to sit opposite him, but he pulled out the chair beside him. When she sat, he pulled the chair by the leg, and it scraped on the floor. He let go when the chair was touching his, when they were so close she could smell him. Driftwood and sea salt and something sweet.

"Read." He handed her a journal and then leaned over her shoulder as she read it. She could feel the warmth of him, his arm resting lazily on the back of her chair. For one tiny second, they could be back at Anchorage Inn.

The entry was dated twenty-three years ago.

> Pregnant. Which is a blessing, of course, but also something that terrifies me. I'll be handing down this curse to yet another member of our family. He'll have a life of adventure chasing down the island, but unless he meets someone to share his mark with, it will be a lonely existence.
>
> My beautiful wife already doesn't deserve this life, though at least she can still belong, she can still live in the memories of the world around her. What of me? What of our future baby? A local fertility theurgist has declared it will be a boy, a healthy boy born in the early days of the flowers.
>
> My wife has started making a blanket for him, fluffy sheep wool, a little leather, and the personal touch: she's crushed hundreds of daises, letting their perfume soak into the leather and wool. She claims the blanket will always smell of their nectar, until the end of days.

"Daisies. That's why he smelled so sweet."

"Huh?"

Had she said that out loud? "Nothing." Cordelia waved her hand at him and continued to read.

> I've found nothing more of the library, though I have some suspicions. A man in the old days of Krionia wrote of an old book building. It's said to have a hidden space, though he didn't write where, with a hidden secret, though he didn't write what, and a hidden book,

though he didn't write what it contained. He was convinced, however, that the book holds great treasures of the future and the past.

I doubt the treasure part, but it's a lead I'd still like to follow up on. But the last storm of the season has passed, and our baby boy will soon be arriving, and I've been thinking of hanging up my adventure boots, just for a few years. When he's older, I'll take him with me, as my father did, and his father, and every father before.

We've decided to name our son Jaspar, a strong name, he who guards the treasure, a name that will encourage him to guard our secret with his life. And who knows, maybe he'll be the one to finally find Qualaris.

34

"YOUR FATHER WROTE THIS?" CORDELIA ASKED.

Jaspar nodded. "Now we just have to find Krionia." He sighed.

"But we're in Krionia."

"What?" His head snapped up.

"Before The Greatest of Wars, Keru was known as Krionia. It's been over a millennia now, but..."

"No, it's brilliant! I'll write Kimbal at once, and he can—" Jaspar stopped short, choking on his words, and he felt the stark reminder like a physical slap. Silence hung between them. He wouldn't write to Kimbal at once. He would never write to Kimbal again.

It had been so easy to forget that the captain was gone. He'd had no funeral for closure, no real proof even that Kimbal was dead. Simply the words of a woman who claimed to be his daughter.

Jaspar could pretend, if he didn't dwell on it too much, that no time had passed and the captain lived on. He'd often go weeks without contact, until he received word that he was needed. Or until he'd had a reason to write to the captain himself. But now he'd never send another letter. He'd never receive another letter.

"Jaspar." Cordelia's voice was soft, and her hand on his arm was gentle. He should have shrugged her off, should have pulled her away, but the kindness in her eyes settled his churning thoughts.

"I'll..." He licked his lips, clenched his jaw, and swallowed. "We can travel there next week."

She nodded, and he stared at the walls behind her, eyes unfocused. If he couldn't have the captain back, if he could never again set sail for an adventure with his mentor, he could at least have his daughter, right?

"If you're coming with me?" His voice was hesitant with uncertainty, but he sighed in relief when she nodded her head.

"When are we leaving?" she whispered in a small voice.

His mind spun with logistics, planning, packing, choosing supplies and routes to take. "Two days."

She nodded again, and her hand dropped from his arm. Jaspar felt an unexpected loss with the removal of her touch. Did she miss the captain, too? Was that why she wanted to be with Jaspar and follow him from one clue to the next? Was she trying to replace her lost father with his apprentice?

But then, maybe he had done that, too. If the captain weren't here, who else could fill his shoes besides his daughter? And she could even remember him, how convenient. But when he looked at the woman before, he did not think of his lost friend, he did not think of the man he'd admired. He thought of how comforting she'd been when he was ill. Laying with his head in her lap, her fingers soft in his hair, and her humming soothing him to sleep.

35

AFTER AN ENTIRE MONTH WITH CORDELIA, JASPAR HAD let his guard down little by little. He tried to tell himself they'd been friends before, but it felt strange to admit to such a friendship when he didn't remember it. And yet they must have been friends, close friends, because she'd been to his home and he'd told her his secrets, secrets of his mother and father that he'd never shared with anyone, not even Kimbal.

He'd spent every day with her, every morning, noon, and night, and still he did not remember. They talked about nothing, and everything, and a lot of things in the middle. And he found he missed her during those hours she spent at the lake practicing her magic.

She tried to tell him about the four months he'd missed. He'd only really learned that he'd spent months in Alaro looking for her and that they'd been attacked by Sidons. But she always stopped herself just shy of saying everything. He wasn't sure how he knew, but he could tell that she held something back.

All the while, there were dreams. Dreams of people he didn't know, places he'd never been, emotions he'd never known existed. He dreamed over and over of another Jaspar, one who laughed and played cards and stole the touch of a beautiful woman. One who slept in the same bed, under the same roof, and woke up in the same village. A village where people knew him by name, recognized him on the street, waved and said hello like they'd seen him the day before and would see him the day after.

She'd told him so little of their supposed friendship. But every new reveal was something that hinted at a truthfulness to her words, and yet he could barely fathom the idea of knowing someone so well, of letting someone know him so well.

Even with the captain, who had been his only companion, he'd kept at bay. There had been a few close shaves when they needed to rely on each other for survival, and the captain had saved Jaspar more than once. Which was perhaps the only reason he really allowed Cordelia to stay. Though he still couldn't bring himself to understand or imagine the captain was gone. It still felt like any day, he'd receive a letter, or the old man would simply show up.

But being with Cordelia wasn't that different than being with the captain, really. Someone to talk to, to share the space with, though sharing living quarters was still new to him. She would bring him coffee, food, and tea whenever he needed it, without being asked, without him even realizing he was hungry or thirsty until it was already there. And gradually, he'd let her in a little more each day. Mostly, he talked aloud to himself, a habit of spending all his time alone. But now there was someone to hear him. Someone to use as a sounding board for some of his more outlandish theories.

Often, she simply listened, nodding and encouraging his enthusiasm. But there were times when she...grounded him: noticing some small fact he'd overlooked or recalling other journal entries he'd left at the cay. Each day they'd spend by the table, her keeping him company reading newspapers about who knows what, and him studying the legacy left to him. She usually fell asleep first, and he would wake her in a voice that had grown gentler each day.

When she wasn't looking, he found himself watching her. Most of the time, she was quiet and contemplative, content with simply being near him, even if it was so boring, all she could do was read outdated newspapers. But he was uneased by her presence as it continued to pull his focus in ways he couldn't explain.

The way she twirled her hair as she read. The way she smiled with her eyes when he got particularly excited. The way she pulled her legs to her chest when she was tired and rested her chin on her knees. The way she'd *hmm* when he'd asked a question she knew he didn't need a real answer to. The sway of her dress when she stretched after sitting too long. Each moment felt foreign and yet somehow familiar.

Her mannerisms, the parts of her that he was getting to see more and more, were burning in his mind like a tiny collection of random facts about Cordelia. His eyes would notice even the slightest movement from her, and his thoughts would immediately drift, and he'd lose all cohesive memory of what he'd been doing. Like right now.

"Where are we going?" She ran fingers through her freshly washed hair, wrapping and twisting it into a long braid. But several tendrils escaped, framing her face.

"There's a hotel north of here, should be close to the upcoming festival where we'll have plenty of opportunities to seek information. If nothing else, it will get us in the right direction."

"How far?" She fixed the collar of her dress, the blue the seamstress had chosen matching her eyes perfectly.

"We'll need to walk quite a ways. It could be hard on you." He paused, thoughts lingering on her many injuries. Was he putting her in danger? Asking too much of her fragile state?

"I'll manage. I'll be sure to get plenty of rest tonight."

He nodded. He was surprised by how at ease he felt with this determination of hers, surprised at how much he liked the idea of her accompanying him. Of anyone accompanying him. He couldn't deny they had known each other, that they had been friends. Because she had been a friend to him these last four weeks. She had *cared* about him.

It was there in her actions: the way she listened intently when he spoke, the way she reminded him to rest, never letting him overwork or stress himself away. It was there in all of her words: the way she comforted him, the way she talked to him, the way she knew and understood exactly what he was trying to say, even when he wasn't sure himself.

Her heart was on her sleeve, always open and unyielding. It was unfamiliar to him, and yet, he knew it to be true. He didn't remember her, but it was clear she *knew* him. She understood exactly how to calm his overthinking mind, she could sense when he was overwhelmed, when she let him vent all of his frustrations, take them all out on her without saying a single word, just letting him know he was heard.

Jaspar may not remember her, but as he laid down to sleep he could see exactly how she had made an impact on his life and perhaps just why he would have made friends with someone like her. Someone kind and understanding, someone open and so emotionally available, someone who reminded him he was human.

36

JASPAR'S LEGS SANK DEEPER INTO THE SAND, THE quickness of it pulling and yanking his whole body until it was up to his knees, his thighs. The movement of the sand stopped somewhere around his middle, and he forced his arms with all of his strength, shoving his body forward, his fingers digging into the sand until they bled.

His body didn't budge, didn't twist. Tightness constricted around his lower half until a tingling numbness set in, and he couldn't feel his legs or feet.

"Cordelia!" He screamed so loud it was almost a roar, the pain and fear morphing into a sound he'd never made before. The strange, blue-silhouetted men dragged her across the sand. She kicked and pulled and yanked, fighting them as best she could. Ocean water sprayed the men, attempting to suck them in, but the water simply moved around them, as if they were immune to her powers.

Cordelia opened her mouth to scream, but no sound came out. Jaspar watched in frozen horror as she dragged her feet, clawed her hands down the men's biceps, opened her mouth as wide as she could and attempted over and over and over to scream.

Jaspar couldn't understand why no cry would accompany her pain. He turned his head in a circle, attempting to see anything familiar. But the sand was chilled, a strange silver and black color, and had an odd, comforting texture. It was the softest, least grainy sand he'd ever felt, as if the ocean had created the sand to match its texture.

The trees surrounding them had strange triangular leaves and long, curved trunks, bare of any branches until the very top. The wind swirled, but the trees barely swayed, as if the gale that attacked only drowned Jaspar in sand, leaving the rest of the beach untouched.

He spit out large mouthfuls of the strange sand, the taste clogging his throat and crunching between his teeth. Cordelia was farther away now, further down the sands, until he could barely see anything but the blue shadows of her and her captors.

It's going to be okay, my friend.

Ki-Kimbal? Jaspar spluttered, shocked to see the hazy image of his former mentor.

The captain looked as he had in his life, lively despite his age and peppered hair. His smile was waned as he watched Cordelia get dragged along the sand.

Help her! Jaspar pleaded, unfathomed by the captain's calm demeanor when his daughter was in danger.

You'll find her. I believe in you. I'm trusting you. The captain placed a hand on his shoulder and feeling slowly returned to Jaspar's feet and legs.

But how—

A loud cannon boomed, so deafening the ground trembled beneath it. The great captain clutched his chest before his eyes went wide, and his clear, translucent body crashed onto the sand. Jaspar lunged forward, surprised when he could slide out of the sand with ease.

Kimbal! Jaspar reached, but his hand went through the man's chest and shoulders, as if he were nothing more than vapor. The wind returned, swirling the sand around them and when Jaspar opened his eyes again, the captain's body was gone.

Humming reached his ears, and he turned to see the silhouette of a figure walking toward him. A woman? A man? He couldn't tell.

I would not be so sure. The figure said in a singsong voice that was both feminine and masculine, as if two voices were speaking instead of one.

Where is she?

She is with the sands of time.

Jaspar spluttered, his words slurring as a strange darkness slowly filled his vision. *Where the blazes is that?*

Where snow meets the ocean, and mountains touch the sea.

Where the world's serpent guards a cave of withered trees.

The darkness grew so much that the light was slowly disappearing, and the figure, almost in view now, was nothing more than a gray shadow gliding toward him, the sand untouched by the strange phantom's feet.

In the highest of norths, and the center of all things, rests the treasure of truth and love and dreams.

The figure was getting closer and closer, until it was standing in front of Jaspar, his vision barely taking in the form of legs under a swaying cloak. Or maybe it was a dress?

The smell of sulfur irritated his nose as the figure came to a stop in front of him.

Please, Cordelia, I need to save her. Sand still dried his tongue, and his voice came out in a desperate, pleading rasp.

Awaiting beyond the cave is a shoreline of black sand and white shells, there is the land of Qualaris, beneath a crimson and blue full moon.

Jaspar felt a hand on top of his head, both heavy and light. And then the blackness finally swallowed him whole, and he could see no longer.

37

Jaspar was thrashing in his sleeping, muttering incoherently. Cordelia approached with caution. Her first instinct was to wake him, to tend to him, to ease his troubled mind. But she was uncertain how this Jaspar would react to being awoken, especially if his unconscious mind was already disturbed.

"Jaspar," she whispered quietly, trying to coax him awake. She repeated his name a little louder and gently shook his shoulder.

Jaspar was on his feet in two seconds. He had pulled a knife from under his pillow and was looking around the room with wild eyes. It reminded her of when he'd awoken on the beach, and she'd realized the man she loved had been lost to the sea.

"Jaspar." She kept her voice calm and even, fearful of the knife in his hand and how he had used it on her the first time he'd awoken on the beach. He was panting through his nostrils, shallow breaths that forced his chest to rise and fall in rapid succession.

He raised the knife high, and she retreated, her back hitting the wall of the small bunker.

"Who are you?" he growled. "Why am I here?" His eyes wandered around the room several times before landing on hers.

"My name is Cordelia." She held up her hands. "I'm the daughter of Captain Kimbal." It hurt her to explain to the man she loved who she was for the second time. How much of her life would now be spent trying to gain his trust?

141

"Kimbal..." Jaspar closed his eyes tight and shook his head. "Yes. Kimbal's daughter. And Kimbal is gone." His voice cracked on the last word, and he sank onto the bed. His eyes were glossy, and he looked up at the ceiling, as if trying to keep the tears in.

"Are you alright?" It felt like a small question to ask, considering the mental state he was in.

"No." Jaspar licked his lips and let his head droop.

Cordelia fought hard against the urge to comfort him physically. Merely a few weeks ago, she could have held him in her arms, ran a hand through his hair, hummed to him until his burdened mind found peace. But how could she comfort this man, so unlike the Jaspar she feared she could never get back.

"How can I put you at ease?"

He whispered something under his breath. "You said that before."

"Yes."

"I..." He coughed and stood abruptly. "Just leave me alone." He put on his boots and grabbed his cloak from the hook by the door. He had the knob turned and the door opened before he turned back to her.

"I'm just...going for a walk?" There was a strange inflection in his voice, as if he wasn't sure why he was telling her where he was going.

"Alright."

"Er, alright," he said. Cordelia felt her heart tug as the man she loved, the man who didn't remember her, the man who may never remember her, walked away, slamming the door behind him.

38

JASPAR HAD RETURNED FROM HIS WALK PRETENDING AS if the nightmare and his reaction had never happened, and they left for Keru as planned. Cordelia had been hesitant to speak, unsure of what might set him off or confuse him further.

"How far is our walk?" Cordelia asked as they left the bunker through the dark tunnel. Jaspar tossed a fireball in the air, and it bobbed in front of them as they walked.

"About fifteen miles."

"Oh."

He shook his head. "It sounds farther than it is. It's a flat walk, and if we can keep a steady pace of...about two miles per hour, we should get there by mid-afternoon."

She sighed, her breath visible in the cold air.

"But we can stop to rest as much as you need." He lifted her under the arms to help her out of the well. He held onto her just long enough to ensure her steady footing, and Cordelia missed his embrace immediately.

Cordelia felt like the former Lady Kimbal, when she'd first arrived at Anchorage Inn, and she'd been so worried about her poor skills holding others back. Like, if she dropped a whiskey barrel, how much coin would Gladys lose? When she'd damaged the oysters by shucking them with her hands, she'd been so concerned about ruining dinner for all their guests. Jaspar, *her*

Jaspar, would have been so quick to support her. But would this man feel burdened by her slow and injured pace?

"How long would it normally take you to walk? If you weren't accompanied by an injured person."

He scratched his neck. "By myself? I can usually do three, three and a half miles per hour."

She nodded and tried to conceal her frown behind a clear expression.

"Cordelia." His voice was softer than she'd heard it recently, and it reminded her of the Jaz she'd first met, the one who cared for her wounded hands, walked her to her room in the dark, and gave her his cloak the first night they'd met.

"We can take as many breaks as you need. You're not slowing me down in the slightest."

It was the kind of statement her Jaspar would have made, comforting her when she was doubting herself or worried about letting people down. She thought of her dream of him, and not letting him go, and not giving up on him.

With no idea where they were headed, she let him lead the way. The weather had been getting colder and colder now that December had arrived, and they were in a more northern country. Though Vales was the coldest continent, the northern borders of Keru were a close second.

"We can take our last rest here," Jaspar said. They'd been walking nearly all day, only stopping twice so far. It had been too silent of a walk, but Cordelia had wiggled a few small conversations out of Jaspar. Mostly theories about where they were headed and what they might find. But just hearing his voice brought so much comfort to her.

They approached a small township and found a local tavern to relieve themselves and grab a quick meal.

"The lamb stew, please. And do you have any bread rolls?" The waitress nodded and left the table just as Jaspar returned and took his seat with a confused scowl on his brow.

"What?"

"You ordered for me."

She bit her lip. "I'm sorry, I—"

"How did you know what I'd want?"

The waitress returned with tea and coffee, and Cordelia quickly looked for a way to change the subject.

"We're a little over halfway there, correct?"

Jaspar shook his head, taking a sip of his coffee. "Only about two hours left. But I'm glad we're taking a break. It's freezing out there. Reminds me of when Kimbal and I got caught in the Scaparion Mountains." His lips frowned.

"Would you tell me about it?"

He raised a brow to her.

"I know nothing of his adventures; he never shared them with me when he was alive." She ignored the prick in her eyes. "I wish I could see that side of his life."

Jaspar nodded. "We'd been following a lead on another descendant."

"A relative of yours?" She couldn't hide the surprise in her tone, and Jaspar gave her a sad smile.

"My greatest grandfather lived forty-two hundred years ago; that's thirty generations of descendants."

"Have you found others, then?"

"Sadly, no. But there have been mentions from time to time in various journals."

"Did you find a descendant of his then? In Scaparo?"

Jaspar shook his head as the waitress returned with their stews. "No. The person in question had died many years before, and he'd lived a long and public life as a Talmudist. The entire mountain village remembered him and his family."

"So, no curse." She tore her roll into small pieces, tossing them into her stew. His face cringed, and she fought back the smile of remembrance. Of a night at Anchorage Inn. The first time they'd shared a family dinner together. And he'd teased her for ruining a perfectly good roll.

He cleared his throat. "No curse, I'm afraid. We'd spent the entire day at the village and should have slept there for the evening," he scoffed. "It was my fault. I thought the moon would be enough to light our way after the sunlit hour had passed."

Jaspar's eyes got a glossy and distant look for a moment before he spoke in a sad whisper. "He saved my life that night."

"How so?"

"Kimbal and I had climbed a few mountains together before, but I'd been climbing all my life. I got careless and shifted from one cliff's edge to the other too quickly. The moonlight hadn't lit my path well enough, and I stumbled onto a precarious cliff that crumbled as soon as I landed on it." His face fell as if remembering his own foolhardiness.

"Kimbal had always used a rope when climbing, and he was able to wrap it around my unconscious body and carry me to safety. I was in his debt from that moment on," Jaspar broke off, coughing and clearing his throat. "Sorry. It's still hard for me to believe that he's..."

Cordelia wanted to tell him that she knew all too well how hard it was.

~

THEY PAID FOR THEIR MEAL AND RETURNED TO THEIR walk, and Cordelia's mind spun with the desire for more: she wanted to hear of all of her father's adventures. Of all of Jaspar's. She wanted to know more about their lives, the parts of them she'd never seen before. The parts of her father she'd never get back.

"Before." She wrapped her small shawl tight as a soft snowfall began and they turned onto the cobbled path. "You said my father saved your life more than once."

Jaspar swallowed and nodded his head.

"There was another time in the Mikirian Capital when I'd unintentionally antagonized the wrong man. Kimbal got me out of there just in time for the man to forget me and for me to try again."

"Try again?"

"You forget I am not remarkable. I can have as many first impressions as I like. If I anger someone, it's easy for me to walk away and come back a day or two later. If I have the time, that is."

"Hmm." This thought had never occurred to her, and she

wondered if, thanks to the talisman around her neck, she would be afforded the same skill.

"Now, I have a few questions for you." Jaspar's tone had turned from playful storyteller to serious interrogator.

"Alright."

"You said before that you'd been through hell and back for me, more than once."

She pulled her lips to the side but nodded.

"What did you mean?"

She tried to contemplate how to tell him anything without telling him of their story, of his betrayal, of hers, of the lies and secrets they'd kept, and how they'd found their way back to each other.

"Need-to-know?" he asked.

"Yes. Perhaps just the highlights?"

"That seems safe," he said.

"You...betrayed my trust."

"That's all?"

Her stomach twisted, not just at the memory of that betrayal, of him leaving, but also of how *this* Jaspar dismissed her pain so easily.

"There was a great deal more to it."

"But you're still here. You forgave him? I mean, me?"

"You're easy to forgive, Jaspar."

His brow scrunched as if this answer didn't make sense to him.

"Can you tell me more about my father?"

Jaspar sipped his canteen of coffee before returning it to his belt satchel. "Actually, I have a theory. I can share it with you. If you're interested."

"Of course!"

He laughed at her outburst.

"Sorry. I meant, please confide in me."

His face turned inward. "Confide in me..." he mumbled under his breath, and she wondered if some small part of him remembered their time in the courtyard, when they'd grieved the captain together. The book had mentioned memory flashbacks; was he having one now?

"Jaz?" She touched a gentle hand to his shoulder, and he jerked. He stopped walking and glared down at her, and she inwardly chastised herself. "I'm so sorry, I forgot."

"You claim to know me so well and yet you didn't remember that I don't like to be touched?"

"I *do* remember. It's just—"

"Just what?"

She gave him a wane smile. "I used to be the exception." She should have been more guarded with her words, but they had slipped out too quickly. Before he could analyze her answer too closely, she steered the conversation back to her father.

"You were about to tell me about your theory?"

"Oh. Yes." He returned to walking, and she sighed in relief before following after him.

"Do you know how your father died?"

39

HER VOICE WAS SAD AND SMALL, AND HE HAD TO WALK closer to hear her over the sounds of the growing wind. "The healers said he had a heart attack."

"I've been reading some of my journals, and I made quite a few notes that I don't remember. Mostly, I log my thoughts so that I don't forget anything. Or logistics so I can plan ahead. But there's a lot of...evidence that he *knew* he was going to die."

"Such as?"

"Mentions of him getting more and more curious about my curse and if I wanted to live my life instead of breaking it, for starters."

She bit her lip, and he felt a tad guilty at having upset her.

"And?"

"I don't recall us ever having such...deep conversations. But there were multiple annotations of similar discussions. Not much to notice if you read a random entry, but when you string all the clues together, it's...suspicious."

Her eyes grew soft, and she stopped walking. "So, he didn't have a heart attack?"

"I think he did, but that doesn't mean it wasn't intentional."

She pulled the cloak tighter as the snowfall increased. "Explain."

"You said your father was found by the Guardians of the Talian Sea?"

"Yes."

"Did you not wonder why he wasn't found by his crew?"

"I...actually, that hadn't occurred to me. Why *wasn't* he found by his crew?"

"Because he wasn't with his crew."

She scoffed. "He couldn't possibly have managed that ship alone. He was a great captain, but even he had limitations."

"He was found on a *ship* early in the morning. Did you clarify *which* ship?"

"No. He only had one ship," she whispered, and he leaned closer to hear her.

"He had two. The one issued to him by the crown, and a personal one man ship."

"But why would he use his own ship for a mission?"

"Maybe he *was* on a mission, but it wasn't sanctioned by the crown of Mikiria?"

"Who else would sanction it?"

"Himself," Jaspar shrugged, reminiscing on all the times the old man had told him of his solo adventures. His heart tugged at the thought that the great captain would never again sail the waters on that boat.

"You think he died trying to find Qualaris?" There wasn't as much skepticism in her tone as he would have expected.

Aside from the captain, it was rare he'd meet anyone who believed the improbable, who believed in the island. It was another element of Cordelia, another detail to catalog as he learned more and more about the only *friend* he had. Even if he didn't remember meeting her and how their friendship had bloomed, he could see traces of their common ground in moments like this.

"Not necessarily. The last mention in my journals from your father, he was certain he'd found a man who could lead us to Qualaris, a man who knew secrets about my greatest grandfather."

"Why were you not with him then?"

"I was in Scaparo. My last memory..."

"Jaz?"

He tried not to wince at the nickname. He didn't remember

why she sometimes called him this, but he'd learned from context that it was a sign of their familiarity, and it felt oddly affectionate.

"My last memory is making plans to meet him. I had been in Scaparo when I received his letter. And I stopped at home—"

"The cay?"

"Yes." He kept forgetting she'd been to his home, that he'd shared that piece of himself with her. "I arrived late that evening, only to find the cay had been ransacked in my absence."

"And you thought it was my father?"

"The cay is protected; only those who have already been there can know where it is. I knew it was your father. I've never brought anyone else there before." *Until you,* he thought.

"How long have you lived there?"

"Since I was a boy. Since my parents..." He let his voice trail off. "Kimbal was always hiding things, always worried they would land in the wrong hands. I don't know what he was looking for, or if he found it. I sorted through everything there, and from what I could tell, nothing was missing."

"And that's your last memory?"

"Yes. I remember finding the cay ransacked and then...nothing," he shook his head. "Nothing until I woke up on that beach."

She sighed, her eyes misty with unshed tears.

"Are...are you alright?"

She nodded. "It's...hard. I haven't spoken about his loss very much. I sort of grieved internally until—"

"Until?"

"Until I met you."

He felt the strange urge to comfort her, to embrace her, and his hand had just lifted when the soft snowfall shifted unexpectedly into a deadly ice tornado.

40

JASPAR WRAPPED HIS CLOAK AS TIGHTLY AS HE COULD, tucking the fabric into the belt of his pants to keep it in place. He ensured his satchel was clutched tight around his torso, eyes searching for shelter. But the cobbled road was empty, the fields were barren from winter, and the town they'd left was three miles back. They were less than an hour from the Deserin; if they could just push through, they could find shelter in the city.

"Jaz!" Cordelia shouted as the tornado of ice pulled her cloak, her body shifting as she fought against the push of the wind. He reached for her waist, pulling her back to him, ignoring the spark when his cheek met the skin of her forehead.

"What's happening?" He shouted over the howling winds. But Cordelia didn't answer as she was pulled from his grasp, sucked into the spinning vortex of the tornado. He saw dark shadows of her figure as it whirled in the winds, and she slowly grew farther and farther away from him.

His fire powers came to his hands, but they were of no use to him on the ground. He could melt the snow at his feet, but what good would that be to an icy cyclone?

"Cordelia!" he shouted, but even he couldn't hear his voice over the gale-force winds.

He searched the grounds around them for something, anything to give him purchase, but there was nothing. He cursed under his breath before chasing after the cyclone, running as fast as his long legs would take him. But just as he worried the cyclone would be too far gone, the winds stopped.

His feet slowed in shock. Cordelia was standing in the field, her eyes closed, her arms held gracefully above her, making a wide u shape. The wind slowly came to a stop, ice returning to its snowy form, dried leaves and branches falling back to the earth.

Cordelia lowered her arms, blood trickled from her nose, and he reached her just in time to catch her. She hadn't lost consciousness like she had when creating the waterfall, but she was close to it. Her cheeks red, eyes drooping.

"Cordelia?"

"M alight." Her words were slurred, and he dropped to his knees, bringing her with him, letting her lean into his chest. It was unnerving how little the closeness bothered him, how much relief he felt from their embrace.

"How the blazes did you do that?"

"Hmm?"

"You just controlled an ice tornado."

Her hair blew in her eyes and face, and he tucked it back behind her ears, pulling her a little closer to block the slowly calming winds.

"Ice is just water."

"Controlling ice goes *far* beyond the abilities of a Danthem, Cordelia. Ice and snow may be made up of water, but they're weather-born, not earth-bound. Power to control them...it's unheard of."

"Hmmm."

"Cordelia?" Her eyes slipped closed, her body going limp, arms dropping to her sides. His gut twisted at the unexpected fear of losing her.

"Cordelia." He shook her several times, but when she didn't respond, he took in a heavy sigh and clutched her close to him. He'd carried her before, back at the bunker when she'd passed out after overuse of her magic. But he'd tossed her over his shoulder then, uncaring about her comfort and simply wanting to ease his own burden.

This time, he couldn't bear the thought. He wanted to be able to see her face, wanted to be able to look in her eyes when she woke, wanted to watch her sleep and to know she was safe. He tucked her legs under his left arm and wrapped his right arm behind her shoulder, careful not to jostle her injured body.

Her face was still red, which could be from the cold winds or the exertion, he wasn't sure which one. Her eyes were closed, her lips slightly parted.

His mind was telling his body what to do, telling him to bend to her head, to leave a kiss on her skin. He shook his head, clearing the inexplicable desire and walking forward to the Keru capital of Deserin.

There was still another half an hour to go, but he would carry Cordelia as long as it took to keep her safe. He wasn't sure why she mattered to him so much. All he knew was the inner voice in his head, telling him that losing Cordelia would be too great a risk, that losing Cordelia meant losing a piece of himself.

41

JASPAR SIGNED FAKE NAMES TO THE HOTEL LOGBOOK, assuring Cordelia it would be enough that even if the inn-keepers forgot someone rented the room, they wouldn't notice until morning. She was still adapting to living by anonymity, but Jaspar had a lifetime of experience. She leaned onto the wall for support, her head still light, her body still heavy.

A loud laugh caught her ears, and she saw a lively family in the dining hall across the way. The chandelier bright, the light reflecting shimmers around the room. The walls weren't papered but painted, colored to mimic the ocean waves and a life at sea. The tables were elaborately carved, with matching chairs and cushions. The hotel was luxurious, the kind of place she would have visited as a lady, and yet all Cordelia could see was the family.

She was wistful when she returned her attention to Jaspar and the maître d'hôtel. "You may follow our staff to your rooms."

"No need, we'll walk ourselves." Jaspar took the key. He hesitated a moment before offering his arm to Cordelia. She wanted to take it, wanted the assistance as her body was still exhausted. But she knew he'd already had to carry her nearly twenty minutes before she'd come to. And she didn't want to burden him further.

"Cordelia?" Jaspar wiggled his arm, but she shook her head, taking the stairs slowly and gripping the banister tightly with each step. His arms twitched at his sides, clenching and unclenching into fists, but he didn't comment.

This Jaspar wasn't the one who'd grown accustomed to her touch, he was the one who still had boundaries, and breaking them even a little could make him uneasy. She'd been careful not to let herself too close, and she told herself it was for his benefit, but truthfully, it was also for hers. Without his memories, a touch meant so very little to him, but still so very much to her.

"Thank you," she whispered when they reached the room, and he held the door aloft for her. She let out a breath, her body ready for rest, her mind barely paying attention as she closed the door behind them. The room they entered was as opulent as the rest of the hotel, with two matching beds and a small sitting area around the fireplace.

Between her injuries, walking all day, and her overuse of her magic, she was in and out of the luxurious bath in minutes. The hot stones and azure basin offered the best bath she'd had since leaving her manor, but her body wanted sleep, and it longed for a night's rest in a real bed.

She stretched out of the bath, relieved her ribs and injuries were healing, albeit slowly. When she returned to the room in her nightdress, Jaspar was already sitting on the bed, reading through a journal, his arm behind his head.

"Are you hungry?" Jaspar put down his journal and stretched as he got to his feet. "I snuck into the kitchens." He smirked, and Cordelia took in the smell and sight of fresh pollock, vegetable roots, bread, and even a small bottle of hops, though after the day they'd had, all Cordelia wanted was water.

"Thank you."

They ate in measurable silence, Cordelia contemplating what was ahead for them, trying to imagine how hard the unknown would be to navigate. Jaspar coughed, choking on his food.

"What?" Cordelia followed his gaze. Without thought, she had given him her carrots and taken his radishes for herself. *Her* Jaspar wouldn't have batted an eye, but this Jaspar was clearly dumbfounded. "Sorry. I-I know you don't like radishes."

"I don't." He didn't make any more comments, but his expression changed a little when he started to eat his carrots. "I was thinking, maybe we should stay here a day or two. Lie low, feel out the area."

"Okay."

"And perhaps you should write to your, er, people? The ones you mentioned at Anchorage Inn?"

"Are you trying to ditch me again?" She took a sip of her water, ignoring the bite in her tone.

"No." His voice was firm, a small comfort to her. "I meant... you've been gone a while. People...families, they worry about each other, right?"

It was a genuine question. Something he knew happened but hadn't experienced himself.

"Alright."

"There's a festival to celebrate The Cold Days, and there'll be lots of people and vendors visiting. May be an opportunity to make some coin."

"Alright."

"Cordelia," his voice was strained, and some of his early curtness was back. "Please talk to me."

"Hmmm?"

"You keep saying 'alright.'"

"I'm tired and—" She cut herself off. She was tired, but the small gestures of their dinner together, and the mention of Alaro was also making her homesick.

"And?" He'd set his knife and fork down, his attention only on her.

"Nothing."

They stayed quiet for the rest of the night, until it was time to sleep and the sconces were snuffed, and Jaspar reignited the fire with a languid wave of his hand. Cordelia chose the bed closest to the fire and was immediately engulfed in luxury. Sleeping on her bedroll had been fine, but she had missed the feel of a real bed.

"Are you asleep?" Jaspar asked, his voice low under the crackling of the fire.

"Not yet."

"How are you feeling?"

She knew he was referring to her loss of consciousness. "Still tired. But I'll be fine by morning."

"Cordelia?"

"Hmm?"

"How long do you plan on staying with me?"

"Not this again." She rolled over to face him. Their beds were a few feet apart, but the fire gave the room a soft, hazy glow, and she could make out his expression. He looked...contrite?

"No." He gave her a feeble smile. "I don't mind the company. I was merely...curious."

"I suppose," she sighed. "I don't know. I guess, if you really don't want me here, if you ask me to leave, I'll go."

"Okay."

She clenched her teeth and pursed her lips. "Is that what you're asking?"

Cordelia waited, counting her breaths, and twenty exhales later, he finally spoke.

"No." His word was crisp, and she heard a muffled *night* as the fire purred her to sleep.

42

THE SNOW MELTED TO WATER UNTIL IT HAD ALL evaporated, and the dry ground caught fire quickly. Janus let his rage out on the fields, the trees, the nearby creatures and homes. Everything within his sight was set ablaze, and fury rolled off of him in dark red clouds.

The weather mage coughed as the smoke invaded her nostrils, her ears, her mouth. The smoke receded, and she fell to her knees, her head swaying as she coughed until her lungs were clean.

"What kind of weather mage can be defeated by a mere Hagan and an untrained Danthem?" Janus growled, his body lit aflame by his outburst.

"I'm so-sorry. I don't know." zhe coughed. "Danthem's can't control snow. I don't know how she—"

"Control snow?" Janus let the fires recede, the sound of the charring earth still lingering in the air.

The weather mage nodded eagerly. "She stopped the snow. She overpowered my spells. I-I don't—that's never happened to me before."

Janus's voice was a low growl. "It's never happened to *anyone* before." He let his hand drop to the woman's head, siphoning all of her magic for himself. He felt his body grow stronger, felt his muscles tense and his bones stiffen. It would hold him for the time being.

The weather mage dropped to the ground, her body wasted without its power. He snapped his fingers, and Alaria appeared, spear in hand. "My lord." She bowed her head.

"This weather mage is of no more use to me."

He heard Alaria snap her fingers and he growled at her refusal to participate in the death of the weather mage. But moments later one of his Sidons stepped in. He heard the slash of the blade, the crack as the daggered tip met skin and bone and then the ground below.

"Clean this up, Alaria."

"Yes, my lord." She removed her spear. "And what of the Danthem, sir?"

"She's no longer your concern." He smiled to himself. The great captain's daughter was no mere Danthem. And she wasn't the *captain's* daughter. She was *her* daughter.

The pieces came together in his mind. What a gift that his greatest grandson should be bound to the witch's daughter. Janus liked to think he was in control of his fate, that the world bent to his will. But this was destiny.

He'd stumbled upon Jaspar, thinking he was no more than another Hagan. He'd stumbled upon the captain's daughter, thinking she was no more than another Danthem. He'd found his greatest descendant, and the only descendant of Bygonia.

He'd planned to steal their magic, to siphon their powers for himself and waste their bodies when he was done. But their powers would be far beyond that of simple theurgists. Their powers would be far greater than the world had ever seen.

Fires of anger erupted from his skin, and he cooled himself with indifference. He was a fool to have separated their memories months ago. He had thought they would be easier prey on their own. But he needed them together, now. Their love could be what brought him back to the island.

A plan slowly started to form in his brilliant mind. A wicked plan for a reunion with Bygonia, a return to the island. He sneered, the grin of a triumphant man, one step closer to revenge.

43

"How does this work?" Jaspar held Cordelia's talisman in his hands, inspecting the blue stones and the starfish shape.

"If you're looking for an explanation other than *magic*, I haven't got it."

He let the talisman fall and watched her tuck it back under her dress. She'd explained, finally, why no one remembered her, and it wasn't the same as his curse. It was more that she wasn't someone remarkable. Her appearance would be so altered that no one would recognize her. The talisman hid her features so that there was a vagueness to her, a mediocrity that didn't suit the enchanting woman who stood before him.

"But it does work, right? Because you look as beau—" He coughed and cleared his throat. "You look as you've always looked to me."

"It doesn't work on you because we're so—" She cut herself off, biting her lip.

"Need-to-know?" he asked, but the more often he asked, the more he'd been hoping for answers. Then he remembered how sick he'd felt when he'd learned of his greatest grandfather.

"Er, no. I don't think so. Just know that it doesn't work on you."

"Alright."

161

She straightened her dress, the dark-blue fabric bringing out the light blue of her eyes. She pointed to his neck, and he fixed the lapel of his collar.

"Does it work as well as my curse?"

"I'm not sure if it's the exact same, but when we used it in Woodvale, it worked in similar ways. People didn't find me remarkable enough to remember, but also my features were masked, and those who knew me did not recognize me."

She crossed her arms over her chest, her full attention on him.

"With my curse, some people forget me almost instantaneously, some it might take a day or two."

"I know."

"Er, right. Well...does yours work as quickly? Does it take longer?"

"I'm afraid I can't answer that. I haven't used it enough to really know."

"We should have a cover story, then. You said before we were... married? That it was my idea to..."

"You told the others we were traveling to celebrate our recent union." She opened the door and waited for him to follow.

"Oh." They made their way down the stairs, Cordelia moving stiffly, and he wondered if she was still in pain, if her injuries were still bothering her. She hadn't complained even once, and he got the impression she was hiding her discomfort for his benefit. He fought the inclination to place a hand on her lower back.

Outside, the festival was loud and could be heard even from far away. The chilly winter air did little to deter eager vendors and shoppers, and the streets began to crowd the further they walked.

"What should our story be this time?"

"What?" He leaned in, barely able to hear her over the growing noise.

"Siblings, maybe?" she asked.

"Why wouldn't we just keep pretending we were wed?"

Her expression was one of incredulity. "I didn't think you'd really want to commit to something so intimate. Not to mention..."

"Not to mention what?"

"Well...do you think you could manage fabricating affection for someone? For me?"

"I did it before, or so you've told me." He shrugged.

"It won't seem genuine." She shook her head. "Let's just not."

"I'm not incapable. What did I do before?" He asked. She'd told him they were friends, so why was she suddenly so hesitant to fake a romance they'd already feigned before?

"Cordelia, if this talisman works as well as you say, then we should be forgotten by everyone we meet within hours. Maybe even sooner, depending on the level of power it wields. We mostly need to blend in, and that's easiest to do when we believe our own deceptions."

She bit her lip. Air expanded within him, and then he let his body relax and give in to the impulse it had felt for days. He wrapped his arms tight around her, pulling her into him. He had no explanation for his actions, except that he had often felt an unusual longing to touch her, to hold her, to be near her in the simplest of ways. He had fought the urges nearly every time, but now was a perfect excuse to give in and see what it really felt like to hold someone, to be held in return.

He couldn't recall the last time he'd hugged someone, though it had to be before his parents had died. And yet embracing Cordelia was natural, familiar even, as if he'd done it every day, as if he could do it every day for the rest of his life. A scene from a tavern came unbidden to him, a crowded and noisy bar, the smell of lavender, the feeling of acceptance...

She was rigid under his arms, hers locked by her side. "What... what are you doing?" She stammered.

"I'm trying to get comfortable around you." He grew annoyed and impatient when she stayed frozen. "Cordelia, can you handle this or not?"

She sighed and it was heavy in the air between them. Then he sensed her body move. She rose to her toes and dangled her arms around his neck. She leaned close, her hair tickling his nose, the scent of her intoxicating in a way he hadn't prepared for.

It was surreal, almost fantastical, the way she fit perfectly into him, the way she knew just how to angle her head so that she didn't nudge his chin. The way his hand knew exactly where to rest on her back, holding her up as she stood on the highest points of her toes. The way her fingers grazed his hairline, the slightest brushing of skin. He felt a delicate spark when her lips brushed his neck, but she didn't seem to notice.

When her arms fell, his did not, and he was reluctant when she slipped out of his grasp. "Alright?"

He nodded once, and then followed her out of the trees and into the crowd. The Cold Days Festival was one of the largest in Keru. People came from all over the world to share goods and services, to celebrate the end of one year and the start of a new one, to eat and drink the most delectable recipes.

The crowds were thick, and they had to keep very close not to be separated by the hordes of moving people. They searched through the people and vendors for anything useful. It would be beneficial to find some warmer clothes and shoes, especially since they may need to go to Vales, the coldest country in the world. Not to mention healing ointments and medicinal aids were always handy.

They could also use food and perhaps some weapons, even just offensive ones, in case more Sidons were in their future. Jaspar couldn't recall their wreck or their supplies. He was taking it on Cordelia's words that his ship was back in Woodvale, evidently too damaged to travel long distances.

Cordelia said they'd lost nearly everything in their wreck, so it was hard to pinpoint exactly what they would need. They tried to let the festival tell them, inspecting each booth and hut as they passed them by, evaluating the goods and services inside.

Jaspar's eyes caught on a caduceus sign, and he shoved through the crowd. A large man with freckled skin was smoking a purple pipe inside the tent. He gave off an aura of monotony, as if this was the dullest festival he'd ever attended.

"Sir?" Jaspar asked when the man didn't acknowledge his entrance.

"How may I help you?" The man blew purple smoke from his pipe, the smell of which was sour and pungent.

"I need a medical kit." They'd used nearly their entire store tending to Cordelia's many injuries from the Sidon attack.

The man didn't move. "What kind?"

"Small. Traveling case."

The man finally stood, his languid movements didn't change as he retrieved a small pouch. It was made of old pigskin and was fraying in several places. The man shuffled around a few crates and boxes, tossing random items in the pouch. Healing salve, needle and thread, a vial or potion of some kind.

Jaspar thanked the lazy man, handing over a large portion of their coin before exiting the tent. Relieved to leave behind the stink of smoke and the unpleasant man, Jaspar turned to Cordelia, only, Cordelia wasn't there.

"Cordelia?" He looked through the throng of people, but her height didn't allow her to stand out in such a crowd. He refused to panic, instead keeping an air of nonchalance and meandering through the festival slowly. But he thought of her exertion from the day before and the hunting Sidons, and he scanned the crowd for dark-green cloaks.

Each person dressed in blue drew his attention, or anyone with brunette curls. He let his eyes linger in every tent and booth, searching through the sea of faces. But Cordelia was nowhere to be found. How long had it been since he'd seen her? An hour? More? The festival was miles long and wound around several times over. There had to be well over a hundred thousand people here. How was he to find one woman?

"I know who you are looking for," said a croaking voice like that of an old frog. A woman of at least a hundred, with skin practically translucent and eyes clouded over, shook a stick in front of him.

"Er, my wife?" The word felt new and distant from his lips, and he wondered if Cordelia had been right, that he couldn't feign affection well.

The woman smiled. "You are not looking for your wife. You are looking for the missing piece of your soul."

His soul? Did she mean the memories he had lost? Did this woman somehow know of his amnesia?

He moved left, avoiding a woman pushing a heavy cart of chickens and eggs. "And where would I find my soul?"

"Wherever your heart tells you to look." The woman lifted a shaky arm and waved her hand in front of his face. "I suspect you cannot be separated too long."

"Oh?" So his memories were coming back soon, then?

"Because fated souls do not last long on their own."

"Fated...what?" He felt a push on his back and stumbled as a man with a child on his shoulders bumped into him. They each murmured apologies, and when Jaspar turned back to the ancient woman, she was gone, but a familiar hand was on his arm.

He looked down, and she was there, hair falling from its braid, face flushed, hands carrying a small satchel.

"Where the blazes have you been?" He pulled Cordelia into him, away from the urgently moving crowd.

She stepped back, her expression revealing her confusion. "I dropped off a few letters and stopped at a clothing vendor." She handed him a thick woolen cloak, and he noticed that she was wearing one as well.

"Oh."

"Are you alright?" She lifted her head to inspect his face.

"I'm fine. I thought you'd left." He snatched the cloak, wrapping it around his shoulders.

"Always hoping to be rid of me." Her eyes were downcast, but there was hurt in her expression.

"No, Cordelia, I—"

"Just follow me. I've found a theurgist."

He shrugged, but she'd already started walking, craning her neck to see over the throngs of people. "So? The festival is crawling with magic users."

"This one is different. He recognized me immediately."

Panic was slowly creeping into his mind, and he distracted himself by following her swaying hair through the throngs of people. "How?"

She reached under her shirt and pulled out the talisman.

"He said he was the one who made this."

44

THE OLD MAN WAS WAITING FOR HER WHEN CORDELIA returned with Jaspar. His wispy hair blew in the harsh winter wind, and his nose was pink from the chill.

"Lady Kimbal, you have returned." He gestured for them to come inside, and they entered the tiny tent, his many jeweled pieces making tinkling sounds as the breeze swept through them.

Jaspar kept close to her, closer than he usually dared, and she wondered if he'd really been frightened at their momentary separation. She struggled not to cling too much to the thought, she was already trying not to overanalyze their earlier embrace. The one that had felt so familiar it hurt her.

"How is the forgotten man?"

"For—you know who I am?" Jaspar's face gave nothing away. Was he angry? Confused? Indifferent? Curious? She couldn't tell.

Klingbiel looked at Jaspar's chest. "Have you lost it?"

"Lost what?" Jaspar asked. "How do you know me?"

"I made a very special talisman for a friend of mine, a captain I think you knew."

Jaspar's lips parted. "Kimbal," he whispered, and the old man bobbed his head.

"Please, sir." Cordelia pulled the seashell necklace from under her dress. "I'm wearing the talisman now."

"Ah. And have you been recognized?"

"No, sir."

"What am I missing?" Jaspar asked, his eyes darting between Cordelia, the theurgist, and the talisman.

"My mind allows me to see the world as it truly is." His words were ominous, as if the truth of the world was a perilous and disturbing thing.

"I see," Jaspar huffed, and the old man looked down to his empty chest. "What did my talisman do?"

Cordelia held her breath.

"It broke your curse for as long as you wore it."

Jaspar's eyes went impossibly wide. He looked from the old man to Cordelia and back to the old man. "I was remembered? By more than just her?"

The old man smiled.

"Why didn't you tell me?" He rounded on Cordelia, eyes glaring.

She bit her lip. "I did. Sort of."

He glared at her. "Telling me I lived in Alaro for four months is not the same as telling me I was *remembered* in Alaro that whole time!"

"I've been a little uncertain about what to tell you."

"The truth would be nice."

"I would be cautious if I were you," the old man interjected. "Memory loss is a traumatic occurrence. Too much information too quickly could overwhelm the mind."

Cordelia held a hand to the old man. "See? Just like that book said."

"Fine." Jaspar's eyes narrowed. "What *should* I know? Can you give me a...a summary?"

Cordelia bit her lip, indecision warring in her mind. "You came to Alaro and told everyone you were a man named Jaz, a young traveling fisherman."

"Oh." His face smoothed. "That's not too bad. I've used that cover before."

"You lived at the local tavern for four months and became acquainted with the staff and patrons. Made friends with the locals."

"Why did I leave? I mean..." He lowered his head to hers, keeping his voice low. "I had a chance at a normal life, why would I leave that behind?"

Cordelia wavered foot to foot, uneasy. She'd kept too much from him, but she'd been fearful the truth would cause more harm than good.

"Have you a reason for your visit, Lady Kimbal?"

"Cordelia, please." She ignored the raised brow from Jaspar. "I was wondering, do you have any magic or charms that can restore memories?"

"Restore?" The man peered up at Jaspar, tilting his head left and right. The old man clicked his tongue. "I do not have a talisman for that."

Cordelia's body slumped, but she straightened her back quickly, not wanting to appear defeated. "Thank you for your time, sir."

"Before you go, Lady Kimbal?" She didn't have the energy to correct him of her lost title a second time and simply took a step to him as he whispered in her ear. "I do not have a talisman for amnesia, but memories have a way of coming back. Give it time."

He gave her a toothless smile, and she tried to bob her head, hopeful his words would ring true. They left the old man, wandering back to the commotion of the festival. Jaspar's eyes stayed on the old man and his tent as they walked, and she fumbled with the talisman under her dress, wishing it contained a different magic.

A group of street performers took up space in the main walkthrough, and she and Jaspar ducked between a row of tents. "We need to see if there's a historian or topographer here, or professor, or records keeper, anyone who might know about the library."

Cordelia shivered and pulled her cloak tighter against the cold. She was relieved that Jaspar had dropped the subject of his missing four months and latched onto his new task. "Alright, what do we look for?"

"Vendors or tents with books, quills, parchments, anything scholarly."

They searched the festival for nearly the whole day but found no one who seemed capable of helping them, though Jaspar assured her more people would be traveling in as the week went on. The sun had now set, and the evening cold was settling in just as the early night's festivities were starting.

The street performers were singing and dancing in the town square while onlookers clapped and danced along. It reminded Cordelia of another time, another market, when they'd shared a dance, and her heart ached. Jaspar seemed completely oblivious to anything joyful happening around him, a man solely on a mission.

They made it back to the inn just before midnight, and despite the quickly filling town, Jaspar had secured another room for them, though they'd have to share a bed. Jaspar and Cordelia were making their way down the hall to their new room when she heard the name *Delia,* and her heart stopped.

45

CORDELIA STALLED IN HER TRACKS, HER HEAD TURNING left. Her eyes were wild and searched.

Jaspar turned back to her. "What are you—"

"Shhhh."

Jaspar heard muffled voices coming down the hall but couldn't distinguish what they were saying or who they belonged to. She cursed under her breath.

"Corde—"

"We need to hide," she said, tugging his arm.

"Why?"

"I heard our names, so would you please just hide and be quiet?" She ran them down the hall, turning a corner. "I don't know which one of us they're looking for."

She shoved him into a hall closet and pushed up against him so she could close the door tightly. He stood with the wall pressing into his back and Cordelia's body touching his. Her head met his chest, her hands near his stomach, her legs brushing his. He gulped, the sound audible enough that she heard him and tried to back away. Her back stopped at the door, and only an inch of space between them was gained.

"I'm sorry, I didn't mean to—"

"I don't mind." His words echoed in his mind, as if he'd said them once before, as if he'd told her once before. Flashes of a dark room, a cool washcloth, Cordelia's lingering touch on his face...

Jaspar swallowed and shook his head, clearing his thoughts. "I mean, it's not like there's a lot of space in here." He closed and opened his eyes several times, letting them adjust to the dark, dank closet. Cordelia was shaking, her breathing heavy. Was she cold?

"You said you don't want to be heard, yet your breathing is louder than any whisper I've made," he grunted. She shook her head, clearly frustrated, but her eyes were wide.

"Wait, are you..." He searched her features. "Are you scared?"

"Of course I'm scared; we're being hunted by Sidons, and I just heard our names! Last time someone spoke of us, they tried to drag me off!" Her face was pointed at his chest, but her gaze was unfocused, unseeing. "I can't fight them by myself," she mumbled.

"What do you mean by yourself?"

"Maybe I could escape, though?" She tilted her head, her hair brushing under his chin.

"Why would you fight—"

"Or hide?" She wasn't talking to him, he realized, she was talking to herself. The voices grew closer outside the hall, and he heard men murmuring in a low Velshian accent.

Tendrils of Cordelia's hair fell from its braid as she shook her head. "But how long would it take them to find me? If fighting them alone is my only choice, how long would I last?"

"Cordelia," he hissed. "Why would you be fighting them alone?"

Her chin lifted, and blue eyes met brown in the dark. "Do you see anyone else here?"

"What? I'm here." He waved a hand at his body the movement in the small space brushing his fingers to her chin.

"And?" There was a bitter bite to her voice he hadn't heard before, and for the first time, he wondered if his amnesia had burdened her as much as her presence had unnerved him.

He was taken aback. "I saved you before."

"I couldn't ask you to endanger yourself like that, Jaspar. Last time they were here, they were seeking someone of your name."

His heart tugged, his body pulling him closer to Cordelia, and it took great effort to keep himself anchored to the spot. "Cordelia, I—"

"Shh. They're coming."

"Gladys and them alright, though?" A deep voice spoke.

"Kevin..." Cordelia whispered.

"Who?" Jaspar murmured.

She put her ear closer to the door. "Three brothers. Friends from Alaro."

Right. He'd had friends. In Alaro. Where he'd lived for four months. Where he'd been remembered. What must that have been like?

"Taylor apparently badassed the Sidons with some leftover war training."

"And Trevyn," Cordelia whispered.

Another Velshian accent answered the first. *"Good man, that Taylor. Though I don't remember him hanging around the bar that much."*

There was a new strain to the voice in the hall. *"He's been there almost every night since Delia left. Keeps hoping she'll just walk in the door."*

Cordelia whimpered.

"Who's Delia?" Jaspar whispered.

"I am. It's a...nickname."

There was a tsk-tsk, and Jaspar could see shadows under the door. *"She still missing? Wonder where she is."*

"Dunno, do I? Marcel wrote that she kept going on and on about some man at the inn. Asked me if we'd heard of him, but I never knew anyone named Jaz."

Jaspar's throat clenched tight. Cordelia had said these men were their friends, but they'd forgotten Jaspar, just like everyone else. Everyone except the captain. Everyone except the woman who stood so close he could practically feel her heart racing.

"Why would we have heard of him?" the man named Kevin asked.

"Delia said he was at the inn for months. That he'd been living there." The man named Treyvon answered.

"Huh. You'd think we would have noticed him."

"*That's what everyone said. No one knows who he is or remembers seeing him, but Delia was adamant.*"

"*Any post for us, Iverson?*" the man named Kevin called down the hall.

"*Desk had one letter from Diarmuid.*" A new voice with the same accent was getting louder and louder and the shadowed footsteps stopped in front of the closet door.

"*I see two letters there, Ivy.*"

"*Ah, well, one of them isn't addressed to all three of us.*" There was a singsong in his voice, like teasing.

"*Give me that!*" the man named Trevyn spat, and there was a light murmur of good-hearted laughter.

"*What did Diarmuid say?*" Kevin asked.

"*Same as Marcel. Sidons attacked, but they're alright and Taylor was a badass.*"

"*Did they really cut open Gladys's throat?*" One of the voices was clearly disturbed.

Cordelia shook where she stood, and Jaspar felt the sudden urge to stroke her back in comfort. Outside the hall, he heard the rustling sound of paper.

"*Yes. Diarmuid said Taylor killed three Sidons, scared the others off, then carried Gladys out of there in one swoop.*"

"No...no, no, no..." Cordelia whispered, and he heard the voices and footsteps retreating down the hall.

There was a low, impressed whistle. "*Never knew he had it in him.*"

Cordelia sagged forward and Jaspar saw her face fall, her eyes swimming with unshed tears. His arms caught her before she could drop to her knees. Her head hit his chest, her body trembling into him.

Jaspar's hand dug into the fabric of her dress, one arm pulling her in by her lower back, his other hand anchoring her to him by the nape of her neck, a soft spark from her skin to his touch. Her soft curls tangled in his fingers.

"Cordelia?" He spoke into her hair, and she lifted her head from his chest as if realizing for the first time she was wrapped tight in his arms. The tiny closet grew impossibly smaller when he bent his head to hers, his mouth near her forehead, her warm breath intoxicating the skin of his throat, his heart racing as it had never raced before.

46

CORDELIA TRIED TO SLEEP, BUT GUILT AND SHAME coursed through her thoughts, leaving behind tiny pricks of fear. Gladys had been attacked. Sidons had been searching for her and Jaspar in Alaro. Her family was in danger. It was remarkably fortunate that Taylor was there that night, that he had saved them, that he was even capable of doing so, but it shouldn't have been necessary.

They'd been forced to take a room with only one bed, as the hotel had been filling more and more each day with visitors for the festival. And though there was a mountain of space between them, Cordelia felt comforted by Jaspar's closeness.

She felt the barest of touches, her hair moving back from her temples. "I know you're awake."

She reluctantly opened her eyes, meeting Jaspar's in the dark.

"I'm sorry about your friends." His voice was soft, reassuring.

"Me too."

"Were you close to them?"

She nodded and saw his thoughts turn inward.

"Was I?"

Need-to-know. He knew they'd been friends in Alaro, knew that he'd made a home there with the local tavern and its patrons. She could share this with him. He wouldn't care as much as she did about their safety, but it was a fact that shouldn't irritate his wounded mind.

"Yes."

He shifted, rolling his body to face hers. "I need to ask you something." He seemed nervous, fidgeting with the cloth of his shirt. It was new for her, to see this version of him be anything other than controlled and levelheaded.

She leaned back into the pillow, gazing up at him, wishing the distance between them was smaller, wishing she could reach out and smooth the worried wrinkles of his brow. "I'm listening."

"Earlier, you didn't want me to help you. If the Sidons returned again."

It wasn't what she was expecting. "And?"

"When we were friends before. Would I...would *he* have helped you? With the Sidons, I mean."

"Yes."

His brows knit. "And yet you thought I shouldn't."

"Should you?"

His fingers moved, trailing circles on the quilted space between them. "Would the Jaspar you remember protect you?"

She smiled to herself. "No, he would say I could protect myself. But he would..." How much could she tell him? How much *should* she tell him? Part of her wanted him to know everything, but she was frightened that if he didn't care, she'd never get that part back. It was all she had left of Jaspar, *her* Jaspar, memories of a time when he'd cared for her, memories she wanted to protect.

"What?"

She chose her words carefully. "He would believe in me, and he'd be there if I needed him."

They were quiet for a long moment, Cordelia watching his hand trail along the fabric of the quilt the same way he'd once left traces of affection on her palm.

"Cordelia?"

"Hmmm?"

"I wouldn't...won't let anyone hurt you. Not if I can stop them."

She tilted her head, her brows knit together. "But I—"

"I know. And I know what I said before, but...it's different now."

"How so?" Had he remembered? Did she dare to hope?

"I know you, now." He shrugged, and she felt her heart deflate, just a little.

"Oh." She could think of no words to share.

"And...we're in this together." He yawned and let his eyes shut, ending their conversation and leaving Cordelia breathless and confused, and maybe just a little bit hopeful.

47

THE COVERED WAGON BUMBLED AWKWARDLY ALONG the cobbled road, the snow thick on the fields that passed. Klingbeil had only a few hour's ride until he'd reach the shore, where he'd board a carrier ship with the brothers and return home to Alaro.

The roads were cleared, and Klingbeil could've waited a few days before returning to Alaro, but he missed the comforts of home and was eager to relay to Gladys and Taylor that Cordelia was alive and well. Though they wouldn't remember her forgotten companion, he could tell them she was safe and in good company.

A loud crack echoed through the empty fields, and Klingbeil felt the wagon lurch and nearly keel over. He fell from the driver's seat, his hands holding tight to the reins. Addi, his old and faithful donkey, squealed as she attempted to stall the wagon. She braced her hooves into the ground, and finally, it stopped.

Klingbeil dropped the reins and steadied on his feet, patting the old donkey's head. "Shhhh, it is alright girl." He stroked her back once before inspecting the wagon, thinking he must have cracked a wheel. All of the wheels were well intact, but the axis beam across the back two wheels had cracked apart. Upon further inspection, Klingbeil saw an arrow jutting out.

"What the—" Something solid and fast flew by his ear, and he ducked in time for another arrow to imbed itself in the undercarriage of his wagon. Alarmed, Klingbeil turned. He was surrounded by Sidons, their translucently green and slimy skin glowing in the early morning hour.

A female Sidon with yellow-tinted skin and purple hair sauntered forward, her webbed feet taking awkward steps as she approached him. "You are the theurgist, Klingbeil." It was a statement, not a question, and Klingbeil remained quiet.

"The craftsman with a fondness for talismans?"

Klingbeil nodded. It wasn't the first time he'd been sought out for his magic, but he was uncertain if these Sidons were friend or foe, though the arrows pointed at him weren't exactly promising. "What is that you need?"

The female played with her slimy hair, twirling it around and around in her fingers. "I'm Alaria, and I want a talisman."

"I am afraid that could take several days. I have not brought my supplies," he lied. "What is it that you are seeking?" He couldn't fathom any talisman he could create that would be of any use to a Sidon, but given his current predicament, he was hardly in a position to deny her.

"Oh, perhaps something like what you gave my friend." She smiled, but it was cruel and eerie.

"Your friend?"

"She is so young, and beautiful, and yet...no one remembers her, or recognizes her."

Klingbeil's face went slack, his hands fisting at his side. "I cannot help you, madam. I must ask you to leave at once." How did this Sidon woman know? Was his magic waning? Had he given Lady Kimbal a poorly crafted protection?

The Sidons laughed, but Klingbeil stood his ground. Alaria shook her head, her features forlorn. "Why won't you help me?" She pouted, the action making her already unpleasant features more disturbing.

"I asked you to leave." Klingbeil gripped his own talisman, resting safely in his pocket, always there should he need it. He hadn't had to use it in years, hadn't felt the need to conceal himself from the world.

"I don't want to." She pouted again, and he heard the snap of a bow-string as another arrow was released. This arrow embedded itself in the ground, dangerously close to Klingbeil's legs. He wanted to escape them, but he wanted to know why they were here more.

"Why would I help you?"

"I know a pretty girl," she said in a singsong voice. "I know who wants her and why. And I know where she is."

She was bluffing, she had to be. Otherwise, she wouldn't be here asking for his help. But still...did his talisman not work for Lady Kimbal? Did it have flaws? Was she in danger?

"My lord is in need of your magic, Master Klingbeil, and I need a talisman."

"Your...lord?" Since when did Sidons have lords?

"She wasss referring to me." A darkened voice turned the air around him. A voice so low, so cold, goose bumps rose on Klingbeil's flesh, and he involuntarily shivered. The immortal sorcerer approached him from the forest. He stood three feet taller than Klingbeil, with sunken, black coal eyes and skin ashen gray. Crimson smoke lingered around him, like an aura of evil blood that misted around the monster.

He didn't have to introduce himself, didn't have to say his name. Klingbeil would recognize Janus anywhere. He gripped the talisman tighter in his hand, wondering how well his magic would hold up against an enchanter as powerful and wicked as Janus.

"I will not help you, Janus. But I think you already knew that."

"Oh you *will* help me...guardian." He said the last word with triumph, as if he were proud to reveal such a secret.

"What is it that you want, Lord Janus?" Klingbeil spat the name like acid, keeping eye contact with the sorcerer and hoping everyone's attention was focused on their conversation and not the talisman in his fist.

Janus released Klingbeil's gaze, clasping his hands behind his back and beginning to pace. Klingbeil took the opportunity to twist his hand, the talisman becoming a bracelet on his wrist, and watched with satisfaction as the face of every Sidon turned slack and unfocused.

Janus stopped his pacing and turned his gaze directly on Klingbeil. The demon's wicked mouth curled into a terrifyingly haunted smile, and Klingbeil's soul was disheartened by the lack of his own magic. It had never failed him, not once in his one-hundred and twenty-three years. And now, when he needed it most, he'd found a foe immune to his powers.

Janus took two steps forward, towering above Klingbeil. He gripped Klingbeil's biceps, boiling hot on his skin and burning through his clothes. He yanked Klingbeil's arm from his pocket and ripped the talisman bracelet from his wrist, nearly taking the hand with it.

Janus held up the dolphin-shaped pendant, arrogance and victory in his eyes. "Ah, now thisss isss just the kind of thing I'm looking for."

48

"ARE YOU ALRIGHT?" CORDELIA NUDGED A DISTRESSED Jaspar. His brow was beaded in sweat, and chills racked his body. He'd been thrashing in his sleep. They'd spent the entire day of the festival searching for answers only to be let down time and time again, and it was no wonder he'd have troubled sleep after hours of nothing but rejection.

"Just a dream..." He shook himself, and she felt the bed move under his weight. Tonight, they'd had to book a small room again, with only one bed, though it was a large one with plenty of space for both of them. That was, until he rolled over, placing himself mere inches away.

His words were cautious, unsure. "It was...like déjà vu and I thought maybe it happened before, like a memory had...resurfaced somehow."

The words of the old theurgist echoed. *Memories have a way of coming back.* "Do you want to tell me about it?"

"I was in bed, or some bearded version of me was. And you were stroking my hair, and I didn't mind the touch, and you gave me tea and watched over me as I slept." His voice grew more and more bewildered with every word.

Her stomach lurched from the memory, sweet but a little stained from his inability to experience it with her. "You had a fever."

"And you took care of me?"

"Yes." She couldn't fight back the blush, and despite the dim room, he noticed.

"What?"

"Nothing."

He met her gaze, his eyes leaving the quilt. "Cordelia, I've lost four months of my life. Please."

"It's a fond memory of mine, that's all."

His forehead creased. "Fond that I was sick?"

"No, no. Of course not." She let herself smile. "That was the first time you kissed me. I don't think you meant to, or maybe you did. But for me, it was—"

"Why would I kiss you?" His voice felt loud in the quiet room. Gone was the moment of bewildered interest, and back was the Jaspar who distrusted the world.

"Why would I kiss you?" he asked again.

"It was...we were..." How could she explain?

"You said we were acquainted, you said we were...friends. Why would I *kiss* my friend?" Her lip trembled, and Jaspar moved closer to her on the bed.

"Cordelia, what aren't you telling me?"

49

CORDELIA SWALLOWED BACK HER ANXIETY, HER FEAR OF what she had done.

"You were...I mean, I was...I didn't want to overwhelm you. You'd gotten so sick that first night. And you said only facts, only need-to-know. I thought if I told you...I wasn't sure..." why couldn't she find the words to explain?

"Cordelia." He was fully sitting up now, his legs tangling with hers on the bed. "Why did I kiss you?" There was a pause between each word, as if it took great effort to get them out.

She forced herself to sit up, her arms uncertain underneath her weight. "I don't think you realized it happened," she said, as if this explained it all away. "It was just a brush of skin, that's all."

His nostrils flared. "You said it was the *first time* I'd kissed you."

She swallowed.

"How many times have I kissed you?"

The whirring sounds of panic were back. Her blood ran cold, draining from her face and her head until all that she could do was stare at him, lost in the turmoil that she had caused.

"Cordelia, answer me." His voice was firm.

"I don't know."

"But it was more than once?"

"Yes," she mumbled.

His eyes narrowed. "More than just my lips to your hand?"

Her voice was growing smaller and smaller. "Yes."

"And did you...did you ever kiss me?"

Unable to speak, her head nodded.

"Did I..." His brows knit together, his shoulders sagging. "Cordelia, were you in love with me?"

Words. How did she form words? How did she create sentences and deliver them into the world through her mouth?

"Answer me!" His voice was no longer angry, just strained, maybe a little unhinged, and then suddenly soft. "Please."

"I don't know what to tell you. It's...not...need-to-know..." It wasn't a whisper, it was a breath between them, so barely there, it evaporated as soon as she'd spoken.

It wasn't just the *need-to-know* holding her back. That was a flimsy excuse for her cowardness. She could try to explain their friendship. But she couldn't explain months of togetherness. She couldn't explain a bond that was all-encompassing. She didn't want to tarnish the times they shared when she knew he'd reject her memories of them.

Jaspar leaned closer to her, clutching the quilt between them. "*I* need to know. I woke up a month ago on a beach with some girl telling me my mentor was dead and I had amnesia and that we were friends, and now you're telling me we were...what? What were we to each other?"

Everything. She wanted to tell him she was his everything and he was hers, and none of this should have ever happened to them. "We were...I was..."

"Cordelia. Were you in love with me?" He repeated each word individually. His voice gave nothing away, but his eyes were pleading, wide in desperation, and she wished she knew what answer he wanted from her.

She tasted the salt on her lips and pinched her eyes tight. When she opened them again, she focused on the features of his face. His deep brown eyes, his strong jaw, the softness of his lips.

"Yes, Jaspar. I am in love with you." She refused to say it in the past tense, she refused to pretend she no longer cared for him. She wanted to ease his pain and suffering, but she needed to preserve her heart, to preserve what she had left of their connection.

"Was I...did I love you back?" He was skeptical, barely capable of believing it, and she could see it all in his eyes.

"I can't answer that for you."

"Cordelia." He tilted his head to her.

She gulped. Her mind flashed to the days before he'd lost his memories, before the shipwreck, when they'd shared all their devotions by the fire at the cay. He'd never said he'd loved her, but then again, had he needed to? She wanted to tell Jaspar, *yes,* but instead, she confronted another fear.

"You don't believe me."

"No," he scoffed. "I mean, why would I?" He shuffled closer across the bed.

"Can you...can you prove it?" Was it her wishful heart, or did he sound...hopeful? Longing? Like he wanted it to be true, like he needed it to be true. But how much of her soul could she bear to him until she had nothing left for herself?

50

"WHAT KIND OF PROOF?" CORDELIA SHIFTED ON THE bed, retreating to the edges of the mattress. She tucked her legs underneath her, her hands folded neatly in her lap. Her deep blue nightgown shifted, covering her legs to the knees, and her long curls were pulled over one shoulder, cascading down to her lap.

If Jaspar squinted his eyes just right, he could see a glimpse of the lady she once was, the lady he'd always pictured when the captain had mentioned his daughter. What would the captain say now, knowing that his daughter claimed to be in love with Jaspar?

"I don't know." He dared to take her in, to seek something familiar in her deep blue eyes. He shifted, moving closer to her on the bed. "I guess, you could tell me why?"

She gave a nervous laugh. "*Why* do I love you?"

"I mean…" He scratched his neck. "I mean people in love they…know each other, right? And we know each other?"

"Yes."

"Quite well?"

She nodded.

"Well, what do you know about me?"

"I…" She licked her lips, drawing his attention to their supple shape and curve. "everything, maybe?" She shrugged. "But I don't know how to prove that."

"Tell me something, anything."

"Like what?"

He searched his mind. "What's my favorite color?"

"That's all the proof you need?" She smiled.

"Just humor me, will you?" He tilted his head, and she mumbled a soft agreeance. "What's my favorite color?"

"It changes with the seasons." There was a fondness in her voice, like she was smiling with her words. "In the summer, you like yellow. In the fall, you like orange. In the springtime, you like green." Her cheeks flushed. "In the winter, you like blue."

It was close, closer than anyone else could have guessed, and yet not quite right. "Mostly, yes, but in winter, my favorite color is actually—"

"Silver," she interjected, "sometimes white. But you changed it to blue when I got my new dress, the one that matched my eyes." She touched the fabric on her legs, her night dress bringing out the brilliant ocean color of her irises. His vision swam, a dream returning, of her on a dock, kissing his hand, his fingers wrapped in soft blue fabric as it hung on the curves of her body.

He blinked, his thoughts clear. Knowing a favorite color was hardly proof of love, just proof they knew each other well enough to share a conversation. "My favorite food?"

"Soup. You only eat it hot, and you always dunk whole pieces of bread into it." She laughed softly. "It used to annoy you that I'd tear my roll into tiny pieces."

He recalled their lunch at the tavern, when she'd thought to order him a roll and he'd cringed at the sight of her destroyed bread.

"What else?"

"You always chew peppermint first thing in the morning, not just for hygiene, but because it helps you wake up."

He nodded, accepting that so far, her answers were right but hardly proof of anything other than observations. Observations she could have gained in the last few weeks they'd spent together.

"True."

"You like to sit on the barstool but not the chair because your long legs get cramped without the extra room."

"Yes." And yet observations didn't usually come with explanations. Sure, someone watching him would notice how he ate and where he sat, but would they know *why* he had these preferences?

"You love sailing. And even though you've done it your whole life, you still find it freeing." Her fingers dug into the fabric of the blanket beneath them, as if securing herself to the bed.

His heart started to race. She knew so much. Too much. More than anyone in his whole life. *This wasn't real! How could this be real?* He'd spent four months with her, or so she'd told him. And all that time, she'd been getting to know everything about him. Tiny, tiny details that may not have seemed like much. And yet they crowded him, suffocating him in a way that was both painful and addicting. He wanted more, needed more.

"Go on."

"You don't like when people complain. You think there's too much to be grateful for in a world where everyone can remember you."

"True." This time, the word was like water in his mouth, pouring out of him without warning.

"You laugh with your whole body, and you bring out the best in me. You're always there to help me when I need it and support me when I don't. And you like when I look after you, when I remind you that you're not as alone as you think you are."

He had no way of knowing if this were true, but he was starting to see how it *could* be true, and that was just as compelling. What would it be like to have someone that made him feel a little less lonely?

"You used to hate being touched, and would always avoid it if you could, even sometimes flinching at accidental contact."

He could no longer speak; every word in his head slowly replaced by one: True. Every word she said was true. So. Perfectly. True.

"Except now." Her words hitched. "You like when I stroke your chest, and it soothes you, and it eases your racing mind while you rest."

Her arm moved and he stilled. Her hand was splayed on his chest, palm over his heart, and her thumb moved in soft, swirling circles. And it should have been unpleasant, should have unnerved him, but it just felt...pure. His hand moved of its own accord, wrapping into one of her ringlet curls, watching it fall.

"You sleep with your arm tucked under your head, and you don't like the covers over your shoulders."

He was completely bewildered now, eyes wide, mouth dry and hanging open, his body leaning toward her.

Cordelia.

He wasn't sure if he whispered her name or felt it. It wasn't just her melancholy or the validity of her words. It was the way she was looking at him, like he was the center of her universe. Like no one and nothing else mattered in the whole world. Like no one and nothing else existed except for the two of them.

Her eyes streamed tears down, and there was no embarrassment, she held nothing back. Her face red and puffy, her lips trembling. The more she spoke, the more she choked on the words, as if she were forcing them out. His heart raced so fast he was certain she could feel it beneath her palm, and yet her touch never wavered.

"You like ale if it's hot and whiskey if it's cold. You're proud of your Hagan powers but wish that people wouldn't fear and misjudge your kind."

His hand was moving, lifting his body up, urging him closer to her, his attention hanging on her every word. If he moved just a few inches further, he could feel her breath, touch her skin, kiss his lips to hers...

"You miss your parents, your mother more than your father, and you sometimes feel guilty at their loss and your survival."

His face moistened, and he realized he was crying. Not streaming tears like hers, but more than he could remember crying in years.

"You love sailing just before dusk when the sun and moon share the sky. You love the peace of reading by the moonlight, and you love...you *loved* me."

Ho-ly ships.

His hand reached for her, grazing her cheek with his fingers, a thumb wiping her tears. Her hand was still on his chest, and she gripped the fabric of his shirt tight in her fist.

"Cordelia..." Her name was like air, escaping his lungs, floating between them, something tangible in the space they shared. For the first time in his life, he wanted to be with another person. His lips were a breath away from hers when her eyes disappeared behind their lids and her fingers unfurled his shirt.

She twisted her head out of his grasp, removing the warmth of her hand from his chest.

They stared at each other for too many heartbeats, Jaspar unable to put into words how he felt. Cordelia opened her mouth several times to speak but couldn't choke back her sobs. She took away her gaze and scooted herself to the very edge of the bed, but a wall between them had fallen.

"Thank you for telling me," he whispered.

Her eyes grew thoughtful. "Should I have told you sooner?"

"No, you were right. This whole memory loss has been...overwhelming. It's left me very uncertain, and I'm not sure I would have believed you before."

She nodded, and his eyes were enraptured by hers. The most brilliant blue he'd ever seen. The blue that had changed his favorite color. Had he once loved those eyes?

He reached a trembling hand out, tucking her soft curls behind her ear, wanting to see her face when she answered him. "When did I tell you I loved you?"

She licked her lips and swallowed, and he let his hand rest on her shoulder. "I don't think you actually said those words..." she whispered.

"But you know?"

She let the time slip between them longer than he would have liked, but eventually, she said, "Yes, I believe that you loved me."

He let his voice soften. "For the first time, I *really* wish I had my memories back, it would be...quite something to remember what that was like, to be loved..." He let his words fade.

"You're still loved." Her smile was forced, but he saw the truth of her heartbreak in her eyes.

"I suppose I am." He pulled his hand back. "You know so

much about me."

She nodded.

"Cordelia," he licked his lips, swallowed. "You're extraordinary. You're probably the loveliest person I've ever met. But I never imagined love in my life, and I don't remember what happened between us."

"I know." She closed her eyes, and he caught another tear as it fell. His thumb lingered on her cheek a bit too long and he felt her shiver.

He forced himself to let her roll away, to let her rest, and to try and sleep himself. But his brain couldn't stop replaying every word. Every. Single. Word.

Because they were all true. Incredibly, *unbelievably* true. It had stirred something in him that had long since been lost: possibilities. So many possibilities he'd never imagined. Eating meals together, walking along the beach, sailing with the setting sun and the rising moon, sharing a cup of tea by the fire, letting down his guard so easily that he could sleep beside someone. So many wondrous, extraordinary things, a life he never could have dreamed for himself, and it had all been with her.

He fell asleep with her last words lingering in his thoughts, ringing in his ears, haunting him like a bittersweet song that wouldn't end. *You loved me.*

51

"I'm TELLING YOU THAT BIRD IS INVALUABLE, NOW follow it!" Five days into The Cold Days Festival, Cordelia had nearly stumbled when she'd seen Frân soaring high above the crowds. It had only been five days since she'd sent a letter to Hygonia. Could her soulmother be here already?

Jaspar stuck to her like sap as they meandered through the crowds. It took nearly half an hour to make it to the stables, but Cordelia knew Hygonia's booth at once. A green hut, almost like a carved wooden box, with flowered vines latticed across every inch of the outside.

When they walked in, the remarkably beautiful goddess was waiting with open arms. Cordelia ran to her, smelling the fresh floral scent on her deep burgundy gown. Today, the demigoddess looked like a plum carnation, her exquisite fat body wrapped in a dress so soft it made velvet envious. Around her head, a tiny halo of daisies was entwined in her mysterious, multicolored hair.

"I wasn't sure you got my letter." Cordelia looked up into a face more angelic and divine than could possibly be imagined.

"Frân received it with just enough time for me to make it here, though I am sorry I could not come sooner." Hygonia's eyes traveled from Jaspar to Cordelia, a question lingering in the air between them. Frân soared in a circle above before landing and resting near a tall sunflower, munching on what looked like a fresh ear of corn. Cordelia was grateful to see the return of his dark eyes.

Hygonia pulled Cordelia into another hug and Cordelia winced, the movement tightening her still-healing wounds. Though they'd met before, being in the presence of a demigoddess was often overpowering, and Cordelia's emotions ruffled under the enormity of it. She squinted at the goddess as her bright aura illuminated the space.

"Thank you." Her voice was slow, slurring slightly, as her soulmother healed her injuries instantly. Cordelia took her first painless breath in over a month.

"What the blazes are you?" Jaspar was staring at Hygonia with squinted, suspicious eyes, and Cordelia remembered their first encounter with her. Meeting a demigoddess can be very taxing on the senses.

"Pardon?" Hygonia asked, ushering both of them inside and providing them each a cup of hot peppermint and lavender tea.

"Sorry. That's actually part of why I wanted to see you."

"Cordelia, you did not mention any injuries in your letter."

Cordelia bit her lip. "I know." It had been far too difficult to put words to paper, and Jaspar had warned of the possibility that the letter would be intercepted. So she had kept the message brief, simply telling Hygonia where she would be and requesting a visit.

"Thank you for healing me, but Jaspar needs you more."

Hygonia eyed Jaspar up and down. "He looks to be in fair health."

"He has amnesia."

"I am sorry to hear that, Jaspar." Hygonia's aura dimmed, and Jaspar's eyes squinted back to normal. Cordelia handed him the tea, but he didn't drink it.

"Please, sit with me." Hygonia sat on a pillow of flowers and Cordelia joined her, but Jaspar stayed on his feet.

"I'm not drinking anything or sitting anywhere until you tell me what the hell just happened."

"Oh, dear, there is so much to explain. You better drink that if you want an answer." Hygonia said. Reluctantly, Jaspar sat down, keeping his distance from Hygonia and ignoring his tea.

"My name is Hygonia, Jaspar. And we have met before. I am Cordelia's soulmother."

"Why were you glowing like a lighthouse?" he asked.

"I was healing Cordelia's injuries. Though I would be fascinated to hear where they came from." The goddess turned her sharp gaze to Cordelia.

"Sidons."

"Again?"

"They attacked the ship we boarded. We survived thanks to Frân and my magic, but I was injured, and Jaspar..."

"What do you mean thanks to Frân?" Hygonia eyed her bird curiously.

"He came to the ship. He helped me channel my magic, and then he delivered a message to you that I was safe."

Hygonia shook her head very slowly. "I got a message from you by mail, Cordelia, three days ago. And Frân has not left the village."

"But I..." Had she imagined it? It all happened so quickly. The ship sinking, her magic trapped inside her panicked and broken body, and then the bird was there, and he'd saved them. Or had she...hallucinated it? But what of the bird coming back to them? What of when he'd come to their hotel window?

"And he assisted with your magic?"

"Yes!" She told Hygonia of her recent abilities, how she could hold her breath for nearly twenty minutes, how her eyes were unincumbered by exposure to the water, how she had controlled an entire ice storm.

"That power comes from within you, Cordelia."

"Cordelia?" Hygonia's voice came from far away.

"I don't...I must be confused. It was all so..."

"In times of great strain, our memories are not always reliable. Perhaps your injuries clouded your recollection of events."

"Makes sense since Jaspar *lost* his memories altogether, why wouldn't mine be muddled?" But something in the back of her mind told her it wasn't a muddled memory, it was something she couldn't explain, but it had happened. Hadn't it?

"Lost his memory." Hygonia inspected Jaspar, who was merely

gazing at her as if he couldn't understand how she existed. Cordelia remembered the first time she'd met Hygonia, how she'd been so overwhelmed by the demigod's beauty that she could barely speak.

Hygonia turned back to Cordelia. "How are you, my child?"

"I'm alright."

"Cordelia, it only harms *you* to lie about your state of well-being."

"I'm fine. You've healed me."

"I was not referring to your physical injuries." She looked between Cordelia and Jaspar.

"I can't remember anything," Jaspar blurted out.

"I am sorry to hear that." Hygonia set down her tea and pushed Jaspar's cup to him. "Drink, please."

Jaspar smelled the cup, wrinkling his nose.

"She won't hurt you." Cordelia's words must have rang true to him because he finally took a sip. Relief quickly replaced his features, and his shoulders and chest relaxed, his expression unburdened.

"Better?" Hygonia asked, and Jaspar nodded. Cordelia told Hygonia everything that had happened in the last five weeks, from the Sidon attacks to the journals they'd read in the bunker, and Hygonia listened with rapt attention.

"Cordelia, are you sure it wise to chase this secret across the world, particularly without your soulfate?"

"Her what?" Jaspar said. Hygonia raised her brows at Cordelia.

Cordelia shrank back. "I hadn't explained that part to him yet."

"Why ever not?" Hygonia seemed outraged and Cordelia shrank back.

"He's already lost his memory, and he doesn't trust me, and everything I've read or heard said too much too soon could worsen his brain trauma."

"I trust you," Jaspar said with conviction.

"Oh."

"Will you let me tell him?" Hygonia asked, and Cordelia bit her lip, indecision warring in her mind.

"Yes," Jaspar said. "If it will help me to understand why she's here and why Kimbal..." His voice trailed off, and Cordelia swallowed a sob.

Hygonia turned her serene, twinkling eyes to Jaspar. "We are beings of flesh and bone, Jaspar, and within each of us is a soul. Our souls are what keep us tethered to our lives and to this world. And some souls are meant to walk the earth alone, but some are meant to be paired. Your soul is paired with that of Cordelia's."

Jaspar's expression was one of incredulity. "What the blazes does that mean?"

"Let me ask you a question." Hygonia laid her hands in her lap, the gesture mimicking a butterfly landing on a flower petal. "Do you care about Cordelia?"

"Er, yes."

"Even though you only met her six weeks ago?"

"Yes."

"Why?"

"She's...nice." He shrugged.

"And do you feel drawn to her? Eager to be in her presence, longing for her touch, desire for an embrace?"

Jaspar's cheeks flushed, and his voice was quiet. "Yes."

Hygonia smiled. "And you do not know why."

"No." His shoulders sagged, and his voice grew low. "But I *do* care about her."

"Yes, and you trust her even though you have never trusted anyone. Not even Kimbal had your full confidence."

Jaspar nodded, eyes locked on Hygonia.

"It is because your soul trusts hers, it recognizes its counterpart in the world. You may not remember the time you spent with Cordelia, Mr. Marlow, but your soul does." Hygonia's voice had turned soothing, and Jaspar seemed to dissolve under these words, his eyes heavy, his head jerking back.

52

"Is he..."

"Oh, yes. I think he took too long to drink the tea." Hygonia tsked as Jaspar toppled over, asleep in the goddess's magnificent flowers.

"No matter," Cordelia sighed, trying not to focus on the revelation that Jaspar had wanted to embrace her. "It might be easier this way."

"What might be easier, dear?"

Cordelia tilted her head. "For you to heal him."

Hygonia's beautiful face wilted. "I can only heal the body, not the mind or soul."

"But he's lost his memories. You need to heal his mind." Cordelia waited, but the goddess was still, her expression clear. "So, he'll just what? Never remember me or us or...anything?"

"I am sorry, Cordelia."

"Don't be sorry, just fix it!" Cordelia pinched her eyes. "Please."

Hygonia frowned but stood, gliding across the room. Her aura lit slowly as she inspected Jaspar, examining his head tentatively. "Did he have any other wounds or injuries from the wreck?"

"Just cuts and bruises. A scratch from an arrow."

Hygonia spun. "An arrow? Show me."

Cordelia, taken aback at the sudden sense of urgency, stumbled forward, lifting Jaspar's shirt to show the tiny mark on his abdomen, just beside his belly button. Hygonia traced the air above the mark and sighed before laying his shirt back down.

"He does not have amnesia, Cordelia."

"But...but his memories—"

"Have been veiled, not lost."

"I don't understand."

"The arrow that shot him was poisoned, tipped with maligned quartz stone."

Cordelia racked her mind, searching for any remaining images she had of the arrow, but it looked like any ordinary arrow tip to her. "What does it do?"

"Rather the opposite of clear quartz, which is a gemstone usually linked with memory improvement."

"Alright." She was slowly nodding her head. "But if he's been poisoned, you can heal him, right?"

"I cannot." Hygonia reached a hand to Cordelia.

"Why not?" Cordelia's voice rose again, and Frân cawed as if upset by the sudden outburst.

"Poisoned stones can only be counteracted by heavily guarded magic."

"You're a goddess!" Cordelia jumped to her feet, but Hygonia remained maddeningly calm.

"I am a *demi*goddess, and I have limitations, Cordelia. Do you think I would not heal him if I could?"

"Please," Cordelia whispered. "There has to be something?"

Hygonia's beautiful face frowned, and her shoulders drooped, making her look like a slowly waning flower.

"Haven't I lost enough already?" Cordelia let the tears come, devastation and frustration colliding.

"Cordelia, I may not be able to bring forth his memories, but I believe that you can."

Cordelia's ears perked up, her back straightened. "How?"

"Your love. Your souls are fated, his soul is tied to your soul."

"Wait, true love? Really, Hygonia, that's your solution?" Cordelia scoffed.

"What stronger magic is there than the purest and most exquisite devotion of love?"

"But you said it could only be counteracted with a heavily guarded magic?"

"That is what love is!" Hygonia clutched Cordelia's hands, her eyes beseeching. "The most precious of all magics is the bond shared between those who love."

Cordelia watched Jaspar's rising chest, his steady breathing in his sleeping state. If their roles were reversed, what would he do? "What if it's not strong enough?"

"Do you have such little faith in your bond?"

Cordelia watched Jaspar sleep and thought of his fingers twirling soft touches in her palm, her head sleeping on his chest, and his boisterous laugh. "How?"

"A moment of pure intimacy."

Cordelia sighed, rolling her eyes. "True loves kiss? *Seriously*? You've read too many fairytales, Hygonia."

"Fairy tales have a core of truth in them. And not a kiss, necessarily."

"Then what is it? What is a moment of pure intimacy?"

"It could be a kiss, or an embrace, like the sparks you felt when you two both shared your vulnerable sides back in Alaro. His soul has to be open to accept yours, as it was before. You cannot force it. If he is protecting himself emotionally, it may take some time to reignite."

"But he loved me before."

"He does not remember those days and nights with you, Cordelia. He does not remember falling in love. He remembers being Jaspar, who was alone and never had anyone's love or affection, and who never knew or imagined any kind of love in his life until you. And even that took time, months."

"I have to make him fall in love with me again and then kiss him, and then that will heal his memories?"

"That is my hope, yes."

"Your *hope*?" Cordelia turned to Jaspar, fearful her outburst had woken him, but he slept on.

"It is not as if I have a great deal of experience with amnesia and fated souls. It is not the kind of occurrence you see on a daily basis."

"You've been alive for how many millennia? Surely you've seen it a few times."

Hygonia had a sudden interest in the wall and was observing it very closely.

"You have! Tell me." Cordelia threw herself at the goddess's feet, eagerly awaiting her words, hoping for reassurance.

The goddess exhaled, her aura dimming like the waning sun. She pulled Cordelia up with her arms so that they sat face to face. "I have seen it three times. Though I have never seen it ignited by a poisoned arrow."

"And?" Cordelia waited, but Hygonia stayed silent. "*And*?"

"The first time, the woman's memories were restored with the very first kiss. The second, the man regained his memories after months spent falling in love a second time."

Cordelia bit her lip. "And the third?" Hygonia's eyes softened, her lips drooping into a frown that marred her perfect features. Cordelia's voice grew quiet. "Hygonia, what happened to the third pair?"

Hygonia gripped Cordelia's hand tight in her own, her soft skin like the silk of a rose petal. "The two souls spent several years together, and they grew quite fond of one another. But the woman never fell in love with the man again. After a while, it was too hard on the man, and he sought to end his suffering when the woman fell in love with another and left him behind."

Cordelia's mouth dried, her lips parted, her world shattered. That was their fate: true love's kiss, fall in love again, or die alone and broken-hearted. Cordelia's blood grew hot, and Hygonia wrapped her in a tight hug. She thought she would cry again, but she was too angry, too frustrated.

"I barely recognize him. I thought if he could just have his memories back..." Her eyes lingered on Jaspar's sleeping form.

"Why do you not recognize him?" asked Hygonia, following Cordelia's gaze and inspecting Jaspar's sleeping features.

"He's..." Cordelia tucked messy hair behind her ear. "He's so different...when he awoke on that beach, he was...angry and distrusting of me, of the world. He's like an entirely different person. Sometimes, I see pieces of the old him, but they're buried deep."

"He *is* someone different, Cordelia." The goddess gave Cordelia's hand a tight squeeze. "You fell in love with a different man. The Jaspar next to us has no memory of love, his only companion is an old captain that he sees a few times a year. He spends his days and nights entirely alone, and he has shut himself off from the world around him. Even your father, his closest companion, had always been kept at arm's length."

"But, when I met him in Alaro, he was none of those things. He was...confident and thoughtful and fun and..." But memories started to resurface that told her otherwise.

How short tempered he'd been in the beginning if her careless ignorance caused her injuries. How slow he'd been to converse with anyone the first few weeks at the bar. How even when she'd stumbled on him crying in the courtyard, he'd flinched at the touch of her. How, for weeks, he'd been careful to avoid touching anyone at all. How he'd been light and social but had never really given away anything about where he came from, his past, who he was.

"You met a Jaspar whose heart was not as closely guarded. Someone who was vulnerable after the loss of his only friend. Someone who, perhaps for the first time in his adult life, had been hopeful. Hopeful that a talisman he did not understand could offer him all the things in life he had never dared to want. Someone who was subconsciously desperate for comfort and companionship."

Cordelia nodded through her tears, untrusting her words to come out.

"He will wake soon; let us not spend our limited time together in sadness. And, Cordelia?"

"Hmm?"

"Do not lose hope just yet. Sometimes love comes back around."

53

"ARE THERE NO ROOMS AVAILABLE?" CORDELIA ASKED AS Jaspar leaned on the hotel desk.

"Not many left," he said, avoiding her eye. It had been hard to meet her gaze since Hygonia's reveal nearly five hours before. He'd barely heard a word the demigoddess had said after she'd explained his soul was paired with Cordelia's. They'd spent most of the evening there, Cordelia and Hygonia laughing and talking like old friends and Jaspar simply staring at Cordelia with new eyes.

"Sorry, sir, I'm afraid this is all we have left. We've been booked up for the festival."

"We'll take it."

"Very well, sir." The man took his coins, and Jaspar refused assistance as he and Cordelia made their way to their second-floor room.

"Why was he apologizing?"

"They only had singles left. It'll be a much smaller bed than before," Jaspar said, climbing the stairs.

"Oh." Cordelia's face fell, her lips in a perfect pout. He tried not to let it distract him, but his mind wandered. He'd loved her once, had kissed those lips...

The room was as opulent as the others, but small, and the large, ornate beds from the previous rooms had been replaced by a single, elegant bed. They were quiet for a long while. Cordelia excused herself to bathe and change for bed, and Jaspar dressed himself quickly. He'd normally tried to sleep in his day clothes, but his breeches were dirty, and all he had left was a large undershirt and night trousers.

Each second that passed had him aching to ask until, by the time Cordelia finally stood next to him by their tiny fire and tiny counter, nearly an hour later, he burst out.

"Fated souls? Were you ever planning to tell me?"

Cordelia bit her bottom lip. "I thought about it but you said *need-to-know*. And you'd already been so disbelieving that I could be your friend or that I could love you, or that you could love me back. I didn't think it would matter to you, and to be honest, this hasn't been easy on me either."

"Why wouldn't it matter?"

"Jaspar." She shook her head. "I bore my soul to you three nights ago, and it wasn't enough. What would my saying we were fated souls have changed?"

He wasn't sure what to say. He'd been too afraid to confront her words, but that didn't mean he didn't believe her. His thoughts never drifted far from that conversation, from all that was revealed that night. *You loved me.*

"The woman, she's a healer?"

"Yes." Cordelia stretched, the movement shifting her night dress so that he saw a slip of her thigh. The bruises from the Sidon attack completely healed.

"But she didn't heal my memories."

"She's not the one who can."

"What does that mean? Is there someone else who can?"

Cordelia's face burned. "That's not what I...I shouldn't have said..."

"Cordelia," he groaned.

"She thought your soul would remember mine, and that a touch of our...connection would be enough to restore your memories."

He let her words come together in his mind, let their meaning give him strength.

"What kind of touch?" He took a step toward her, and she

took a step back, bumping into the counter that held their mirror and hand basin.

"Something intimate."

"Intimate how?"

Her skin flushed, her lip trapped in her teeth. "A moment of vulnerability."

"Such as?"

She tried to take another step back, but the counter blocked her path, and instead, the empty water basin rattled. Jaspar sighed, reaching for the basin and moving it to the floor.

"Cordelia," he said slowly.

"A kiss," she said softly.

"I...I've never done that."

Her eyes dimmed, and he recalled their conversation...*that was the first time you kissed me.*

"I have done that."

She nodded.

"But I don't remember it," he whispered.

"Do you want to remember?" Her voice was small. He took three steps forward and stood in front of her, her eyes looking up at his.

He moved slow, his head bending down, until his heart was beating in his throat, and he finally gave in to the longing he'd been denying for weeks.

And then...he laid his trembling lips to hers.

First, slow and gentle and very hesitant. Every muscle clenched tight, and it was like he did remember her, or at least his body did. He'd never kissed her before, never kissed anyone, and yet his hand knew just where to rest on her back as she stood on her toes, and her fingers felt like silk in his hair. Her chin was tipped back just so, and he bent at the perfect angle to meet her lips. It wasn't clumsy or impatient but familiar, natural, as if kissing her was as easy as breathing. Something his body knew how to do without thought.

The kiss was tender and sweet but quickly turned to passion and fire. Jaspar deepened the kiss as sparks ignited from his lips to hers, pulling her in and lifting her up, her thighs clutched tight in his hands. He felt her body respond, her legs wrapping around his waist. He set her on the counter, let her back lean into the wall. He kissed her more urgently, letting his desire control his body.

One of his hands was tight on her thigh, the other possessively grasping her back. Her hand in his hair was gentle, and she pulled him closer, her other hand slipping beneath his shirt. It warmed him inside and out, somehow delicate and unrestrained.

He couldn't explain how every part of him seemed to ignite. The way she felt in his arms, like a piece of himself he didn't know he was missing. Her skin under his fingers like a touch he wanted to memorize. Had he done this before? Held her? Kissed her? Stroked her cheek? Touched her hair? Felt her lips on his like two souls needing to connect?

His pulse thrummed, every nerve in his body responding to her kiss, the feel of her mouth on his, of his hands freely roaming her body. He whimpered, or maybe she did, and her hand in his hair tightened, and the slight sting of her nails on his scalp sent a thrill through him. It was heady and divine and *everything* he never knew he wanted. And then it stopped.

Her hand hit his chest, pushing him back, hard. He stumbled, gasping for air.

"I can't." Her eyes shined with stalled tears. He stepped back, and back, and back, allowing her to hop down from the counter.

He swallowed an almost audible gulp, his hands still longing to hold her, his lips feeling the absence of hers.

"Did it work? Do you remember?" Her voice was pleading, beseeching, and he wanted so badly to say yes.

Jaspar shook his head, and she nodded, her eyes closed. He took a step toward her, but she turned, walking away from his outstretched hands.

"I'm sorry. I shouldn't have..." But he didn't want to apologize, he didn't want to take back the kiss that had triggered something inside him he didn't know was there.

"Jaspar." She let out a sigh and sat on the bed, her shoulders slumped. "Please understand my side of things."

He lowered himself, sitting beside her, careful to keep his distance. "Alright. Tell me."

He tried not to be distracted by the memory of touching her

thigh as she sat down and her night dress shifted. Her face was sorrowful, and it was all he could do not to comfort her.

"I know you don't remember being us. But I do," her voice broke.

"The soulfate thing, right?"

She shook her head. "It's so much more than that. It's...it's hard to go from what we had to this...indifference." She waved a hand between them.

He flinched. "I am not indifferent to you, Cordelia." He couldn't explain what she was to him, but in the few short weeks they'd spent together, he'd grown...fond of her. Maybe it was the soulfate bond, maybe it was just her, but he had cared for her more than he'd cared for anyone in living memory. And this night, that kiss...it only pulled him closer to her.

Her eyes watched the fire. "You have no idea. The things we've done for each other, the things we were meant to do."

"Can you tell me about it?"

"About what, Jaspar?" She faced him. "You look like him, and smell like him, and sometimes you still act like him, and you're here!" She reached out and clutched his chest, her fingers so tight on his shirt they were turning white. "It's like I'm haunted every single day by this phantom of a man who doesn't exist anymore. And it's not your fault, or my fault. It's been so hard to let him go knowing I still see his eyes every day, still hear his voice, still feel him so close to me. And I've been trying, and I've gotten fairly good at hiding my emotions, but like this." She gestured between them. "I can't. When you kiss me like that, Jaspar, I just can't."

Kiss her like that. "Like what? Is that how it was before?" Their all-consuming kiss had been a new experience for him. His lips were still swollen from the feel of hers, his scalp still tingled from the lingering of her nails in his hair.

She nodded her head and pulled her hand back. "Since the night you showed me your mark, there have been no walls between us. Not until that morning on the beach. When your eyes looked into mine and saw a stranger."

54

REFLEXIVELY, JASPAR'S HAND WENT TO UNDER HIS ARM, his birthmark, the mark of a cursed man. "I gave that to you?"

Cordelia blinked. "Does that surprise you after everything you've learned?"

"I suppose not." His mind turned, thoughts of his family and the cursed mark marring the pleasure he'd felt when her hand was on his back, and her lips were on his, and her fingers had been in his hair. Had those fingers really touched this mark?

"I just never thought I'd share it with anyone after my Aunt Dierdre."

"You never planned to marry before." She said it as a fact.

"Before what..."

Cordelia didn't answer, and she didn't need to. *Before* he'd met her, he'd never thought of having a future with someone *before* he'd met her.

"Did I...did the me before, did he tell you about my aunt?"

Cordelia shook her head. "No. Was she important to you?"

"She's why I never thought I would marry," Jaspar said in a matter-of-fact tone.

"But your father married, and his father, and generations more before that. You wouldn't exist, Jaspar, if your family hadn't found a way to love beyond the boundaries of their curse."

"That was different," he shrugged.

"How?"

"No one married for love."

"No one?"

He moved closer. "I don't think it was that hard in the beginning. A thousand years or so ago. Arranged marriages were the common union, and it wasn't unusual for partners to meet the day of the ceremony, but in recent years, people marry for love, and that can be much, much harder."

She leaned up, letting her feet dangle over the side of the bed. "And your parents? Were they in love?"

"Yes. My father first. He'd been in love with her for years. Mother took some time. He revealed his mark early, then courted her, then told her the story. I think he wanted her to know before they married, before they had children."

"Do you regret...giving it to me?" Her voice grew smaller with each word.

"I could never regret what I don't remember giving."

She nodded, thoughtful. "Are you upset that you can't give the mark to someone else now?"

She hid it well, the choke in her voice, but he heard the sob catch at her words. Her beautiful face was hidden in the shadows of the room, but he knew the eyes that held him captive would be sorrowful. "I want to tell you no, but..."

She nodded.

"It's not you, Cordelia." He leaned forward, catching her hands in his. "I think you're...divine. You're kind, thoughtful, clever. Beautiful." He tucked a curl behind her ear and felt her blush heat his skin.

"And it's so easy to be around you, to be myself. If I were the type of man who thought of that kind of future, you're my ideal partner in ways I didn't even know I needed."

He felt saddened by the truth in his words, and if it hurt him to say them, he couldn't imagine the pain Cordelia felt at hearing them aloud.

Cordelia was everything he'd never allowed himself to want, never allowed himself to seek for. But there were *reasons* he'd never allowed it. And he had no idea how the past of him had overcome every fear and given to her the one thing he could never take back.

"I just...I never planned to marry, to share my mark with someone. But it's one thing to deny myself of that, it's entirely different to know I'll never again have the option."

"If..." she pulled her hands away from his. "If you found someone else...maybe you could still find a way? You couldn't give her your mark, but maybe Klingbeil could craft another talisman. Or Hygonia—"

"But I thought..." he leaned away from her. "So, if I found someone else, someone to love, someone else that I wanted to share my life with, you could...accept that?"

"Yes." There was a firmness to her voice that didn't match her sorrowful expression.

His heart told him to reach for her, to embrace her, but he controlled his wayward thoughts.

"Jaspar?"

"I just"—he shook his head in bewilderment— "I've never heard of something so selfless."

"I want you to be happy. After all that your family has endured, after the years of loneliness you've had without your parents, don't you think you deserve that?"

He shrugged. "I don't know what I deserve. If the legend you told me is true, then my grandfather deserved his curse."

"But you don't!" She turned to face him, her dress shifting again, his eyes lingering on her skin. "You're not him, Jaspar. If I ever meet my mother, *I'll curse her* for punishing generations of innocents over the wickedness of one man."

Jaspar gave a small laugh. "It doesn't matter. I appreciate your offer, and perhaps a talisman could work, but I never really thought I'd show my mark to anyone. It just caught me off guard to know I'd done it already. I wish I knew why I had made that decision. It's so much worse than not having memories of what happened. I don't have memories of why I made those choices or how I felt."

He closed his eyes and lifted his shirt above his head, revealing to her the birthmark on his ribcage. A compass, but where there should have been the compass star was the shape of an oval with undulating edges. He inhaled, sharp and shuddering, before lifting her hand and placing it over the strange symbol. His skin tingled at her touch, but not because of the magic of his mark. Maybe it was the magic of their bonded souls. Or maybe it was the passion of their kiss, the heat of which still warmed him.

"I never even considered sharing the mark because it's a risk. I'm risky with my *life,* Cordelia, but I never was with my heart."

"But you showed me."

"Which is why I struggled with believing you. Obviously, you knew me, and I knew you, and if you can see and touch this mark without any magical reveal, I must have shown it to you in the past. But I had always assumed I'd end up like the other half of my family. Alone."

"You're here, more than a thousand years have passed, and you're here. There was plenty of love along the way."

"Maybe."

He stared at her hand, still resting on his mark. He swirled his fingers in circles on the back of her hand. They'd moved of their own accord, reacting to her touch, to the vulnerability of this moment. Had he removed his shirt for her before? Had he touched her like this before? Had she him?

"My Aunt Dierdre. She was my father's sister." Jaspar recalled her portrait, a tall woman with dark skin, even darker hair, and the saddest eyes imaginable. "She died before I was born."

"What happened to her?"

"She was in love. She shared her mark with a man that she'd long since admired. But when he learned of the curse, he rejected her."

Cordelia whimpered. "Jaspar, I'm so sorry."

"She had one person to share herself with, one chance at happiness, and she had been refused. My father said it destroyed her. And she..."

"You don't have to say, if you don't want to."

He gave a hollow smile. "See, there you go again, saying the perfect thing."

Cordelia waited patiently, allowing him ample time to decide how much he wanted to share with her. He took comfort in her hand still resting on his mark, her skin soothing him inside and out.

"She went out to sea with my father and my mother, who was pregnant with me at the time. She was on the bulwark, looking out at the ocean, and she just...walked off. Sunk beneath the sea before anyone could reach her."

Jaspar turned to face her, and her hand moved, tangling in the hair of his chest. He moved in, his hands resting on her hips, pulling her closer.

"So you see why, right? Why it's so incredibly unreal for me to wake up one day and find out that not only did I share my mark with someone, but she didn't reject me? She knew of my history and my family and my curse, and she stayed with me anyway? She *loved* me anyway?"

She let her hand walk from his chest back to under his arm and stroked the mark again. She leaned down, and his whole body stilled as she laid the gentlest of kisses on his mark. His heart raced at her affection, given so freely, and he longed to feel her lips on his again.

When her eyes met his, her voice was the softest prayer he'd ever heard.

"Do you think it's possible...after what we've been through..." She brought her hand to his mouth, stroking her thumb across his lip.

"Cordelia..." Desire bloomed in him, and he gripped the hips of her dress tighter, fighting the urge to let his lips touch hers again. His head tilted down, his hand on her throat, thumb on her lips, his body following the impulse to kiss her again.

"Do you think it's possible you could love me again? Someday?"

His first thought was that his answer should be *no*. He'd never allowed himself to love before, or to want to love. He was hardwired to reject love. And yet some part of him, the same part that still thought of her lips on his, desperately wanted to tell her *yes*.

But then she must have seen the indecision in his expression because she blinked, and sadness showed through those ocean-blue eyes. She nodded, as if accepting an answer he hadn't actually given.

"I'm sorry, Cordelia," he answered truthfully.

She sighed, and piece by piece, they rewound. She licked her parted lips and leaned away from him. He stroked her cheek once before letting his hand fall. She removed her touch from his chest, and he unfurled her dress. He let his hands linger on her thighs until she scooted back from his embrace, and he returned to the other side of the bed.

Jaspar laid down, keeping as much space as he could between himself and Cordelia, though every inch of him longed to be beside her. Her back was to him, but he watched her chest rise and fall with each breath. He let his hand move on its own, pulling the covers over her shoulders and letting his fingers stay too long on her neck. She didn't react to his touch, but he knew she was awake, knew she felt him, and that was enough, for now.

But how long would it last? He clearly wasn't going to remember anything from before, but that didn't mean that there was nothing between them now. Hadn't their kiss proven that some piece of their affection still lingered inside him? Maybe he didn't remember falling in love with her, but did that mean he couldn't fall in love with her again?

He thought of the last five weeks. How she had refused to leave him, how she had nearly sacrificed herself to save him. How she had brought him coffee when he worked late and how she always let him explain his outlandish theories before contradicting him. How her words and touches had comforted and soothed him even when he didn't know he needed it.

She rolled over to face him, her eyes sleepy but open, and his hand moved from her shoulder to her face. His thumb stroked her cheek, and she reached out, slowly pulling his hand away. It was gentle, but the rejection still stung. She set his hand back on his side of the bed and tucked hers under the covers, but she didn't roll away. Her eyes finally slid closed, and eventually, she drifted to sleep.

Maybe he didn't remember falling in love with her, maybe he never would, but he remembered every moment with her since he woke up on that beach. Every second of the last forty-five days. Every lingering touch and lasting kiss.

Her words lulled him to uneasy sleep. *Do you think it's possible you could love me again? Someday?* If she'd given him time to react, time to speak, he could have said *Maybe. Maybe someday*...in fact, he might be half in love with her again already.

55

TREVYN WALKED PURPOSEFULLY, CLIPPING HIS STEPS AS he and his brothers made their way out of the village and toward the water.

"Look, they offered us a fair-priced ride, and it's the best deal we're gonna get." His brothers followed after him. "We already missed our first ship waiting around for the theurgist."

"I told you," Iverson said, following his brothers up the shoreline, "I think something happened to him."

"Klingbeil must have changed his mind," Trevyn said dismissively as they reached the docks. "We waited an extra day and a half for him. I'm not waiting any longer."

"Trev, it wouldn't hurt to extend our stay by one or two more nights," Kevin said, clear neutrality in his voice. As the oldest of the brothers he often tried to play peacekeeper, but Trevyn was tired of traveling, tired of working one odd job after another for extra coin. It had taken over a month of cleaning the ships of other fishermen, but they'd finally saved enough coin to get back to Alaro, and Trevyn was eager to go home.

"It's this one over here," Trevyn grunted under the weight of his bag as he steered his brothers toward a graying freighter. "We'll be stuck in the cargo hold, and we'll have to help with maintaining the sails, but at least it's a ride back."

Kevin followed after his youngest brother, but Iverson stayed on the dock.

Kevin stopped and looked back over his shoulder. "Ivy?"

Iverson was glaring at the ship, his face pale under the small cluster of freckles beneath his eyes. "Something isn't right."

"What is it?" Trevyn took a step back toward his brothers.

"I don't know. Something doesn't feel right." Iverson was looking back at the lively festival, only a mile up the shore from where they stood. Thousands of people had come from neighboring villages and countries, sharing in the celebration of a new year, and they were leaving behind a boisterous and happy energy.

"It's just a feeling." He shook his head.

"About what?" Kevin asked.

Ivy was looking at the large freighter awaiting their boarding. "Like my gut is telling me not to get on this ship. Things just aren't...lining up." He shrugged.

Trevyn rolled his eyes. "What in the barnacles are you talking about?"

Iverson scowled. "First, Delia won't stop talking about some guy no one's ever heard of. Then," he held up his hands and started ticking off each sentence with his fingers, "she runs off to Woodvale without word back home for weeks. Then, our ship is attacked and sank by pirates. Then, Sidons attack Anchorage Inn, nearly killing Gladys. And now, Klingbeil is missing?"

"He isn't missing," Trevyn sighed, "he must have changed his mind, is all."

Kevin examined his brother closely. "Iverson, there's nothing connecting any of those events, it's just...life," he shrugged.

But Iverson didn't respond, he just stared back at the festival.

"I think..." Kevin placed a hand on his brother's shoulder. "Maybe you've got a bit of vertigo from the shipwreck. We'll be fine this time around."

"No," Iverson said emphatically. "It's not like that." Iverson shrugged out of his brother's grip.

"Do you want to stay?" Kevin asked, and Trevyn scoffed. He wanted to help the old man as much as anyone, but he also had Marcel to get back to, and he'd put it off long enough. They'd already spent more time in Keru than he would have liked.

"Are you coming or not?" a man from aboard the freighter yelled down, reminding the brothers that the ship wouldn't wait for them.

The brothers all stared at each other for nearly a minute before Trevyn let his bag drop. He groaned and rolled his eyes before hollering back at the man, "I guess we're not."

56

"BE POLITE AND RESPECTFUL," JASPAR SAID AS THEY approached the unusual tent. The outside was made of moss and pig leather and all around people from the festival were walking in wide circles, angling around one another. "Don't speak unless spoken to. Don't ask any questions."

"Do you trust her?" Cordelia asked, her eyes questioning the stall. "No one is coming within a foot of this..." She let her eyes wander around them. "Her shop."

"It's not a shop. And she's a high priestess. People often fear what they cannot understand. Hold on," he sighed. "We want to be presentable."

Jaspar smoothed his shirt, but the wrinkles remained creased. He bent down, tucking Cordelia's hair back into its braid. His fingers sparked as they grazed her cheek, and he saw her throat bob. He pulled his hand back, stuffing it in his pocket.

Cordelia blinked and peered into the tent, her eyes skeptical. He'd been so certain a girl who believed in the island would have no trouble believing in those who could see the future, but she was apprehensive about visiting the oracle.

"Cordelia, the festival is almost over, and we're no closer to finding information than when we arrived."

"What about everything Hygonia told us?"

He let her words sink in and kept his voice gentle. "I wasn't referring to my memories."

It *had* meant something to him, everything he'd learned from Hygonia. And everything that happened after. But he'd spent his whole life only thinking of the island, and he had little reason to dismiss it for some fairytale of love. Even if he did feel something for Cordelia, it wasn't enough to overshadow his life's promise.

"Come on. She'll be expecting us." Jaspar held up the sheer cloth for Cordelia to enter.

"How does she know we're here?"

Jaspar rolled his eyes. "She's a seer."

Cordelia frowned but entered the tent, and Jaspar followed. He was surprised to see the old woman he'd met on their first day at the festival. She sat with her legs crossed, a roped rug beneath her, a glass ball floating in front of her. The ball was clear, but inside, he could see swirls of purple, leaving a lavender haze around the tent. The dark, curtained walls kept the room dim, but Jaspar could see Cordelia's confused face in the low light.

"You may sit." The woman kept her eyes closed as she spoke, and Jaspar and Cordelia sat opposite her, mirroring her crossed legs.

"You have come for answers, young Hagan."

"Yes, wise one." Jaspar bowed his head, but Cordelia stayed still.

"You must seek the stall with the answers on the walls. Maps and knowledge are the treasure they sell, but only you are the one they will tell."

Cordelia lifted a brow.

"Your memories have not returned." It was a statement, not a question, and Jaspar remained silent until she spoke again. "I cannot see if they will."

Jaspar nodded. "Thank you, wise one." He almost stood to leave, but her purple orb turned black, and a new haze of gray filled the space. A cold hand found his and squeezed it tight. He thought it was Cordelia, reaching to him in fear, but Cordelia was frozen. She did not move, speak, or breathe. Jaspar noticed the smoke in the orb no longer swirled, and the sounds from the festival had halted.

"You seek your memories, but they are still blurred." The wise woman squeezed his hand tighter, her frail hand on his shaking. "Your soul cannot be reawakened without her."

Jaspar opened his mouth and closed it several times, desperate to seek answers, but she had not asked him a question. It was rude, disrespectful even, but he wasn't sure her words made any sense. What *her* was the wise woman talking about? Cordelia? Was the oracle referring to the soulfate bond Hygonia talked about?

"Ask your questions while you can, before time returns and the world spins again."

The world spins...time returns...he looked back at Cordelia, who had not moved since the purple orb had turned black. Time. The oracle had frozen time.

"Why have you stopped time?"

"Our words are a secret I do not wish to share. And that is why they will fade to nothing more than air."

Jaspar grew frustrated at her strange, unhelpful riddles. He'd never visited an oracle with such vague fortunes before. All the others he'd seen had been very straightforward, answers given in curt sentences with very little room for interpretation or confusion.

She'd said to ask his questions...what did he ask her first?

"Cordelia." The name came to his lips without thought. "Is she...is she really my fated soul or whatever?"

The oracle smiled a toothless grin. "A powerful essence, our souls, one that cannot be broken, once we are whole."

"So...yes?" She didn't answer and instead started to chant.

"Tick, tock, tick tock," she said, nodding her head back and forth like a pendulum of a clock. He was running out of time.

"Her love is...pure," he said, and the old woman gave the slightest nod. "Was mine?"

"You already know the answer there, seek another, and I will share."

"Er, right."

"Tick, tock, tick tock," she said again.

"Why does Janus hunt us? What does he want with us?"

221

"You do not know your true destiny, but you will find it at the end of the sea."

The end of the sea? Jaspar was starting to have more questions than answers.

"Where is Qualaris?" he finally spat out, hoping there was still enough time to answer this last question that should have been his first.

"The island waits for no one, it remains hidden from sight. But those who have already been there can find it in the night."

"So...look for it at night?" Does that mean moonlight would reveal its location? Stars? Constellations? This riddle could mean any number of things.

"Her heart is pure. That is why I am here, to leave a secret in your mind."

Her words had stopped rhyming, and when Jaspar blinked, the old woman was gone. In her place stood a beautiful silhouette, a cloaked dress billowing behind her, her face hidden in the darkness.

"You should not have come here, Jaspar; the oracle cannot give you the answers you seek." The voice was ethereal, a whisper and an echo he thought he'd heard somewhere before.

"But she—"

"She has told you nothing of importance, and her riddles will only muddle your thoughts. But you are so close, and you shall not leave empty-handed."

"What do you mean?" Jaspar cocked his head from side to side, trying to see the woman's face.

"I will answer your questions. Yes, Cordelia is your soulfate. I know your deepest fears, Jaspar. Even the ones you hide from yourself."

He took a sharp breath. "You do?"

"Her love for you is sincere and endless; it will never waver. Never." She gave a gentle smile. "Janus hunts you for your magic, he knows he cannot find the island without your connected souls."

"And Qualaris?" He beseeched the shadowed figure. Was she going to tell him the location of the island? Could it be that easy?

"As long as you know where your heart is, you will know where the island is."

Jaspar tumbled her words in his mind. "That doesn't make any sense. My heart is right here." He clapped a hand to his chest.

"I will take today away from you, take away this last hour so your mind can be at ease."

"Take away..." *No.* She was going to remove this from his memory. Always his mind was being manipulated, thoughts and memories stolen from him, just as the memory of him was stolen from others. Why could he not hold on to the moments of his life? "No! Please! You've told me so much, how can you take it away? I don't want to forget!"

"That which is forgotten can always be found again. You need only remember: Cordelia."

"Cordelia?" He shook his head, understanding lost on him.

"She is the key to unlocking that which has been lost for centuries." The woman began to walk backward, sinking farther into the shadows.

"Wait!" He leaped up, reaching for her, and fell forward, his head and body colliding with something solid. He blinked several times in the darkness. He was tangled in something, some kind of scratchy material, like canvas.

He groaned, holding his head in his hand. He jerked his arms in and out, trying to disentangle himself from the tent.

"What are you doing down there?"

"Cordelia?" Jaspar finally tossed the tented canvas from his head and Cordelia was staring down at him. She offered him a hand and he took it, hoisting himself back onto standing legs.

Jaspar turned in a circle, trying to recall how they'd gotten to this side of the festival and why he had been trapped under a broken tent. All his mind could think of was Cordelia and he shifted so he stood closer to her.

"Are you alright?" she asked, and he felt relief at the concern in her voice.

"I...fell, I think." He tried to get his bearings. His eyes scanned the stalls around them until he saw a sign. A quill on top of a map, with a small compass in the corner. He must have been headed there and gotten distracted somehow.

"A topography studio." Jaspar shook his head and placed a gentle palm on Cordelia's lower back, ushering her inside. He couldn't explain why, couldn't explain how, but he felt the strongest urge to keep Cordelia close, and he'd grown tired of ignoring his instincts.

57

Jaspar pulled back the curtain, the scent of cherry ink and dusted parchment pungent in the air. Cordelia was close behind him, and he tried to keep his hand on her lower back, hoping the closeness would calm his nerves, but she walked out of his grasp as soon as they'd entered the shop.

"Greetings. How may I assist you?" a young woman greeted them, dark hair and dark skin silhouetted by the brightly lit stall.

"We've been researching, curious about a library I read about once," Jaspar inquired, for perhaps the dozenth time. He relayed all the information he could recall and handed over the piece of paper with the ruins of the library's location.

"Hmmm."

The woman donned a pair of large spectacles and inspected the ruins closely. "Your translation appears accurate, but I'm afraid I'm not familiar with this particular library or location."

"And what about that symbol there?" Jaspar said, pointing to a smudged ruin in the shape of a bird.

"Hmmm," she said again, turning the paper in her fingers. "It could be *ar* or *ou*." She adjusted her glasses and turned the paper again. "I'm afraid it's too damaged to give a confident answer."

He felt Cordelia's shoulders deflate beside him.

"Thank you for your time."

"However," the woman fixed him with sharp eyes. "There's a ball tomorrow evening, a fundraiser in honor of the newly appointed chancellor of the Keru University. There will be plenty of scholars there, perhaps one of them will have the answers you seek?"

Jaspar and Cordelia left, thanking the scholar for her time and her words.

"Are you going to attend the ball, then?" Cordelia asked as they walked back through the festival, the crowds thicker than the night before.

"Yes, *we* are." He nudged her shoulder as they walked through the crowd, and he was relieved when the barest of smiles played on her lips. The lips he had kissed.

"We'll need clothes." Her eyes wandered around the festival, and he knew she was seeking a seamstress.

"We'll manage." A loud pop caught his attention, and Cordelia halted in her steps. He followed her eyes and the sound heavenward, where the street performers were shooting flaming arrows. Each arrow had a different tip, and they lit the night sky. Brilliant colors of the world ignited above, a spectacle that caused cheers and admiration from the many festival goers.

But all Jaspar saw was Cordelia. The way the light reflected in her wide eyes. The way her mouth curved in the tiniest smile. The way his arms longed to wrap around her, to hold her close, to watch the display and share the moment together.

Something familiar stabbed his chest, his breath caught, his head suddenly pounding. A small firework appeared in his mind, the sound of a lute, of children laughing, the smell of bread and fresh citrus. The look of adoration on Cordelia's face, the feeling of longing and desire pulling at him, ripping him from within.

That doesn't taste anything like a grape. A voice, Cordelia's, maybe? *I wish we could stay longer.* And his own voice? His fingers tingled, the feeling traveling up his arms and across his collarbone and then throughout his entire body.

Jaspar. Jaspar.

But this time, it wasn't a memory; the real Cordelia was gripping his bicep, repeating his name.

He shook his head, and she dropped her hand, the feeling of her touch still imprinted on his muscles.

"Are you alright?" She tilted her head up, her eyes seeking his.

He nodded. What could he say? What had he even experienced? Was it a memory? A broken dream? Unexplainable déjà vu?

"Perhaps you should head back and get some rest. I'll get our clothes for tomorrow evening."

"No, I'm alright." How could he explain to her something he didn't understand himself? But the rest of the evening was just as strange. He had another pained moment at the seamstress, when Cordelia sifted through blue fabrics, searching for a dress, and he heard his own voice in his head, that blue was his favorite color. He could practically feel the soft fabric between his fingers.

"Jaspar?"

"I'm fine!" He growled. He closed his eyes, pinching the bridge of his nose between his thumb and finger.

"You look ill."

The book from the parochial had mentioned nausea and headaches associated with memories. Is that what this was? Was he remembering things? He'd had flashbacks before, but they were small visions in his mind.

This time, he could feel them physically. They ignited his senses: he could smell the bread, he could hear the lute playing, he could feel the fabric between his fingers. The memories could come back disjointed, as feelings and emotions as much as actual visual experiences. Had their recent kiss ignited something after all, but with a slight delay?

"Perhaps you're right." He started walking, reaching a hand to hers and holding it tightly in his. He wasn't sure why he'd done it, it was as if his hand acted on its own. And yet, his fingers laced with hers were flawlessly matched, as if her hand was literally designed to fit perfectly into his. Was this the soulfate bond?

"I need to ask you something." He stopped their walk, sitting down on a bench beneath a willow tree. "Do you think..."

"Jaspar, you're starting to worry me." She looked at their hands, still laced together, now resting on his lap. He should have let her go, but he didn't.

"Were we...did we go to a festival? Before, I mean."

Her eyes brightened. "Not a festival, but a market. It was similar, though more shopping than festivities." Her face went pale. "Did you...did you remember?" He wished he could ignore the pain and longing in her voice.

"I don't know..." He cleared his throat, eyes downcast. His thumb was stroking the back of her hand, swirling across her skin. When had he started to do that? "I remembered something about grapes and blue fabric, and...it's all jumbled together."

"Need-to-know?" She ventured, and he could tell she wanted to say more, but she was holding back, protecting his mind even though it meant hurting her.

"Yes."

"We went to a market, we had to get supplies and I'd never been. I was meant to go alone, but..."

He saw the indecision in her eyes. "Is it need-to-know?"

She shrugged. "I don't think so; it's just logistics."

"Let's venture it matters, anyway."

She nodded. "You wanted to accompany me, and we spent the day together. You led me around, letting me explore all new things, helping me navigate the stalls and learn to barter and trade with the vendors. And that was where," she picked at the hem of her sleeve.

"Where?"

Her smile was warm, and maybe a little wistful. "Where I got my new dress."

Her words from the second night of the festival came back to him, that his favorite color in the winter was silver or white...*But you changed it to blue when I got my new dress, the one that matched my eyes.*

He lifted her chin, examining the color of her irises, his thumb grazing her eyelashes, her deep, ocean-blue gaze holding his. Maybe it was the memories that had come back to him in his dreams. Maybe it was all the truths she'd known about him. Maybe it was the tingle he still felt at the memory of her lips on his. But he wanted to kiss her, wanted to kiss her like he had never wanted anything in his entire life. Which was why his gut clenched tight when she ducked her head out of his grasp.

She stood, straightening her shoulders and wiping her hands down the front of her dress. "It's getting late."

She was right, he knew she was, and yet his hopeful longing followed them all the way back to the inn.

58

CORDELIA LET THE SALTY AIR EXPAND WITHIN HER, accompanying her orb of magic and releasing it back into the water. Testing her powers at the lake had been helpful, a good start. But the ocean was where she felt the most connected to her magic.

She let droplets swirl around her, creating an orbiting ring. She moved a hand, and the ring returned to the ocean without a single ripple. The waters had been cold when she'd taken her first steps, but her body now matched the temperature. Despite her breath visible in the air, Cordelia was as warm as if she were in a bath of hot stones.

She longed desperately to reach the very depths of the sea, but feared it was too far below. She'd been training with her magic when she could, in between visits to the festival. She came when they had the time to spare, or when she needed to escape.

Her body and soul still clung to Jaspar, still felt the need to stay close to him. But it took a toll on her all the same. She'd hoped that the memory of their kiss would linger in his mind as it had in hers, but so far, he'd seemed as complacent as ever.

There were small moments where she saw him stare at her when he thought she wasn't looking. Or when he'd let a hand linger a little long on her back when they walked through the crowd. Or even a caress of the cheek when he was vulnerable. But she'd bore her soul to him, three times now, and he'd never given her even the slightest hope. Rather the opposite, in fact.

He'd told her he didn't understand why past Jaspar had given her his mark. He'd asked her to step aside if he someday sought the love of another. He'd even rejected her idea that maybe he could love her again...someday.

Cordelia shuddered when something tickled her feet and she glided below the seawater, letting the ocean swallow her. Swaying around her foot was a feathered sea star, its oddly translucent and weightless limbs dancing in the freeness of the ocean.

The sea star spun with the grace of a ballerina, its black and white feathers twirling in the waters. She let her fingers dance above the star, let its carefree manner and joy absorb into her. When the sea star twirled away, she felt lighter and swam further down.

She'd never reach the bedrock, as she had at the lake, but the further down she went, the more plants she saw. She had remained close to the shore, not wanting to venture too far away from the land. Bright pink and ginger coral reefs marked the space beneath her, like an underwater sunset. Small orange and white fish swam in and out of the corals.

She thought of the cay, how one of Jaspar's ancestors had built it over the coral reef. He had been a powerful lapis, a rare magic that gave theurgist power over the elements of rock and sand and dirt. The longing for Jaspar returned, and she imagined an invisible hand pushing it down, deep into the recesses of her soul where it could no longer poison the happiness of the ocean.

She blinked her eyes, focusing on the brilliant sea colors, the carefree, happy sea creatures, and the world that had given her a new home when hers had been left behind. She missed Alaro, she missed her father, and she missed the man who had once promised his life to her. But for now, she had the call of the sea to cradle her.

59

AFTER AN ENTIRE WEEK AT THE INN, CELEBRATING THE festival with the rest of Keru, the final night had arrived. Jaspar and Cordelia had spent days searching through stalls and booths, meeting people and being forgotten, and yet they had hardly learned anything new. There were some rumors of burned or destroyed monuments, lost centuries ago, but much like the island, many seemed to think they were more myth than history.

On top of that, staying at the inn as new guests every single night was quickly racking up their debt and they'd been forced to take odd jobs here and there to make extra coin. Jaspar had mostly focused on manual labor, lifting and hauling goods for local vendors or overindulged guests who'd bought more than they could carry.

Cordelia had cleaned a spare stall or two and had even offered her help behind the bar of the hotel when the crowds were over-powering the wait staff. It had been enough to earn them the coin needed for their stay and to have a small amount set aside, but there was no telling if it would be enough for the next leg of their journey.

Jaspar walked out of the washroom with his hair pulled back in a neat ribbon and his new, dark-green blouse uncuffed at the wrists. He was fiddling with the buttons, the fabric flopping about. Cordelia approached him.

"May I?"

He nodded. She took the sleeve from him, clumsy and nervous fingers buttoning it together.

"I feel ridiculous," he grumbled, and she straightened his tunic.

She admired his strong jaw, his flawlessly characterized nose, the perfect, early stubble of his slowly growing beard. It reminded her of when they'd first met. "You look handsome. And you'll fit in well with the nobles."

His expression wavered from annoyance to something unreadable.

"What?"

"Nothing, you look...that's the dress you picked?"

She peered at her reflection quickly, taking in the suede of her navy-blue dress and the matching ribbons she had entwined in her braided crown. It was the closest she'd looked to the lady she once was.

"Is it too much?" She peered up at him, but Jaspar didn't answer her, he just licked his lips and started adjusting his shoes. She shrugged it off and pulled tight her elbow-length gloves, grabbing a small valise and wrapping the tiny, beaded strand around her wrist.

She had spent most of her life dressed like this, in the finest fabrics and the latest fashions, but now she missed her ordinary clothes. The return of the corset was grotesquely uncomfortable, not to mention dreadfully difficult to tighten on her own. Even now, she was convinced it was somewhat lopsided, but Jaspar hadn't mentioned it, so it must not be bad enough to reveal their cover.

Tonight, they were visiting nobles in town for the festival, celebrating the new year. Their goal was simple: seek out the oldest, most educated nobles in the dance hall and earn their ear. They could try to sway the conversation to the ash library in an organic way, but if the night wore on with no news, they would push the subject harder.

"Name?" Jaspar asked her.

"Cordy Kimber. I'm traveling with my cousin before I start

finishing school in the spring."

Jaspar nodded. "Marl, I'm your cousin and a recent graduate from Mikirian University. I'm writing a paper on abandoned historical sites and am researching a lead from an old tome."

Cordelia let out a low sigh, her hands unable to tie the ribbons on the back of her collar. She was about to admit defeat and tuck them under her dress when firm fingers moved her hair. He made short work of tying the ribbon, the touch familiar. Her mind wandered to a time so similar, and a laugh escaped.

"What?"

She could tell him. That they'd done this before. That she'd once tried to tie her own ribbon and she'd tangled it in her hair. That it was so tangled he'd had to cut her dress free. That it was the first time they'd touched, and there had been a literal spark when skin met skin. But what would be the point if he didn't remember?

"Nothing, it...tickles." The warmth of him faded away and she stepped forward, holding the door open for him.

"Shall we?"

They walked side by side down the stairs and corridors, following the sound of music and laughter until it was so loud Cordelia could barely hear her own thoughts.

"I'll go to the lecture hall first." Jaspar stopped in the foyer, the ballroom on one side and the lecture hall on the other.

"Am I not joining you?"

He scanned the heads entering the large lecture hall. "I don't think they allow women."

She scoffed.

"I'll find you later, alright?" He tucked a curl behind her ear. But was it a sign of affection or simply adjusting her appearance for the ball?

"Are you nervous to go without me?"

She shook her head. "It's not that. I've no idea how to go about seeking information like this."

The crowd grew larger, and Jaspar leaned in. She repeated her words and felt his soft breath on her neck.

"Try to blend in, ask questions when you can, don't give yourself away though. We have to walk the line between curious and demanding."

Jaspar did just that, mingling in with the crowd of men entering the hall until she could barely make out his silhouette among the many suited men. Cordelia patted her dress, touching her chest to ensure the protective talisman was safely around her neck. She pinched her cheeks for color before entering the ballroom.

It was like being transported back in time. The live band, the elaborate gowns and waistcoats, the table of dance cards, the trays of refreshments floating around the room. The smells of various perfumes mixing with the aroma of fresh food and fire into something that should be distasteful but mostly just felt reminiscent of another time. Not too many months ago, this had been her life.

"May I add my name to your dance card, my lady?" A tall, dark-haired man with tanned skin and a huge smile bowed before her. In another life, her heart may have fluttered, and she would have exchanged giggling glances with her friends.

"Certainly, sir, thank you for your kind offer. My dance card is currently open." She offered him a light dip of her head and allowed him to sign her card. Her dance card filled quickly, and she spent too many hours dancing with strange men and not enough asking questions.

No one seemed to care about the library, her inquiries, or even her thoughts. The men simply wanted an opportunity to boast about themselves, their wealth, accomplishments, and families. And of course, they took the time to offer Cordelia shallow compliments on her fine hair and dress.

They inquired about her family and background, though she knew that wasn't out of interest but compatibility. No noble would want to be caught courting outside their own class. The abstruse charade was exhausting, and she couldn't remember how she'd forced herself to endure such superficial exchanges in her past life.

Now Cordelia longed for late nights at the bar, discussing fishing techniques and new whiskey recipes. A finger on her palm, a whispering laugh, an arm on the back of her chair, and the ecstasy of a blossoming love.

60

"And that is how we plan to move forward in the future, focusing our scholarly interests in new inventions and setting aside the art of mapping." A whispered echo followed these words, bouncing off the acoustic walls of the large lecture hall.

"Thank you, Chancellor Bennett." The host of the evening, a young pale man in a white suit, waved an arm over the crowd. "Shall we have a round of applause for tonight's speaker?" His booming voice was met with polite claps, and Jaspar fought the urge to scoff at the lot of self-righteous men that surrounded him.

Chancellor Bennet bowed deeply.

"Thank you, thank you. Before we join the dancing ladies and our fellow men, I'd like to open the hall to questions." The chancellor was dressed in a gold suit, the brilliant color drawing out his dark skin. He seemed to glow bright with both ideas and pride. He awaited the questions eagerly with his hands clasped behind his back.

Jaspar thrust a hand forward and was surprised when he saw no one else had any inquiries.

"Yes, the young man in green?"

"Does this mean you will no longer offer topography studies at the university?"

The chancellor nodded, though his lips pouted in a grimace. "I'm afraid so. We've spent centuries mapping the globe and we've neglected other subjects in that time. I'll focus my tenure on inventions and leave the world drawings to the next generation, if they're needed at all."

"So, you think we've discovered all the world has to offer?"

Jaspar couldn't see who had spoken but the voice came somewhere from his left.

"I do." The chancellor held up two hands as murmurs around the room grew louder and argumentative. "Please do not misunderstand. I spent the first ten years of my education sailing the globe and illustrating atlases, and I have a great deal of respect for the craft. However, I see no necessity to continue the study in the near future."

"What of the places yet to be discovered?" A different voice asked, and he was met with words of agreement around the hall.

"I don't think there are many left. But if you have suggestions, please share." The chancellor chuckled as if he thought no one would be able to suggest anything at all.

"The Lost Island!"

Jaspar jerked his neck so hard it pulled a muscle. The voice was fragile, and Jaspar turned to see an old man with fair skin and white hair. The hall erupted in laughter, and it was clear many thought the old man senile.

"I have mapped the world myself, sir, and I've never seen any sign of Qualaris." The chancellor spoke with amused patience. "Are there any other questions?"

The old man tried to talk again but was pulled back by the hands of a younger man, his son perhaps, and was led away from the hall. Jaspar followed after them, pushing through the crowd of scholars, uncaring of what the chancellor had to say but desperately curious about the man who believed in the island.

"Pardon me! Sir!" Jaspar caught up with the men as they reached the door.

"Er, yes?"

"The island—"

The younger man pushed the old man toward the exit. "Please leave my father alone. He's confused, he didn't know what he was saying."

"You don't speak for me, Jackson." The old man shoved his son away, and Jaspar seized the moment.

"Do you truly believe in the island?" He tried to keep the desperation from his tone.

"You don't live as long as I have and not believe."

"What can you tell me of the island? What do you know?"

"Alright, that's enough. How dare you play on the mind of an old man." The son tried again to pull his father away.

Jaspar shook his head. "I'm not playing on anything. I believe in the island."

The son pulled back, incredulity in his eyes. "You're mad."

The old man leaned in, lowering his voice so only Jaspar could hear. "If you're a believer, don't let that chancellor stop you. Find somewhere else to study."

"That's enough, Father." The son led his father toward the exit, and they fought as they left the hall. Jaspar stood dumbfounded, his eyes blinking rapidly.

He hadn't felt this kind of energy since he'd first met the captain, and a fresh wave of guilt overcame him. How helpful it would have been to have Kimbal here now. How comforting to share the joy it was when they encountered a believer in the island.

And just like Kimbal, just like Jaspar, just like Cordelia, there were still those who believed, and as long as there were, he wasn't really alone on his journey. There were whispers he could follow, there were answers in the world, all he needed was to find them.

61

CORDELIA TOOK A MOMENT TO ENJOY A MUCH-NEEDED break, sucking in a gulp of wine and patting a gloved hand to her brow.

"Pardon me."

She turned to the voice, tender longing already in her heart.

"Are there any spaces left on your dance card, my lady?" Jaspar was bowed at the waist with his hand outstretched. She took it in hers, and when he pulled her close, the entire room faded away.

There was no band, no music. No budding and wizened scholars. No lords and ladies in fancy attire. No hotel staff and attendants. No shimmering candle lights and crackling fires. There was only Jaspar and Cordelia.

"I'll always save a space for you."

His lip quirked, but then his passive nature returned. The Jaspar from before was still there, in his movements and voice and in this dance. His palm spanned her lower back, a gentle nudge until her chest was almost touching his. Their hands entwined, tight together, and when they swayed onto the dance floor, it was graceful, effortless.

He pulled her close, and she felt the barest touch of his chin against her temple. "I don't know about you, but I've had very little luck learning anything other than the estimates of every noble's coffers." His voice was a hum in her ear, and she swallowed away thoughts of a simple head turn and twist of the neck and rise of her toes that could bring back their kiss.

"I've had several conversations of the same nature." He twirled her once and pulled her back, perhaps a little closer than the dance called for. "Did you learn anything of importance from the lecture?"

"They'll be eliminating topography studies at the university for the foreseeable future."

"Oh." It wasn't a topic she'd spent much time on herself, until recently.

"And there was an older man, a believer of the island."

"Is that...unusual?" She'd rarely heard of anyone who believed in the island before meeting Jaspar.

Jaspar shrugged, and she dipped low and turned back as the dance demanded. "It happens from time to time, but it's been a while."

A dancing couple passed through them, and Cordelia turned about with the group of ladies before returning to Jaspar. He pulled her in, slowly leading her away from the crowd so that they were dancing on the edge of the room, away from the voices and gazes of those around them.

"Your card is full." Jaspar nodded, his nose to the dance card ribboned around her wrist.

"There are more men than ladies tonight," she sighed. "It's a wonder any of us would have room on our cards left."

"Any good dancers?"

"None as fair as you." She smiled as he twirled her once more. She felt her heart race when he pulled her back to him. She was close enough to raise her lips to his, but she didn't dare. His cheek was near her forehead, his breath leaving a soft caress in her hair.

"Mostly men who want to brag about how wonderful they are and why every woman should desire to marry them." She rolled her eyes and Jaspar laughed, a soft and quiet vibration on her cheek as he lowered his head.

"Have you considered marriage, then?" He smirked. "Did you accept any proposals?" His voice was a low murmur, a private conversation, words from his lips meant only for her ears.

"There's only one proposal I'd ever accept," she whispered. Cordelia knew she shouldn't have said it, but her heart had responded to the voice of the man she loved.

"Jaspar." She cleared her throat softly. "I'm sorry, I shouldn't have—"

His fingers gripped her waist tighter, the slightest pressure, and then she felt his chest on hers. His hand released hers, coming to rest on her neck, tipping her head back.

"That should probably burden me with anxiety." His eyes studied her face, from her lips to her hairline and back.

"Does it not?" She tried to laugh it off, but inside her heart was a hammer against her sternum.

He tilted his head to hers, his breath warm on her lips. One shake of his head and their noses brushed together, his eyes boring into hers, stealing her breath.

"Cordelia." Her name was so delicate from his lips, like a purr in his throat. "What if I—"

"Pardon me, my lady, but I do believe it's my turn on your dance card."

The purr in Jaspar's voice turned to a growl, and for one heart-beat, Cordelia wasn't sure he'd let her go. His eyes stayed affixed to hers, but then a slow blink, three strides back, a single bow. With each step, he was farther and farther away from her, and yet the feel of him remained, like an indentation on her body that could never fully fade.

An old pale man with a monocle and top hat held out a hand to her, and she politely took it. Finally, she had a partner with age and wisdom, but all she wanted was another dance with Jaspar. The man was just as reluctant to engage in intellectual conversations with her, and Cordelia forced herself to show enthusiasm for the old man and his grandson, who were stupidly rich and irritatingly connected.

"My grandson is also quite the accomplished equestrian."

"Lovely," Cordelia mumbled. It was as lovely as finding out that the man's grandson was an accomplished rower and swordsman and came from one of the finest families in Mikiria. She had just resigned herself to endure more compliments of the grandson when her ears perked. "Pardon, sir, could you repeat that, please?"

"The painting." He gestured over her shoulder to a large portrait of an old lighthouse. "Pity it burned down. It would've been the greatest honor to visit the site. Invitation only, of course, but our family has always benefited from such fine requests."

"When did it perish?"

"A few centuries ago."

Perhaps the translation had been wrong, *AR or OU*. What if Jaspar's research had yielded no results because he'd been looking for a library, when he should have been searching for a lighthouse?

"Would you mind, sir." Cordelia stopped dancing and bowed her head to the man as the music ended. "My cousin is a scholar and quite fond of historic sites. Would you be so kind as to tell him of the lighthouse?"

"Certainly, my dear. And in the meantime, I'd like to introduce you to my grandson, Russel. I think he'd very much fancy a dance with the finest lady of the evening."

62

"YOU MUST BE MARL." JASPAR LIFTED HIS EYES FROM HIS conversation. He'd been speaking with a man of his own age who had a similar interest in scholarly sites of an abandoned nature but was currently only interested in discussing a church he was helping to redesign.

Jaspar was relieved to be saved from the conversation where yet another noble wanted to boast about themselves. That was until he saw who had interrupted them. It was the man from before, the man who had stolen Jaspar's dance with Cordelia.

"Yes, sir." Jaspar and the old man offered the same slight bow, a soft inclination of the neck. Cordelia stood just behind the man, her beautiful curls escaping their braided style, her face flushed from an evening spent dancing, her lips pulling his attention when he should have been listening to the old man.

"Lord Reginald Gauder, at your service. Your lovely cousin said you were a scholar."

Cousin. Right. She was supposed to be his cousin, and Jaspar was looking at her like she was the most perfect creature to ever exist. Maybe she was.

"Yes." Jaspar cleared his throat, removing the lump of yearning that lodged his words. When he spoke again, his voice was crisp and clear. Intrigued but measured. "Yes, I have recently taken an interest in historical sites, your lordship."

"Indeed. Come." The old man turned but then stopped. "Miss Kimber, my grandson Russel would love a turn on your dance card." He left Cordelia with a man Jaspar didn't want to admit was good-looking. Cordelia smiled at Russel, and with great difficulty, Jaspar let the old man lead him away from Cordelia.

Jaspar followed Reginald to the edges of the ballroom, where many works of art lined the wall. He stopped in front of a large portrait of a lighthouse. The painting took up most of the wall, and Jaspar had to stand back several feet and look up to admire the entirety of it. Swirls of design covered the canvas with colors both faded and vibrant. A small city, surrounded by water, with boats of every shape and size floating on its surface.

In the center of the city was a cliff, tall, foreboding, jutting from the sea like a small mountain. Atop the cliff stood a lighthouse, towering high above the city, reaching up until clouds encircled it. No, not clouds. Billows of smoke. Painted flames of orange, red, and yellow were reaching out from the lighthouse windows, reflecting off the blue waters below.

Jaspar's mind returned to the ruins he'd read, the descriptions he had translated...he searched for Cordelia in the crowded hall, but she was lost in a sea of dancers. She had found their lifeline though. She had found what they needed.

Jaspar sipped his whiskey and gave his full attention to the old man, who now donned a pair of tiny spectacles and gazed upon the painting with an earnest expression. "Lord Reginald, what can you tell me of the lighthouse?"

"It was called The Pharos of Talian. Centuries before the world we know today existed, there was a society built on technology and architecture, dedicated to discovering all the secrets of the sea. The lighthouse was constructed to bring home explorers who traveled the oceans in search of unfound land. It was more than four hundred feet high, and many considered it the greatest wonder of the world."

Jaspar searched his memory, only recalling small mentions of an ancient lighthouse, but he'd never given it much thought before.

"It was built several millennia ago by the Great King Michael, for whom the Mikirian nation was gifted its name. He had sailed the world searching for the perfect home and found it on the sands of the tiny continent. He wanted everyone near and far to see his home, no matter how small it was, and built the tallest structure on land. It was said to be so tall, it reached the heavens above and could be seen from the greatest of distances.

"My ancestors were once invited to tour the great building, before the earthquake of course." The pride and pomposity was so thick in the lord's voice Jaspar was impressed he didn't choke on it.

"When was the earthquake?"

"I believe it's been just shy of five centuries."

Lord Reginald pointed to the burning sectors of the building. "It burned for an entire day and night, leaving behind rubble and ash, the only remaining pieces of what was once considered to be the greatest architectural monument in human history."

Jaspar's shoulders sagged. "Is there nothing left of it?"

"Oh, there's always a little something left of everything, my boy. Nothing is ever truly forgotten."

If only that were true. "Where would I find this site? If I wanted to visit it?"

He turned to Jaspar, tilting his head. "Do you have a team at your disposal?"

"Er, no, sir." Right, he was a college scholar. "It wouldn't be a sanctioned investigation. This is merely for my own curiosity."

"Ah, of course." The lord cleaned his glasses, placing them back on his nose, a little crooked. "Well, you would find it in the north. Off the southeast coast of Vales, there's a tiny toll, all that's left of the small continent and its lighthouse. I'm afraid there's not much there; many scholars have already searched for remaining artifacts or relics and found very little."

Jaspar nodded. "Yes. I think it would simply be awe-inspiring to look upon the space it once held."

Lord Reginald smiled when they returned to the ballroom, craning his neck and looking beyond the crowds. Jaspar followed his gaze and his lips tightened. Cordelia was now enjoying a mead with the man's grandson, listening intently as he spoke. It was as if no one else was even in the room. Jaspar swallowed, his mouth dry.

He had no reason to feel ownership of Cordelia, even if Hygonia had said they were fated to one another. He didn't remember her, and hadn't she already told him that he was a ghost of the man she once knew? And hadn't he rejected her love when she'd offered it to him many times?

And yet, how could she love Jaspar and flirt this carelessly with some man at a party? And why in the name of Mikiria did the sight of her with another man fill him with anger, frustration, and something he'd never felt before. Something acrid and burning a hole in his gut and churning a fire within him. Something a little too akin to jealousy.

63

"AND WE'LL NEED TO LEAVE EARLY TOMORROW," JASPAR said, unbuttoning his blouse and kicking off his boots. Cordelia had let her hair down, and it now cascaded behind her back. She pulled the long tresses over her shoulder, letting them rest as they fell down to her elbows.

"And how are we traveling to this lighthouse ruin?" She handed Jaspar a cup of coffee as he sat beside her in front of the fire.

"I'll get us a ship in the morning. It'll take the last of the coin we've earned, but it'll get us there."

"How long?"

He smacked his lips after taking a drink of his coffee. The lips that had kissed Cordelia only two nights ago. "Hard to say. All I know is it's off the northeastern coast."

"And we're going to sail around until we find it?"

"You have a better idea?" He set down his mug. He took Cordelia's now empty tea mug, and she closed her eyes as his fingers brushed her skin, still tingling from the dance, the closeness of his embrace. It brought back so much for her, and yet she was certain it meant so little to him.

"Is this what your life has been?"

"What do you mean?" His brows knit together.

"Searching for clues, chasing random tiny scraps of information, hoping it leads somewhere?"

"Yes. Why?"

She swallowed. "I've been wondering why it's so hard for you to grasp, for you to believe that you once had a home and a life and someone to—" She blinked, quickly stumbling through her words. "It must seem so dull in comparison."

"Compared to chasing a curse around the world by myself?" He shifted so that his long legs were stretched out in front of him, his hand tugging on Cordelia's dress as he leaned back on his arms. "It seems sort of perfectly ordinary. I never imagined something so," his eyes squinted, "permanent."

Cordelia could think of no words in response and let her eyes watch the fire dance and gleam shadows on the wall.

"Did you have a good time tonight?"

She sighed. "Not particularly." *Unless you count the greatest five-minute dance of my entire life.* "Why?"

"I saw you dancing. It looked as if you were...enjoying yourself."

Was there resentment in his voice, or was it wishful thinking? "I was raised a lady, Jaspar. I may not have played my part these last six months, but I still remember it well."

"Didn't seem like a part. You were smiling and laughing. Especially with the last man."

Her brows creased. "Yes. He was quite amusing. We did enjoy a laugh or two at his grandfather's expense."

"Oh?" Jaspar practically growled, and she had to fight back a laugh.

"My dance partner has already found a very suitable match for himself, but his grandfather doesn't approve. So he has no interest in me, and I have no interest in him. We were merely two people enjoying a ball."

"Why does it matter if his grandfather approves?"

"You must understand society life is often about marrying for advantage. You never want to marry too far below or above your station." She let her voice drop to an exaggerated whisper. "It's scandalous." She was relieved when he gave a half-smile. "The grandfather doesn't approve of his grandson's choice because he thinks it...too out of reach."

"How out of reach?"

"About as out of reach as one could get." She smiled. "Russel is in love with the princess."

"What princess?"

"What do you mean *what* princess?" She let her legs drop, shifting when her feet nudged Jaspar's. "How many princesses are there?"

"Russel is in love with Princess Marie?" Jaspar sat up quickly.

"They met when Russel was competing in an equestrian tournament at the palace. The princess was the one officiating the ceremony."

"Why wouldn't his grandfather approve of a princess?"

Cordelia spoke with great patience. "Jaspar, she is a *princess*. Can she marry a commoner?"

"Oh." His face fell. "I see."

"If she marries Russel, she'll lose her place in the royal family, her inheritance, everything. She'll be a disgrace on society, a mockery of her title."

"But they love each other." Jaspar's voice was warm in a way she hadn't heard since before the shipwreck.

Her voice softened. "Sometimes, love's not enough."

"Will she give it all up for him? Do you think?"

"Oh yes. He didn't confirm as much. But he let slip they had plans of their own."

A small smile played on his lips, just enough for one dimple to appear on his cheek. "At least someone will get a happy ending, then."

Cordelia felt her heart sink and she got to her feet, wiping the dusty floor from her dress. She removed her silk boots, gloves, and sash. She was walking to the washroom when her fingers tangled in the mess that was the buttoned back of her dress.

Gentle fingers brushed the tendrils from her neck, and she stilled instantly. Heat flushed her cheeks as his assured fingers loosened each button until half of the dress was undone, more than enough for her to manage on her own.

His hands lingered on her back, a soft caress of skin to skin, the spark that sealed their connection igniting. She felt the barest of touches as his breath warmed her neck before he pulled away.

"Thank you." Her voice was breathy, giving away every desire she should have been trying to hide.

Jaspar mumbled under his breath, and Cordelia turned back to him.

"Jaspar?" His eyes met hers. "Why did you care? If I had fun with Russel?"

"I was...confused. I thought you were still in love with me, I mean the other me."

"I am in love with *you*." There was no hesitation in her words, no doubt or lack of conviction. Despite all that had happened, her love had never changed or wavered. How could it?

"But I'm not *him*."

"You are." She took a dangerous step forward and touched the space where his beard was slowly growing back. He was so far away her fingertips were all that reached, and though he closed his eyes when her fingers met his skin, he didn't pull away. "You're still kind and generous and clever. When I look in your eyes, nothing has changed."

Too many silent seconds ticked by, and she let her hand drop, blinking away the hurt of his absent thoughts.

"How many men did you have to dance with?"

She blanched a little at the change in subject. "A dozen or so."

He nodded. "It wasn't because there were few ladies."

"Pardon?" She met his gaze again.

"You said your dance card was full because there were so few ladies to dance with."

"Yes," she whispered.

"It was full because you..." His hand ran through her hair, a ringlet twisted around his fingers. "You were the most beautiful woman in the room."

She touched the talisman to her chest, the one that masked her true features to anyone but Jaspar. "No one can even truly see what I look like."

"I can."

Those were his last words before he laid for bed, and she retreated to the washroom. She closed the door and let her head rest against the wood, adrenaline spiking through her bloodstream, her breaths coming in short pants. She kept the sconces unlit, the curtains closed, letting her imagination flash through her mind in the dark.

She replayed every moment, every touch, every lingering stare. The waltz when he'd held her closer than necessary. His disappointment when their dance had been interrupted. His jealousy over her dance with another man. Her skin still tingled from where he'd touched her neck, where she'd dared to give herself too many moments of false hope.

But the hope was short-lived when she replayed another moment. She'd been perhaps the most vulnerable she'd ever been in her life. The night she'd bore every piece of herself, exposed every raw emotion she'd ever had, and asked him the one question that was perhaps the most important. Her heart had broken in ways she couldn't even imagine that night. And she let the moments of his small acts of tenderness fade away.

Instead, she held on to the moment that would be her only antidote for hopeful longing.

"Do you think it's possible you could love me again? Someday?"
"I'm sorry, Cordelia."

64

JANUS LET HIS RAGE OUT ON THE CARGO SHIP, SENDING flames in every direction, charring everyone and everything in his path. The smoke billowed into the clouds above, bathing them in darkness, leaking ash and embers like rain. Janus had been waiting like a fool for a delivery that would never come, and someone was going to pay for their mistake in charred flesh.

"What do you mean they never boarded?" He shook the portly shipmate, leaving welts on his pale skin.

"They...they changed their minds." The shipmate's words stumbled out, fear and confusion haunting his thoughts. Janus grunted and threw the man across the burning dock, not following to see if the man survived or not.

The brothers had been essential to his plan, and he needed all three of them. It was bad enough that the first batch of Sidons had managed to sink the brothers' ship but had failed at actually capturing them, now they'd slipped through his grasp once more.

"I gave very clear instructionsss," Janus growled as the ship's men stood in a row, some already coughing and succumbing to the smoke billowing around them. "Thisss ship wasss not to leave the dock without the brothersss."

The men did not answer, they stood and trembled in fear. Janus was growing impatient. Each carefully laid plan of his had backfired in so many ways. Every time he'd ordered others to do his bidding, they had failed over and over. The Sidons had let Cordelia escape three times, three of his Sidons died at the hands of a mere homemaker in Alaro. His only loyal and competent abettor was Alaria, and recently, she'd had a long list of failures trailing behind her.

"Where isss your captain?" Janus asked a young shipmate who was coughing uncontrollably. If anyone were to provide him answers, it would be the man Janus had clearly overpaid to offer the brothers a trip to Alaro.

"I'm here, Lord Janus." The captain emerged from the flames, his long, braided blond hair blowing in the smoky wind, his proud head held annoyingly high.

"What do you have to sssay for yourssself?" Janus approached the man, fascinating himself with ideas of torture and retribution.

"I let them pass, my lord. They refused to board, and I left them in Keru. The fault is mine and mine alone." There was no fear in his voice, he stood resolute and strong, as if the fire and Janus were no concern of his.

He wasn't afraid for his own life? So be it. There were other ways to frighten a man. "Your daughter isss at home, isss she not?" Janus picked lazily at his jacket.

The man's eyes widened, and though he tried to mask his features, Janus knew he'd hit his mark. He no longer had time to seek the brothers, by now, they could be with the witch for all he knew. But he did have more use for the ship captain.

"I tell you what. I'm feeling...forgiving today. You have one lassst chance to prove yourssself to me."

The man nodded once, and Janus slapped his hands together, instantly extinguishing the flames around them. "You will take my men to the lighthoussse, you will take them to the mountain, and then, you will give them passssage back with their prisssonersss. Or"—Janus let a flame dance in his palm—"I'll sssee if your daughter likesss to play with fire."

65

THE DREAM WAS HAZY, AND YET JASPAR COULD SENSE his awareness. He stood on a dock he didn't recognize, the sun high, golden and beaming. The ocean was restless, waves of white foam crashing into the ships, the docks, the sand. He lifted his head to the sky, allowing the sun to blind him until all he saw was the back of his eyelids. But then the light was gone.

He was on a ship. Not just any ship, the captain's ship. Dozens of people lined the benches. And a girl stood by an altar at the front. Not a girl, Cordelia. And not an altar, an open casket, with the captain's body. Cordelia was mournful in maroon, and her song was a cry in the air, an ache that he felt in his heart.

The ship swayed, and he was overcrowded. Faceless people surrounded him, each wore an expression lacking any features. Their missing noses and eyes and mouths disturbed him. He waved his arms to fight them off, but they were translucent, disappearing like vapor.

The air shifted, clear skies turning to haze and smoke. Cannons boomed. He was on a different ship, one he didn't recognize, one that was being attacked. He watched himself and three bearded men hustle around the deck, he jumped to get out of their way, and he stepped back until he stumbled over the edge of the boat and into the icy ocean.

Water filled his ears and nose and burned his eyes. Out of the darkness, a blue haze approached him. It swam closer and closer, gliding through the water with grace and ease. It was Cordelia. Only, she wasn't the Cordelia he knew. She was wearing a maroon working dress with a white apron. Her hair was braided to the side, and she wore an old pair of worn slippers. She spoke, but it turned into bubbles in her mouth.

He studied her lips, reading his name in their movements. *Jaspar...I can save us...just hold on...*

She held up her hands, palms out, and Jaspar was lifted through the water, flying to the surface. He soared high above the waves and landed on a boat deck, his ship. He stood up, perfectly dry, and he was docked to the cay. He jumped down to see himself, with Cordelia, sitting beside her in the sand.

He was laughing and smiling, and she nudged his shoulder with her own. His arm wrapped around her, pulling her to his side, leaving a kiss in her hair. She craned her neck, and his lips found hers. It was soft and gentle, the perfect kiss of complacency.

The Jaspar beside Cordelia whispered something, and she smiled warmly in return. Jaspar tucked a hair behind her ear and leaned in for a kiss, looking at Cordelia with an expression of pure devotion. They turned to see dream Jaspar, and the Jaspar of the cay and Cordelia rushed at him. Jaspar wielding fire, Cordelia wielding water, and when they reached the shore, the Jaspar of the cay faded away.

Dream Jaspar watched from his ship as Cordelia looked for *her* Jaspar and then realized she was alone. She stumbled around in the sand, desperate, searching. Her eyes landed on the boat, hopeful, joyful. She called his name, but he turned his back to her. And then he was sailing away, and her voice was still calling his name. And it grew louder and louder and louder until it was the only sound in the world.

66

"Jaspar!" Cordelia's voice was loud, shrill in his ear, and he felt her shove his side, hard.

"What? What?" He sat up in a jolt, eyes wide, knife in hand. Cordelia was kneeling by the bed, still in her nightclothes. Screaming and shouting came from the halls, slamming doors, and...water? Rushing water?

"We. Need. To. Leave," she hissed at him, panic straining her lovely face. He was out of bed in a flash, donning his boots and grabbing anything useful. His knives, his new journal, his bag. He reached a hand back for Cordelia, but she was already at the door.

She heaved it open, and a wall of water cascaded into the room. The water lifted him, taking him with the rushing current, and his body collided hard with the wall. When the water receded, he followed Cordelia down the hall amid the masses of people trying to escape the slowly flooding hotel.

Cordelia winced and squinted, staring at the water with great frustration.

"Cordelia?"

"It won't work," she whined, letting a family with a group of small children go past them. "My magic...I can't even feel it, let alone access it."

"You mean, you can't stop this?"

She shook her head, lips pouting.

"It's alright. It doesn't matter." He reached for her, but she was already moving, trudging through the three feet of water with the throngs of people trying desperately to escape. Suitcases, clothes, and personal items floated down the halls and stairs. Hotel staff tried to keep doors open, to shuffle people through in a calm and orderly fashion. But there was too much panic, too much chaos.

Their room had been on the top floor, where the flood had barely reached and began to seep the floors. But the lobby level was completely underwater, and the staff was evacuating people through the open balcony doors of the second-floor ballroom.

A group of men pushed past, and he lost sight of Cordelia. He searched for her, but the shoving crowd dragged him out. The water flowed from the hotel to outside, where the street was flooded with great torrents of water.

People tried desperately to navigate the chaotic flood. Carts and festival goods floated down the main street, the tents and huts of the vendors submerged under thirty feet of water.

"Cordelia!" Jaspar saw no sign of her in the guests that had fled the flooded hotel. No sign of her in the many people still exiting from above. No sign of her in the throngs of people swimming down the main road.

He heaved in a breath and dove under the surface. The water stung his eyes, and he strained himself to keep them open. He could see the damaged hotel, the entire first floor and half of the second completely submerged. The legs and bodies of animals and humans kicked and slashed, trying desperately to tread the water. Debris and belongings from hotel guests and festival vendors trapped beneath the surface.

He broke through the surface and gasped in the air, panting. His salt-stung eyes scanned the top of the waters and the crowds of people. Then, when he felt his whole world had stopped spinning, she popped out of the water. She squinted, her arms high above her head in the shape of a u. Her body shook, blood slowly dripping from her nose.

"Cordelia!" He swam to her as quickly as his long legs would allow, but between the current of the water and the many people, it took him nearly ten minutes.

"What the blazes is going on?"

"That's not me!" she shouted indignantly. Shrieks filled the air as the glass windows from the top floor of the hotel burst, flying in all directions like a hailstorm of sharp shards. Jaspar tucked Cordelia to his chest, shielding her. Water overflowed from every orifice of the hotel: every door, every window, every gate.

"If that's not you, then what are you doing?" He wrapped an arm around her back. She tried to push him off, but he scowled. "You're two seconds from passing out, and you've got a nosebleed." This time, when he wrapped an arm around her, she sank into his embrace, allowing him to help keep her afloat.

He used the sleeve of his night-shirt to wipe her face, letting his fingers linger too long on her blue lips. "Please tell me you're alright," he said gently, and she gave a delicate nod. "If that's not you, then who is it?"

"I don't know," she said through panted breaths. The quietness of her voice unnerved him and he pulled her closer.

"I can't use my magic. It won't work. I can't feel it at all." Tears poured down her pale face, her lips still slightly blue.

"Let's get out of here." He steered them to the shoreline. Many people were struggling to evacuate the waters, opting to follow the current and try to find shelter along the way. There were some who had found ropes and tied themselves to wood poles, attempting to ride out the flood.

"Where exactly are we going?" Cordelia shouted over the rushing waters.

The water's strong current had not slowed, and he kept Cordelia close, fearful she'd be washed away in her exhausted state.

"I'm still working that out." His eyes found the docks. In the chaos of the flood, the harbor had been abandoned, and several boats sat idle, the docks lost beneath the flooded waters. Indecision warred his mind.

"How much coin do we have?"

"I'm not sure. Maybe a thousand coppers?"

Jaspar cursed under his breath. "I hope it's enough."

He guided them to the docks where fate had provided them an opportunity: a for-sale sign on a small veleiro, oak wood with gray edges.

"Hand me your coin purse."

Cordelia shifted awkwardly, reaching into her soaked dress pocket. "What's your plan?"

Jaspar swam them to the boat and tied the purse coin to the top of the pole next to the for-sale sign.

"Jaz!"

He ignored her, pushing her onto the deck.

"That's not how purchasing works."

"Well, this isn't how water works!" He waved his arm out of the flooding capital. "Do you have a better idea?"

She pouted and began to help him untie the ship, and they climbed onto the mercifully dry deck. The ship was small, only two sails to navigate. There was no cabin and only three blankets and two creels aboard the deck.

"Tie off that—" Jaspar spun in a circle. While he'd been navigating the ship, Cordelia had drifted back to the open waters.

"Cordelia!"

Her eyes were wide with terror, and he followed her gaze to a group of men in dark robes, a shiny pendant on their chest. He pulled her by her sleeve, noticing that she was still in her nightdress.

"Get on the boat!"

"No, wait!"

"Now, Cordelia!" He growled, and she shoved and kicked him.

"Jaz!" Her hands cupped his cheeks, demanding his stare, and his whole body stilled at the touch. Her eyes locked on his, and his mind muddled back to a bar where she'd held his bearded face in her hands, a blizzard raged outside, and his lips were close to hers.

She dropped her hands when she had his attention.

"Those are not Sidons," she said clearly, and Jaspar blinked away the memory. The men, drifting through the waters with ease atop currackes, wore robes of deep navy blue. The pendant on their chest was silver and the shape of a sea turtle. They sheathed bronze swords instead of bows and arrows. And though it was hard to tell from the distance and the water, Jaspar could swear their skin had a cerulean glow to it.

"Cordelia." He leaned his head toward hers, keeping his voice gentle this time. "Please come back to me."

"But—"

"I don't know who they are, but I don't think they're our friends. They may not *be* Sidons, but they dress very similarly. And whoever these men are, they showed up just as an unexplainable flash flood terrorized the very hotel we were staying in, and your magic stopped working."

Her eyes darted back to the men, but then she nodded and returned to the ship, helping him tie off and raise the sails. The darkness of night gave little light, but the moon and stars would have to be their guide. Jaspar didn't know who those men were. He didn't know why her powers weren't working. All he knew was he had a ship, and he was getting Cordelia as far away from danger as he could.

67

CORDELIA SETTLED NEXT TO JASPAR AS HE LAY BENEATH the stars. The deck wasn't particularly comfortable, but the wool blankets were warm and had stayed dry in the benches of the small boat.

"That one"—Jaspar leaned over, pointing north— "is Ursa Major." Every inch of the left side of her body felt the warmth of Jaspar, and she forced her mind to focus on the stars and shapes above.

"And what is its purpose?" So far, she'd learned that Jaspar, and many other explorers, used constellations to navigate the waters. She'd known this from her father, of course, but no one had ever taken the time to show her the shapes and explain their meanings.

He sat up, leaning his back on the bulwark of the ship, and she followed his lead. "The tip points directly to the Northern Star." She leaned her head back, letting it rest on the ship's wall.

They'd been sailing all day, and she'd never felt the sea sickness she had back on the cay. Perhaps she was more acquainted with the waters now. When the night sky had risen, Cordelia finally understood the peace Jaspar felt on a ship.

With the sun resting and the moon and stars shining, the waters were beautiful in a way she had never appreciated. The light from the moon and stars danced off of the darkness of the ocean's surface. And the sky reflected the water in its infinite depths. Above, there was an endless sky of stars, and below, there was an endless ocean of waters.

"When I was a boy," Jaspar's voice was soft. "I used to sail the seas with my father and my mother. My mother didn't like sailing." He smiled, wistful.

"We would spend our evenings staring at the stars, and my parents would tell me such magical stories. About the constellations and the gods who named them and the many places one could visit, if only they studied natures map in the sky. I've never had anyone to share that with."

She gave a wane smile. "You can share anything with me."

"Hmm." He nodded. "Guess I can."

"Thank you for telling me." She longed to reach for him, but she kept herself guarded. Though Jaspar had opened up to her a great deal more, confided in her and let his guard down, even touching her freely at times, like now, when he pulled the blanket up to her shoulders, she hadn't forgotten his declarations. He may have warmed to her, but he'd also made it clear that love was not in their future.

Each day spent with him was like another piece of herself she tucked away. Any small smile, any carefree laugh, any accidental brushing of skin. She saved every moment, cataloging them away for later. A day would come when Jaspar would no longer need her company, and she wanted memories of him and their time together.

Perhaps he would find another, as he predicted before, and she would step aside, as she'd promised. Perhaps he'd grow tired of having a companion to search the seas for and wished to return to his journeys of solitude.

"Cordelia?"

"Hmm?"

Jaspar was handing her the woolen blanket, and she wrapped it tight around her shoulders, laying back down on the deck. Jaspar lay near her, but not quite beside her, several feet separating them. She hummed to herself, tracing small circles on the back of her hand, reminding herself of another time.

A time when she didn't fear Jaspar's growing indifference or boredom. A time when she didn't worry his devotions would belong to another. A time when she didn't feel alone in his presence. A time when Jaspar had kissed her lips and promised his life to her.

68

"IT'S BEEN TWO DAYS, JASPAR, THERE'S ONLY SO MUCH ocean in the world." Cordelia sat on the bench as the boat glided effortlessly through the open waters. "Perhaps the old man was wrong or confused. Or perhaps there's nothing left of the lighthouse and its toll."

"Cordelia." Jaspar heaved a sigh, tying off a rope and coming to sit beside her. "My family has been chasing an island no one believes existed for more than two thousand years. I'm not giving up on a lighthouse after only two days." He squinted in the sunlight, taking the water canteen she offered.

"Did you ever think of giving it up?"

"What?"

"The dream." She took the canteen back, and he propped up a leg, letting his arm dangle over the side of the boat. "Just staying on this boat, living out at sea. No more chasing, no more running, just...sailing."

He scoffed. "This boat that we acquired two days ago?" He tapped a finger to her forehead. "What's churning in there?"

She let herself smile, and a picture started to form in her mind, of another life, one she was so close to having just two months ago. Her voice was soft when she finally spoke.

"It could have been so simple, you and me. I thought it would be, and even with Qualaris and Danthems and Hagans and Sidons, I thought I could still see it."

She heard a tight intake of breath. "See what?"

"That shiny, happy ending."

"Cordelia, are you sure you're up for this?"

She turned to face him, her leg nudging his on the bench. But he didn't pull away.

"For what?"

"Are you prepared for this life? To follow me around the world looking for an island? Knowing that I may never get my memories back? Knowing that we may never find the island? Knowing—"

"That you may find another." Her voice was so soft he hadn't heard. But she couldn't bear to say it again, and when he asked her to repeat herself, she changed her answer.

"I don't see a future for myself that you're not in. I can't imagine a life that doesn't include you."

There was silence between them, and Cordelia stared at the open waters, watching the sunlight reflect off the water in blinding rays of gold.

"You didn't answer the question," he said softly.

She let herself say the words she'd been committed to for weeks. Perhaps even since that day on the beach. "I don't mind. If you don't get your memories back."

"You don't?" His voice was laced with disbelief.

"Obviously it would be a relief if you could remember, but I..." *love you*. "I'll stay with you as long as you'll have me." A thought struck her. "Plus, I thought maybe..."

"Maybe what?"

Despite her sense of self-preservation, or perhaps a lack thereof, she had allowed herself to hope that his feelings for her would shift and change, just as that of her Jaspar once had. But she'd long since given up on the notion of love and now could only hope for open and trusting companionship.

"Maybe after the last two months together that you were starting to...I don't know...trust me?"

Cordelia was grateful he didn't answer quickly, grateful he

took the time to register her words and carefully think through them.

"I trust you more than I've ever trusted anyone."

"But?" She could hear it, the silent reluctance at the end of his sentence.

"But I'm worried it's just...that soulfate thing. You're the only one who remembers me, and we're *destined*," he said the word like it was the strangest sound he'd ever heard, "for each other. Is that the only reason that I feel so..."

"So what?" She should have better control, should have reeled herself in, but her words came out a gasp of pure hope. Like the night he held her in his arms, and they danced in the dark, and she admitted to a future she'd once longed for.

"I don't know. It's like...it's like I'm drawn to you, just blatantly aware of you. My thoughts drift to you when I'm idle. And my eyes follow you around the room. And my hands twitch constantly around you." A shaky finger touched her face. "And that kiss...it never leaves my thoughts, Cordelia."

69

JASPAR HAD NEVER FELT SO HELPLESS, SO EXPOSED IN HIS
life. And yet something felt right, something clicked into place like
it had always been meant to be there.

He leaned closer to her on the bench. "I may not remember
him, but some part of me does remember you. Or at least, parts of
you. The last two months with you have been like...a dream. And
maybe it is the soul thing," he shrugged. She bit her lip, and a pool
of desire warmed in his chest. "But maybe it's just you."

She lifted her head. "Jaspar?"

All the air left his body, and it felt like they were standing on a
precipice, one they couldn't come back from. Their kiss before had
been to try and cure his amnesia, to break the cage that trapped his
memories. If he kissed her now, it would be for no other reason
than...because he wanted to.

"I know I...I want to remember. Our kiss was only meant to
bring back my memories because it was a moment of *pure* intimacy. But I was so skeptical of everything you knew about me, of
the soulfate bond, of sharing my mark with you." He swallowed
his panic and licked his lips.

"What if it didn't work because...subconsciously, I wasn't
ready to remember before? Because I didn't allow myself the
possibility?"

"You don't know what you're asking for," she breathed, and he could hear the vulnerability in the strain of her voice.

Cordelia's eyes were heavy, lidded to hide her sorrow, but he knew she was hurting, that every minute where he didn't remember took something away from her. He wondered if she was hesitant because she hid how hard his memory loss had been on her. She didn't complain, she didn't blame him, but he knew it had taken a toll to love someone who didn't remember loving her back.

Cordelia didn't move, didn't reach for him. But she also didn't pull away. Had he felt this trepidation before? Had their love scared him in his past life, or was it also laced with the same anticipation and affection that flowed through him now?

And yet, even though he knew the ghost of his love plagued her, her love had not wavered. Had she always been so certain, so sure of her feelings? But, the other Jaspar had shown her his mark, so he must have been just as certain.

Images fluttered in his mind, fragmented memories of his dreams. Things he knew had happened versus things he vaguely remembered from a dream or an inexplicable flashback. Holding her in an unfamiliar and crowded tavern. Dancing with her tight in his arms at the ball two nights ago. Kissing her hand in front of the fire at the cay, tucking a hair behind her ear on the ship. Letting his lips brush her palm in a fever filled haze, her fingers engraving their love and devotion into his chest.

Reality and memory were becoming so interwoven, did it matter which was which? Did it matter which Jaspar cared more for her so long as they both did? He didn't need to remember a past where he loved her, all he saw in front of him was a future where someday he could. Maybe someday sooner than he'd ever imagined.

Maybe the kiss before hadn't worked not because they weren't really fated, not because they weren't really in love, but because he wasn't ready to believe it. He wasn't fully ready to accept that he loved someone, or that someone was capable of loving him. But things were different now.

A finger ran along the curls cascading over her shoulder, down her arm. His eyes dropped to her lips, her neck, and back. He closed the distance between them. She didn't move, even though he knew she wanted this as much as he did.

But Cordelia was waiting, letting him decide for himself. Patient. Kind. Respectful. Selfless. How did any version of him, past or present, deserve a love like this?

It was like the earth stopped spinning, every second somehow frozen, only his thrumming heartbeats measuring the time.

Beat: he let his left hand rest on her hip. Beat: he tugged her closer to him. Beat: his right hand tangled in her curls. Beat: he felt her breath on his face. Beat: his nose tucked next to hers. Beat: his lips met hers, tender. Beat: the tiniest of kisses, soft and fleeting. Beat: her hand on his chest. Beat: her fingers stroking his jaw. Until all the beats of his heart caught up at once, and he was kissing her with no hesitation.

70

CORDELIA'S WHOLE BODY WAS ON FIRE AT HIS TOUCH, at the longing she'd felt for his affection. Her heart raced as Jaspar pulled her closer, his arms wrapping around her. This time, when she sank into the kiss, he kissed her back. Their kiss before, when they'd tried to bring back his memories the first time, had been all passion. But this felt...more akin to how they'd kissed in Woodvale.

There was affection, there was tenderness, and she longed for what it could mean. But the longer they kissed, the more she realized it hadn't worked. It was like he remembered her even though she could already tell he didn't. Like his body remembered her, but his conscious mind had not recovered his memories.

Something more passionate, more urgent, sparked between them. His hand was wrapped tight in her dress, carrying her to him. This kiss was more than anything she'd felt. More than their kiss in Keru. More than their kiss in Woodvale. More than their kiss on the cay.

The kisses with Jaspar at the cay had a sense of decorum, boundaries maybe. They had once spent months hiding their feelings, and when they'd finally kissed that night by the fire, it had been building into something gentle and intimate.

But this was all lust, only desire controlled his body. Cordelia felt her eyes burn and knew she had to protect what little piece of her heart she had left, had to hold on to the tiny piece of *her* Jaspar that was still there. The Jaspar that had loved her.

The briefest moment paused their kiss, and his name fell from her lips, and he went still, body rigid. He leaned back, the spell between them broken. She placed a hand on his chest, letting her other fall from his neck. He pulled back, reluctantly, the space between them not far enough. She could still feel the warmth of his breath, could still see the closeness of his eyelashes, could still sense the charged energy sparking from where his lips had touched hers.

"It didn't work, did it?" Cordelia heard the pleading in her voice as she removed herself from Jaspar's warm embrace, the feel of him still pulsing through her. He was slack-jawed, as if his thoughts were still in the moment. He licked his lips and gave the smallest shake of his head.

"It's alright," Cordelia said more to herself than to Jaspar. She was touched that he had even tried, that he had even wanted those memories back, but the knowledge that it hadn't worked, twice now, crushed any hopes she had left that it could ever work. The more time that passed, the more solutions they burned through, the more she felt it was hopeless. His memories would never come back.

She thought of Hygonia's stories, of the three people who'd had the memories of their soulfates taken from them. There'd been a happy ending for two of them, but the third person... She didn't want to end up like him. She didn't want to feel the loss of Jaspar so deeply that it consumed her until nothing living was left.

How long could she hold on to Jaspar before he would need to move on? Was she holding him back for her own selfish reasons? Could she simply remain a close confidant, a friendly partner on their lifelong adventure?

But his mark meant that he may never fall in love again. He would have had a chance before, with the mark and memory to share. Hadn't the others in his family done just that? Hadn't they fallen in love, shared their mark, and bore children that could carry on both the curse and its legacy?

"Cordelia," he breathed her name, like the whisper of what

could have been, or maybe that was how she heard it because she knew that's what she wanted to hear. For him, it was just a kiss from a girl who loved him. But for her, it was the reality that she'd never again have the love he had once given to her.

His heart had sealed away the part of him that cared for her. Maybe staying with him all these weeks, forcing him to take her on a journey that belonged to him and his family, was keeping him from living whatever life he was meant to live without her. And wasn't that the most selfish thing she could do to him? Who was she to determine who he spent his time with, who he shared his life, adventures, and secrets with?

"It's alright, Jaspar." She moved away from his grasp, but he stayed still, his arms still trying to wrap around her. The feeling of him felt hollow, a hug from the man she loved, but not the man who loved her. She gripped his wrists, lifting them from her side and shifting out of the warm space between his arms.

She tried to give him a wane smile before letting her eyes drift back out over the water. After a moment, he walked back to the sails and the steering. She was slowly resigning herself to the possibility of a future in which Jaspar never remembered her, never found love for her again. And she thought she could do that.

She could love him enough for the both of them, even if it meant burying her love in the shadows of her broken heart. Hygonia had said she could break through, that their love was strong enough to overcome the poison that had stolen Jaspar from Cordelia, but she'd been wrong. Love wasn't enough.

71

JASPAR'S LEGS SANK DEEPER INTO THE SAND. HE WAS somehow conscious that he was asleep, but the dream felt so real and vivid that he was suffocating in it. He tried to wake himself, tried to free himself of the strangely familiar nightmare. Had he had this dream before? Fought back the demons of his fears in another life?

The quickness of the sand pulled, yanking his body. It reached his knees, his thighs, his torso. He dug his fingers in, anchoring himself to the land as he continued to sink.

"Cordelia!" Why was he screaming for Cordelia? Was she here? He turned his head left and right, looked up and down and beyond, but saw no signs of her. No footprints in the sand, no shadows beneath the moon. He was alone on the strange shoreline.

The sand began to warm, slowly burning hotter and hotter until it scorched his skin, as if he were in a bed of coals, as if embers were sinking into his flesh.

"Only you can stop the pain. Only you can stop the fire." It was Kimbal's voice, echoing around him, but Jaspar remained alone.

"Kimbal?" He shouted for his friend, but only the whistling of the wind responded.

"Your memories are blocked by your own self-sabotage. You do not believe yourself worthy of love and so you cannot accept it." It was a different voice now, female, patient, kind.

"But I accepted it before!" he screeched into the night, frustration at the past months of loss weighing him down, sinking him farther into the burning sand. A whirl of wind took the sands, creating a tornado, lifting him free until he could crawl out.

He hunched over, on his hands and knees, panting. He inspected his skin for burns, but his flesh wasn't red, it was...shiny, pale. The more he looked, the less pale it was, and the more it appeared...blue, almost cerulean.

"What's happening to me?" he asked the emptiness around him, and the female voice returned.

"I only have a moment before you will awaken."

"This nightmare, I've had it before." It was a question more for himself than for the disembodied voice.

"You can release your memories, you can free yourself."

"How?" he screamed in desperation. Hadn't he been trying to do that for weeks? Hadn't that been why he'd kissed her yesterday?

No, a voice told him. No, he had kissed her because he *wanted* to, not because he truly hoped to remember a time from before. A time he didn't have any reason to get back to.

A swirl of vapors appeared before him, an image playing inside. The shipwreck, Cordelia trapped, and the Jaspar from before desperate to save her.

"We do not have much time. Any minute now, Cordelia will wake you from your troubled dreams." A figure stepped through the vapors, the images of Cordelia and Jaspar dissolving in the air.

"Listen carefully." The voice grew louder as it approached him. The silhouette of a person, the curves of a woman, the voice of an angel.

"Sands of time can do more than shine if their silver runs black as the night. Questions change the sand, and wrong answers will keep the silver bright. But screams will never make a sound, until one of your answers is right."

Jaspar was still thinking of the shipwreck, the vision of his own face so filled with devotion.

"Remember my rhyme, Jaspar, remember you are the Celarestar!"

"I am the cele..." His body shook, and he was fully clothed. Metal-plated armor, a navy-blue cloak, a sword at his waist.

"You are the Celarestar..." The voice grew distant, a whisper in the wind, until all he heard was the name of his heart.

Cordelia.

72

Jaspar's eyes snapped open, his forehead dripping with sweat, a quiet voice in his ear, a mild hand on his shoulder. Cordelia, always Cordelia.

"Jaspar?"

He was lying on the deck, face down, the wool blanket wrapped tightly around his legs. Jaspar disentangled himself, taking in as much oxygen as his lungs would allow and letting it out in long rasps.

"Are you alright?" she asked, her gentle hand resting on his shoulder.

The dream was fading fast, something about a star, his skin pale, no blue skin, the lightest shade of cerulean blue. And Cordelia was there. No, it was someone else...but who. And was there a song? A poem or riddle? He couldn't recall. The longer he was awake, the more he tried to cling to the dream, the faster it slipped away.

"I'm fine."

He wasn't sure why the dream had affected him so greatly, he couldn't seem to recall what it was about or what had happened. And yet it had caused an anxiety so strong it had stayed with him even after waking.

Thoughts of the dream fell away as memories of the afternoon before filled his thoughts. Her kiss still lingered on his lips, her smell, her touch, everything he'd ever seen her do, everything he'd ever heard her say. It was all burned into his mind, and memories of the past or not, he wouldn't soon forget how it felt to have her wrapped in his arms.

"Where are we?" he croaked, and she offered him an already prepared canteen of water. So attentive. So thoughtful.

"I never pulled the anchor."

"Right." She may have been the daughter of a sailor, but she'd never learned to sail herself. "Let's remedy that, shall we?"

"Pardon? Remedy what?"

"You're going to learn how to sail."

"What? Now?" The wind whipped her hair around, and she jerked her head to shake it out of her eyes.

"No time like the present."

Cordelia bit her lip, and he saw the indecision, the uncertainty, but he knew she was capable, she just needed to trust herself.

~

"HOLD ON TIGHT ENOUGH IT WON'T SLIP FROM YOUR fingers, but loose enough you can easily move and shift around the spokes when you need." He stood behind her, his hands resting on hers, guiding her placement on the spokes of the wheel.

"Why don't we quit while we're ahead?" Her voice shook.

"Nonsense, you're doing great!"

"Liar." There was something in her tone, a resonance of before. Images flew back to him, a dark cellar, a walk through the cold night, him lying in a bed, her fixing a blue dress in the moonlight, him holding up a pair of worn slippers three sizes too small for his feet but the perfect size for hers. He rubbed his eyes, inhaling the cold, salty air and exhaling his sudden anxiety.

"Where did you go? I need your help!" she shrieked, and he realized he'd stumbled back, let go of her hands, left her to steer by herself. He was a step away from returning to assist her when he stopped. She didn't need him. She was steering, gliding through the water with ease, navigating the boat and its sails as if one with the ocean waves.

"Cordelia," he whispered, bewildered, excited, in awe.

"What?" Her hands were steady, strong, the ship never wavering, but he could hear the panic in her voice.

"Cordelia," he said more slowly, "you don't need my help. You're already sailing."

"I...I am?" A simple stutter, but when he moved to step in front of her, she was smiling. A grin he'd never seen before or perhaps one he had forgotten. Had he once seen it in a loud tavern filled with people just before he'd embraced her?

There were tears on her cheeks. "My father...if he could see me now. If I could only share this with him." Grief constricted both of them, but it felt new, different. They still missed him, but they were starting to feel pieces of him again. In the sails that swayed in the wind, in the stern that glided through the water with ease, in the moments that they wanted to share with him but would never be able to.

"He'd be proud," Jaspar told her, knowing it to be true. He could practically see the captain's face beaming at the image of his daughter steering a boat as if she'd been sailing all her life.

"There!" Cordelia shouted, pulling him from his thoughts. He followed her outstretched arm and saw the tiniest pocket of land to the south.

"Great," he mumbled. Of course he'd wanted to find the lighthouse, but he'd also wanted to stay in this moment. He'd let his feelings for her distract him from his lifelong mission for the island. He thought of her words from before: that they could simply sail the waters forever, forgetting about curses and lost islands and family legacies. What kind of life would that be?

"How long?" Cordelia asked, her knuckles white on the helm.

His eyes measured the distance across the water. "Maybe two hours?" But it took nearly three before their ship finally reached the shore. Cordelia steered the entire way, satisfaction evident in her expression even as she stretched out her back and shoulders.

Jaspar dropped anchor several feet from the sand, and they hopped into the water to walk the rest of the way. Tiny pockets of droplets surrounded Cordelia as she waded through the water, like air, landing on the sand with dry feet and clothes.

Jaspar dragged his soaking and soggy clothes, his steps labored, collecting sand on his boots and pants as they trudged their way forward.

"Can I take the water?" She tilted her head. "I've seen you do it with fire. You sort of...absorb the embers and the ashes."

He nodded. "Try to think of the water as something that already belongs to you. You're just picking it up again."

She reached for him, cautious. "May I?"

He cleared his throat and nodded.

She let gentle hands rest on his shoulders, closed her eyes, and hummed. For a moment, they stood like that, but then...tiny tickles of droplets of water suddenly pulled from his clothes, hair, and shoes and danced in a swirl before returning to the beach.

"Cordelia."

She opened her eyes. "I...I did it?"

"Of course you did." She lifted a hand, as if to touch his face, but then pulled both her arms back and stepped away.

The toll was small, too small to be any part of the world that he recognized. The sand was dark, almost dirty, and the grass growing was brown. The trees around them were dry, ashen. Everything on the island seemed to be just a little dark, as if it were dying.

"Jaspar?" Cordelia spoke his name slowly. She was staring so high up her neck looked craned. Her eyes were wide, her lips parted. Jaspar looked up, and up, and up, and there before them, towering into the heavens above, was what remained of The Pharos of Talian.

Jaspar took three steps to stand beside her, unable to remove his eyes from the lighthouse. He stumbled in the sand, and a strong, steady hand caught his arm.

∼

IT WAS JUST AS MAJESTIC AS IN THE PAINTING, ONLY now, it was as brown and gray as everything else on the toll. Once there had been magnificent, stain glassed windows, but all that was left were cracked fragments around the edges of large, gaping holes. The building of white and silver marble bricks had been reduced to nothing more than rubble and rock encircling the base of the once towering structure, which resembled a broken tree. It was still standing, but something about it felt ambiguous, half-finished, or half-destroyed, somewhere between awe-inspiring and heart-breaking.

Cordelia walked ahead, and he ran, putting himself between her and the crumbling lighthouse. If she found this odd, she didn't show it, simply following him, her expression one of admiration and intrigue.

They walked around what was left of the base, inspecting it for openings or doors that had yet to be blocked. Several gaps seemed a rockslide or two away from allowing entrance, but neither Jaspar nor Cordelia could move the heavy stones. It was as if the lighthouse had barricaded itself from the world.

Jaspar tossed a heavy chunk of marble behind him, peering around another and trying to determine if he should move to another section. He heard a sharp scream, and his neck jerked him around. His lungs emptied, his heart hammering in his chest. He walked faster, around and around and around the lighthouse. His walk became a jog and then a run, and then he had encircled the entire lighthouse to no avail. Cordelia was gone.

73

"THANKS." IVERSON SHOOK HANDS WITH THE CAPTAIN before jogging back down the dock to his brothers.

"Alright, they've agreed us fair passage to Alaro, so long as we in debt work to them when we arrive," Iverson said, clapping his hands together and grinning at his brothers. It was now their third attempt to make it back to Anchorage Inn, and though he couldn't explain why he had been hesitant to board the last ship, he was glad his brothers had trusted his instincts.

"*In debt work to them?* What the barnacles does that mean?" Trevyn asked, shielding the sun from his eyes with his arm, the golden beams bringing out the natural orange highlights of his flaming red hair.

"Gladys?" Kevin asked.

Iverson nodded. "She won't mind, she'll need someone to replace our inventory anyway."

"Again, what the barnacles does that mean?" Trevyn said, snapping his fingers to get his brother's attention, annoyed at the continued conversation without him.

Kevin let out a heavy sigh at Trevyn's usual impatience. "It means we recommend work for them in the area, if they earn enough to cover our passage, our debt is paid." He returned his attention to Iverson, handing him a canteen. "How long did they give us?"

Iverson took a long swig of the cool water and wiped his mouth on his blouse sleeve. "Six months."

"Is that long enough?" Trevyn pondered aloud.

"Should be. Depends on how many buyers we can find them in Alaro." Iverson tossed his rucksack over his shoulder and led his brothers to the moderate fishing ship that had granted them passage. It was large enough to crew half a dozen men and could easily catch plenty of fish. The problem would be selling such a large supply to the small village of Alaro.

"Gladys'll take their orders, but who else in town?" Kevin asked.

"Dunno, do I?" Trevyn shrugged, trailing after his brothers down the docks.

"I'm hopeful Gladys will spread the word, maybe tell a few of the noble families in town," Iverson said.

"She don't know any nobles." Trevyn smirked.

"She knows their staff, which is far more important as they're the ones who make the food purchases," Kevin said, thinking that if nothing else, Taylor could be useful in spreading the word.

"Oh, right." Trevyn shrugged as he followed his brothers up the creaky ramp to the ship, shaking hands with the crew and thanking them for their generosity.

"Alright, so how long until we're home?" Trevyn's face brightened.

"*Home* is it?" Iverson nudged his brother, elbow to elbow. "We're from Vales, Trevy." He spoke slowly, as if trying to explain the sun to a small child. "Vales is our home."

"Hoist anchor!" a man shouted as the crewmen made the arrangements to set sail, and the brothers, used to doing the work themselves, jumped in to assist.

"My home," Trevyn grunted as he helped two crewmen pull back the lever for the mainsail, "is wherever I make it."

"Ah," Iverson sighed, letting out the ropes to free the side sails. "And you've made your home in Alaro, have you?"

"We all have," Kevin said as the brothers and the crewmen settled into the ordinary routine of setting sail on open waters.

Soft, ocean air breezed through the deck, and the brothers felt peace at the familiar steady rhythm that the waves of the Tilerian Sea offered her travelers. "Spend more time in port there than anywhere else."

"All I know," Iverson said, leaning against the bulwark, "is I'm ready for a hot meal, a warm bed, and a fresh start." He clapped a hand on each of his brothers' backs, letting his arms dangle around their shoulders, grinning into the sunrise. "Things are looking up, mates."

74

COLD. CORDELIA WAS COLD. AND DARK. IT WAS DARK. And quiet. So, so quiet. She listened intently but only heard the faintest whooshing. The wind howling in and out of the broken window frames of the lighthouse. The waves of the sea lapping the sands from far, far away. She blinked open her eyes.

She was lying on a chilled, rocky surface. The darkness around her was broken by tiny fragments of light entering through the spaces between crumbling rocks and broken walls. The ground beneath her body was sharp, piercing into her skin and sides. She rose to her feet slowly, pushing herself up and feeling a tightness in her shoulder.

Her head was heavy and tipping, and she was down again, this time on her hands and knees. She rose more slowly this time, allowing her head time to adjust. She took inventory of her body and her surroundings. There was a cut on her hairline and scratches and newly forming bruises all along her arms and torso. But for once, she had managed to avoid any serious injury.

Cordelia saw nothing but the rocks and jagged-edged spaces around her. The tiny fragments of light peeking in did little to illuminate the space. She had no idea how far she had fallen or where she was, just that she was somewhere beneath the rubble of the once glorious lighthouse. She didn't know how much time had passed, how long she had been unconscious. The light outside was orange and red, had she been here all day, or was it a mirage from some of the stained glass windows that gave the same colors as the sunset?

"Jaspar?" she called out, but no one answered. How far away was he? Would he be able to find her? What could she do but stand there? Wait and hope that Jaspar found his own strange way into... wherever this was.

She kept her hands outstretched, taking small steps forward, her ears hearing nothing but the distant ocean. She counted each footstep, channeling her fears into determination. Over a thousand heartbeats later, her hands collided with something solid and damp and hard.

She felt the surface, pushing with all her might, and it gave, just a little. There was the tiniest crack of light at the bottom of a giant stone, a small piece of the legendary lighthouse. The stone would not give or move under her weight. She sucked in a breath, trying to squeeze her body between the stone and the wall, seeking the tiny glow beneath her feet.

Behind the rock was a small room, and her eyes squinted in the suddenly brighter light. The light was coming from an opening above her, where the red sun was bursting through a large space that had once been the wall of the lighthouse. The red and pink shades of the setting sun lit the room with an unusual glow, and Cordelia fought back alarm. If the sun was setting, that meant she'd been unconscious for nearly five hours.

The room was empty but for a few crooked and broken framed art pieces, an overturned table, and a crumbling staircase that led to a caved-in roof. Cordelia allowed her fingers to graze the ancient paintings, so withered from age she could barely discern their previous state. One could have been a portrait of the lighthouse, perhaps, but she couldn't be sure.

She left the disillusioned paintings behind, examining the floors, stairs, and doorways. Beneath the stone steps was a small, wooden door hanging from its hinges. She approached it slowly, listening intently. It was only a half door, the kind that would lead to a servant's quarters or a small storage closet.

When she entered the room, the door closed behind her, and

she heard the tumbling of rocks from above. She wrapped her arms around her head, ducking, but nothing fell on her. Instead, the small light from beyond the door had weakened, and when Cordelia tried to open the door, she was met with great resistance. She cursed, realizing that she had trapped herself inside the tiny room.

She felt her breaths sharpen, knew panic and hyperventilation were mere seconds away. She thought of Jaspar, *her* Jaspar, and pictured him here. A hand on each of her shoulders. Breathing with her. In, one, two, three; out, one, two, three.

Palpitations slowly faded, and the feeling returned to her nose and lips. She opened her eyes, turned from the door, and entered the tiny space under the stairs. There was an empty fireplace, rocks and stones caving in the left side of what was once a mantle. Light trickled in through a crack in the rumbling roof above her. Was it big enough to climb through?

The room was lined with dusty bookshelves, a chair and rug rested in front of the fire, and there was a small desk between two of the bookshelves. It was as if someone had hidden a study underneath the lighthouse. Perhaps someone who used to work at the lighthouse slept here? But there was no indication of daily luxuries such as cooking utensils or a washing nook. Just books, and a chair and a table.

Cordelia squinted, shoving her face close to the walls. The small light did little to illuminate, and she worked hard to read the spines of the books, taking in the varied collection. Some were science, herbs, and apothecary. Some were magic, elemental, and potions. Some were history, maps, and ledgers. There were even a few literary choices, though she wasn't familiar with the narratives, just the authors.

Cordelia left the shelves behind, her fingers brushing dust from the desk. She let her eyes take in the room as she walked around, feeling the coldness of the stone, smelling the dust, listening to silence. She turned, her eyes landing on the chair opposite the once-lit fire, and screamed.

75

JASPAR HELD THE FIRE IN HIS HANDS ALOFT, KEEPING IT
close in case he needed the protection more than the light. It had
taken nearly half the afternoon to remove enough rocks to find his
way beneath the base of the lighthouse. He'd been stumbling
around beneath it for hours and had yet to find Cordelia.

He had no idea where she had fallen or where she was now.
He'd long since given up shouting her name. She could have hit
her head, she could be unconscious, she could be too far away to
hear. He refused to think of the other reason she may not be
answering his calls.

The distant sound of falling rocks caught his ears. A tiny patch
of light behind a large fallen stone. The stone wouldn't move
beneath his force. If he couldn't move the stone, there was no way
Cordelia could. But something was telling him to look, something
was pulling him beyond the giant brick, a hook in his chest leading
him forward.

There was the smallest gap between the stone and what
remained of the wall behind it, but Jaspar's shoulders couldn't fit
through. He climbed up the stones around him, forcing his way
through the slightly wider opening at the top, landing with a hard
impact on his ankles on the other side.

It was an atrium, or what was left of one. The long-lost elegance of the lighthouse was evident beneath the ruins of time. The frames that had once hung from the walls were tinted in sapphire and bronze. The caved-in windows still had remnants of the painted glass, surviving only by the plaster holding them on the windowsill. The crumbling staircase had been carved from the finest granite, and it still sparkled beneath the tiny rays of the setting sun and rising moon.

Beneath the staircase was an oak door, carved edges, with a gold handle. The door was blocked by rocks, but not dust, and Jaspar wondered if this was the tiny rockslide he'd heard before. He was close to leaving the empty room behind when he heard the most terrifying and gut-wrenching sound in his world: Cordelia's scream.

It had come from behind the blocked door under the stairs. He wrenched the rocks apart, shoving and prying. His fingers were still raw from digging his way under the lighthouse and the skin beneath his nails bled. Finally, they gave way, and he let them fall, ignoring the pain in his legs and feet as he kicked his way through the door.

He forced his way into the room, fire in his hand, fear in his chest, determination in his movements. It was nothing more than a study, probably belonging to the previous master of the lighthouse. Bookshelves, a dilapidated fireplace, a cushioned armchair, and...

"Cordelia."

Her face was contorted, half-moon eyes stretched with terror. She didn't seem to register he was even in the room with her. He was at her side, taking in the sight that had frightened her: a skeleton was in the chair, a mug of some forgotten and dried-out beverage in one hand. The clothes of several thousand years past hung from the bones, and the stench of death had long since left the air.

Jaspar wrapped an arm around her, both in seeking to soothe her and in feeling her solid form, knowing that she was there, reassuring himself that she was alive. Her arms didn't return the gesture, they hung limply at her sides. Her chest was still, she was barely breathing. He hugged her tightly and lifted her in his arms, carrying her to the other side of the room, as far from the chair and the body as he could manage.

He tried to set her on her feet but couldn't bring himself to let her go. He lowered them and sat on the cold, stone earth, Cordelia still in his arms. He let her rest in front of him, her body so rigid it didn't move even as he set her down.

"Cordelia." He brushed the hair out of her eyes. "Please." Her irises were on him, slowly receding the whites, her trembling lips sucking in oxygen until her whole body slumped forward. His arms caught her, pulling her to him and holding her tightly against his chest.

She was too in shock to cry or sob. He breathed her in, the feel of her in his arms, the smell of her in his lungs. Lavender and the sea salt of the ocean. He kept hold of her back, his hand spanning across her shoulders. He murmured into the crown of her head, "It's alright." His chin dropped, his lips chaste in her hair. "Just breathe."

Finally, she calmed and lifted her head. "You're here."

He nodded. "I'm here." He stroked her hair.

"Who was—"

"I don't know."

She brushed dust from his shoulder, and another touch of brushed fingers came to mind, one with snow and a shovel and his hand warm on the barstool behind her. He blinked his memory flashes away.

"Are you alright?" He peered into her face. Lines of worry were returning to her eyes, but she'd lost the wide pupils, and her irises had returned to the normal blue that had quickly become his favorite hue. She did what he so often saw: closed her eyes, pursed her lips, and completely hid her emotions behind a mask of apathy. Only now, he knew the contours of her face so well, her mask hid nothing.

She disentangled herself from him, his arms unwilling to let her go, following her as she slowly got to her feet. "What is this place?"

"If I had to guess, I'd say it was once the suite of the lighthouse master."

She wrapped her arms around herself, and he wanted to be there, wanted to hug her so she didn't have to hug herself. She started to move back into the room, but he pulled her back.

"Wait here." He searched under shelves and the chair and the desk until he finally found a trunk in the corner of the room, opening it to reveal several blankets inside, which he used to cover the skeleton. "Alright."

Her focus immediately went to the chair, but he saw her relax when she noticed the blanket instead of the body.

"Thank you. Do you know how to get out of here?"

"I uncovered the door."

She nodded.

"You're hurt." Her face flinched before his hand reached for her hairline, a small patch of blood had congealed her hair to her skin. He tipped her head, inspecting the cut, and flashes came back to him, another cut, another touch to her head, another time when he'd said those very same words.

She touched his hand, bringing him back to the moment, and he let the unexpected flashback fade away. They had been happening more and more frequently since their time at the festival. He wasn't sure what had brought them on. It could have been the revelation that she was once his beloved, or that they were fated to one another, or maybe it was that kiss, kisses...

"I've had much worse," Cordelia mused, and he let his hand fall from her wounded forehead.

He saw her tug her shirt sleeves down and run her hands up and down her biceps. The sun was long set, and the moon did very little to warm the night air. It was getting colder and colder, the air so chilled they could see their warm breath forming tiny puffs as they spoke.

She started to hug herself again, and he reached for her, the sense to comfort her a reflexive reaction of his body. But she was walking away from him, her eyes wandering around the room.

"If you want to leave, we can." He looked into the eyes of the woman who loved him, and though he couldn't remember a second of the time they had once spent together, he wanted to, desperately. Because he'd never been loved like this before, and Cordelia deserved to be loved back.

She shook her head. "We went through an awful lot of trouble to get here, may as well take a look around."

They began combing through the room. Pulling down books that seemed relevant or important, flipping through a desk full of letters, finding two talismans similar to the one Klingbeil made. An hour had passed, and they'd accumulated a stack of items to sift through, mostly books, letters, and notes.

"Is any of this even valuable?" Cordelia sorted through the papers, separating items into small piles. "How can we possibly tell?"

"You learn to look for keywords or symbols or anything that could resemble a map or a hint of the island of some kind."

"It's just a bunch of books and papers," she whined, tossing an old letter on a stack of twenty. Her eyes drifted to the blanket covering the skeleton in the chair. "Did he die hiding something? Protecting it?"

"I doubt it. Probably died in his sleep or during the quake that rocked the lighthouse," Jaspar scratched his neck. "Heart attack, a fallen stone to his head." He shrugged.

"Thank you for coming. You're much braver than I am. I almost feel foolish for reacting so harshly to the body, but it was just...I've never seen a...skeleton before. I suppose it was a bit of a shock."

"I've never seen one before either." He took a letter from her hand, helping her organize the books they'd gathered.

She tilted her head. "But when you came in, you barely even noticed."

"That's because when I came in, all I saw was—" He stopped himself. *You*, he'd almost said, *all I saw was you.*

"Was what?"

He let his eyes shift to the chair, unable to let his face reveal what his words could not, and he saw a small, carved shell. Barely there, but clearly intentional and unmatching any of the plain stones around them. Cordelia followed his eyes.

She fell to her knees, tracing the shape of the tiny shell. "It's like the one at Shell Cottage."

"The one where?"

"Oh. Nevermind."

She tried to pry at the shell, as if she could scratch it off the floor with her nails. Jaspar had originally thought the floor was made of earth and stone, nothing more than the rest of the lighthouse.

But Cordelia had seen what he had not: lines. A grid of lines and grooves all along the floor, like stones placed together. It had been crushed and evened so much that the centuries had practically left the ground smooth.

Jaspar plucked his knife from his boot and joined Cordelia on the floor. He dug into the rock, forcing it until it finally dusted and crumbled. The shell stayed intact, but the stone brick did not. Jaspar brushed the rocks and pebbles and dirt and revealed a small leather pouch, big enough to fit a grapefruit, and sewn onto the front was a symbol. A compass star overlaying an oval with undulating edges.

76

JASPAR HELD THE SURPRISINGLY LIGHT LEATHER POUCH in his palms, eager and hesitant to open it. What could be inside that was kept this hidden? Was it more than hidden? Is it possible there was a small booby trap that released when they opened the pouch.

On his first adventure with the captain. They had traveled to the edge of Scaparo and had discovered a small wooden box. They'd cut open the seal, and a brown powder had escaped, burning their hands and leaving their skin boiled for weeks. Could this pouch have a similar protection? Grief clung to him as he recalled the moment. It was when he'd first truly trusted the captain. And now he was gone.

"Jaspar." Cordelia's voice was unexpectedly strained. "We are not alone," she whispered, her jaw clenched tight. Jaspar listened intently, trying desperately to hear what she had, to sense what she had.

He touched a gentle finger to her elbow and kept his voice low. "Grab whatever you can and run."

Jaspar reached for a scroll, but before his fingers could wrap around it, the door behind them squeaked open. There stood four Sidons, the same that had hunted them in Keru when Cordelia had nearly sacrificed her whole body to protect him. He placed himself in front of her, wrapping her behind him and tucking the pouch in her hands.

He summoned a ball of fire, aimed and ready. But the Sidons just stood there, arrows notched and aimed.

"Hello again, Hagan," a slippery voice purred, and the violet-haired woman from before pushed through the Sidons, her spear tight in one hand at her side. "I had hoped you'd be here...Jaz." She smiled as the name left her lips, and Jaspar noted she didn't have the yellow and sharp teeth of a Sidon, but the simple canines of a human.

Jaspar swallowed, wishing he could silently communicate with Cordelia to hide the satchel. She remained quiet and still behind him, her heavy breathing the only indication of her fear. He wondered if she was recalling their last encounter when she'd suffered such brutal injuries. The memory of it brought fresh anger to Jaspar, and his orb of fire grew bigger.

"Come with us willingly, and no one will get hurt," the woman said.

"Over my dead body," Jaspar growled.

The female smiled again. "That won't be necessary."

Before Jaspar had time to react, the female Sidon took her spear and stabbed it into the earth beneath their feet. A fissure erupted from the pierce, and cracks fractured the ground as it shook.

The female cursed as Cordelia was thrown back and Jaspar fell below.

"Not him!" The female cursed, and Jaspar's hands found the edge of the fissure, clinging desperately. Cordelia screamed, and he didn't know if she'd been captured or hurt or killed.

He grunted and tried to pull himself up, but a sneering Sidon stomped on his fingers, and he lost his hold. The empty space below swallowed him, and he had just enough time to register the darkness before sharp pains of cold ice pierced his skin.

77

Jaspar slammed painfully into an underground lake, leaving a small hole in the iced-over surface. He floated quickly to the top, but the lake's frozen ceiling wouldn't give under his fists or feet. He reached for his knife, remembering too late that he'd left it above when they'd cut free the pouch.

The darkness was all around him, and he tried desperately to summon his magic, but fire didn't light underwater, and it was useless to him now. His chest clenched tight as he tried desperately not to inhale the icy water.

He pressed his body along the endless sheet of ice above him, searching for the hole where he'd fallen in. If he could just get a palm, a finger above the ice, he could melt his way free. But his body was heavy, his lungs were giving out. His arms and legs jerked, and then he felt his body still as it began to sink.

Jaspar had come close to death many times in his life. As a boy, when the great forest of Mikiria burned to ashes. As a teenager, when his first attempt at rock climbing had ended in a painful broken leg at the bottom of a precarious cliff. As a young man, when the captain had given him the antidote just moments after he'd accidentally taken a poisoned mug from a stranger at a pub.

But as the remaining air left his lungs and the fight in his body gave out, he wondered if this was the way to go. A strange sense of calm had come over him. He was very aware that he was drowning, that his body was in pain, that his lungs longed to fill with oxygen. And yet, all he thought of was Cordelia.

Her ocean-blue eyes full of love and wonder. Her beautiful smile full of life. Her sweet, lavender smell, soft touch, and the sound of her humming in his ears. He wasn't sure which flashes of her were memories or dreams, but they all blurred together into just the feeling of her.

Even now, he thought he could see her, in a brilliant blue light beneath the lake. Swimming closer to him, words turning to bubbles under the water. And he tried to speak to her, to tell her every thought left to him, every feeling left in his soul.

He would die, and she'd never know that he loved her. That the Jaspar of the past had loved her. That the Jaspar of the present loved her. That every version of Jaspar to ever exist would always love Cordelia Kimbal until the icy waters that trapped him froze his body, mind, and heart.

78

"No!" Cordelia screamed as Jaspar fell over the fissure and into nothingness. She tried desperately to wrench her arms free, but the Sidon's slippery grip was strong.

"You fool!" The female Sidon swiped her spear beneath the Sidon who had stomped on Jaspar's hand, and he fell into the fissure below, his scream growing quieter and quieter until it could be heard no more.

"Bring the girl!" the female Sidon screeched, her wild, dark eyes peering into the cavern below.

The Sidon holding Cordelia's left arm gave a pained groan and slunk to the floor, a bronzed dagger in his chest. Cordelia whipped her head around the space, searching for her rescuer. She heard the hiss of a sword unsheathing and then saw the sharp, bladed tip jutting from the stomach of her other Sidon captor.

With free arms and legs, Cordelia could finally escape, but fear kept her locked in place. A man, as cerulean blue as the Sidons were green, stood beside her. He wore navy-blue robes with the broach of a sea turtle and had a bronze shield in his hand. He yanked his sword free of the now-dead Sidon, wiping the yellow-colored blood on his cloak and aiming the sword at the half-Sidon, half-human woman.

"Celarestars," the female breathed, fear trembling her lips and voice.

The strange man beside Cordelia raised his sword to the violet-haired female, slicing into her left calf and releasing from within her a high shriek that reverberated around the crumbling room.

She pulled her spear back, arching it high and aiming it at the strangely blue man, piercing him in the thigh. As the two fought for purchase, Cordelia told her body to move, to run. She still held the heavy pouch in her hand, and she quickly tossed it over her neck, fastening it tightly to her bodice.

She felt around her, wondering if the ocean was too far for her to summon her magic. But she didn't feel the ocean. She felt cold, fresh water, somewhere beneath her feet.

She followed the feeling to the edge of the fissure that had swallowed Jaspar, and though she couldn't see it with her eyes, her magic let her sense the underground lake below them. She wasn't sure how far below, or if Jaspar could've survived the fall.

One of the cerulean men continued to fight the violet-haired Sidon, but the other was now approaching Cordelia. He reached a hand to her.

"Wait! Please do not leave." There was something oddly familiar about his relaxed accent. "You must come with us."

She looked from the man to his sword to the dark unknown below and walked off the edge.

79

THE LAKE WAS COLD BUT NOT UNCOMFORTABLE, AND she found that although she wasn't in the ocean, she could still move freely through the water. Her eyes searched for Jaspar in the dark and she bobbed for a moment, letting them adjust to the new lighting.

A strange spark in her chest pulled her down and to the left, and she saw Jaspar's limp body slowly sinking to the bottom of the lake. She reached him quickly, wrapping her hands around the chest of his blouse and dredging him up.

She separated the ice from the water with tiny droplets and created a small hole. When they broke through the surface of the lake, warm air cleared the goose bumps from her already dry skin. Jaspar remained unconscious and heavy. She worked hard to pull him free of the waters and dragged him off of the icy surface of the lake.

There was no shoreline at the edge of the lake, only mud and large cliff edges. She pulled Jaspar to the warm stone, and he rolled over, expelling water from within his lungs and breathing heavily. His eyes were bloodshot, and his skin had an unusual blue hue from the lake.

"Jaspar?"

He turned cautiously toward her, and slowly, his breathing began to even, and he reached a hand to hers. They sat for several moments, lowering their heart rates and letting the adrenaline subside.

"Any idea how they found us?" Jaspar finally asked.

"Which ones?"

Jaspar titled his head. "*Which ones?*"

"Oh, they must have appeared after you fell."

"Who appeared?" Jaspar's shoulders stiffened and he glanced around the small cave.

"I don't know what they were. They had bronzed weapons and blue robes, and their skin was..."

"What? Green?"

"No, not like the Sidons. It wasn't slimy, it almost shimmered. Like water sparkling in the moonlight. And their skin wasn't green, it was blue, cerulean blue."

Jaspar's hand touched a spot on his ribcage where she knew his mark was hidden beneath his shirt.

"What? What is it?"

"It's vague." He shook his head. "I thought I remembered something, but then it slipped away."

"Why are you touching your mark?" She nodded to where his hand still rested on his ribcage.

"What—oh." Jaspar looked down at his hand as if he hadn't noticed its location. He pulled his hand away slowly and looked it over.

"What? What is it?"

"Er. Nothing." He shook his head and very slowly got to his feet, reaching down to help Cordelia stand.

"Any idea where we are or how the hell to get out?"

"No."

"You saved it!" Jaspar pointed to Cordelia's chest. She looked down, remembering the pouch they'd found in the lighthouse.

"I'd nearly forgotten." She pulled out the pouch and heard the gasp from Jaspar when he saw that it was still dry.

"It better be worth it," Jaspar mumbled, and Cordelia tucked it back under her clothes.

"It's not our priority at the moment. We need to find a way out of here."

Jaspar tossed a ball of fire into the air, and they felt their way around the cave, searching until finally, Cordelia found a small opening between the rocks. It was narrow, so narrow they had to walk single file and Jaspar had to hunch over. But after climbing for several minutes, they'd found their way back to the beach.

The sun had long since set, and the moon was high in the sky alighting the shoreline and the lighthouse with a silvery glow. Jaspar kept his flame close by, and Cordelia kept her magic orb strong in her chest, but there was no hint of the Sidons or the strange cerulean men Cordelia had seen.

The small boat they'd acquired remained docked, seemingly untouched, and Cordelia couldn't help but feel a sense of false safety. There was no ship in sight; how had the Sidons gotten here? How had the strange cerulean men? Where were their vessels now?

"Do you think it's safe?"

Jaspar continued to search the grounds with his eyes. "For now, it looks like they've gone. But I won't be letting my guard down anytime soon."

"Nor I."

"I don't know who those men were, Cordelia. But if they were looking for us, they'll be back."

80

HER NIGHTDRESS DID LITTLE TO KEEP HER WARM AS THE cold, winter air swirled around the boat, rocking it back and forth. Jaspar lay not far from her, his breathing measured, even. One hand behind his head, the blanket rested just below his shoulders, his palm on his chest, fingers splayed out.

They'd sailed for hours, Jaspar wanting to get as far away from the toll as possible. The lighthouse had remained in sight for nearly a day before Jaspar finally dropped anchor. Exhausted, they'd laid down for bed almost immediately, only Cordelia remained awake.

Her mind spun, keeping sleep far away. She was still apprehensive of falling asleep without knowing where the Sidons and the strange blue men were. She wondered about the pouch, which they had decided to open in the morning so that Jaspar could have ample light and time to check for any safeguards it might have.

But it wasn't just thoughts of attackers and strange men and mysterious pouches that kept her awake. It was Jaspar. Her mind kept drifting back to the time and space before the Sidons and the strange men and the lake. She thought of the way he had held her. His arms tight around her, like he couldn't let her go. His chaste kiss in her hair, a reflex he couldn't control. His steady breathing calming her, pulling her back from panic.

She felt the blanket jerk beneath her and saw Jaspar toss a lazy hand in the air and a fire burned above them, floating and warming the space. He lifted his arm, wrapping it around her, pulling her into him.

"I can't sleep with all of your teeth chattering and shivering." His face was unreadable, his tone apathetic.

His body was warm around her cold skin, so gentle and familiar it was painful to be there. Painful and yet everything she'd ever wanted. Her body refused to stop shivering, and Jaspar wrapped the blanket tighter around them. He turned to his side, their legs tangled together, his arms so broad they wrapped all the way around her. She was so close she could smell him, driftwood and sea salt and something sweet.

"Are you scared?"

Scared? Yes. But she knew he was referring to the Sidons and the strange men and the skeleton in the lighthouse. She nodded into his chest, and he let his chin rest on the crown of her head.

"I'm not going to." His sigh tickled the tendrils of her hair. "I'm not going to let anything happen to you."

She nodded again. "Does it ever feel impossible? I know you don't like that word, but it just," she sighed. "I've only been living this life for a few months, and it's already taking a toll on me. How have you done it all these years?"

His shoulders shrugged, and she slipped closer, his arm wrapping tighter around her back. "I don't know. I guess I don't know any difference. It's been this way my whole life."

She thought of those four months in Alaro, months when she knew Jaz, but Jaspar still lingered. Had he continued to search the world for clues even while staying at the inn? How much of his time there had he spent hours looking for the island?

"In some ways, it feels like the island is closer than it's ever been. And in the others, it seems like I'll just never quite get there."

His head shifted, and she pulled away to meet his gaze. There was something hesitant in the way he spoke. "I never really thought of another life until I met you."

She bit her lip. "But does it matter if you can't remember it?"

"No, it's not that at all. I don't *need* to remember it."

They sat up and he let his eyes linger in hers for one moment too long before releasing her. She was no longer shaking, no longer shivering, her body warmed by him and the fire.

"I may never remember those four months. And I may never know how you grew to trust and care for me. But I think..." He let his voice trail off, shifting on his leg, letting his eyes flick to the fire. Cordelia kept her gaze on him, and when he turned to face her, she saw a glimpse of the Jaspar she'd first met in Alaro. Kind and honest but guarded.

His eyes turned back to her, his expression curious. "I'm starting to see it now."

"See what?"

His hand touched her before she was ready, fingers tracing her jawline before twirling in her hair just once. "How he fell in love with you."

81

JASPAR MOVED SLOWLY, GIVING HER AMPLE TIME TO
pull away, but she wanted this as much as he did. He wrapped an
arm around her waist and moved himself closer to her. Cordelia's
hand was light on his bicep, and he could sense the slightest
tremble.

He leaned in, breathing in her scent, and let his lips touch hers.
Soft, slow, a brush of skin to skin. But when she didn't pull away,
he kissed her again, letting himself get lost in the moment.

It felt like their first kiss, even though it wasn't. But when
Jaspar had let his lips touch hers, that strange spark had reignited,
but anew. There was no attempt at breaking a spell. No hidden
agenda. It was simply born of desire. And it wasn't the first kiss,
but it was better.

It was easy, natural. When her fingers glided into his hair, and
his arms wrapped tight around her, and he felt her warm him
inside and out. Like thawing his deepest fears with just her touch,
her very presence.

Their kisses before he'd been hopeful for the return of his
memories, almost willing them into existence, only to be distracted
from that goal by the intoxication of her. They paused, for one
moment, their foreheads touching, but when she breathed his
name, he pulled her close once more.

Cordelia sighed, but in a resigned way, in a way that made him

306

feel as if she hated the walls between them. She'd been holding back, he knew, for weeks. Fearful of what to reveal and when and how. And he'd selfishly been obsessed with his own loss, with the fact that his memories were gone. He hadn't given enough attention to how this had hurt her.

Her breathing hitched and her lips tightened on his, the tiniest of nips, the sensation sent a thrill through him. A thrill that mingled with feelings he'd never had, with possibilities he'd never considered. This was a level of affection, of devotion, he never thought he'd experience.

Her fingers tightened in his hair, and he pulled her even closer, until she was nearly in his lap. His hands were in her dress, on her thigh, touching any part of her he could. Once, he was afraid of any human contact, and now he needed her skin to skin so much he craved it.

The boat rocked, a wave crashing in, and Cordelia was pulled from his grasp by the cruelty of gravity. Cordelia's eyes met his, and he hated the sadness he saw there. Her expression cleared almost instantly, hiding her emotions with the grace of someone who'd spent years growing up in a society where they had no place.

"Cordelia..." But he didn't have any words for what he was feeling, because he'd never felt it before. Then again, maybe he had; he just didn't remember.

She shifted, pulling further from him, and his arms lingered around her waist, wanting to bring her back. She lifted his left arm, placed a chaste kiss on his palm, and then returned it to his lap. And he knew what she was going to say.

That they should get sleep, that they should rest and prepare for the next leg of their journey. He could see it in her eyes and thought maybe the kiss meant something different to her. For him, this was all so new, but did she feel like she was kissing a ghost? Is that why she pulled away?

He wondered if this was born of self-preservation, like she wanted to hold onto the old Jaspar, the one who remembered her. But the person he was now had grown to care for her, as well. Could that be enough?

He reluctantly let her go and she laid down with her back to him. His gaze lingered on her, watching her chest rise and fall with each breath as she drifted to sleep. His heart still raced, and a desire he hadn't prepared for clutched at the recesses of his mind.

He'd never known...love like that of what Cordelia gave him. And it was something new, something he desperately craved but had never been willing to allow himself to dream of. But he wanted to dream of her, to wake up with her, to feel her in his arms every day. He didn't need to have those four months back to tell him what his heart already knew.

Cordelia was his, and he was hers. And this was what forever and happiness and perfection felt like. And as dreams overtook his thoughts, the taste of her lingered on his lips, and the feel of her lingered in his mind.

82

"THIS IS IMPOSSIBLE." JASPAR THREW HIS HANDS UP, nearly knocking over the table. They'd taken refuge at a hotel on the shorelines of Vales, eager to bathe and rest after nearly a week on the boat.

"Improbable." Cordelia smiled to herself, twirling a tiny scrap of parchment in her hand. It was one of many that were scattered on the table around them. They sat by the fire, letting the sunlight creep through the windows. It was nearly nightfall, and it'd taken them two days to reach dry land. Jaspar had been adamant about being on stable ground before opening the satchel, so fearful of booby traps and safeguards.

But the pouch had opened with ease, revealing nothing but dozens of tiny pieces of shredded parchment.

"That really only applies to things that exist, not things that can't be done." They'd made no mentions of their kiss or their conversation from two nights' past. It was as if neither had happened, and Cordelia had done well to keep her distance. Only her thoughts were safe, he need never know she still wanted him as long as she could let him have peace.

"Patience." Cordelia let herself be smug as she lined up the parchment with another fragment.

"While you're enjoying your little puzzle game." Jaspar's

fingers touched her temple, tucking back the hair that had curtained her face, "don't forget to eat."

She ignored the tingle left behind by his touch, gently pulling away. She had kept her promise to herself, to put distance between them, to accept that he'd never love her again. But he seemed incapable of staying away from her. She took the offered bread, grateful to eat something other than fish.

"This map is of the cliffside, I think."

She tore her eyes from her parchment puzzle, blinking them into focus after staring intently for so long. "Which map?"

Jaspar brought the atlas he'd purchased from the local bibliognost over to her. She leaned over his bicep to inspect the small, smudged map.

"How can you possibly tell?"

His lip twitched into the barest of smiles. "I love that you can see a picture in scraps of paper but can't see through a smudgy map."

She told herself to ignore the choice of words, that the word *love* meant nothing to him and far too much to her.

"This edge here." He pointed along the jagged line on the bottom right corner of the page. "That's where we are. And the lighthouse is here." He pointed just beyond the line of trees on the map. "And the other side of the cliff." He wrapped an arm around her back, pulling her in and putting the map between them. Then he pointed across the page where a blurry circle had been painted on in dark, maroon ink. The map faded off, almost like the maker had stopped sketching it. "This is where we need to go."

"Into nothing?" she deadpanned.

"You have other plans, do you, Lady Cordelia? Off to a party or a dance? Perhaps young Russel sent you an invitation to supper with her highness?"

She rolled her eyes, returning to her fractured parchment. Her breath caught in her chest. She tilted her head, taking in the shapes, the shadows, the image before her. From this new angle, she could see the likeness of the drawing she hadn't before.

"Cordelia?" Jaspar's palm was warm on her elbow. She lunged at the table, her hip crashing into the wood in a painful impact.

But she hardly noticed, throwing pieces together, shoving them into place with clumsy, trembling fingers until, miraculously, they all formed one single picture.

"Is that..." She felt the heat of Jaspar's words behind her, felt him lean over her shoulder, taking in the same sight as her.

"Yes." She nodded, her voice nothing more than air from her lips. "I think that's my mother."

83

TIME FELT SUSPENDED AS CORDELIA ABSORBED AN image so reminiscent it felt burned in her mind. It was like looking in a strange, foggy mirror. Dark curls, pale skin, brilliantly bright blue eyes. A tattoo, a mark, a compass star with a heart pierced by a trident. Cordelia's mark was hidden behind her ear, but her mother's was on her chest, centered in the middle of her collarbone.

Cordelia traced the lines of the mark, charcoal smoothing, paper crinkling, the image growing clearer and sharper in her mind. The more she looked at it, the more the woman reminded her of Hygonia. But then again, they were twins. Cordelia had never seen herself when looking at Hygonia, but this shredded sketching of her mother felt like a distorted reflection; there was so much of herself in the face that stared back at her.

"She looks like me," Cordelia squinted at her mother's face. "Except that she's..."

"Not nearly as remarkable." Jaspar's voice was objective, completely dry. He could have been saying the ocean was wet, the night sky had stars. "And your mark is much smaller and better concealed." He brushed her curls back, scrutinizing the tiny compass behind her ear as if reminding himself it was there. Her skin warmed under his touch and his fingers slowly left her hair.

"Do you think your greatest grandfather drew this?"

"Who else?" Jaspar circled the table in the limited space of their small room, inspecting their pieced-together puzzle from every angle. He paused, tilted his head, touched a space beyond her mother's hair.

"Map." He thrust his hand across the table, and Cordelia handed him the map he'd just shared. He turned it in his hands, flipping it upside down. He laid it next to her mother's hair, and Cordelia gasped.

The lines of her mother's hair formed a perfect edge with the map, curvy, jagged, and just a little askew. Where the circle connected with the image of her mother, there was now a bluff. Not just a cliff, but a mountain, one that shot into the sky and across the continent. It was north, or northeast, and the terrain on the map was jagged, uneven.

"It's the Eiran Mountains."

"In northern Vales?"

"Yes." Jaspar's mood had changed. He was now hurriedly gathering their things, packing them away, tucking the books and papers and journals into their newly purchased satchels.

"Have you ever been?" he asked.

"No."

"Well, you're going now." He took in the image of her mother, quickly cataloging it into his mind, clearly identifying each individual paper, before sweeping them back into the pouch.

"Jaz!" Cordelia lunged forward, but he stopped her effortlessly with a hand on her hip.

"We have to go, you can piece it back together later."

"It's the middle of the night." Cordelia yearned to see the image of her mother again, ripping the pouch from Jaspar and clutching it tightly.

"I know we can't leave right this second." He took the pouch from her hands, tossing it on the table and leaning back against the fireplace mantel. "But we should still plan to leave early."

"Fine."

"Fine." He crossed his arms over his chest and relaxed his shoulders. She wanted nothing more than to walk forward, to step into him, to feel his arms unfold and fold again with her in his chest. But instead, she reached for the pouch, tossing it on her cot.

Jaspar continued to pack their things and tidy the room. By morning, they'd be able to wake and leave before the sun rose. She laid down, letting her eyes stare out the window at the moon, her adrenaline far too spiked for sleep.

Jaspar snapped his fingers, dimming the fire before laying on his own cot. "It'll be a long walk. And a lot of hiking."

Cordelia feigned a yawn and watched Jaspar's cheek dimple. "That's the first time I've seen my mother. I didn't realize the resemblance."

"You do look *a little* like her." Jaspar nodded, lifting his arm behind his head.

"It feels like a foggy mirror."

"No, you're much..." He pursed his lips. "There are differences."

"Such as?" She scoffed.

He turned to face her. "Your hair," his hand brushed a tendril by her temple, "there's a shine to it, especially in the moonlight. And your...lips are fuller." His eyes dropped to her mouth, his finger trailing down her jawline. "And your eyes...there's no color in existence to compare to the blue of your eyes." He brushed her lash with his thumb.

Her lip trembled, tremors reverberating from everywhere his skin had met hers. She swallowed her longing, feigning a stretch to hide her desperate need to separate from him.

"I need to ask you something." He reached for her hands, rotating them so that the scars on the backs showed in the dim moonlight. "I've been wondering where these came from. And then, the other night, I had a dream of me wrapping your hands on the docks. And I thought maybe it's like before." He squeezed his eyes shut. "I thought maybe they weren't dreams. They were memories."

84

Jaspar inhaled sharply, his tongue dry. He'd been certain just days ago that what he felt for Cordelia was love, but doubt had quickly crept its way into his mind. What if his feelings were motivated by the fear of death? What if it wasn't love? What if it was the soulfate bond? What if it was residual feelings from before he'd lost his memories?

Cordelia lifted her head, propping it up with her hand. "Was it like the dreams you described before?"

He nodded. He let his mind fill with the disjointed images of his sleepless thoughts. "But also...random flashes. Little slices of time. Like something I'm observing or feeling but not doing."

"Do you want to tell me about them?"

"I want to know if they're *genuine*. Will you know? If it was a dream or a memory?"

She sat up on her cot, pulling the covers around her shoulders. "Maybe."

He sat up, and flickers of his visions, both the dreams and the déjà vu, came back to him.

"I was sick, a fever, I think, and you were there. You made me laugh and sang me to sleep. That was when I...kissed you, right?" He bent his head, questioning, curious. He thought of the feeling from the dream, of his lips grazing the skin of her palm, of the

315

happiness and trepidation the dream Jaspar had felt from the tiny moment of intimacy.

"You had a fever. I stayed at your bedside for two days." Her voice held nothing but conviction.

"And we were...together then? We were...fated souls or whatever?"

She fought back a smile. "We've always been soulfates, but no, we weren't *together* then."

"But you took care of me anyway?"

"Yes."

He wanted to ask why, but he wasn't ready to hear the answer. "And by the docks, your hands were bandaged, and you were crying." She lifted her arm in the light, and he saw the tiny scars on her fingers and the back of her hands.

"I had injured myself shucking oysters and you had tended to my wounds."

"But we weren't together then either?"

"No, we'd only just met then." She inhaled sharply.

"But I helped you. I...took care of you?" The words pained him. Hadn't he taken care of her several times in the past two months? Hadn't they taken care of each other? But this somehow felt different. This other Jaspar didn't have the knowledge of lost memories. Had he simply grown to care for her on his own?

"Is that hard to believe? That you would care for someone?"

He pulled his legs up, refusing to allow the thought to cloud his mind. "I was...crying, under a tree."

"Yes. You were grieving a lost friend. It wasn't until later I realized it was my father."

Guilt clutched his chest. He'd barely had time to register the death of the captain. It still felt like any day, he'd receive a letter with plans for their next adventure. For the first time in his life, he fully understood why people had funerals and services: the living needed to see the dead, or they'd never accept the loss.

"What else?" Cordelia pulled her legs to her chest, resting her chin on her knees. He'd learned that she sat like this when she was feeling particularly vulnerable, a way of hugging herself, of holding herself together.

"We were in a bar, a tavern, I think. And you had a bump on your head, and I whispered something."

She hid her warm cheeks behind her knees. "Perfect."

"What?"

"I was worried about how the bump looked. And you said I was perfect. I don't think you meant for me to hear you." Her voice was reedy, like the words were so fragile they'd whither when they left her mouth.

"We were by the fire at the cay, and I bowed my head to you, I kissed your hand."

A tear spilled down her cheek, she didn't wipe it away, but he saw her throat bob with the controlled effort to fight back the rest of her sobs. "You had made a promise to me...a vow."

He was almost afraid to ask. Hadn't she before said they weren't married? That they weren't betrothed? What then could he have promised her? "What kind of vow?"

She shook her head and pursed her lips. "Need-to-know, Jaspar, need-to-know."

"I *do* need to know!" His shoulders went stiff, his head bowing lower to hers, eyes fixed without wavering. "I've never made a vow to anyone. Well, except—"

"Your family."

He recalled the captain and what Cordelia had said of his letters. He didn't remember vowing to protect her, but he'd made that vow to the captain all the same. The only vow in his living memory was the one to follow the curse, to find the island, to dedicate his life to its discovery. "What did I promise you, Cordelia?"

She bit her lip and blinked her eyes, soft, slow tears soaking into her skin. "That I would always come first."

His forehead creased. "First? First how?" When she didn't answer, he reached for her, but she jerked away, out of his grasp. "Cordelia?"

He saw it then, the moment when she took back control. She closed her eyes, took two deep breaths, and her face cleared, neutral once more.

Her voice didn't falter, but was clear, strong. "Before the island, before the legacy of your family, before the curse."

Jaspar couldn't help the pang of jealousy he felt for this other version of himself. The version that was so loved and cared for. The version that had all of these little moments of pure joy. The version that made the most beautiful woman in the world blush with one word. The version that would promise his life and soul to another person.

"You'd planned on giving up this life." She let her hand circle the room. "No more traveling, no more searching for clues, no more running."

He heard his own sharp intake of breath and felt his body slump under the weight of her words.

"But I didn't want you to give it up. So, instead, I promised that I would dedicate my life to helping you. And you promised never to care more about the island than me."

"I said that?" There was no denying his disbelief.

"You promised on your life."

"Is that how we fell in love?"

Cordelia pulled her head back, letting her knees fall. "I don't know. I can't speak for you. For him."

"But for you?"

"Yes, I think...I think it was...so many moments of togetherness, that you started to feel like another piece of me."

His chest pulled across the space between them, an invisible string linking him to her. "How did you know?"

"That I loved you?"

Jaspar shook his head, sitting up and facing her. "How did you know that *I* loved *you*?"

"Well, to be fair, you didn't actually confess such a thing."

"And yet you knew? You were certain."

She nodded. "It was...little things, a lot of little things. But you weren't..." She pouted her lips, looking away.

"What?"

"You didn't exactly hide your affection, from me or others."

He drew back. "I didn't?"

"I think it wasn't really a matter of how it was just... inevitable." She shrugged.

"Because of the soulfate thing?"

She shook her head. "Because of us. We were just...because of us."

He tilted his head down to hers. "But why did you care about me so much?"

She shook her head, bewildered. "You think so little of yourself?"

"No." He frowned. "But...I'm trying to understand how much of...whatever we had was because of this soul bond."

"You're kind...generous and thoughtful, and you were there for me at a time when I didn't realize how badly I needed a friend."

"How so?"

"You believed in me, even when we'd just met, and you found me annoying and thought I complained too much." She smiled at some fond memory he'd lost. "I was insecure, and you encouraged me to prove myself to everyone, to know that I could do what others never thought I could, what I myself even feared I couldn't. You cared for me when careless mistakes had left me injured.

"We were both attentive, even from the very beginning. We shared a grief, a loss, and even though we didn't realize we were grieving the same man, it was comforting to go through it together."

She bit her lip, and he nodded, urging her to continue, to share more. "You made me feel cherished, cared for. And with you, I felt loved. You never said it, but it was there in your actions."

"And now?"

"Now what?" Her brows lifted. "Now do I still love you?"

He nodded once.

Cordelia tilted her head to his, moving the tiniest fraction closer. She stayed silent for so long he almost asked again, but finally, when she spoke, her voice was shallow once more, as if she couldn't hold on to her façade of apathy. "Yes, Jaspar. I still love you."

"Me or the me you remembered?" He rejected the notion they were the same person. How could they be when everything he learned about the other Jaspar seemed so distant to him?

"Both. Not just who you were before, but who you are now and every day for as long as forever." She yawned, rubbing her eyes.

"And...why did I care about you?"

She flinched, and he cursed his own name. "I'm sorry, that was crass."

"It's alright." But he heard the pain she held back. "This must be so strange for you. Hearing about your life and feelings from another person."

"You're great, you are. And I do see you as my..." He stumbled over the right word. Friend wasn't strong enough, but what other word could he use? "My companion, now that we've spent so much time together."

"But, when you say that I loved you...I wonder how much of my affection before had been because of the convenience. Not the soulfate anomaly, but because you were there, and you remembered me. It sounds crude, I know, but I'm just trying to make sense of everything."

"You wore the talisman for months, Jaspar. You could have loved any woman in that bar."

"But I loved you." He saw her wince a little at the words.

"We bring out the best in each other," she said finally.

"Like back at the bunker?"

"What do you mean?"

"You always knew what to say and when to say it. You sort of... kept me grounded. You reminded me when my brain got lost on a track it couldn't follow, making sense out of my chaotic thoughts, even when I couldn't."

"Hm."

"I could see how that kind of...friendship would be important to me, but...it doesn't sound like love." And it was nothing compared to the emotions he felt for her now.

"No." Cordelia blinked back tears. "I suppose not."

He had more questions, more thoughts, but he could hardly organize them into words, and remorse needled him at the pain his words had caused her.

"Sorry. I should probably let you sleep."

She nodded, biting her lip and wiping her tear-stained cheeks.

"Thank you. For answering my questions." He wanted to apologize for hurting her, for upsetting her and making her cry, but his hurt hadn't been intentional, and he felt the words hollow in his throat.

She nodded and rolled over, her back facing him, hiding her face and her pain.

"Cordelia?"

But she didn't answer, and after several heartbeats, he realized she had fallen asleep. He closed his eyes, but when he finally drifted to sleep, it was with a heavy heart and a strained mind.

85

Jaspar was certain his legs would fall off if he took one more step. His feet were made of heavy, leaden bricks, his lungs nothing more than empty sacks in his chest. But Cordelia hadn't complained even once, and he didn't want to bring her momentum down with his.

They'd walked to the very edge of the map, where the Eiran Mountains stood tallest in the world. They'd been on foot for five miles when they finally reached the cliff, and even Jaspar's determination was starting to falter. A rock dislodged itself beneath his foot and he slipped, his knees slamming into the jagged mountain.

"Alright," Cordelia panted, helping him rise back to his feet. "What exactly are we looking for here?" She planted her hands on her hips, squinting in the sun and letting her eyes scan the mountain. Jaspar tried to center himself, focusing only on the beauty before him.

The indigo sky held few clouds, allowing the sun to paint the view with brilliant shades of gold and orange. The water's edge was in sight, drifting along the endless horizon. Trees and foliage littered the base of the mountain, the usually green and lush landscape hidden beneath winter snow. Birds flew high in the sky, small drops of color among the blue ocean waves sparkled in the setting sunlight, and yet all he saw was her.

Jaspar straightened, brushing dust from his pants. He

inspected the map once more, noting the small circle shape. Cordelia snatched the map from him, nearly ripping it in half.

"What? What did you see?"

She turned the paper, slowly spinning it in her hands. She looked above, beyond the mountain, her eyes searching. "What if it's a cave?"

"Huh?"

"Look." She pointed directly to the circle shape, then turned it on its side and folded the paper just slightly so that the circle became an oval. "What if it isn't something that was circled on the map. What if someone was *adding* a cave?"

Before he could answer her, the ground trembled; it was slight at first, so small Jaspar wondered if he'd imagined it, but then it shuddered again. The uneven, stone surface beneath his feet weakened, Cordelia barely caught the mountain to hold herself up. An earthquake was attacking the mountain, shaking the trees and rocks loose.

Jaspar caged Cordelia, hiding her between himself and the mountain as rocks tumbled down the side. Dust flew around them, coating their eyes and hair, and Jaspar closed his mouth to the taste of dirt and sand. The mountain shifted so loud he could barely hear his own breathing.

He pushed Cordelia back onto the side of the mountain, his chin on her head, anchoring himself to her, an arm on either side of her head. Cordelia clutched his shirt, her fists wrapping in the chest of his blouse. And then it stopped. The ground was steady, firm beneath their feet. Pebbles tumbled down the side of the mountain, slow and lazy, as if no longer urgent.

Something cold pulsed in his veins. Jaspar lifted his head, the earth coming back into focus, his world solid and safe in his arms. Her face was covered in dust, her eyes wide, her shoulders taut. He exhaled all of his panic.

Her hair was soft under his lips, and he felt her body relax as he drew her closer, hugging her tightly. He had just enough time to breathe her in before the earthquake shook the mountain once more.

86

Cordelia felt Jaspar's hot breath on her shoulder as his hair tickled her cheek. The mountain around them shook, but he stayed firm, solid, protectively wrapped around her. Over the sound of falling rocks was a strange wail. Not quite a roar, though just as loud, and not quite a howl, though just as high. The earth steadied as the quake dissipated.

"Bolter," Jaspar grunted.

"Bolter?"

Jaspar pulled twigs from her hair, and she wiped the dust off his brow.

"Slide Rock Bolter. It's a type of whale."

"I don't know how to tell you this, but we're on a mountain!"

Jaspar laughed, a full and real laugh, the first she'd heard in weeks. "It looks like a whale, and sounds like a whale, but it's a land creature."

"And let me guess, its natural habitat is mountain ranges?"

"Come on."

She let him lead as they made their way farther up the path, climbing the mountain higher and higher. The beast let out another strange, roaring howl, the ground shaking. Jaspar stopped, his eyes unfocused. "It's over there!" He pointed northeast and started to climb in that direction.

"What? What do you mean *it's over there*?" She chased after him, clutching the skirt of her dress in her hands.

"Come on, we're losing it!"

"Why in the name of Mikiria are we *chasing* it?" Her voice echoed off the rocks around them.

"Do you want to find the island?"

"Not if it means getting crushed and eaten by a mountain whale!"

"Bolter." He stopped again, listening to the howling creature and turning further east.

"Jaspar, this is lunacy! There's no way I'm—" Her words were drowned out by a scream so shrill her ears hurt.

Not more than two hundred yards to their right was a cloud of swirling, falling dust, forced out by the giant, leather-skinned whale sliding down the mountain.

Cordelia stopped breathing. The Bolter was so disturbing and so unique, she couldn't help but stare. Dry, green leather skin wrapped around a body so girthy it was wider than the Anchorage Inn's entire length. The beast was so long it spanned at least fifty yards, its underbelly edged by lines of grappling, hooked claws.

It roared again, revealing rows and rows and rows of dagger-sharp black teeth. Its eyes were so sunken in Cordelia could see no irises, only the carvings of where the eyes should be and a hooded temple.

"Come on, I'll explain later!" When she didn't move, Jaspar bent down, wrapping his arms around her legs.

"No!" she screamed, but he picked her up anyway, grunting under her weight but running up the mountain. He made it twenty feet before depositing her on the ground again. Cordelia watched in abject horror as the swirling dust settled and the whale turned, slithering like a monstrous, blundering snake. The whale howled, cocking its neckless head to the sun before climbing back up the peak.

Each hooked claw dug into the earth as it crawled up the rocky mountainside. The beast shook the ground beneath each clawed grip, the sun glittering off its scaly skin.

"Cordelia!" The pain in Jaspar's voice was so like him, the *him* she remembered, the him that cared so deeply for her, that it pulled her eyes. "Can you walk or not?" Unable to speak, her mouth dry and her throat silent, she nodded her head.

They climbed high, running, panting, and forcing their bodies to move faster than they normally would. The beast was almost up the mountain, but so were they. Finally, Jaspar stopped climbing, rushing toward the beast as it continued to climb. They were thirty yards away from the whale, but it didn't notice them. It slithered into the largest cavern Cordelia had ever seen, a thousand feet in diameter at least. The ground tremored again, another howl echoed, and then the beast was flying down the side of the mountain once more.

87

"Is it later yet?" Cordelia asked as she followed Jaspar into complete darkness. He gripped her arm a little tighter. The cave was quiet, and they'd walked deep enough that the sounds of the beast and its afternoon fun of sliding down the mountain were almost out of earshot, the tunnel suppressing noise from the outside. Cordelia had been counting her breaths and steps, a way to try and center herself. But she lost track after the first five hundred.

Jaspar stopped, and his hand fell from her arm. A small orb of fire lit the tunnel, and Jaspar tossed it in the air so that it floated above them. He started to walk down the cave, Cordelia and the tiny ball of flame trailing after him. "That was a Slide Rock Bolter. They're land whales that live on mountains and cliffs, and they're rather fond of goats, birds, and, as their name suggests, sliding down the mountainside."

Cordelia caught up and her breath hitched, still winded from the climb. "And why are we roaming around its cave?"

"It's the one from the map," he said with conviction.

"Are you sure?"

"It makes perfect sense. Their caves are miles long and burrow from one side of the mountain to the other."

"You mean, we'll walk through this cave, and at the end—"

"We'll be the other side, yes."

"But what about when the bolter comes back?"

"Do you see how big this cave is?" He held his arms out around him. "Even if it shows up, we've got plenty of space to press into the wall and wait for it to slide by." Jaspar continued to walk without a care in the world. It was almost a scene from another life, the buoyance in his step, the carefree expression on his face.

"Cordelia, do you have another plan?"

~

"I don't believe you." Cordelia laughed, the sound echoing off the walls of the cave.

"It's true! Your father had me hanging on by my literal fingers. I swear he took his time just to add suspense."

"He wasn't that dramatic." Cordelia shook her head.

"Oh, but he was. And..." Jaspar rolled a sleeve on his arm, showing her his elbow. "I have the scars to prove it!"

They'd been walking for nearly six hours, trading stories about the life he'd forgotten in Alaro and his adventures with her father. How they'd once been trapped in a vaulted chamber, only to discover the iron bars lifted easily. Another time, they'd been sure they'd found an undiscovered toll, only to arrive in the middle of the ocean with nothing around them for miles and miles. And this time, of how they walked through another bolter cave and the ground had given out, Jaspar had fallen through, and her father had been the one to save him, to pull him back.

"I wish I could have seen him like that, could have gone on adventures with him." She fought back the urge to cry. "I'll never get that time back."

"I never got to see him the way you did," Jaspar admitted. "He was fun on an adventure, sure, but he never let his guard down, not fully. And neither did I. There was always a seriousness to him, a determination."

"Yes." She smiled fondly.

"Huh." He shrugged.

"What?"

"I figured at home he would have been calmer. I always thought it was the danger that kept him guarded."

Cordelia shook her head. "No, he was always that way."

"I was guarded too, though," Jaspar admitted, looking ahead as they walked.

"More so than now?" she chided but he stopped, his expression serious.

"I'm never guarded with you, Cordelia, even when I try to be."

"Oh." She wished she knew how to respond, hadn't he been guarded these past two months? "Are you sure?" She smiled but knew the teasing wasn't real.

He shrugged and started walking again. "I'd never have gotten a night's sleep around you if I was."

A strange silence overcame them as they both remembered the captain, both the man they knew and the man they'd heard stories of. Cordelia had shared tales of her childhood with Jaspar, and though her stories were about treasure maps and hidden trinkets, he hung on her every word. Perhaps they were both missing the captain, and it was nice to think of him, to talk of him, without the sadness of grief. It wasn't that she no longer mourned her father, rather, it was his memories were becoming fond, instead of haunted.

"Cordelia..." Jaspar's voice was soft, uncertain. She wiped her eyes and lifted her head. In her distraction, they'd reached the edge of the cave.

"Are we..." She lost her breath, taking in the large rock wall in front of her. She tapped it, shoved it, pushed her entire body into the stone. She turned back to Jaspar, his eyes wide.

"Jaspar, are we trapped here?"

88

"NOT THAT I'M NOT HAPPY TO SEE YOU BOYS SAFE, BUT we *were* hoping you'd bring Delia when you came back." Gladys poured a round of whiskey for the three returned brothers, Kevin, Trevyn, and Iverson. Trevyn watched the door, bouncing on his feet.

"We never saw her. At least you got a letter." Kevin pointed at Gladys as he and Iverson found two empty stools in the crowded bar and Taylor vacated his seat for an anxious Trevyn. Taylor took two strides and stood behind Gladys, recalling the feel of her in the empty space between them.

He saw her back stiffen, but she otherwise gave no indication he was there. "Important thing is the three of you are safe and made it back here. What's next for you boys? Find another ship?"

"Eventually, though it will cost us plenty of coin." Iverson sipped his whiskey.

"You boys stay as long as you like, you can pay me back when you get coin and help out around here until you do," Gladys said.

"Thank you, Gladys." Kevin sipped his whiskey as Trevyn continued to stare at the door, as if willing it to open.

"We should have been here, Gladys." Iverson hung his head. "What happened with the Sidons..."

The mention of the bottom feeders' attack brought Taylor's

blood to the surface. He had come very close to losing Gladys that day, and any time it was mentioned, he felt the same as he did at that moment: like there was no world he could live in without her in it.

"That's admirable of you, but she's well protected." Taylor's voice sounded oddly possessive, but it wasn't a lie. It was the reason he was at the bar tonight in the first place. It had been tormenting, trying to return to work, worried about what was happening at the bar in his absence, worried about her.

He'd only lasted three days before he'd handed in his resignation, packed a bag, and demanded a room in exchange for work. Gladys was hesitant, skeptical, but she had conceded. Every day, he spent at the bar keeping her safe, and every night, he slept in the next room, guarding her from afar. It had been the most blissful form of torture, to be so close to the woman he loved and yet still so far removed.

"Any idea what they wanted?" Iverson asked.

"No. But they haven't returned, so they must have found whatever or whoever they were looking for." Gladys shrugged, but Diarmuid huffed behind the bar, carrying trays of sausage and bread.

"What?"

"Got nothing do with that. It's cause Taylor went rogue on their asses. They'd be dead fools to come back here." There was a peculiar, shared pride between Taylor and Diarmuid, more gratitude from Taylor that his everything remained safe and whole, but he'd deduced that Diarmuid liked the excitement after so many years in the kitchen.

"Should we look for Delia?" Kevin asked, helping himself to the sausage Diarmuid had delivered.

"Here, you may read it," Taylor said, handing over the agonizingly short letter from Delia.

> *My dearest family,*
> *I'm sorry I haven't written to you sooner.*
> *I cannot tell you particulars of where I am or what I am doing, but please know that I am safe.*

I love and miss you all terribly, but I can't come home. Not yet.

I've found a piece of my father again, a way for me to hold on to him, and I can't bear to let it go.

All my love,
Delia

"Not very detailed, is it?" Kevin grumbled.

"We know she is safe, but that is of little comfort," Taylor said. "It would ease a great burden from us if she were home." Gladys went breathless at the word *us,* and he wondered if it carried too much weight, if he shouldn't have spoken for both of them.

Gladys crooked her neck and Taylor leaned in, auburn hair filling his sense. "Wonder what she's off doing, though." Her sultry whisper nearly did him in, but he remained the calm, moderate man he'd worked so hard to be in her presence.

"We'll get her back soon enough." He let his knuckles linger by her hip for one single beat of his heart. The door creaked open, and a startled Trevyn nearly fell from his stool.

The young blacksmith had few expressions and even fewer words, but the crease between his eyes smoothed, and Trevyn stood on shaky legs. Taylor removed his gaze; he'd always been unable to watch the intimacy of another couple. Perhaps it was his bitter heart, the longing that he never got to have such moments of his own.

Gladys abruptly dropped her apron, disappearing behind the swinging kitchen door.

"Er, hello there," Trevyn said, cheeks as red as his hair.

"Hello." Marcel nodded his head back.

"Pardon me," Taylor said curtly before following after the woman he loved.

89

"Gladi?" Taylor knocked again on her door, raising his voice, though he knew she could hear him.

Far too many seconds passed, and Taylor's knuckles were raised to knock again when she finally pulled open the door.

She wasn't crying, she rarely did, but he could see the glimmer of something deep in her fierce eyes. "I'm fine, Taylor."

He followed her in, closing the door behind him. She sat on her bed, the plaid quilt wrinkling just slightly. But for once, his eyes weren't lingering on her. They were focused on the painting hanging opposite her bed. From this angle, the painting would be the first thing she saw every morning and the last thing she saw every night.

He took careful steps, letting his fingers touch the bumpy, painted canvas. A simple cottage home with a white fence and lavender trees in the yard.

"After all these years..." Taylor let his voice trail off.

"Yes." Her voice was close. In his distracted state, he hadn't noticed her leave the bed. Now, she stood just behind him, staring at the painting of the home he'd once planned to build for them. His eyes found hers, and she took two steps back.

Three strides and a turnabout the room, and he was there before her. She backed away until she bumped the wall behind her.

She remained silent, staring at something on Taylor's clavicle.

He looked down to see the small scar barely visible under the crook of his shirt. The scar was from the war, as so many of his scars were.

"That could have been us down there." Gladys inched forward. "All those years ago, that should have been us. You should have walked in the door, and my world would have stopped, and you'd embrace me." Her hands lingered in the space above his biceps, but skin never met skin. "I shouldn't have let you leave. We could have had so much time together."

Taylor looked at the woman he'd loved for thirty years, examined her every feature. Wrinkles of time had creased her radiant eyes, years of laughter framed her full lips, wisps of silver streaked her brilliantly auburn hair. But she was every bit as breathtaking as she'd been at nineteen.

"All this time." His timbre was low, like gravel trapped in his windpipe. "I've never loved anyone but you."

Space suffocated around them, his knee pushing her legs and backing her into the wall. He bowed his head, letting her catch her breath, giving her the chance to push him away. Her grip was tight on the sleeves of his shirt, and he breathed her in, when she crooned his name, her lips dangerously close to his, Taylor knew there was no turning back.

90

AFTER MONTHS AWAY FROM HOME, AND MONTHS AWAY from their second home of Alaro, Iverson was ready to settle down for several days. The shipwreck had cost them everything, but he was beyond grateful that he still had his brothers. And weeks in Keru kept them from earning real wages or attempting to get a new ship. But now, they could forge a plan.

Gladys had given them each a room in exchange for work at the inn, and he settled into the one down the hall. He was hoping they could find work in Alaro, save coin, and someday earn enough to buy a new ship and head back onto the waters. Kevin had ideas of taking out a loan, but Iverson doubted the credit of a Velshian would do them much good in Mikiria. And Trevyn didn't seem to mind one way or the other, so long as they promised not to leave Alaro.

Iverson stretched his back, clicking the door closed behind him. He lit the fire and unpacked his rucksack. He was fumbling with his jacket when a button popped off the sleeve and rolled under the dresser. He scoffed before lowering himself to the ground and reaching around under the drawers, aimlessly hoping to retrieve the tiny button. But his hand found something else.

It was hard, and the texture felt like canvas or maybe old leather, a book? He reached further under the chest of drawers until he could fully grip the mysterious object. He sat with his back leaned onto the mattress, examining his find.

It appeared to be an old black journal made of dyed leather. He wondered whose room this had been before his. He flipped absently through the pages and was debating whether he should return the journal to Gladys when a name inside caught his eye. *Cordelia*.

Cordelia's room had remained untouched at the end of the hall since she'd left. Gladys refused to check it out to any guest and refused to move any of her belongings, convinced that at some point, the girl would come home. Who would have once stayed in Iverson's room that would have a journal about Cordelia?

Iverson dismissed his discomfort at reading someone else's private thoughts, his curiosity getting the better of him, and flipped to the first page. He didn't recognize the handwriting, but it was easy to tell who had written in the book after just a few sentences of reading. Iverson had grown up on the waters and was not the most gifted reader, so he read aloud quietly to himself, taking his time on each word.

Cordelia will forever be cherished, if not by me, then by others. But I fear her mother will come for her someday, and I may not be there to protect her when the time comes. Though I do not know his name or identity, I know the man, the demon, who seeks her will never give up, not until he has what he wants. Jaspar will keep her safe for me, if I ask that of him, and so will my trusted friends in Alaro. But my brave daughter may need more.

I've made arrangements to travel to Scaparo and seek out a true guardian for Cordelia. I've never had much use for them in the past, but I am confident that their binding vows will prevent them from revealing any secrets of my daughter.

Iverson flipped through a few more pages, curious why the lost captain's daughter would be in any danger, but much of what he saw were similar vague entries, or logistics about someplace the captain was searching for.

He yawned, stretched, and decided the book could wait until after a long night's rest. But when he tossed the book on his dresser, it fell to the ground, cracking the spine and splitting the seam. It remained held together by the ropes and pages, and Iverson examined the pieces, trying to determine how to mend it.

His mouth parted, his curious mind spinning. Along the back binding of the book, where the pages should have been sealed, was a peeling paper. Iverson flipped a knife from his boot and cut at the book's bindings, revealing two pages that had been hidden, tucked into the book's spine.

He pulled them out gently, anticipation in his heart. He shouldn't be reading the captain's secret journal, nor should he be reading a hidden message locked inside it. And yet...

> *My suspicions are correct! It is a truly Eureka moment for me. Jaspar is the answer, the solution to all of my problems. He has no idea he is a Celarestar, that he was born to guard the island, that his marked skin and protective nature are natural instincts from thousands of years of guardianship.*

An unusual but familiar symbol was etched next to this passage, and Iverson touched a hand to his underarm in wonder.

> *I have always been a believer in destiny, in fate, and how could I not be now? When the greatest grandson of the cursed captain turns out to be a born guardian of the very island he's been hunting for generations! He must be the one to break the curse, I am most certain of it. And he will surely protect my Cordelia once he learns how invaluable she is.*

I believe fate brought my baby girl to me on the waves of the sea, and fate brought Jaspar into my life on the waves of the sea, and now fate will ensure my daughter and my only friend are safe by the waves of the sea! If only I am lucky enough to find my end of days out at sea, then the ocean will truly have gifted me the most incredible of lives.

But there is so much I still do not know, so much I will need to plan! I must see Jaspar, must invite him to join me as I search for this last protection. I've read passages of an enchanter, a powerful one, I'm hoping he will help me. Perhaps he can place a shield charm on Cordelia, one that will outlive my life charm once I am gone.

I have made plans with Taylor to keep Cordelia in Alaro for the foreseeable future, not that she often ventures out of her home, but just until I can ensure her safety. The enchanter travels a great deal, and he goes by many names, many aliases. But how am I to find the right man?

"Good evening." The voice that interrupted Iverson's thoughts was cold, deadly, and came from the shadows of the night. Hadn't he closed his door when he entered the room? And yet now, it stood ajar, and a tall, foreboding darkness filled the doorway. "I think, young fishermen, the captain wasss looking for me."

91

"Ivy? Are you up yet?" Kevin rapped on the door, confused that he was awake before his usually early-rising brother. It was well past sunrise, and though he wanted to let his brothers rest after months of traveling and working, he felt too much sleep was a waste of the day, and they could rest more after a hard day's work.

A door creaked at the end of the hall and Trevyn's head popped out, his brown mane slick wet from bathing, a ribbon on his wrist.

"Morning." Trevyn yawned, buttoning his blouse.

"Late night?" Kevin lifted a brow, and Trevyn's cheeks blushed, but he didn't respond to his brother's goading.

Kevin met Trevyn in the middle of the hall, not wanting to shout too loudly and wake the other guests of the inn. "Gladys said there are a few townsmen looking for builders. They're erecting a new schoolhouse by the fields. Could be good work for us."

"Yeah, alright." Trevyn yawned again, running a hand through his wet hair and brushing his fingers through his long locks. "Long project?"

"A few months." Kevin shrugged. "I doubt it will be enough for a ship, but we'll be able to pay for our lodgings and start setting aside more coin. I know Gladys said we could work for our rooms, but she can't need that much help that it would pay for all three of us."

"Yeah, I don't want to impose either." Trevyn wrapped his ribbon around his hair, tightening it at the back of his head. Beside his dapper younger brother, Kevin felt unruly with his bushy beard and thick mane. He halfheartedly patted his coarse hair but gave up quickly when it stayed much the same shape.

"Better wake up sleeping beauty and get started," Trevyn said. "I'd like a nice breakfast before we walk halfway across town and lift lumber all day." Trevyn flattened his blouse, and Kevin followed him back down the hall.

"Not visiting the blacksmith today?" Kevin tried to sound singsong, like Iverson when he teased their youngest brother, but he didn't have the same gentleness in his gruff voice, and it came out more aggressive than he had meant it to.

Trevyn, to his good nature, laughed it off. "Better wake up Iverson before you make a fool of yourself," he smirked.

Kevin rapped gently at the door again, but Trevyn nudged him aside.

"Ivy!" Trevyn shouted.

"Will you hush!" Kevin shoved his brother.

"What?"

"Do you want to wake the whole village?"

"What do I care? It's after sunrise, most people are awake anyhow." Trevyn shrugged and pushed past his brother. He pounded on the door, and it creaked open, revealing an empty room.

The brothers stepped cautiously inside. The bed and mattress were shredded, the reed stuffing pulled out. The drapes on the window were ripped and hanging haphazardly from their hooks. Candles had been overturned, melted wax leaving long trails along the carpeted rug. The dresser was on its side, drawers pulled out and turned upside down, their contents littering the room. The mirror on the wall had been broken, and there were shards of glass scattered across the floor.

"Kevin..." Trevyn's voice had grown soft, and Kevin detected the fear in his young brother's eyes. Trevyn sank to his knees, inspecting a poker stick for the stove heater. It lay haphazardly on the earth by the fire, surrounded by shards of glass from the broken window, the sharpened point covered in dark, sticky scarlet red. A pool of blood lay beside the poker and red drops lead a pathway across the floor, the bed, and along the sill of the window.

"What's all this shouting about?" Diarmuid demanded as he kicked open the door with his cane. "You could wake up..." The grumpy man's voice trailed off as he took in the scene, his eyes scanning the room and then the brothers.

"What the—"

"He's gone." Trevyn's voice cracked slightly, and Kevin felt his chest constrict with the realization weighing on them. "Iverson is gone."

92

"IT'S A MAZE," JASPAR SAID, AND HE SCANNED THE TOPS of the tall rocks, realizing they were a formation, an intentional layout and design.

"I was never very good at those," Jaspar admitted.

"I've never been in one, so we're about to find out if I'm any good either." The ground trembled, and somewhere on the other side of the mountain, the bolter was sliding down the side with glee, its howls just barely audible from this distance.

Jaspar took a stance in front of Cordelia, a fireball in one hand and a knife in the other. "Stay close."

The space was tight, merely ten feet wide, and the farther they walked, the stone pillars that blocked them started to obstruct all noise and light. The path twisted and curved so many times Jaspar lost his sense of direction. They could be heading north or east or west or south, he had no idea. He longed for the stars of the night sky to give him guidance, but nightfall was hours away.

"How will we know which one to take?" Cordelia asked, peering down each pathway at the first fork in their path.

"We won't, not until we reach a dead end and have to trace our steps back."

"We could split up, I'll take the left, and you'll take—"

"No. I'm not leaving you," Jaspar said. She looked as if she wanted to argue but must have thought better of it. "We'll go left."

"Because?"

"Because...instincts." He turned the corner, and she followed him, and on and on it went. It wasn't just the path that made the maze difficult to navigate. There were sounds, like the sawing and grinding of rocks, and he could swear, at one point, he heard crying. Cordelia was convinced a bird whistled somewhere in their midst, and the temperature changed drastically from hot to cold, depending on which pathway they walked down. The ground was inconsistent, muddy down one path, stone down another, or sand.

Twice, they ran into dead ends and had to trace their steps back. Each new pathway was twisted and winding and confusing. When they reached a new fork, this one with four pathways available, Jaspar grew frustrated. There was no way to turn back now, no way to give up on the maze and simply try another path. They were trapped here, and who knew how many hours had passed, who knew what time it was?

"What was that?" Cordelia whispered.

"What? I didn't hear anything."

She closed her eyes. "It was like a...slither, a snake maybe?"

"A *mountain* snake?"

"Oh, but a mountain *whale* is perfectly acceptable?"

He rolled his eyes and fought back a smirk. "A *bolter*, and yes. Snakes would freeze up here, they live at the bottom where they can burrow and keep warm."

She spun in a circle. "There it is again!"

"Cordelia—"

"I know what I heard and—" Her words were cut off by a scream as she dropped to her chest, her chin smacking into the ground with a sickening crunch.

Jaspar looked down to see a monstrous serpent, twenty feet in length and at least three in diameter.

"Jörmungandr." He barely believed it to be real, and yet the terrifying mythical monster was before him, slithering away with Cordelia tight in its grasp. But how was it on the mountain when it lived far beneath the sea? And why was it wrapped tight around Cordelia's ankle and pulling her, yanking her away with alarming speed?

"Cordelia!" He ran after her, hurling fire at the snake, but it was hard to avoid hitting Cordelia in the process. The blackened body of the serpent seemed to know its way around the maze, and it navigated each twist and turn with ease, and within three corners, it had disappeared from sight. Cordelia's screams grew quieter and quieter, farther and farther away.

Jaspar ran through the maze, dead end after dead end forcing him to retrace his steps. His heart raced, fear pumping adrenaline throughout his entire body. Hours passed, the sun slowly falling lower and lower in the sky, and he had not found Cordelia.

He tried to break through the rocks, to climb to the top of the thirty-foot stone pillars, eager to see above the maze and beyond. But it was no use, Cordelia was gone, and Jaspar was no closer to finding her than he was to finding that damned island.

93

HYGONIA COCKED HER HEAD AT THE UNFAMILIAR BIRD caw that did not belong to her Frân.

"Fågel?"

The bird was a near-identical twin to hers, except for whitened eyes. She hadn't seen him in decades, and she felt her heart race. She was terrified of what the bird could mean, but also eager with anticipation.

The door squeaked open, and several men entered, all with translucent, cerulean skin and long locks. They wore navy-blue robes with a silver sea turtle pendant, and each carried a bronze sword with ocean waves engraved in the hilt. She should be distrusting of them, uncertain if they were Celarestars who supported her sister, or those who opposed her. But the presence of her sister's bird, Fågel, reassured her.

"Is she here?" Hygonia asked before the men could speak. A tall Celarestar approached Hygonia and bowed deeply, his voice thickly accented.

"No, Your Majesty. We have been ordered to take you home, it is not safe here."

"What of Cordelia?"

"Others have been assigned to her highness; they are seeking her now." He stayed bowed, and Hygonia tapped a finger to each of his shoulders.

"You may rise, brave protector. I would like to wait for Cordelia. Surely Bygonia would understand—"

"You will come with us, now, please." The Celarestar looked pained at having to interrupt and contradict her. "Our instructions were very clear."

Another Celarestar stepped forward, dropping to his knees and bowing his head. He held out a scroll of kelp. Hygonia ripped the scroll from his hands, eagerly devouring the words of her isolated sister, her heart sinking.

"Will Cordelia be alright?" Hygonia's fear for her own safety was small compared to that of her concern for her niece.

"Our bravest guardians have been dispatched and will bring her home quickly. We live to serve." The cerulean men all touched their hands to their temples and bowed their heads.

"Very well, very well." She whistled, loud and high, and Frân and Fågel flew to her side, each landing on a shoulder. "You will join us," she told Fågel, and the great bird nodded. She reached a hand behind her, and Frân took a step to her finger.

"I can trust no one more than I trust you," she whispered. "Will you go to her? Please ensure that the Celarestars bring her safely home?" Frân cawed, nipping her hand before soaring through the opened door and beyond.

Hygonia didn't carry any belongings with her, as a demigoddess, she had very little need for earthly possessions. Instead, she wrapped an orchid-inspired cloak tight around her shoulders and donned a pair of dandelion gloves.

"How are we traveling?" She followed the Celarestars to the street, noticing empty pathways. They shuffled quickly into The Woodvale Forest, keeping to the shadows, the many trees and plants comforting Hygonia as she thought of seeing her twin again for the first time in centuries.

"Our gateway rests in the local harbor, if we leave now, we will arrive there no later than—"

Hygonia heard a whistle on the wind and the young Celarestar stalled in his steps, blood gurgling slowly from his lips. He clutched the arrow in his chest, his eyes widening. He seized the demigoddess' hands, falling to his knees, uttering one word with his dying breath.

"Run."

94

THE CELARESTARS SURROUNDED HER, A CIRCLE OF strength ready to fight, whomever should attack. Arrows flew from every direction, clanging against metal as they bounced off the shields of her protectors. She couldn't see where the arrows flew from, the woods and many flowers surrounding her cottage concealed her enemies.

Hygonia didn't need the trees to reveal her attackers, she knew only one who would dare hunt her, and only one whose minions used arrows and bows as weapons. She clenched her teeth, her mind working, her body growing tight with fury. Hygonia pulled every rooted plant and tree she could, encircling herself and her remaining protectors, praying that Janus would focus only on her and leave her peaceful village safe and untouched.

The arrows suddenly stopped, but Hygonia didn't let down her plant stronghold and the Celarestars kept their shields raised. She grunted as thousands of piercing knives bled through her entire body. The Sidons were cutting through her many trees and vines and plants, each blade of the knife like a cut to her own skin.

Soon, the plants and trees were retreating, returning to the earth and dirt they'd come from. Hygonia swayed on her feet, the invisible scars left by the Sidon attack draining her vitality. Her head felt heavy, and she wished she could heal herself, that her powers would be stronger, could be stronger.

As a demigoddess, she should be far more formidable than a mere sorcerer, but she could feel something thick inside her. Something unrecognizable was blocking her magic. She fought through it the best she could, but the plants around her slowly started to recede, retreating back to their homes in the dirt.

The arrows flew once more, but her Celarestars were prepared, once again lifting their shields to create a barrier around her. Arrows flew beneath the shields, knocking men down by their legs and feet. They stood as tall and powerful as they could, and Hygonia reached out to each of them, healing them with her magic, but it was a slower process than it should have been. Her magic was weak, barely there at all. And she struggled to heal the men as fast as the arrows were flying.

She heard a cough, followed by another and another until the men chorused with hacking around her. She felt her nostrils burn, her throat tighten. Smoke, charcoal black, and laced crimson red billowed from the ground up, like a rising fog of deadly vapors. One by one, the men surrounding her dropped, the smoke suffocating them beyond their ability to breathe.

Arrows flew again, now taking to the skies, a caw screeched above. Hygonia saw with great pain as Fågel spiraled down from the sky, landing in a lifeless heap at her feet. Tears came to her eyes as she channeled her healing magic, but the bird was already dead, an arrow speared through his tiny heart.

Hygonia lifted her skirts, ready to run as fast and as far as she could, but a hand pulled her back by her long hair.

"Now, now, my sssweet flower, I'm just getting sssstarted."

95

THE VOICE WAS LIKE A HISSING GROWL IN HYGONIA'S ear, a heated breath on her neck, burning into her flesh. Something cold and heavy dropped over her neck, metal burning as it hit her chest. She smelled her hair, singeing from his grasp around it, and jerked with her weight and force, yanking herself free, leaving behind feet of her hair that Janus had burned off.

He was even worse than she remembered. His skin was so sickly it was practically ashen gray, as if he were made of the dust and coals from his many fires. The smell of sulfur hung around him, accompanied by a deadly cloud of smoke.

She called her powers, ready to use every plant in the forest at her disposal, but nothing came to her.

"Yesss." His voice slithered as he walked by her and whispered in her ear. "Very ussseful. I am most eager to tessst it on your beloved twin."

Her eyes fell to the talisman around her neck. It was shaped like a Jörmungandr and made of a strange, red metal. "How did you—"

"Klingbeil...taught me a few new tricksss." His voice slithered out like a snake.

Her heart sank. "You killed him."

"Don't be ssso melodramatic." Janus snapped his fingers, and a Sidon slunk forward, dragging the old theurgist behind him. He

350

dropped what was left of Klingbeil at Hygonia's feet. His eyes were unfocused, his body unmoving, his chest barely rising and falling. His skin sagged on his bones, as if pulled tight and stretched out.

"What have you done..." Her voice had lost its commanding force. She channeled the plants around her, the earth beneath her feet, the air in the sky. But nothing came, no magic, no power, no ability to heal.

"It'sss entirely futile. I have blocked your magic beyond even your capabilitiesss." Janus smiled, a sludgy, black liquid blood trickling from his mouth. He wiped it on his sleeve, turning away from her.

"What do you want?"

"Oh, come now, my sssweet flower, we're far passst that. Sssurely you can be at no losssss why I am here." He clasped his hands behind his back, glaring down at Hygonia. Despite being exceptionally taller than the average human, Janus still stood at least a foot taller than her.

She turned her face into an expression of tranquility and ignored Janus's taunting.

"Asss you know, I've been working for centuriesss to clear my good name."

Hygonia scoffed and a rage of fire shot from Janus, burning the grass by her feet. She stepped back from the burning, and Janus growled, his expression sneering in fury.

"Don't you dare. You have no idea how much I have sssuffered."

"Not nearly enough," she spat, and a flame shot from his hand to her face. Had her powers been present, she could have deflected such an attack with ease, but the talisman made her vulnerable. The flames hit her square in the chest, and she staggered back, nearly losing her footing.

"Your filthy twin left me to rot in eternal ruin and shame, leaving my dessscendantsss with a curssse that made each and every one of them ussselesss. Generation after generation of disssap-pointment. Ssso imagine my sssurprisse when I dissscovered that my contemporaneousss grandsson, my only living progeny, wasss the fated love of none other than the daughter of the very demon I'd ssspent centuriesss hunting."

Hygonia spat at his face. "She is not a demon."

His monstrous hand slapped down on her face so hard it dropped her to her knees. The forest floor shook and trembled as she fell, and a blind fury escaped her lips in a snarl.

"She'sss asss evil and foul asss you are, and sssoon she'll under-ssstand the full extent of my wrath. Centuriesss of ruin will devour that island if it isss the last thing I do." He smiled, wide and wicked, more black sludge dripping from his sharpened teeth.

"And I'll be damned if Jasssspar and his little Danthem witch find it before I do."

Hygonia rose to her feet, fisting her hands at her sides, forcing her shoulders to stiffen. She prayed the other Celarestars were more successful, that they had taken Cordelia and protected her, that they were returning her home safely at this very moment.

"You know of the prophecy." The words had escaped her before she could stop them, the sheer terror and shock pulling them from her.

"Yessss." He rounded on her, as if to strike her again. His voice turned to a dangerous, deadly whisper. "I heard the pretty poem that sssaid Jasssspar isss to be the death of me. But what that little prognosssticator didn't know wasss how ssstrong I would become, how indessstructible. No one, *no one*, will be the death of me. I will live forever, and that little pyromaniac will burn with hisss sssodden witch."

Janus snapped his fingers, smoke flickering around his hand. Two Sidons came forward, carrying a small boy with dark, cropped hair and fair skin.

Hygonia felt new disgust and hatred, more than she thought she was capable of, at the idea that he had kidnapped a child. She inspected the child closer, the tiny vial in his hand. "No..." She shook her head, summoning powers that wouldn't come.

"Yessss." Janus ripped the bottle from the boy and several Sidons were on Hygonia in an instant. They grabbed every part of her body they could, pinning her down. She worked hard to keep her mouth closed tight, even biting the hands that tried to pry them open.

"Enough." Janus gripped her mouth, ripping her jaw until she heard a sickening crack. The liquid was surprisingly sweet on her tongue, but the bitterness of defeat felt like venom. Janus had sunk to a new low, using the child of a guardian to create the serum of truth, a potion so powerful even she could not resist it.

"Now, my sssweet, sssweet flower." Janus snapped his fingers, and the many Sidons gripping Hygonia released her. "You're going to tell me absssolutely everything, ssstarting with the location of that forsssaken isssland."

96

WATER DRIPPED ON IVERSON'S CHEEK, THE SMELL OF mildew pungent in his nostrils. He opened heavy eyes, crusted from hours of unconsciousness. The hard earth beneath him was made of stone, as were three of the walls that surrounded him.

"Hello?" His croaky voice echoed back to him. A large iron gate enclosed the three stone walls, trapping him in a ten-by-ten large cell. He had nothing more than a bucket of water, a bedpan, and a holey blanket.

Where was he? How long had he been here? How had he gotten here? It came back in intense flashes. The demon attempting to capture him, Iverson fighting him off, the demon shredding the room until he finally hooked Iverson in the gut with the poker from the fire. That was his last recollection before waking up here. He supposed he was lucky to be alive after such a stabbing, but it was hard to appreciate that at the moment.

"Hello?" he called again to no avail. In the distance, there was a hall with sconces lit and he looked up to see the dripping water from the ceiling. There were three other cells opposite him, and he'd guess one on either side.

He held his heavy head in his hand, searching his mind for how he arrived in this strange dungeon.

"The handsome prince awakens," a girlish voice called, and he blinked open his eyes. A beautiful woman with deep, gray eyes and violet hair approached Iverson in his cell.

"Sorry to have brought you here so roughly." She reached a slim arm through the bars and handed him a wet cloth that smelled like lemons and wood. She gestured to his arms, where dozens of deep cuts latticed his skin.

"Where am I?" he asked.

The woman smiled and handed him a small shot glass of whiskey. "For the pain."

He nodded and took it with relish before wincing as the cold, witch-hazel-soaked cloth touched his wounded skin.

"What's your name?"

"Iverson."

She smiled and bowed her head once. "Alaria."

"Er, nice to meet you. Mind telling me why you've locked me up?"

She pouted. "I didn't lock you up."

"Who—"

"That would be me," the demonic voice from before thundered down the hall. "Alaria, ssstop playing with the human; we have work to do."

The man was tall, dark, foreboding, like the violence of a fire brought to life in human form. Though Iverson wasn't sure the man was human.

Behind him, the man dragged what looked to be an enormous and bloody flower, but as the shape came closer and closer, Iversons' stomach churned. It was a woman. The most beautiful woman he had ever seen, with soft features and hair in every shade of the rainbow, even now covered in mud and blood, it shined.

"What have you done to her?" Iverson gripped the bars in his hands. He felt inexplicably protective of the flowery creature, who seemed far too incredible to have been so beaten down.

The demon did not answer, instead tossing the woman into the cell beside him like a wilted flower.

"Miss?" Iverson asked the silence, but the woman remained unconscious.

"She is of none of your concern." The demon turned red eyes on Iverson.

"Alaria, now!" he shouted, and fear marred the purple-haired woman's lovely features as she hurried after him. "My grandssson and hisss little witch are waiting for usss."

"What are you?" Iverson dared to ask, and the demon gave a gleeful, eerie smile.

The man sparked an orb of fire, hurling it at the cell wall. Iverson held his arms to catch the burn, shielding his face. The fire seared his flesh, the smell of it burning in the stale air.

The demon lowered himself, reached a stony hand through the bars, and pulled Iverson up by the chest of his shirt. His voice was low, deadly. "I am the sssecond coming of Epiales."

97

CORDELIA FELT THE SHARP SURFACE OF THE MOUNTAIN rip through her skin as she was dragged along the stony ground. The serpent was long, slimy, and the dark-green color of seaweed. It gripped her ankle so tight she'd lost all feeling in her foot.

Jaspar's screams had long lost earshot, and all that could be heard was the slithering of the snake and the grunting of Cordelia as she tried desperately to wriggle herself free, but to no avail. She kept her head tilted up and to the side, avoiding scraping her face or mouth along the ground. The snake rounded corners fast and hard, her body jerking with each swift turn. She was nearly on the verge of passing out when her suffering finally came to a blissful stop.

She slowly opened her eyes, first the left, then the right. The snake lay motionless on the ground, its body slowly relaxing and uncoiling from around her legs. Cordelia's eyes traveled up to a Sidon, yielding a sword, the snake lay in two pieces at his feet. She stumbled, screamed, called her magic, but there was no water on the rocky mountain.

She was in a clearing, several pathways leading in different directions in a large circle. The center of the clearing was a sundial, golden in the light of the setting sun. But as she looked around, she realized it wasn't a circle; it was an oval. Each pathway that led out of the clearing was perfectly placed, so that entire clearing resembled the symbol that marked Jaspar as a cursed man.

"There is no need to fear us," the Sidon said, and as he stepped into the sunlight, Cordelia realized he wasn't a Sidon. His skin was tan and cerulean, and his cloak was a deep blue, like the depths of the ocean. On his lapel was a similar pendant to the Sidons, only his was bronze, not coral, and bore the resemblance of a turtle instead of a Jörmungandr. Were these the same men who had confronted Cordelia beneath the lighthouse?

"Who...are you?"

The man bowed his head, and Cordelia saw scarred lines covering the length of each side of his neck. No, not scars: gills. "We are here to escort you home."

"Home...I'm not going home." Why would she go back to Alaro with these strange men? And who were they?

"I'm afraid it is a matter of life and death, Princess."

She pointed a finger to her chest. "Princess...?"

A faint voice echoed around them, bouncing off the walls of the stony maze. "Jaspar?" She turned her head in all directions. Which pathway had she entered through? Her name was heard again, louder this time, and her heart raced faster until finally she saw him.

He rushed out of a corridor far to the left, nearly a quarter kilometer from where she stood in the middle of the giant clearing. Their gazes met, and she saw his wander around the scene. He ran to her, a ball of fire hovering in his hand.

She moved to meet him, but the cerulean man grabbed an arm and held her back. "Unhand me!" She yanked and pulled, but his grip did not loosen.

Jaspar arrived, panting and angry. The cerulean men bowed a curt head but otherwise gave no indication he was there. She tried to pull away again, but their grip was too strong.

"Who are you? What do you want?" she asked, but Jaspar's voice was louder.

"Let her go, now." His fiery orb hung above them, and she wondered why he had not used it yet.

"We will not let her go, brave protector. We have come to take her home."

"No one is taking me anywhere!" Cordelia screamed and stamped her heel into the strange man's foot, hard, but he didn't budge. Jaspar hurled his fire at the man holding Cordelia, but a shield appeared, the fire bouncing off and soaring back to Jaspar, who snuffed it out instantly.

"It is not safe here. You must come with us." The man's deep voice was pleading, his eyes wide with a concern Cordelia didn't understand.

"I don't—"

But before she could speak another word, an arrow pierced through the man's chest. His grip released Cordelia's arm, and he fell to his knees. He gasped, eyes slowly losing their life, wheezing out a final word before his chest no longer rose and fell. "Run."

98

JASPAR'S FURY BURNED HOTTER THAN HE'D EVER experienced before. He'd never heard of cerulean Sidons, but he recognized their swords and uniforms. They were the same men he and Cordelia had seen at the hotel in Keru two weeks ago.

The men holding Jaspar loosened their grip for the smallest fraction of a second, surprise and anguish at their dying friend. He used the opportunity to burn their hands, but they hardly noticed. He kicked and pulled until he was finally free and ran to Cordelia, gripping her hand tightly in his.

"You heard the man, run!" He made it three steps when another arrow soared through the skies, this one lodging into the back of Jaspar's left thigh. He stumbled, lost Cordelia's hand, and fell to the ground in pain. She dropped to help him, but he shrugged her off. "Go!"

The two remaining cerulean men had regained their composure and were now attempting to escort Cordelia by the arms, pulling and yanking her body as she tried desperately to stay with Jaspar. A roar echoed around the clearing, made louder by the many rocks reflecting its sound.

The Tigraige from months past was slowly approaching them. It was as majestic as it was terrifying, but several injuries still hindered the beast, slowing its movements, its steps labored and awkward.

Another arrow arched high, but the cerulean men raised their shields, deflecting it before it could pierce Jaspar. He eyed the men cautiously, wondering why they had saved him.

Nearly every pathway in the clearing was now inhabited by a Sidon with a raised bow and notched arrow. The cerulean men saw the Sidons at the same time he did, and they faced each other, a private conversation passing between them. The one on the left nodded his head, letting go of Cordelia's arm and holding a small plant wrapped in cloth over her mouth.

"No!" Jaspar lunged for her, but it was too late. She lost her balance, her eyes rolling back, her body collapsing. The cerulean man threw her over his shoulder and fled, his shield twisting and turning with speed as he deflected the arrows. He ran to one of the few empty pathways and quickly disappeared, two Sidons following after him.

"Do not fear, brave protector." The remaining cerulean man lowered a hand, gripping Jaspar's arm and pulling him to his feet. "Fredrick will deliver the princess to safety, and I will stay and protect you."

"Princess...?"

But the man did not answer, he simply took a stand in front of Jaspar and raised his sword and shield. Jaspar ripped off his belt, biting down on it as he yanked the arrow from his thigh. Blood spurted out of his leg, and he wrapped the belt into a tourniquet as tight as he could. All the while, the strange man deflected arrows and protected Jaspar.

"She's not a princess, you've abducted the wrong girl," Jaspar gasped as he tried to stand, placing all his weight on his uninjured leg. An arrow came dangerously close to his chest, and he ducked down at the last moment, nearly losing his newfound balance. The man steadied him.

"You should lean on my back, Sir Jaspar."

"Sir Jasp..." He shook his head. "I am not a knight."

The cerulean man titled his head, as if he'd never heard such a preposterous statement in his life. He pulled Jaspar by the shoulders, forcing him to stand with their backs touching. A roar signaled the closeness of the Tigraige, and the strangely human female Sidon from before accompanied it. The arrows stopped flying, but each Sidon was still holding notched bows.

"I am so happy to see you, *Jaz*." The woman touched her hand to her neck, revealing a talisman much like his own. "Or should I say, Sir Jaspar?"

She had found a way to overcome his curse, using a talisman. Had Klingbeil designed one for her? Was he working for the enemy?

"Where is the girl?" she snarled, but no one answered her. The cerulean man who stood shoulder to shoulder with Jaspar did not flinch, his face was as solid and expressionless as the monoliths surrounding them.

The female snapped her fingers, and the Tigraige sped through the clearing, but the man still did not flinch. Jaspar tried to control his fire, tried to use his magic, but his injuries were draining his energy, and his body felt weak and heavy.

The Tigraige roared, the ground beneath its heavy paws trembling. "Take this." The cerulean man whispered, handing Jaspar his sword. Jaspar took it with no hesitation, holding it aloft, ready to fight off the beast. But the man simply raised a hand.

The beast stopped two feet in front of them, bowing its head low to the ground. "I am sorry for your suffering," the man whispered, and he took a step toward the beast, patting its head. The Tigraige whimpered and leaned into the touch. In the distance, the female was shouting in fury.

"What are you doing? Attack! I order you to attack!"

But the great beast did not attack, he remained yielded, his head still under the fingers of the cerulean man. "It is time to go home, brave warrior." The Tigraige licked a slimy kiss to the man's hand before bolting across the clearing. He ran through the same pathway Fredrick had used to flee with Cordelia.

"Get back here, you mangy cat!" The woman screamed, but the Tigraige never looked back. "He'll kill me," the woman whispered frantically.

"What the blazes is going on?" Jaspar yelled.

"Tigraiges are the majestic creatures of the sea. They do not serve Sidons. I sent him back to the ocean where he belongs." The cerulean man held up his shield as arrows plummeted them.

"Enough." A booming and wicked voice echoed through the clearing. A man misted in blackened crimson appeared like smoke. His towering body jumped down from one of the many tall monoliths. He landed with great force, though the impact did little to slow him down. The earth trembled under his feet, and Jaspar felt a sudden chill ripple around the clearing. The man lifted his head, his face visible in the lowering sun, and in sheer shock, Jaspar dropped his shield and clutched his chest.

99

IT WAS AS IF HE SAW A MIRROR OF HIS WORST FEARS. The man was a mountain of brute strength, his skin sickly, his eyes dangerous. A horrifying echo of fumes glowed around him, black and as scarlet as blood. But what was most terrifying was his face.

He bore the same features as Jaspar, the exact same nose, mouth, chin. He knew in an instant who this man was, who it had to be: the enchanter Janus, his greatest grandfather, the forgotten captain from the legends.

"Good evening." His voice was grating, as if gravel and tar filled his throat. Jaspar clutched his chest tighter, the pain and construction bordering on unbearable. The cerulean man stiffened his shoulders.

"Do not fear, Sir Jaspar, I will protect you with my life."

Jaspar didn't have time to analyze why this strange man would sacrifice himself, why he addressed Jaspar as *sir*, why he called Cordelia a princess. He only had eyes for Janus.

"I have been looking for you, my ssson."

"I'm no son of yours," Jaspar hissed.

Janus laughed, his head rocking back, his mirthless smile gleaming. "Ah, but you are, aren't you? And you were born a *Celaresssstar,* too. I have been waiting far too long for you."

Janus was only a few yards away now, but the cerulean man continued to shield Jaspar. The smoke was suffocating to Jaspar, how was the man immune? Was it something to do with his strangely gilled neck?

"Where isss the witch?" he growled, but Jaspar shook his head, adamant. He didn't know where Cordelia had gone, but even if he had, he would never tell a soul, let alone the most evil and wicked demon to ever exist.

"Shall I loosssen your tongue, child?" Janus clasped his hands behind his back, lazy, leisurely, as if this were simply any other day, any other conversation. A cerise ribbon of ash furled and coiled, making its way through the air. It coated around the cerulean man who seemed immune to its powers. Before the smoke could infiltrate Jaspar's lungs, he used every ounce of power he had left in him and suffocated it with his own vapors.

"Ha! You sssee! You are my progeniture, for who elssse could have powersss so similar to mine?" Janus seemed thrilled with this revelation. "Perhapsss the most impressssive of all my great dessscendantsss."

The female half-human Sidon suddenly appeared behind Janus, and Jaspar realized a coil of smoke was wrapped around her, binding her arms to her sides. She looked fearful as the smoke dragged her forward until she was in front of Janus. The smoke dropped her to her knees, and she bowed before him, trembles racking her body.

"You have failed me, Alaria. You will sssuffer for thisss." His voice wasn't a whisper, just a low, deep rumble. Before she could apologize, the smoke coiled tight around her neck, suffocating her, asphyxiating her in a near instant. She collapsed to the ground in a heap. It took several moments for Jaspar to realize she was not dead, her chest still rose and fell, but Janus had weakened her greatly, and she remained unconscious.

"I do not need Sssidonsss to defeat you, Jasssspar."

The cerulean man shivered. "I am afraid I will not be able to protect you much longer. I have run out of time to explain." He pulled from his pocket a sharp handheld arrowhead. It was shaped like the trident in Cordelia's tattoo and shone like gold in the white light of the newly risen moon.

"What's—" But before Jaspar could utter another word, the cerulean man stabbed his neck with the arrow.

"No!" Janus shouted from somewhere far away as Jaspar's vision grew blurry. Images he could barely decipher flashed before him. A hurl of fire, the cerulean man clutching his chest, collapsing to his knees. A furious scream and roar from Janus, and then his vision went dark as a haze overcame Jaspar. The last thing he remembered was the sound of Cordelia's voice, soft, soothing humming in his ears as the world turned to ash and dust.

100

JASPAR COUGHED AS SMOKE AND SULFUR BURNED HIS nostrils and throat. The ground beneath him was hard, and warm snow slowly drifted from the sky. But Jaspar realized it wasn't snow, it was the ash of a burning fire. He forced himself to rise, shaky on an injured leg with a belted tourniquet wrapped at the thigh.

He blinked open heavy eyelids, searching for Cordelia, but all he saw was black. His heart dropped. Black and empty. No plants or trees or houses or people. He was in the forest of his nightmares, the forest he'd lost his parents in. And nothing was left of the once great lands but the soot and ash of the fire that had destroyed it ten years ago.

"I see you recognize your home." The voice was eerily familiar to him, but the face he recognized at once. It wasn't quite Cordelia's, wasn't quite Hygonia's either, but something akin. It was the face of Cordelia's mother, the woman from the drawing, right down to the mark in the middle of her collarbone.

"Why am I here?" He didn't recognize his own voice as it rasped from him. He coughed, and smoke and cinders burst from his lips. "Cor—"

"Cordelia is with the other Celarestars, they will keep her safe while you fight Janus and find Qualaris."

"But you could take me. You know where it is!" He coughed

367

again, the force of using his voice tore through his throat like tiny daggers.

"No, I am a mere vapor, a messenger dream."

"Dream? I am not awake?" How could he feel this much pain and agony if he was not awake?

"No, Jaspar." She shook her head, sadness in her eyes, and for the first time, Jaspar realized she was translucent. "Janus has captured you, and I am not sure where he is keeping you."

"Why did you bring me here of all places?" he rasped.

"It is not I who brought you here."

"This is my dream?" The darkened lands still held the screams of those who'd died here, and Jaspar clutched his eyes closed at the images flashing in his mind. His mother, his father, his home, burning, charring, disintegrating in the flames.

"It is your nightmare," she said softly.

"Janus..." The disturbing image of his greatest grandfather came to mind, the terrifying, wicked, and sickly man who had hunted Jaspar. He recalled the clearing, the cerulean man, the arrowhead to his neck. His fingers touched his throat, but no wound was there.

"You are not harmed, Jaspar. Not by your Celarestars."

"*My* Celarestars?"

"They are your brethren."

"My...what the blazes are you talking about?"

"The arrow," she said, ignoring his questions. "Was laced with a sleeping tonic. It was imperative that I come to your dreams, otherwise I could not rely on you to find the island and rescue my daughter."

"But you said she was safe!" Jaspar took a step forward, stumbling on his wounded leg.

"She is safe for now, but she will need you when Janus comes. He has gone to great lengths to find the island, and I fear he is nearly there now. You are the only one with the power to vanquish him." Her brow furrowed, and he couldn't tell if she was sad or angry. Maybe she was both.

"What power? I am a mere Hagan!" he shrieked, small sparks of fire ejecting from his hands in absolution.

"You are a born Celarestar. You were prophesied to defeat the enchanter. I do not know how you will accomplish this, simply that you must." Her voice wavered, as if the fear of Janus and the conviction of Jaspar's destiny warred within her.

"How will I find Qualaris? My family has searched for thousands of years to no avail."

"But no one has come as close as you." She waved her hands in front of her body, and a scroll appeared, as translucent as the woman who'd conjured it. He took staggered steps forward. On the scroll was a map, the most detailed map he'd ever seen, and it clearly indicated where Qualaris was.

He reached out a shaking hand, but his fingers snatched nothing but air.

"You must remember this map, Jaspar, for I cannot give it to you in a dream."

He stared intently, noting every undulated continent, every shape of the ocean, every measurement of land and sea between the place where he stood in the dream and the place where his Cordelia was waiting for him.

"How will I get there?" The sky grew dark, and Cordelia's mother turned into a blue haze before him, slowly fading from view. "What's happening?"

"You are waking up, Sir Jaspar."

"No."

"Find the island, find Cordelia, save us all." She vanished, and Jaspar gasped for breath.

～

"Ah, the daring Celaressstar awakensss,." Janus's voice was cold and the earth around Jaspar changed. When he opened his eyes, he was no longer in the burnt forest but in a sunken room. Damp and slimy walls surrounded him on three sides, and a grated iron gate was all that stood between him and the enchanter.

Chains shackled his hands and feet to the ground, and the smell of something putrid and rancid burned his nostrils and pulled at the back of his throat. He fought back a gag and inspected the edges of his dungeon, the dawning of entrapment stifling his mind.

"Welcome to your new home, Jassspar." Janus's smoking body billowed around him, and the enchanter seemed larger than life in the too-small hallway. His massive body was a greater cage than the iron gate, his tall frame nearly reaching the slimy, stony ceiling.

He opened his mouth to speak, to demand to know where he was, but nothing came out. His eyes widened in fear. His mouth went dry as sand.

"You will only ssspeak when I allow you to, my ssson."

He spat at Janus's feet at the word son, and the enchanter reacted faster than Jaspar could prepare for. A wall of smoke and heat flung Jaspar across the dungeon, and he slammed into the floor with burned skin and singed hair.

"Where is the island?"

Jaspar narrowed his eyes. Why did Janus think he knew the location of Qualaris? A soft whimper caught his ears, and he turned to see another cell across from his. Behind Janus, ducking in the corner, more broken than he could ever imagine, was Hygonia. She was dirty, bruised, and bloody, and the whimpers had come from her unconscious lips.

Beside her cell was another, this one imprisoning a man with a dark-brown beard and mane to match. He was bruised and bloodied, and Jaspar recognized his face but couldn't place it. Another whimper pulled his attention back to Hygonia, and Janus followed the gaze.

"The demigoddesss has been ussselessss," Janus hissed, as if disgusted by the mere existence of such a creature. "But you will not be. Where. Isss. The. Island."

Jaspar was surprised when his mouth filled with saliva. "I don't know."

"Ah, but you do. Becaussse wherever the isssland isss, ssso is your beloved sssoulfate."

Jaspar clamped his mouth shut tight.

"Yesssss." Janus smiled, a wickedness curling his lips like the coiling of a snake.

"I don't know where she is. If I did, I'd never lead you there." Another fist of smoke and fire seared Jaspar, his clothes flaming on his skin. He worked hard to keep from screaming, refusing to show Janus any satisfaction at the pain he was causing.

"Liesss," Janus whispered and snapped his fingers. The iron gate closed with a slam, the sound echoing around him, taking his freedom with a bang. Janus stalked off, his heavy footsteps slowly fading, leaving Jaspar and the precious demigoddess imprisoned.

101

"Jaspar," said a whispered but musical voice. The only sound for the past day had been the trickling of water from the ceiling and the rustling of wind from somewhere outside the dungeon. Jaspar had done nothing but lay on his cot, his mind racing, his heart desperate for its other half.

He lifted his head. The demigoddess Hygonia was kneeling, her hand pressed against the door of her cell. Beside hers, the dark-haired man lay on his cot, quiet, thoughtful, eyes staring into the nothingness above them.

A ten-foot hallway separated the cells, just far enough that hands could not reach. He crawled across the slimy floor, his shackles pulling him back just when he'd reached the iron bars.

"I am sorry you are here," Hygonia said.

"Likewise," was all he managed to say as the sight of the broken and fragile goddess tore through him. Janus had covered the remarkably beautiful demigoddess in dirt, bruises, and dried blood. Her colorful hair was greasy and seared at the ends; her dress, designed to look like the petals of an orchid, was ripped and stained with mud.

"You must escape."

"How?" Jaspar asked incredulously. If she knew how to escape, why was she still here?

"I will help you. We will find a way. You are the only one who can defeat him."

The dream came back to him, the conversation with the translucent Bygonia. Had it been real?

"Tell me about the prophecy."

Hygonia blinked. "You know about the prophecy?"

"I know that it says I am the only one who can defeat Janus." He debated whether to tell her of the dream, but he still wasn't convinced it had been anything more than that.

"Yes. You were born to love the daughter of a demigoddess, and together, you are destined to defeat the world's greatest of all evils."

"I don't suppose you could tell me how I am to accomplish this?"

"It is a prophecy, Jaspar, it is not meant to be instructional," her usual musical voice was slightly dimmed, like a fractured song that wasn't quite in tune. "Tell me what your thoughts are," she said after several moments of silence.

"Cordelia," he said with no hesitation.

She tilted her head. "Have your memories been restored?" Her voice was suddenly sharper.

"No. Why?"

The demigoddess squinted. "You have grown to care for her. Again."

Jaspar felt the heat rush to his cheeks, but he didn't try to hide it. "I have."

"And you love her?" Her voice was stronger now, eager. He started to shake his head, but flashes of his time with Cordelia returned to him. The feeling of her lips on his, the warmth of her body when they embraced, the soft tenderness of her touch. Her sweet humming as he drifted to sleep.

Hygonia nodded, her eyes alight, a small smile on her dirty, blood-stained cheeks.

"Close your eyes, Jaspar. Close your eyes and think only with your heart."

Think with his heart? What the blazes did that mean? But he followed her instructions, vanquishing every thought from his mind except for one: Cordelia. He saw nothing but the back of his eyelids for several moments, but then...

"What do you see?" The goddess's voice was deeper, low with anticipation.

"Black sand, green trees, the bluest of blue waters."

"Where?"

He let his eyes focus, and the map from his dream came back to him. He thought of its many detailed images and then recalled the lines of longitude and latitude. But he couldn't quite recall the numbers, didn't quite know the exact coordinates.

"Where snow meets the ocean, and mountains touch the sea." His voice had turned singsong, but he had no idea where the words were coming from.

"Yesss." Hygonia's voice was desperate now.

He kept his eyes closed, thinking only of Cordelia and the map. "Where the world's serpent guards a cave of withered trees. In the highest of norths, and the center of all things, rests the treasure of truth and love and dreams. Awaiting beyond the cave is a shoreline of black sand and white shells, there is the land of Qualaris, beneath a crimson and blue full moon."

"Thank you, my ssson. I've never been prouder of one of my progeny."

The voice that spoke was low, dark, deadly. Jaspar gulped and opened his eyes with trembling hands. Hygonia was gone, and in her place was Janus, a pleased and wicked smile on the evil demon's face. Jaspar tasted bile and iron on his tongue as shame and fear pulsed through his veins.

"No..." he whispered, tears in his eyes and disgrace in his soul.

Janus left with pride in his every step, and Hygonia and Jaspar locked eyes from across their iron bars. Hygonia's face was sad but forgiving, a forgiveness Jaspar knew he did not deserve. The lost island had been protected for centuries, for generations, and he had been its downfall.

All Jaspar had wanted was to save Cordelia, was to find Cordelia, but instead, he had found what had been lost for centuries. A descendant of the forgotten captain had finally discovered the lost Island of Qualaris, and Jaspar had delivered its location to the devil himself.

Acknowledgments

Thank you...

To my dear readers, for spending your time with my stories, you have no idea how much I value each and every one of you.

To all the readers, teachers, booksellers, librarians, reviewers, and bloggers who keep the love of reading alive.

To the many podcasts and reviewers who took the time to read and share MTL. Thank you for your brilliance, patience, and enthusiasm.

To my brilliant team at Wise Wolf, thank you for making every step of this journey more and more magical. I am honored to be a part of your publishing family.

To my cover art designers, who have created such beautiful and perfect covers.

To Tracey for being so much more than an editor. Every note from you has made me a better writer.

To my incredible publisher, Rachel, the hardest working woman in publishing. I couldn't do any of this without you!

To my family and friends, thank you for supporting me all these years and for letting me use your names in my stories.

To my writing community, Abigail Spaggiari, Natalie Glassford, Soumaya Hajji, Heather Schneider, and M. T. Zimny, for endless brainstorming sessions, writer's retreats, sprints, encouragement, and so much more. Writing with you has been a privilege. I look forward to watching your writing careers flourish!

To my mama Desiree for telling everyone she meets that her daughter wrote a book.

To my sisters Lindsey and Samantha: it's hard to find people who will love you no matter what, and I thank every sand in the ocean for both of you.

To my father, Mike, I wish I could share every moment with you.

To Quentin, my forever sounding board and biggest cheerleader. All's well that ends well to end up with you.

Watch for Book Three:
More Than Love

*Dive into a world of magic and adventure in the thrilling
conclusion to the epic* **More Than Life** *young adult fantasy trilogy.*

Jaspar Marlow, after years of relentless pursuit, has uncovered the long-lost
island of Qualaris. But when he unknowingly gives that location to the
evil enchanter Janus, he jeopardizes the very existence of the island and its
inhabitants. Now, Jaspar must break free from Janus's grasp, navigate
treacherous obstacles, and race against time to rescue Qualaris before it
succumbs to darkness.

Cordelia Kimbal was last seen getting captured by a strange, cerulean man
in bronze armor. She wakes up in Qualaris only to realize that the utopia
she envisioned is far from reality. Tasked with confronting the inner
demons plaguing the island's inhabitants and defending against external
threats, Cordelia learns valuable lessons about the dichotomy between
dreams and reality. As unexpected perils emerge, including a mysterious
illness and unfamiliar creatures, Cordelia must rely on the aid of strangers
to ensure her survival.

In "More Than Love," familiar faces return alongside compelling new
characters, weaving a tapestry of intrigue, suspense, and destiny
fulfillment. With unexpected twists and turns at every corner, this
gripping tale will keep readers on the edge of their seats until the very end.

AVAILABLE APRIL 2024

About the Author

Bethanie Finger is a graduate of The University of Southern Mississippi and works as a school librarian. When she's not writing she enjoys hiking, podcasting, and exploring the world. She happily lives in Nevada with her husband, their two dogs, Scamp and Beowulf, and an ever growing TBR collection. Find her online here.